Virtually Yours

For Andi, Jilly, Jeri, Terri, Viper, Muffy, and Ooie,
the Real Virtual Moms.
I couldn't have written this without you.

This is a work of fiction. All of the characters, organizations, and events portrayed in this novel are either products of the author's imagination or are used fictitiously.

Chapter One

Somewhere on the Internet
October 30
Asheley MacDaniel's blog post,
Missing Mac

My dearest Mac, I can't believe it. Has it been a year? Two men in full dress uniform, a chaplain and a captain, solemn faces. I glanced outside that sunny afternoon – my heart lurched. A bad sign when they make the trip to you. A hundred old movies from the 1940s flashed through my head, sad military notifications, you hold your breath for impending heartbreak.

From that moment on, my life became a motion picture, something I was compelled to watch in the dark. No popcorn, no Sugar Babies, a captive audience. It's been a year of mourning, of anger, of survival. Of losing you, and finding... myself.

Somewhere Else on the Internet
October 30
To: jannasbananas, ally1234, missymom, laurelextonsbunch, shootingskye
From: celiasunshine
Subject: Virtual Mommies! Where are you???

Sorry I haven't been chatting as much as I should. My work load has been incredible lately! My boss, Mr. Bass, decided to retire (not that he was worth two cents) so I'm now, *ta-dah*! Queen of Sarasota General. Don't be jealous. My new position is hardly glamorous. I'm doing the work of two people…well, at least a person (me) and a half (Mr. Bass).

Kimber's doing well, shopping around for college. I might need your help, Janna, since you've put two through already. Her boyfriend, Brandon, is sweet. I've still got my eyes locked on those two. I provide enough supervision to keep them from getting *too* close, if you know what I mean. Other than that, it's the same old, same old. You know me…I can handle it. People who can't stand lemons haven't had Miss Celia's lemonade.

Miss you all to bits. What's up with the rest of you ladies?

Love, Celia

***

To: celiasunshine, ally1234, laurelextonsbunch, missymom, jannasbananas
From: shootingskye
Subject: Depression Finished…Again

Celia, good to hear from you! I was beginning to think the Virtual Moms had fallen off the virtual edge of the Internet.

Today I woke up and decided my depression is over. OVER. For REAL.

I know I've said that every week since Trina left me. I know what you're all thinking. *Get over it!* Right? I know it's what my son is thinking.

Rob thinks I'm insane. Right when I think the clouds are ready to part, the fog rolls in. 'Course it would roll in, San Francisco gets that way at times.

Honest to God, I'm going to do something today. Maybe I'll open the front door and look outside. Maybe there'll be something more than fog today.

My mommies, thank you so much for your support and understanding and for putting up with me. I know I'm a whiner. Bear with me; I'll be normal someday. I hope.

Skye

***

To: shootingskye, ally1234, jannasbananas, celiasunshine, laurelextonsbunch
From: missymom
Subject: Halloween, Anyone?

OMG, girls! Sorry I've been off the grid. Been busy making costumes. Kara wanted a Hershey's Kiss outfit, and I had that all sewn up (very punny!) last week. Then what happens? She gets the flu! My poor baby's been out of school all week. As for Kassie, at first she wanted to dress up as Cyndi Lauper during her *Girls Just Wanna Have Fun* phase. Yesterday, she decided she's too "old" to trick or treat. Too old? I guess she realized her big 1-3 is coming up in a few weeks. I wish she'd decided to grow up before I bought a hundred yards of netting!

Earl's been busy with his new project, a high-rise condo on the Strip. He's been working long hours and tries to squeeze us in.

As for me, I'm hanging in. Now that I think about it, I'm missing all of you. We need to get together! Vegas is centrally located, and we have tons of room. Any takers? Let me know, girls. My casa is always your casa.

Love you, Missy

***

To: celiasunshine, shootingskye, jannasbananas, ally1234, missymom

From: laurelextonsbunch

Subject: Thank You Through the Chaos

I know Celia's email to us all was actually directed at me. I'm the guilty one, too busy for friends.

That's why I'm writing an email when I should be doing the laundry, or dishes, or something.

Skye, chin up! You'll work your way out of your funk someday. Missy, I hope Kara is okay. So much scary flu going around these days.

I have to thank each of you for the online birthday party this week. What a total surprise from a great bunch of girls. Honestly, after we signed off, I cried.

As for the rest of my life, chaos would be a vacation. Missy, believe me, if Vegas were in the cards, I'd be on the next plane.

Marcus is doing well in school. I only wish I could find a teaching job closer to home. It's a time suck driving all over St. Louis. However, I'm grateful I *have* a job. I'm living in my minivan, which would be great if it were a Mercedes and not a broken down antique. Things will get worse if Marcus lands on the traveling hockey team. I'm crossing my fingers that he's no Wayne Gretzky. I know. I'm a bad mother.

As for Joe? Please don't ask. You know the economy.

Break's over. Back to laundry.

Love you guys, Laurel

***

To: shootingskye, laurelextonsbunch, missymom, jannasbananas, celiasunshine
From: ally1234
Subject: Insanity x2

Hello from the Tundra!

Looks like we'll be trick or treating in shorts and flip flops this year. Heat wave in Minneapolis, and I prayed for temps in the 30s. Vanessa's dressing up as a fairy princess and the effect would be lost if she had to wear a snowsuit over her ball gown! LOL. Greg and I are already fighting over who will go out and who will stay home to pass out candy. I have a schedule worked out on an Excel worksheet. I hope he follows it, he's been known to cheat. At five, Nessy's just so darned cute, and I'm so blessed to have a husband who gives a lot more than a damn.

Mike and Mike Junior will stop by. Junior's been rather secretive about his costume. He says, "Gramma, you'll have to wait and see." The tease.

I'll send pics ASAP, Ally

***

To: celiasunshine, missymom, laurelextonsbunch, shootingskye, ally1234
From: jannasbananas
Subject: Just a few…

Yo, girls. You know I flew to Paris last weekend…I'm back at Charles DeGaulle, typing this while I wait to catch the next plane home. Penn called this afternoon. Mandy has swine flu! Her entire dorm is being sent home. Rachel's picking her up to bring her back to NYC. My plane leaves in an hour.

Sorry so short. Will fill you in later.
Love and miss you all,
Janna

Chapter Two

Enter a hunky specimen of a man, muscles ripped and dewy, a beacon of manhood shining in dusky light. Like an angel, he approaches, surrounded by a heavenly aura. His long blond hair billows in the breeze, reflecting gold highlights. Her eyes scan the rest of this exquisite specimen. Rock-hard abdominal man-flesh gives way to a trim waistline; beyond are legs of sinewy steel. Salty spray glistens diamond-like from tanned skin. She glances up from her lounge chair, attempting to rein in her startled expression. It's a difficult task, what with a dangerous combination of perfect musculature and captivating smile to overcome. She trains her eyes past the wind-swept sands to the sea, to a faraway point where the horizon disappears.

He catches her gaze with his own. No. Don't look. Turn away. Too late. *God. Those eyes. They are a stunning blue, the color of robin's eggs, of pristine cloudless skies, of fine turquoise, of the aquamarine Caribbean. She could resist. Why deprive herself? He was the ultimate vintage. Oh yes, she could drown herself in a case of this and die a content woman. She feels the oddest compulsion to kiss those lips. Heck, why a kiss only? She could take him, in front of God and everybody.*

Her heart skips a few beats as her face flushes.

Sarasota, Florida

"Grah!"

Piercing, high decibel sirens stabbed into the still night. Celia rolled to her left and found herself a few inches of mattress short. She tumbled to the floor, dragging with her a comforter, sheets, cell phone, an antique Mickey Mouse lamp, and an assortment of dog-eared romance novels from the nightstand.

"Kimber! Jesus, Mary, and Joseph! Turn that thing off!"

Celia extricated herself from the tangle of debris, flicked on the overhead, and surveyed the damage. Her prized Waterford clock! *Damn it.* The tiny square crystal was a wedding gift from her maternal grandmother, a woman of style and substance. With the exception of Kimber, the clock was the only other treasure to survive her brief and unfortunate union with Melvin Davis.

Celia ran her index finger over the wounded crystal, catching her flesh on jagged glass. "Kim-*ber*!"

She returned the timepiece to its place on the nightstand and stomped down the darkened hallway toward Kimber's room. As much as she loved her daughter, the theft of the rare occasion to sleep in on her one day off merited the nuclear reaction. Why was Kimber's "loudest alarm clock in the world" blasting a firehouse wail when Sunday slumber was a commodity more precious than gold?

"Kimber *Marie* Davis!"

She hit the light switch to find the bed made and the room empty, triggering a foggy recollection that Kimber wasn't home. Last night she'd attended a Halloween party with her friend Alyssa and decided to sleep over instead of driving home late. Celia fumbled with the buttons on the alarm, located the 'off' switch, and padded back to her bedroom.

Back at the disaster scene, Celia stared at the ruins of her bedding and caught her image in a mirror. She shuddered. Her dark eyes were rimmed with a spider web of bloodshot whites and her normally obedient wavy brown hair resembled a thorny bush. A soft layer of blubber protruded over the waistband of her pajama bottoms. The blond hottie from her Dream Interrupted would have quickly passed on this frump, but what are fantasies for? The dream. *Blond, good looking – mmm... Wonder if a brain was under the eye candy? Why are the good dreams cut short and the nightmares never-ending?*

"Oh, great," Celia grumbled. "I could have slept another hour." Now she would never attain full climax of her hunk-o-rama fantasy.

She decided to take advantage of her forced rising to get a jump on the day. Celia thrived in her job as a hospital administrator, and with her recent promotion, Sunday was her sole day off. No matter how organized she was – and she prided herself on flawless execution – she had only time enough to complete her To Do list, nothing else. Kimber was self-sufficient and a huge help. Although a huge help, with laundry, cleaning and home maintenance, Celia's schedule was tighter than spandex bike shorts. As sunrise stained the skies, she made a pot of coffee and moved to the computer to check her email.

"*Celiasunshine*." She typed in her screen name followed by her password. "Huh, I don't feel much like sunshine today," she muttered to herself. Caffeine helped, many pots and strong enough to illuminate all of central Florida. "Please, girls, *one* of you make me smile."

"You've got mail!" her computer announced.

She patted the side of her monitor. "Of course, baby doll, I have mail," she cooed. Unlike the spotty and less than stellar appearances of the men in her life, her virtual friends were ones she could count on. She glanced up to the framed photos lining the bookshelf in her den, nestled between a platoon's worth of beanie bears; Virtual Mom meetings at Disney World, Hawaii, Las Vegas. Baby photos, school pictures and camp snapshots captured the lives of the Virtual Kids through diapers, toothless grins, sports and proms. It was one big extended family.

I think I need some good times today. Bleary from a late night of passing out candy to Halloween munchkins, she'd topped off the holiday with a midnight replay of *Carrie* followed by an early morning showing of *Love Story*.

"Ugh," she said aloud, yawning deeply and shaking her head. "No wonder the dream. That'll teach me to mix up my genres."

She first opened a chatty email from Ally complete with Halloween photos of Vanessa dressed as a fairy princess. A rhinestone-studded tiara held back long, curly ringlets, and the little girl's pink dress billowed from her waist like a cotton candy cloud. Ally's grandson Mike Junior, the one-eyed pirate, stood behind the little girl and mugged for the camera. "It was a warm All Saint's Eve in the Tundra this year," Ally opened in her email. "Thank God, because I'd never let Vanessa out in this getup if snow was on the ground!"

One photo depicted Vanessa displaying her plastic pumpkin full of candy loot. Celia felt a twinge of longing for those trick-or-treat days. Her Kimber teetered on the verge of adulthood. Sure, she still dressed up in costume, this year as Sarah Palin – her daughter was a dead-ringer for the ex-governor, down to the

10

bouffant tease and smart glasses – but the days of pumpkin carving, apple bobbing, and candy expeditions were over. Her 'baby' was driving now, had a boyfriend, and was already looking at college choices.

"She's so adorable!" Celia typed back in response. "Junior, too."

Then an email from Janna:

To: celiasunshine, missymom, laurelextonsbunch, ally1234, shootingskye
From: jannasbananas
Subject: New Mommy Anyone?

I know it's been ages since we've allowed anyone new into the group. I'm asking for an exemption this one time. I have a secret to share. A year ago I met this wonderful person online. You all know I contribute to online grief forums, which is where I found her. Asheley MacDaniel is a writer living in North Carolina. Her husband was killed in action in Iraq last year and she's left with a five-year-old boy named Tyler (she writes to stay at home with him). Ashe has few friends and no family. Her husband was an only child, no living parents. She's not originally from NC although she's staying in the area.

Girls, if anyone needs our help, it's Ashe. I'll understand if you want to keep the group closed; however, I know all of you. You have big enough hearts to include her in the loop. She's funny and her child is precious. Most of all, she's lonely and disconnected from the outside world. She *needs* us.

Let me know, k?

Love ya, j

Celia frowned and closed the email. She noticed Laurel on her Buddy List. The IM box couldn't open fast enough.

celiasunshine: *Laurel! What are you doing up so early?*
laurelextonsbunch: *Marcus has hockey practice.*

Celia did the math in her head. It was an hour earlier in St. Louis.

celiasunshine: *At 5 a.m.? That's crazy!*

laurelextonsbunch: *Ice time. Gotta grab it when you can. Some teams are on at 2 a.m.*

celiasunshine: *Joe?*

laurelextonsbunch: *What else? Sleeping in. Getting together with the guys later I guess, for the game.*

Celia's stomach churned for her friend. Joe was a good-natured guy, although not much help in the husband department.

laurelextonsbunch: *I have to run. Marcus is dogging it and I'm late as it is.*

celiasunshine: *Okay. Did you read the email from Janna?*

laurelextonsbunch: *Just replied.*

celiasunshine: *And?*

laurelextonsbunch: *I voted no. It's taken so long to get to where we are. All getting along. No drama. Why mess with a good thing?*

celiasunshine: *I hear you.*

laurelextonsbunch: *I have to run. Let's chat later.*

***

To: AsheMacD
From: jannasbananas
Subject: Gatekeeping

How's it going?
Sent out the email. I'll keep you posted.

***

To: jannasbananas
From: AsheMacD
Subject: RE: Gatekeeping

Yes, ma'am. Should I say a prayer? Get out my lucky rabbit's foot? Grease some palms?
Virtually yours,
Ashe

***

To: AsheMacD

12

From: jannasbananas
Subject: RE: RE: Gatekeeping

LOL. Too funny, Ashe. Don't worry. You're in. Mark my words.

***

Laurel Exton slid the transmission into neutral and prayed for a downhill slope. She strained forward and swayed back and forth. "Come on, darling," she coaxed, "we only… have… to get… a little bit… closer." One tiny burst of momentum was all she needed to maneuver the minivan from the highway to the safety of the gravel shoulder. The dilapidated Town and Country was prone to break down when she depended on it most, and today was one of those days. Marcus peered into the darkness, his worried eyes blinking under a mane of shaggy hair. *Reminder to self: Find time for Marcus's haircut.*

"Mom, I'm going to be late for practice. The coach is going to kill me."

Laurel exuded upbeat and positive. "Marcus, he won't *kill* you. He might take you out of the next game's line-up, that's all."

Marcus pulled the hood of his sweatshirt over his head and slumped in his seat. "So I'm *one* step away from being murdered."

Laurel kept one eye on the road in front of her and another on her son. This was why she got out of bed in the middle of the night? To forego a shower and breakfast, throw on some old sweats, tie her hair into a messy ponytail, and drag her sleepy offspring to an ice rink where she could sit in a frozen stupor for two hours on a Sunday morning? Surrounded by rabid hockey dads? Overdosing on Zamboni gas? And the icing on the cake: the car breaking down – *again.*

Laurel kept her cool. "I'm sure it's that same loose wire. I can fix it. If not, we'll call your dad."

Right on queue her phone rang. Perhaps Joe's telepathy was pushing overtime; it was clear the rest of him wasn't working at all. "Hello?"

"Laurel, it's me, Missy." Missy didn't have to identify herself. Her breathy, little girl voice and Midwestern accent gave her away.

"Hi. If I didn't tell you before, thanks for the birthday surprise. You guys are the best." Laurel wanted to add, "It was much nicer than what I got from my husband," but kept her mouth shut for her son's sake. "Missy what's up? My phone is almost dead, we're late for Marcus's practice, and my car just died."

"Sorry! I wanted to know what you thought about Janna's email?"

"I haven't had a chance to think about it. I voted no. What if this Ashe person turns out to be a weirdo? I'm too old and too busy to deal with that kind of drama. What about you?"

"I keep going back and forth. Part of me wants to be compassionate, and part of me wants to keep our group cozy. You're right. I don't need the drama either. We know Janna. I trust her instincts."

A speeding semi careened within inches of Laurel's disabled minivan, sending a thin wave of slick mud over the car. She fumbled for the wipers. The blades were not much more than brittle shards of plastic, so dull they could barely knife through to the windshield. She pushed on the wiper. The motor whirred. A weak spray of fluid trickled out. "Missy, I'm going to hang up and call you later. If I don't call Joe right now, we're going to end up encased in slime."

***

"What the hell? That Janna…" Celia guided the skimmer along the surface of the pool. She mulled over Janna's request while performing the mindless task. Celia had no time for the chore, but someone had to do it. Her regular maintenance man missed his customary schedule two weeks before. If by chance he managed to make it on time, the work was so careless he might as well have stayed home. What time he did not devote to his cell was spent looking over his shoulder.

"I'm going to have to call that company tomorrow," she muttered. "This can't continue, damn it. Like my schedule isn't jam-packed already?" Celia shook out the captured leaves and twigs onto the pool deck. She bent over to collect the soggy vegetation into a dustpan and dumped the remains into the trash.

Back to the Virtual Moms. Why would she jeopardize the well-being of their group to allow an unknown? *Janna knows the score. What was she thinking?*

Her task complete, Celia made her way back to the kitchen and a quick lunch. Her mind wandered from her current VM annoyance back to her early morning fantasy. She sighed. Real life men were flawed disappointments, though there were always the dashing lords and buff musclemen in the land of her dreams.

Lunch today was a low-key affair, a sandwich of bologna and mustard, its interior laced with smashed up potato chips. Celia contemplated a dessert of leftover Halloween candy. She was in the process of responding to Missy's email when she heard a car pull into the driveway. Dressed in an oversized Buccaneer's tee shirt and faded jeans, Kimber entered the kitchen. Her long, brown hair was pulled back into a loose ponytail.

Thank goodness she had sense enough not to return home in the harsh glare of daylight as a defeated politician.

"Hi, Mom. How's it going?" She slammed the door hard, giving the hinges and frame a rigorous workout. Celia cringed. Kimber sat poised on the cusp of adulthood, yet she could still act like a child on occasion.

"Not bad. How about your party?"

"Oh, my God. So much fun! I had the best time ever!" Kimber's dark eyes rolled and flashed with kinetic energy. *Teenagers.* "I don't think Brandon pulled off the John McCain look though. No one got who he was supposed to be. People thought he was my grandfather. Can you imagine?" She paused for a moment, head tilted, fore finger resting on her chin. "Maybe he *should* have rented that grizzly bear suit like he wanted to. So, did you get many kids last night?"

"It seemed like hundreds. They were still knocking at the door way past eight. I was afraid I'd run out of candy. Where do they come from?"

"Maybe they're trucked in."

"I doubt it." Once she'd landed the plum job at Sarasota General, the first thing Celia did was buy a small home in a gated community so they could live buffered from the outside world. The chance of gypsy bands of inner city trick-or-treaters finding their way inside Gulf Wynds Cay without an invitation and an assenting nod from a security guard was nil.

Kimber scooped up a package of peanut M & Ms and tore into the wrapper. She peeked over her mom's shoulder. "How are the Mommies doing today?"

Celia turned the screen toward Kimber. Her voice rose excitedly. "Look at this photo of Vanessa. She's so sweet."

Kimber gave the monitor a noncommittal glance as she separated green M & Ms from the rest of the candy and slid them across the table to her mother. "Cute."

Celia sighed as she absently popped the candy into her mouth, one piece at a time. She lingered over each long enough to partially soften the outer shell before crunching down. "Ally's so lucky to have a young one in the house. I remember those days like it was yesterday."

"Huh!" Kimber sniffed, "I'd rather not remember. Some of those days were brutal. You'd think you'd be happy now that I'm an adult."

"*Almost* an adult. What's the harm in looking back?"

"Keep looking backward, because I have plans. Don't count on grandkids in your future, not for a long time."

"Good. You're still in high school."

"I have a science report to finish by tomorrow. Can I use the laptop? I want to work outside by the pool as long as it's nice out." Kimber headed toward her bedroom.

"Sure, let me log off. He, you forgot to turn off your alarm! The siren went off at five this morning," Celia called.

"Sorry, Mom," she yelled back.

Celia put her plate in the sink. She'd reread Janna's email several times and hesitated to respond at first, thinking long and hard about the addition of a newbie to Virtual Moms. The group was tight and comfortable, and it hadn't been easy to get to that point. The six moms knew each other well, although some had never met. The last thing they needed was an unknown to upset the dynamic of the group.

Her initial reaction was that of cautiousness. Could she trust Janna, who by all accounts was an excellent judge of character? *Still, you never know.* Celia spent the morning privately emailing the others Virtual Moms to get their opinion.

All except Laurel felt the same. It was a done deal.

Welcome, Ashe.

To: AsheMacD, missymom, jannasbananas, laurelextonsbunch, ally1234, shootingskye
From: celiasunshine
Subject: Welcome to the Group!

Ashe, as the person with the most history with this group, it's my pleasure to welcome you to Virtual Moms. Janna has said some very nice things about you and we hope you will find the group helpful.

Please feel free to respond to any and all of the emails, or not. As moms, we know how hectic life can get...

Celia stopped typing and shook her head. A generic, cordial letter. Friendly, without suspicion, it was a bland cousin to many of the letters she penned for her job. "I can't believe this."

"Can't believe what?" Kimber appeared at the door, textbooks and paper in hand.

Celia straightened a sagging line of Beanie bears on the shelf as she looked at beaming VM faces smiling at her from the bulletin board. Wedding photos and baby pictures, family candids, and snapshots of meeting moms. Also present was a super-sized knot twisting in her gut. "We're inducting a new VM."

"No way! That hasn't happened in what? Twenty years or so?"

She scowled at Kimber. "Har-dee-har. You know we haven't been together that long."

Kimber crossed her arms and returned a steady glare, her brows furrowed. "Uh-oh."

"What do you mean, 'uh-oh?'"

"You have that look on your face."

"I don't know what you're talking about."

"You know, that 'don't cross me or I'll slap you upside the head' look. The 'you're messing with the great Celia Davis' look. The 'I'm a mama bear' look." Celia slapped at the air in front of Kimber. Her daughter shimmied her hips, deftly moving away. "Honestly, Mom. Get a *life*. I mean one beyond the Virtual Moms. Isn't it time you found someone?"

"Don't snark with me, little miss."

"I'm serious. Time is passing you by. I'm a big girl now. Let me go, like a little bird." Kimber cupped her hands together, raised them above her head, and opened her fingers as she balanced on one toe. "And then we shall both be free!"

Celia hurried to close browser tabs. "Damn those third grade drama classes. I should have steered you toward gymnastics," she huffed.

"Oh, Mommy, my favorite Mommy," Kimber sang sweetly. "Can I have the laptop now?"

"Sure." Celia pressed the send button before she could reconsider and logged off.

Chapter Three

Monday, November 2

To: ally1234, shootingskye, laurelextonsbunch, missymom, celiasunshine
From: jannasbananas
Subject: And if there was any doubt left…

My lovely darlings,

I understand some of you have deep concerns about allowing newbie Ashe into the fold. I know the history, yada yada yada – remember, I was here too. If you have been too busy/lazy/forgetful to go to Ashe's blog, I'm pasting an entry below for your perusal.

I cannot believe it. My darling Mac, returned to me not as a triumphant hero, not as my warm, breathing, passionate, sometimes hot-headed, often exasperating one true love full of warm hugs and tender kisses. No, you return a shell, broken and damaged, a body encased in a wooden box…Where can I take my anger when you chose this life? Damn you, Mac. You promised to return. You said you'd be safe. Your CO promised. The President promised.

Liars! Your collective lies have exposed my heart to its core, where it bleeds raw and forever. Our baby does not understand. You will never walk through the back door, ever again. We will never see your broad smile or hear your hearty laugh, be subjected to your pitiful attempts in the kitchen or your terrible jokes. We will never again feel a circle of your love.

Ladies, I refuse to believe any one of you can deny this lost soul a place among us. Virtual Moms to the rescue!

***

19

San Francisco, California

After she'd skirted the walkway and tumbled over uneven dunes, Skye Murray made a beeline for water's edge. She loved jogging the wide expanse of Ocean Beach in her bare feet. The pre-dawn hours were ideal, when she could have miles of sand to herself. She could slip on ratty flannel pants, an old sweatshirt and ear muffs and not have to worry about running into practically naked buff power athletes or confused tourists shivering in their parkas. They frequented the beach in more civilized hours. Her flip-flops, necessary for the long walk back to the house, dangled with her keys from a lanyard laced from her neck.

With each stride, the size 7 sandals pounded against her chest. A stiff winter wind whipped up cold and brutally brisk. She didn't care. She enjoyed the give under her arches and the smooth coolness of packed sand under her toes. Pain was a welcome sensation at this point. She embraced the chilly wilderness feel of this San Francisco beach, so different from the warm southern California beaches near where she had been born and raised. As she found her pace near the water's edge, pelicans circled overhead, while gulls pecked at the sea foam for tidbits from shells of dismembered crabs. Skye picked up her run and sprinted a few hundred yards before she stooped to catch her breath. *I'm so out of shape. I'll never be ready in time.*

A chirp and vibration from her stomach startled her. *Saved by the bell.* Skye fished her cell phone from her pocket.

"Murray Studios," she answered, summoning her best corporate voice through measured gasps.

"Is this a bad time? Are you busy? I know it's early." The crash of surf drowned out Missy's childlike voice.

Skye straightened and squinted into the distance. Through the mist, she could make out a tanker heading west, away from the Bay. "Not at all. Might need you… to call 911," she said, releasing a pant.

"You okay?"

"Sure. Nothing a personal trainer with a mean streak couldn't handle. I decided to take up running again. I'm tired of lying on my ass, feeling sorry for myself. I thought it would be easier to get back in the swing since I'd done it before. I was wrong."

"Take it slow. Maybe you should get a doctor's approval first." Skye smiled at the thought of glamour-girl Missy fretting over her.

"I'll be okay."

"You're nuts, girl. Keeping up the house and running after my kids is enough exercise for me."

"It is for you. Your house is enormous, your kids are younger, and you're still carting them around. Me? I live in tiny apartment and Rob's a self-sufficient teenager. *He* takes care of me. I'm tired of being depressed and under house arrest. I have to do something before I blimp out."

"As if. You're totally gorgeous."

Skye winced and measured two inches of burgeoning spare tire between index finger and thumb. Her muffin top had exploded all over the oven. A mirror would reveal puffy cheeks and frizzy auburn hair in sore need of a trim. If she were so attractive, why did Trina leave her? Thoughts drifted to her long-time love, a woman who was so beautiful, so kind, so *organized*, so *not* her.

Skye shrugged off the sting of the memory. "You haven't seen me lately, Missy. I'm a fat slob. I've got to get out of this funk somehow. This is what I know. I'm planning on running the Marathon. Good thing it's in July. I'll have nine months to train."

"You're running the Marathon again? But…"

"But *what?*" Skye's defenses flared at Missy's sputtering. She checked her indignant reaction.

"What about *Trina?*"

"I'm not doing it for her. I'm doing it for me." *Truthfully told*, Skye thought. *Perhaps I'll be super-fit and gorgeous by then so if I happen to run across the two-timing bitch, she'll drown in an ocean of regret.*

"What if you see her?"

"How? It's unlikely. There'll be thousands of runners. I won't see her. I haven't yet." San Francisco was big enough for their paths to fail convergence since the abrupt break up six months before. It helped that Skye had spent much of that time in bed mourning and the rest avoiding their old haunts. She hopped on one foot and then the other, shook out her arms, and jogged to the north. "The weather's cold and misty today, Missy. I've got to get going to stay warm. What's up?"

"I don't know. I'm lonesome."

Skye grimaced. The wayward husband was behind this conversation. "Where's Earl?"

"I've no idea. He left before four this morning. I don't get it, Skye. We used to be so close. Now we're like roommates working opposite shifts."

"Have you talked to him?" Communication was a key component in any good relationship. Too bad Skye missed all the signs of her own broken system until it was too late.

"How can I? He's never here. Anyway, I thought we'd dish about Ashe."

Ah, the mysterious Ashe. "I scanned the blog. I haven't had any personal contact yet. What's to dish?"

"Don't you think it's odd? Janna must have thousands of friends and she's never asked anyone to join the Virtual Moms before. None of us have."

"I don't have a problem with it, as long as Ashe is decent. I don't need drama."

"I hear you. Remember Melda? I get the heebee-jeebies thinking about her."

Skye shivered. Melda had been the last of the Wizz moms, so named because they were the VM's pissy faction. She'd been ejected from the group eight years earlier. All it took was a cyber-stalking incident where she threatened to kidnap Missy's newborn baby. That was quickly followed by criminal charges and a personal protection order. Skye shook off the memory. "You know Janna. She's got a huge heart, and she's an excellent judge of character. You have to admit Ashe's story is sad. Did you read the excerpt Janna sent? How heartbreaking. I'm with Janna. Let's give her a chance."

"Maybe."

"I have to get going if I want to finish my run. I've got a job later today."

"You do? Fabulous! I'll see you online later. Have a good day."

As Skye puffed toward the Cliff House, her mind drifted to a recounting of her failed personal life. Their relationship might have shown signs of impending implosion, yet Skye recognized them only in hindsight. Perhaps if she'd become a vegan like Trina, they would have had a chance. Skye was an unabashed carnivore and junk food junkie, craving nearly rare sirloin on occasion. Top off the cholesterol and protein overload with an order of In-N-Out animal fries – now that was *true* Nirvana. Perhaps if she'd kept the house and her books tidy, love might have withstood the test of time…and dust bunnies. Instead she was hopelessly disorganized and Trina was an anal retentive neat freak. Maybe if they'd sought counseling, the rancor between Trina and her son Rob might have subsided, the rough edges in their own relationship worked out. Woulda, shoulda, coulda. Did any of it matter? Trina moved out and moved on. End of story.

At least Skye could count on the Virtual Moms to help raise her out of depression. Thanks to Rob, who hacked into her email account and sent off an SOS to her online friends. The resulting responses were overwhelming. A flurry of email jammed her inbox, expressing both outrage and sympathy. The responses made Skye smile. Celia offered to break Trina's legs. As she was part Sicilian, she often offered free appendage breaking as an option for every problem.

Within days, a care package arrived from Minnesota, loaded with lavender bubble bath, scented candles, Godiva chocolates, a bottle of champagne, and a CD that contained an odd mix of soothing classical pieces and down-home country tunes about being wronged. "Now get in the tub and stay there until all of this chocolate is gone!" Ally had scribbled in a card.

Laurel sent a huge bouquet of flowers that filled the house with fragrance.

Janna hopped on the first plane out of New York. Taking charge, she cleaned house, answered the studio voice mail and made appointments. She bought groceries and paid bills. She promptly bagged all of Trina's belongings and showed up on the doorstep of the miscreant's new love nest where she unceremoniously deposited the contents into Trina's arms. "Stupid bitch," Janna had muttered as she skipped down the steps.

"I can't believe I forgot to snap a picture of her when she opened the door," Janna laughed later as she and Skye shared a bottle of sake at the Japanese restaurant down the street from her apartment. "You would have loved it. Her expression was priceless."

Even Skye smiled.

The VM intervention eventually germinated and took root. After six months of inactivity, Skye decided it was time to get back into life. She should have rejoined the rest of the world months before. It had been spinning without her. She wasn't looking for a new love; she'd decided after the breakup to give her heart a rest. No, she was going to reclaim her life bit by bit, and if it took her the next fifty years, so be it.

Skye stopped dead in her tracks. *Why am I mooning over Trina?* She put both hands to her head and shook it as hard as she could before raising her fists to the sky. "No. I am *not* going to waste two minutes over that woman *ever* again!"

Roused from early morning slumber, a one-legged seagull hobbled away from her and took to the sky.

It was then Skye noticed a fisherman within earshot, a young man with two Boston terriers chasing a misshapen yellow tennis ball, and a surfer, long board under his arm, emerging from the shallow water.

Skye's face flushed with embarrassment, although she giggled.

***

jannasbananas: *Yo, Ashe. You available?*

AsheMacD: *Yes, ma'am. I should take a break. This project is especially challenging.*

jannasbananas: *You sure?*

AsheMacD: *What's up?*

jannasbananas: *Checking up to see how my fellow mommies are treating you.*

AsheMacD: *I haven't heard much. Maybe they don't like me.*

jannasbananas: *No way! I should start an email.*

AsheMacD: *If you do, make it a call for recipes. I'm sick of eating macaroni and cheese.*

AsheMacD: *Although Tyler doesn't complain. It's his favorite dish.*

jannasbananas: *I forgot you don't cook.*

AsheMacD: *Not DON'T. CAN'T.*

24

jannasbananas: *I don't get it. All women should know how to cook. It's in our genes.*

AsheMacD: *Not in mine.*

jannasbananas: *Your lack of culinary skills might be problematic.*

AsheMacD: *?*

jannasbananas: *Just thinking out loud. You know, Skye doesn't cook. CAN'T, I mean.*

jannasbananas: *I don't think she can boil water!* ☺

AsheMacD: *So I'm not a freak after all!*

jannasbananas: *LOL. I wouldn't say that. It's more like having two freaks in the group.*

AsheMacD: *Precious. If that ain't true, grits ain't groceries.*

jannasbananas: *Charming, Ashe. Call me a bitch. I know you want to.*☺

AsheMacD: *My Southern upbringing precludes me from using that coarse term.*

jannasbananas: *?*

AsheMacD: *It doesn't mean I can't think it.*

jannasbananas: *I knew I could get a rise out of you!*

AsheMacD*: Let's get serious. What can I do? I mean to soften up the VMs?*

jannasbananas: *Be yourself. Soon enough they'll know you like I do and we'll all be one, big, happy, coast-to-coast family.*

AsheMacD: *Sure. Maybe I should send private messages. 'Reply all' is too out there.*

AsheMacD: *Especially since I know some of them had their arms twisted.*

jannasbananas: *It's called the "Power of Persuasion." You're right, though. Personal messages might help.*

AsheMacD: *It couldn't hurt.*

jannasbananas: *Gotta run and pick up Mandy's prescription.*

AsheMacD: *'K. TTYL.*

jannasbananas: *Good luck.*

AsheMacD: *Thanks. Cross your fingers.*

jannasbananas: *My toes 2.* ☺

***

25

"Oh, my, look at this."

Kitchen classroom B at the California Culinary Academy resembled an operating room, with cavernous, white tile, huge overhead lights, its arena seating surrounding a trio of steel tables far below. Skye and her equipment held court center-stage. Before her were a selection of luscious plated desserts, intricate pastries adorned with fresh orchids and mint and drizzled with chocolate and caramel sauce. Skye positioned her camera close enough to catch the curving tail of a dollop of whipped cream that graced a mousse.

The last thing she had wanted to do was return to CCA. It was, after all, where she met Trina, who was then enrolled in the Le Cordon Bleu pastry program. She'd graduated years before. Chances were nil of running into her in the halls or in one of the kitchen classrooms. Nervous, Skye glanced at the clock. Trina would be at work at the Biltmore Hotel – safe on the other side of town. Still, it was eerie returning to the 'scene of the crime.' Yet, she had to. She couldn't very well turn down an opportunity to work for *Sunset*, now could she?

"How do you keep from getting fat?" she asked a nearby student as her camera clicked away.

"Believe me," a gravelly voice answered, "if you live and breathe food ten hours a day or more, you have no compulsion to eat what you're cooking. It's a labor of love for someone else to enjoy."

Skye paused mid-shot to look up. This student was different, older than the usual group of fresh-faced twenty-somethings. This man's face was lined with wrinkles. The pony-tailed hair escaping from his chef's hat sported more salt than pepper. Arms crossed, the man appeared gruff yet she could feel the pride surging in his voice.

Skye smiled. She agreed with his assessment. She'd dropped two dress sizes during those teenaged years as a Denny's waitress in Riverside. Denny's, where she learned she could serve food, appreciate food, but cooking. Cooking was another story, more like a disaster movie. Couldn't get it, never could. Working in restaurants was where she learned food could be most unappealing when you knew the back-story on the entrée – the grease and guts behind the matter. Skye adjusted the light and turned the plate to catch the dish from a different angle. "You *must* like cooking. Actually, I would say better than like. I can see the love in this chocolate cake."

"Flourless chocolate torte," the student corrected.

"Excuse me. Whatever it is, it's exquisite. Too pretty to eat."

"Thanks."

Skye addressed a raspberry confection supporting a honey-mesh lace heart and adjusted a sprig of mint. She took a few more photos in case, yet knew all would be clear and crisp. Portraits and landscapes were mundane, and nearly anyone could take those pictures. When it came to food photography, she had the gift. Her images could whet the appetites of die-hard dieters. "Thanks, class." She waved as she packed up her equipment. "I'll email copies to your teacher."

She slung her bag over her shoulder and headed outside into the wet mist.

The fog was comforting and mystical, as much a part of the City as the steep hills, cable cars, Alcatraz, and the Golden Gate. Every pore of her body absorbed the moisture. Some thought the fog was a negative; she embraced it. By contrast, the previous week had been blisteringly hot by Bay Area standards, so warm that Ocean Beach had been lined with bikinied bodies catching unexpected rays instead of walkers bundled in parkas. November's blanket of moisture was a welcome relief from October's fleeting heat wave.

Skye strode past the promenade in front of City Hall. She had an hour to kill before meeting Rob after school. Instead of a local school near their apartment, Rob attended an arts school near the Civic Center. It was the best fit for him. He was a decent artist, accomplished guitarist, and his writing had blown her and his elementary school teachers away. With a generous scholarship, she could afford to send him to the Academy by the Bay. She reasoned they could ride the MUNI home together, that is, if he wanted to be seen with her. Although they were close, as her son matured, he wanted less to do with her. His friends were more important to him these days.

Skye headed across the mall to the public library, where she could clear some email while passing time. The bank of computers, free to San Francisco residents, was usually jammed with users. Somehow she managed to find an open machine.

She logged on to her AOL account and read several emails from the Virtual Moms. An early morning, minor inter-group uproar flared after Janna's initial email asking for Asheley MacDaniel to be allowed into the group. Laurel was the first to reply all, balking at the idea of an unknown outsider coming in. Missy responded next, half-heartedly backing Laurel. Ally was supported of Janna; that was to be expected. Both were easy-going with massive capacity for compassion. Celia, the oldest member of the VMs, was oddly silent, bowing out of group discussions. Skye expressed her reservations to Janna privately immediately after reading the first email. Janna had called back within minutes.

"My darling, how can you not want her with us? Ashe is perfect!"

"Listen, Janna. We're at such a great place, the six of us. We know each other. The kids know each other. We understand each other's idiosyncrasies. We've weathered every friendship storm ever imagined. Why rock the boat now?"

"Why not?"

"I don't know if I have the energy for someone new."

"Make some, woman. I'm telling you, this one is a keeper. Smart, generous. Like you."

"Don't snow me, Janna. She is *not* like me. No one is like me, thank goodness. If they were, I'd feel sorry for them."

Janna laughed. "Don't sell yourself short, Skye. Maybe you're not perfect but you're a wonderful woman."

Skye smiled. She could count on Janna's lighthearted quips to offset her gloom. "So, you like Ashe, huh?"

"I'm telling you, she's a perfect fit. Check out her blog," Janna insisted. "*All* of it. It's spare and not very pretty. I'll tell you, I still cry when I read her posts. She's so eloquent about her feelings. Read and you'll see she's not some kind of flake."

After hanging up, Skye followed the link Janna provided to *Missing Mac.* She backtracked to the first post. It was poignant, with each successive entry more gut wrenching than the last. The more Skye read, the more she realized striking similarities to Ashe's life.

Her husband, Lee had died in a freak snowstorm in the Sierras six years before. Ashe's initial words of denial and grief brought forth memories of the days of anguish and confusion following Lee's funeral. The sadness and the longing for someone to fill the gaping hole in the heart Skye found hardest to overcome. The acceptance came much later. It is the ultimate loss when God takes a loved one.

She winced. The pain after Trina's betrayal was altogether different. It was a hurt that could last a lifetime. The finality of death she could handle. Trina was still alive, across town enjoying a new life with a new love. Her memory would be harder to erase.

The only photo on *Missing Mac* was of Tyler, an impish boy with deep blue eyes and a mop of dishwater blond hair bowl cut in a straight line across his eyebrows. His smile was huge and beaming. "What a doll," she said out loud.

She might have been the last to respond, yet how could she not vote yes?

Next in her inbox was a personal note from Ashe. She smiled as she opened and read the contents.

To: shootingskye
From: AsheMacD

I wanted to send you this personal note to thank you, Skye, for allowing me into your group. I've known Janna for almost a year (online). She's spoken highly of the Virtual Moms. I feel like I know all of you. She shared the circumstances of your husband's passing, and I definitely feel for you, being in a similar situation myself.

If you want to know me better, I hope you will read my blog. I'm attaching a link if you want to check it out.

Thanks again.
Peace out,
Ashe

Skye dashed off a quick reply before logging off to head for Rob's school. "Dear Ashe, sorry to hear about Mac. I'm no expert. I hope I can share something that will help you in your time of grief." *What a lovely person*, she thought as she hit the "Send" button and closed out the screen. It might be wrong to question the integrity of this unknown newcomer. Ashe was a lonely human being who needed the connection of sympathetic friends.

After all, like shoes, a girl can't have too many friends.

***

"Come back, my little munchkin." Greg Smith, a hulking man of six foot three was brought closer to earth by the mere fact of being on hands and knees. He trailed after his daughter, a blur of long, curly hair in corduroy overalls topped with a red cape. They circled the kitchen island several times before Vanessa ducked behind Ally.

"Momma, help!"

Ally pushed a wayward strand of hair from her forehead, her hands covered in pumpkin guts. A burst of pie making had been slated for the afternoon, before the little squash turned into a rotten mess. Although Vanessa was fast, Ally was faster. She evaded her daughter's move for cover. "Oh, no you don't. I'm too busy to play. This is Daddy's game. I warned you being chased by Wolf Daddy would be no fun."

"Momma!"

"Sorry. You're on your own."

"I'm going to eat you up!" Greg growled, any ominous tones tempered with stifled giggles. Vanessa responded with shrieks of delight.

"You two. Honestly." The phone rang. Ally smiled as she wiped her hands on a dishtowel, leaving a smudge of orange goo. She retreated to the relative calm of the family room to take the call.

"Smith House," she answered. "Center of mass mayhem and hilarity."

"Are you having a party?"

"No, it's the regular mob." Ally covered the phone and yelled across the room. "Hey, Little Red Riding Hood and Wolf Man? I'm on the phone here. Think you can keep it down?" By that time, Greg had captured Vanessa and the screams dissolved to muted twitters. Ally returned to her call. "Skye! What's up?"

"I'm on the MUNI. Finished a job downtown."

"A job, huh?"

30

Skye lowered her voice to a whisper. "Rob's here. He's at the front of the car. We're pretending we don't know each other."

"I remember those days. I don't think Mike said a dozen words to me in any given month. Don't worry. It'll pass, and when it does, you'll have a man where your boy was."

"So you keep telling me. I'm not sure I can wait."

"You can, and you will. Congrats on the job. You're feeling better?"

"I ran for an hour today."

"No kidding?"

"To be honest, it was more like a half hour. I'm so out of shape, Ally, I should have called 911. At least I got out of the house without being dragged."

"I bet you're calling about Ashe." Ally sank into the couch, pulled her long legs under her, and settled in.

"No. Well, yes. I'm also calling about Missy."

"Missy?" Ally scrunched up her nose.

"She called again today. Earl is up to something and it can't be good. I don't know what to tell her." Skye paused.

Ally used the silence to arrange her thoughts. "Ugh, Earl. I'm sorry, but I never saw the appeal."

"Who did?"

"Maybe she's coming to you because of Trina."

"Like I'm an expert on breaking up? Please. I'm the last person to come to for relationship advice. I'm just most available. Janna is too glamorous, you're too happy, Laurel is too stressed and Celia is too cynical. And no one knows Ashe yet."

"Speaking of which, she emailed me."

"Oh?"

"It wasn't a round robin letter, it was private. She thanked me for allowing her into the group and let me know how lonely she was. She asked me to give her some tips on Tyler. We had a pleasant exchange. It's nice having another mom around with a child in the same age group."

"What about Mike? He's still your child."

"Mike's twenty-six. He's hardly a child."

"What about Mike Junior?"

Ally laughed. "Honey, we will revisit this topic when Rob gives you a grandchild. Take it from me. The difference between children and grandchildren is amazing, even if they're close in age."

"So you like Ashe?"

"Yes, I think I do. Why?"

"Janna's really pushing."

"That's our Janna. When she feels passion for something, she throws all her energy behind it. Why so negative? You haven't been listening to Celia, have you?"

"It's not that. I've been through the relationship blender and what's come out isn't exactly pretty. I have issues with trust, with jealousy. I don't know if I'm capable of being a friend to anyone new right now."

"Don't sell yourself short."

Skye burst out with raucous chortling.

"What?" Ally asked.

"It's funny. That's what Janna said."

Chapter Four

Why Me? Why Us?

My dearest Mac,

According to the World Wide Web, the number of people on the planet is nearly 7 billion.

The number of people in the United States is 300 million.

The number of people serving in the military is 1.4 million. The number of them in Iraq is 92,000.

There have been 1,200 U.S. casualties since the war began.

* Sigh *

So why all the numbers?

You know me, not much of a math head. I'm trying to figure out the percentages. Remember what you told me before you left? Your words still ring in my head. "What are the chances, Ashe? It's so slim, and I'm needed. I'll be in the medical unit, far away from the hot zone." Damn, but you had a way of sweet-talking me into anything and everything. 'Honey' me this and 'Sugar' me that. It made sense. What could I say? I so wanted to believe you.

If it was such a long shot, how the hell did we not beat the odds?

I think about those numbers all the time. I eat, sleep and dream them. One life out of three billion, one out of 300 million, one out of 1.4 million, one out of 92,000.

There's only one I care about. One out of 1,200. The One who used to live here with me. The One who was my soul mate. That was the only One who mattered, and now that One is gone.

The anger explodes when I realize you lied and then I get mad at myself. You were only following orders, but me, I should've said something. I should've kicked, screamed, thrown dishes, barred the way to the airport. I should've burned your fatigues and kidnapped you and Tyler and headed for Canada.

Nope, I kept my mouth shut. You were a soldier, descended from a long line of soldiers going back to the Civil War. It was in

your blood. Instead I smiled, I waved goodbye, when what I
wanted to do was to lock my arms around your ankles.
       Dear God. Why me? Why us?

***

Las Vegas, Nevada

A flash of hot pink and denim flew past Missy Martin, the whirlwind accompanied by the tinkle of charms and the jangling of bangles. "Whoa, whoa, whoa, what's the hurry?" Missy asked as she twirled her daughter Kassie around by the shoulders and gave her eldest the once-over. Her brunette locks were neatly straightened and she smelled of strawberry shampoo. Yet the total picture was miles from schoolgirl innocence. Kassie's plaid skirt had been rolled up at the waistband, the hem brushing dangerously close to the top of her thighs. The shirt she chose came from last year's shopping trip and hugged her pre-teen body, emphasizing every burgeoning potential curve. And what was that on her eyelids? Purple eye liner?

"You're *not* going to school like this, Kassandra Martin. We might live in Vegas, but you're not walking out of this house looking like a showgirl wannabe."

"Mom!" Kassie pouted. "See? I'm wearing tights. And *three* camisoles!"

"Bring the skirt down a little, Kass. And let's tone down this makeup." Missy reached into her pocket for a Kleenex to dab at her daughter's eyes. Kassie backed away before Missy could make contact.

"I'll look like a baby!"

"You'll look decent!" Missy's voice rose with exasperation. Kassie had begun life as a pleasant, mindful child, eager to please and obedient compared to other girls in the neighborhood. In recent months Kassie stretched her wings and pushed the envelope with Missy. It didn't matter the subject. If Missy said 'yes' Kassie said 'no.' When Missy said 'black' Kassie said 'white.' If she decided to change her mind, Kassie was sure to reverse her opinion as well.

Missy shook her head. "You're so pretty, honey. You don't need to resort to these tactics to get attention. Besides, you're not a teenager yet."

"Two weeks! I'll be thirteen in *two* short weeks! Two painfully short, teeny-tiny weeks. Are you going to start treating me like an adult then?"

Missy crossed her arms and frowned. The girls' public school academy had a dress code, not strict, although by Vegas standards it pitched to the conservative side. Yet she understood the desire to fit in. "We'll compromise. Unroll the skirt, Kass. You can have one roll up and that's it. How will anyone be able to concentrate with you dressed up like a hoochie mama?"

Kassie did as she was told, lowering the skirt four full inches. It was still too short by Missy's calculation.

"Let's keep it that way all day, all right? The last thing I need is to field a call from school today." Missy's hands grasped Kassie's skull. She tilted Kassie's face toward her before pounding her own carefully coifed head against it. "Okay?"

"Okay." Kassie frowned.

"Now get to the bus stop. Where is your sister? Kara! Hurry up, girl. You'll miss the bus! You've already missed enough school with the flu."

A pounding of footsteps preceded Kara's arrival. Delicate and petite, the other girls in her class towered over her. She missed school often for sickness, yet managed to keep up. Kara struggled with her backpack, bright purple and nearly as big as she was. A week's worth of homework assignments were crammed inside. "Where's Daddy? I have to ask him a question." Kara asked, as she peered into the kitchen.

"Gone. Early day. You'll have to wake up before dawn if you want to catch him."

Earl Martin was a successful architect. His current project list included a pricey high-rise condominium on the Strip. With a wildly fluctuating economy, the work meant many long hours away from home. Not that she minded. Although she had been an architect in her B.C. life – Before Children – conversations about supply flow issues, the lack of skilled tradesmen, and fussy subcontractors with outrageous demands made her eyes glaze over.

Not that her husband was around much to regale her with stories from work. Missy recently quipped to a neighbor at a subdivision barbecue that Earl was so busy these days she wasn't sure what he looked like anymore. Earl, who had been talking UNLV basketball with the other husbands, was not amused by the smart comment. Missy was unrepentant. The pointed remark was meant to highlight his absentee status.

Missy inspected Kara, making sure she had her lunch and homework zipped up tight. "Give me a kiss, pumpkin." Kara obliged, throwing in a tight hug for good measure. Kassie had given up Mommy-kisses when she entered middle school. Missy extricated herself from Kara's love squeeze. "Okay, off with you! Don't miss the bus!"

She stood at the door until the bus arrived, dutifully waved as it pulled away from the curb, and closed the door behind her.

Ah, peace and quiet.

Missy headed for her spacious gourmet kitchen and poured another cup of coffee. She was lucky. Earl's income was generous, more than enough so that she didn't need to return to work once Kara was old enough for school. While not a life of bonbons, power shopping, and reality shows, Missy's spare time was devoted to her favorite charities. She was a room mom for Kara's class, was active in the PTA, and volunteered to teach illiterate adults to read. Missy was a militant housekeeper, preferring to do most of the work herself. Each night she made sure a home-cooked meal was on the table. June Cleaver was her idol, and Missy neared the pinnacle of Domestic Diva-dom.

She took her mug into the great room and settled down at the computer. A chronic insomniac, she had shared many sleepless nights with the Virtual Moms. Thank God for the Internet and that first Beanie Baby chat room. After strong relationships were forged, they moved on to forming their own private room. Back in the day the online get-togethers were cheaper than phone calls and faster than snail mail, although calls were frequent and friendship balls, Christmas presents, and various collaborative scrapbooks made the rounds. After twelve years, she knew all of the women as though they lived on the same block.

Missy first in-person VM meeting was with Celia, who acted as designated travel companion for her elderly mother's frequent gambling junkets to Vegas. Missy's girls were babies then, still in strollers. Celia's Kimber wasn't much older. They'd spent an afternoon in the mall at Caesar's Palace, unsuccessfully searching the maze-like upscale stores for Beanie Babies, and ended up pushing the kids through F.A.O. Schwartz. Kimber had caused a ruckus when she scaled an elaborate Barbie display and sent it tumbling to the ground. Missy and Celia couldn't exit fast enough, and broke out in hysterical giggles as soon as they left the store.

It was as if they'd known each other forever.

Janna came to town next. As soon as she saw her at the airport, Missy recognized her, she was that familiar. "Look at you! You're so...*tiny!*" Missy had blurted out. Janna, at barely 5 feet tall, was a mere slip of a woman, trim and elegant, nothing like her huge online persona, dominant and flashy.

Janna had laughed. "Look who's talking! You didn't tell us you were Miss America," she replied.

Over the years, Missy had downplayed her looks and hid her resume as high school model, homecoming queen, and first runner-up to Miss Indiana. Flawless skin and an hourglass figure had come in handy, especially in college when she'd set her sights on one handsome Earl Martin. Missy Martin was so much more than a pretty face. She wanted to be known for her creativity, her compassion, and her *brains*.

As luck would have it, Janna's parents maintained a winter home in nearby Laughlin. Regular visits to Las Vegas were penciled in as a matter of family duty, and with it, a standing VM get-together. Missy was impressed by Janna's sophisticated style and entranced by her stories of life in the Big Apple. Janna's daughters Mandy and Rachel, now twenty and twenty-five, were beautiful and well-behaved as children. Missy hoped her own two would turn out as nicely.

As she logged on to her account, the familiar AOL voice announced, "You've got mail!" Of course, there was mail – there would *always* be mail. While it was nothing like those frenetic days when two hundred emails in a twenty-four hour period meant someone was slacking off, the moms still shared daily updates. The Virtual Moms exchanged recipes, jokes and links to free samples, along with news and photographs. As the kids grew up and schedules stretched thin, email volume decreased. Some took to text messaging; others kept in touch by Facebook or Twitter. Missy was old-fashioned and preferred the email loop or a phone call. Watching Janna manipulate her Blackberry made her head spin.

As for the new member, Ashe MacDaniel, Missy was torn. Change was hard; accepting a virtual stranger was harder. After members exchanged a few chatty and welcoming emails, Missy went to Ashe's blog and read her posts on the loss of her husband. Being left a young widow would be difficult in any circumstance. But to lose your husband to war? That was the ultimate sacrifice. How could a person endure such hardship and yet write the way Ashe did? How could she write at all? *If I lost Earl, I don't think I could function.*

Ashe's blog was an eye-opener. Missy knew nothing about military life. How would she, safe in her own bubble? Some posts were uncomfortable and depressing. Something else bothered her… something about Ashe that nagged at Missy. She couldn't put her finger on it; something wasn't right. *Maybe I'm imagining things.* She shrugged off her doubts. The group was solid and tight. Whack jobs like Melda were the exception, not the norm. So much time had passed since that nightmare mom that their protective armor had disappeared.

To: missymom, jannasbananas, celiasunshine, laurelextonsbunch, ally1234, shootingskye
From: AsheMacD
Subject: Re: Re: Re: Welcome to Virtual Moms

I know I've said this before to all of you. Thanks for including me in your group. You don't know how alone I have felt in the last year. I had no one to turn to except Janna. The isolation was killing me. Trust me. This group is what the doctor ordered.

So far, I've received quite a few recipes on cooking for one and a half and a list of politically correct finger foods to pack in my son's lunch. Ally also advised I should take Tyler in to get his ears checked. (I will.)

I have an assignment to finish up in the next few days, so I'll be around although I'm working. Keep the emails coming. I'll read them all. Promise.

Peace out,
Ashe

***

"Damn it to hell."

Celia slammed on the brakes as the light turned red. Her car screeched to a stop mid-crosswalk as an elderly man pushing a walker adorned with pink tennis ball feet stepped off the curb. He shook a bony fist at her while she sheepishly backed up a few feet, taking care not to bump into the blue-haired driver behind her. Florida could be paradise; it was also a haven for antiquarian octogenarians.

"Watch where you're going!" the pedestrian yelled.

"Jesus Jimmy," Celia said under her breath. "I only have twenty minutes." The day started poorly with no coffee in the house and quickly sank to cataclysmic levels when an epidemic of staff members called in sick with the flu. To top it off, Celia had brought an important fiscal report home for study before her big meeting at one, and of course she'd forgotten to bring it back to the hospital. Depending on the time of day and weather conditions, a ten-minute trip could take an hour. She smiled and waved to the old man, one eye on the clock. "Any time now," she whispered.

She was jolted out of her watch by the phone. *Probably the hospital wondering where the hell I am.* She flipped it open without looking. "Celia here."

"Hi, Celia, it's me, Missy."

Celia's eyebrows knit together in concern. She'd anticipated an emergency call from Missy at any minute. Celia's last visit with the Martins had been strained. During subsequent conversations, she deduced that Earl was a sneaky dog, not unlike Celia's first husband. If ever lived a man who required a broken few body parts, it was Mr. Earl Martin. "Is anything wrong?"

"No. I had some free time and wanted to touch base with you. I noticed you weren't responding to email like you normally do."

What could she say? That she decided to take a step back because of the whole Ashe thing? That she didn't like being

39

overturned by the Virtual Moms, or Ashe? "I've been busy with a hospital study," she white-lied. "It's been a bear, super time consuming. I'm actually in the car right now. I forgot the report at home so I had to go back to get it. Meeting at one." *At least that part is true.*

"Sorry to hear that. Is Kimber okay?"

"She's fine. It's my job that's a mess." The light turned green and Celia pressed her foot to the floor. The car sputtered.

"So, what about Ashe? Is that why you're not responding?"

Ashe. The axis of the entire universe rested on the martyred woman. Let's venerate Saint Ashe with the gifts of the Magi. Ashe this, Ashe that, poor, poor Ashe. "I don't think anything about Ashe," Celia replied, annoyed. Any level of compassion she might have entertained had evaporated in the course of this nightmare of a day. *I think Ashe should drop off the face of the earth. I think you're all naïve for letting a virtual stranger into our group. That's what I should say.*

Celia's sarcastic tone went over Missy's head. "It's so sad, what happened to her. And the little boy. What a tragedy."

"Yes. Sad. It's a mess." Celia's eyes fell to the dash. "Oh, my God."

"What? What's going on?"

"Oh, my word. The cherry on top of a killer day. I'm out of gas!"

"Are you kidding?"

"Would I kid about something like this? Freakin' frack, I have to be back in ten minutes. My ass is going to be in a royal sling."

"Sorry."

"I hate to be short, but I've got to go."

"Sure. Go ahead."

"I'll email you later. After I call AAA. Hopefully I'll still have a job tonight."

"Good luck."

***

Missy finished dusting and vacuuming in record time. "It's not so hard. All it takes is a system," she said as she glanced at her watch. She grinned. Noon was an hour away and there would be more than enough time for a shopping trip before the girls arrived

40

home. She had to pick up groceries, of course, and drop off Earl's cleaning. Missy also had Kassie's birthday present to pick up.

Her daughter had been hinting for months that she wanted diamond stud earrings – *real* diamonds, not CZs. Missy had been outnumbered by a knock-out combination of Kassie and the Virtual Moms. "This is a big step for her," Celia told her. "You're only thirteen once." Janna added, "You don't want to see your baby all grown up, but you can't stop it!"

Missy agreed that turning thirteen was a landmark occasion and should be celebrated with an heirloom quality present. She had carefully considered the other baubles on the jeweler's tray. In the end, she agreed the diamonds were understated and pretty, especially if they were small enough to be discreet. To make sure they wouldn't be lost, Missy had screw backs put in place.

Missy tucked the vacuum and cleaning supplies away and hummed as she made a room-to-room inspection, although her home was *House Beautiful* perfect. The bed linens were flawless, wrinkle-free, windows open wide, dust chased, and toys put away. At least one vase of fresh flowers brightened each room, bursting with the color and redolence of far-off spring. In the master bedroom, Missy scooped up Earl's sports jackets and sweaters from the hamper. His worn white shirts were still stiff with starch, much like their owner. Missy smiled. Earl was a decent man, although at times he could be a humorless suit. What happened to the merry prankster she had met in college, the party boy, the one with a mischievous twinkle in his eye? That Earl had been a blast to be around. Somewhere along the line, her husband had turned into his father, serious and dry, so dry he was nearly crispy.

She began the tedious task of turning the pockets inside out. Early in their marriage, she had once forgotten to retrieve an ink pen from an inside pocket. So had the cleaner and an entire load had been destroyed. Missy was too experienced these days to make such a mistake. Earl was meticulous, too. No money, no cigarettes, no strange receipts; the most Missy pulled from his pockets these days were lint balls.

Except today.

Missy pulled a pristine linen business card from the right front pocket of Earl's best silk suit and squinted at it. From arm's length, she could make out the irrefutable scent of Chanel No. 5.

"Marcella Bainbridge. Who the hell?" A name and a printed phone number, no address or company name.

She turned the card around – nothing. *Maybe she's a consultant.* With the economy in the doldrums, a lot of folks were laid off and worked from their homes. On her way out of the room, Missy placed the card on Earl's dresser and anchored it with a bottle of his cologne.

"Don't forget to thank me, honey," she said aloud.

***

To: jannasbananas
From: AsheMacD
Subject: Re: Nothin' special

Janna, I wanted to thank you again for including me in your group. I've already had several private conversations with the Virtual Moms. They're all so nice. What a breath of fresh air! I've been wallowing in self-pity for so long I'd almost forgotten about the world. Your friends are the coolest.

Virtually yours,
Ashe

P.S. What's up with Celia?

***

"Mom! We're home! *Mom*-ma!" Kara screamed as the back door slammed shut.

"So you are," Missy whispered as she turned down the oven. "You certainly are." A beautiful pork loin lay roasting in its own juices. Dinner was poised to be yet another foray into gastronomic heaven.

"What's for dinner? Smells yummy." Kara peered into the oven door.

"Pork loin. Applesauce. Whipped potatoes. Homemade chocolate cake for dessert. Where's Kassie?" Missy wiped her hands on a dishtowel and looked to the back door. Her oldest was not only contrary but pokey, too. It took forever for her to accomplish anything.

"She's coming." Kara opened the refrigerator, her eyes giant saucers scanning the shelves for snacks. Missy pulled her shoulders back.

"You'll spoil your dinner," she said as she closed the door.

"Momma, please! I'm starving."

"How was school? You took it easy, right?" Missy gave her the 'mom' look. Any lingering effects of the flu had vanished. Kara was back to her old self. Missy relented on the snack verdict and relinquished a vanilla wafer.

"The teacher said I did a good job. I was all caught up! Except I need some help with fractions. I don't get it. Can you help me?"

"I'm afraid your father is the math expert. You can ask him."

"Is he coming home on time?"

Good question. The family hadn't shared a dinner in ages. She and the girls ate theirs at a reasonable hour with Earl picking at leftovers or bringing his own fast food later. Missy couldn't remember the last time Earl made it home before 9:30. The girls were in bed by then and hadn't seen him in weeks. Weekends found him away from home. She did her best to mask her disappointment from the girls. Missy could survive without the conversation and affection of their father. Her daughters couldn't. No matter what, Missy would make sure their lives were perfect.

"Why don't you call him?" Missy cheerfully handed Kara her cell phone.

Kara fumbled with the receiver. She frowned. "He's not answering."

"Leave him a message, pumpkin. He's probably out of range. Tell him pork roast and applesauce tonight. Maybe that'll get him home on time." Missy bit her tongue. She hoped Kara would miss the terseness in her response.

Kara left a long-winded, breathless message about two-fifths and four-eighths, would he come home early enough to help her, and there was homemade chocolate cake for dessert.

It broke Missy's heart.

Dinner was another lonesome threesome. It was delicious, nutritious and awesome, yet the table was missing a key family member.

At least Earl had the decency to call Kara back, right in the middle of dessert. "He says if I get up early tomorrow, he'll help me," she reported after hanging up.

"He won't help you," Kassie snarled.

"What time?" Missy's interest piqued. Earl's usual escape from the house was by six a.m. *He's nuts if he thinks she's getting up at five,* she thought. *It's too much for a little girl.*

"Five-thirty."

"You'll never get up," Kassie taunted.

"I'll set my alarm, Momma." Her little pumpkin was earnest.

Missy smiled; inside, she was seething.

As the girls readied for bed, Missy logged on to the Internet. She perused a department store web site in search of interesting bargains. She was soon bored to tears. Missy turned her attention to Facebook. Perhaps if she could take out a few people on Mafia Wars, her mood would improve. To her surprise, her IM chimed.

AsheMacD: *Isn't it late where you are?*

The first IM from the newbie. Missy was glad for the diversion.

missymom: *Isn't it* later *where you are?*☺

AsheMacD: *Tyler's asleep. I'm working while he's unconscious. It's impossible to write when he's awake. Or do anything else for that matter. Night time's the only time I can get anything done.*

missymom: *I hear you. I love my kids. I can get a lot more accomplished when they're in school.*

AsheMacD: *Tyler started kindergarten this year. It was an adjustment. More for me than for him.*

Missy smiled as she remembered teary scenes on the first day of school. By the time she had returned to fetch the girls, they hadn't wanted to leave their teachers and new friends.

missymom: *That's how it is.*

AsheMacD: *A lot of you ladies seem to be insomniacs. That's how I met Janna. Late night in a grief forum.*

missymom: *LOL...you're right about us night owls.*

44

A minute passed without a reply. *Oh, my God,* Missy thought, *I LOL'ed a woman in mourning?* She typed quickly.

missymom: *Oh, Ashe, I'm so sorry.*
AsheMacD: *Sorry? Why?*
missymom: *The 'LOL.' I'm so embarrassed.*
AsheMacD: *No worries. A person has to laugh some time, even if you feel like crying.*
missymom: *I'm not bothering you?*
AsheMacD: *No, ma'am. Call it break time.*
missymom: *OK.*
AsheMacD: *Janna says you're from Indianapolis. You're a long way from home. How do you like Vegas?*
missymom: *It's okay. It's not like you'd think. Everyone is from somewhere else. People who live here don't hang out on the Strip.*
AsheMacD: *Don't you miss your hometown?*

Missy tilted her head and pondered. She had been so busy trying to keep her life organized that she rarely had time to think about 'home.'

missymom: *Not really. I miss my parents and my friends sometimes. I'm busy with my own family now.*
AsheMacD: *I hear that. My life is full with work and taking care of Tyler. It leaves little time for homesickness, or anything else.*
missymom: *It has to be hard to handle a household alone. I mean, after what happened.*

God, Missy thought, *I hope Ashe doesn't think I'm insensitive.*

AsheMacD: *Sure is. We're in similar circumstances, aren't we? Janna told me your husband isn't around much because of his job.*

Missy blushed. What else did Janna tell Ashe?

missymom: *He's busy, yes.*

AsheMacD: *Doesn't your husband mind you being on the computer at night? Mac couldn't stand it. When we were together it was We Time.*

missymom: *I wouldn't know. Earl's not home.*

AsheMacD: *Really? But it's late...*

She glanced at her computer clock. It was late – the next day late. Missy's heart dropped. She'd believed her marriage was more than the animal attraction of frat boy and beauty queen. Once upon a time, she and Earl made a cohesive team, with similar likes, dislikes, and aspirations. Now she wasn't sure who her husband was. Did they have conversations anymore? She squinted into the monitor and blinked back tears. Thank goodness for good, old-fashioned computer illiteracy and technological refusnik-ism. Her disabled web cam meant Ashe couldn't see her.

missymom: *Yeah, well. Business. You know how it is with men. Janna must have told you he's got a huge project right now. It's a multi-million dollar building on the Strip. His calendar is pretty full.*

AsheMacD: *Impressive.*

missymom: *I suppose.*

Missy wished she could type *I'd prefer if he were a real husband and not a silent roommate.*

AsheMacD: *Thanks for inviting me into the group. Janna's amazing, don't you think?*

missymom: *Oh, yes. She's great in person, too. I love her. So tiny! And, well, so bubbly and warm. She must know everyone in New York. You have to meet her.*

AsheMacD: *You don't say?*

missymom: *She comes to Vegas at least three times a year to visit her parents so I've seen her the most. Very nice family.*

Missy heard a car door slam.

Missymom: *Gotta go, Ashe. My hubby's walking in. TTYL.*

46

Missy logged off the computer before Ashe could say goodbye. She brushed away tears and hurried to warm Earl's dinner.

Chapter Five

On the Occasion of Ty's Fifth Birthday

We didn't do much. What could we do? It's not much of a celebration without you.

I'm lost when it comes to the ways of little boys. You know me. No prior experience. Like you, I never thought about having children. Good God, could you imagine? You with your track record of hang-ups and me – let's just say the picture's not pretty. It was nice to borrow our ankle biters from friends and give them back at the end of the day, or even better, to observe the Child Species from afar.

Along came Tyler and our lives changed.

We became parents. Damned good ones too, I think, despite our flawed and off-beat logic. I take that back. You slid into the role with ease, while I approached our tiny human with panic. Five years later and I'm still not comfortable.

I'm not like you, Mac. I'm not easy-going. I don't like talking to strangers. I can't see the world like you could – I don't have your wicked humor. I don't plan parties. I especially don't like birthdays, starting with my own.

On his birthday, I did the good parent thing and we made do. I took Tyler to his favorite restaurant (McDonald's) for lunch where we ate good and greasy (cheeseburgers and fries) and chased down the high cholesterol and sodium overload with a couple of Cokes. Tyler was buzzed on sugar. I then escorted Tyler to Toys 'R Us and told him he could have whatever he wanted. After circling the store for an hour, he chose a GI Joe Cobra. I threw in a Cobra Pit Mobile Headquarters so Joe and his pals would have something to tool around in.

I shouldn't have, I know. I'm trying to plug a gaping hole with a hundred bucks' worth of plastic toys.

I know nothing of war but I got on my hands and knees and played like I did.

You'd be proud. We dusted off all of those terrorists.

Minneapolis, Minnesota

Ally kept one eye on Vanessa, who was whirling in the kitchen, and another on the computer screen. She was waiting for Janna to come online so they could IM and dish about Asheley MacDaniel. However, most of her attention was captured by a five-year-old on a sugar high. Ally knew better. Now she would have to wait out Vanessa's hyperactive buzz. Vanessa, with her cherub's face and long, curly locks, could talk a bowl of Fruit Loops out of the meanest mom on the planet. The "Mean Mom" title was once Ally's, back when she was a struggling young single mother trying to raise young Mike after his father took off for parts unknown. Ally's parenting style swung in the opposite direction with Vanessa. Saying "no" to her late-in-life baby was next to impossible.

The trials of single parenthood ended long ago. Ally hit the jackpot with Husband Number Two. She met Greg Smith on a dare ten years before, long after the sting from the desertion of Mike's dad subsided. It was one fine fall day when Ally and a visiting Janna decided to have lunch in a Grand Avenue bistro. Janna dared Ally with a crisp one-hundred-dollar bill that she would not introduce herself and pass her phone number to the handsome hunk sitting alone at a table across the room. The big brute was dining on a mile-high veggie sandwich accompanied by a mocha latte topped with whipped cream. To Janna's (and Greg's) surprise, Ally got up and did just that.

Greg was a welder by trade, a huge strapping man, down to earth as well as easy on the eyes. A decade younger than Ally, the age difference wasn't a concern for him. Their brief introduction led to a first date, funded in part with the payoff from Janna's bet. Ally tried hard to scare him with tales of the teenaged-Mike and what a hellion he was. Greg was undeterred. He stepped in easily as a strong male figure for the struggling adolescent and included him in their activities. It worked. They hit it off and Greg proved to be perfect. How could Ally not fall in love with the big galoot?

The first thing Ally did was mention Greg to the rest of the Virtual Moms. She sent photographs and forwarded personal email exchanges between her and Greg. Celia was cautious, Missy absent (she was eight months pregnant with Kara at the time), Skye was noncommittal and Janna, the romantic and chronic instigator of the bunch, was over the moon. "I've seen him in the flesh and he's a doll. You can't let this one go," she warned. Even conservative Laurel cheered her on.

Later that year, they married on a beach in Hawaii, with Mike Junior, Janna, and Skye in attendance, followed by a serious case of happily ever after. A pregnancy, however, was much harder to accomplish. A year after Ally and Greg were placed on an adoption waiting list, Ally suffered from bloating stomach, mood swings, and insatiable hunger. She thought her symptoms were signs of early menopause. A trip to the doctor confirmed what she had only dreamed of… she was pregnant!

Fast forward five years. Vanessa had grown into a gorgeous, intelligent, and compassionate beauty. Her daughter was blessed with Greg's thick hair and flawless skin tone. After Vanessa arrived, Ally couldn't stop smiling. She approached each day as a learning experience, so different from raising Mike. Ally's single parent stress had blotted out the small pleasures. Her life in those days was carefully choreographed, a balancing act between work, home, and everything in between. In raising Vanessa, she realized she'd missed a lot of Mike's growing up. Ally was blessed in that she had Greg's support in every way. He was a doting, wonderful father. Sure she wished she had the stamina of her youth, yet she wouldn't trade her lot for anything.

"Come on, babe, let's get ready for school," she said as she drained the remains of fruity loops into the sink. Ally longed for five spare minutes to gossip about the new VM, Ashe. With the mountain of work on her agenda, the email and IM could wait.

"Can I take some candy to kindergarten? Can I?" Vanessa jumped up and down. She'd cleaned up this Halloween as a fairy princess. Some people gave her extra candy for being extra cute.

"I think not, babe. Your teacher would put me on the D List if she finds out about the you-know-whats you had for breakfast."

"Fruit Loops are good for you. Look, Mom. Says 'fiber' right here." She pointed to tiny lettering on the side of the box.

Vanessa was too smart. She'd started reading at three and had long outpaced her classmates. Pretty soon she would overtake her parents and go on to rule the world. Ally took the box and sighed. "Says 'sugar' right here, too," she pointed. "See? Fructose is sugar. This stuff's full of it. That's the part that makes you a crazy baby."

"Crazy baby!" Vanessa squealed in delight. "I'm no baby, I'm a girl. Crazy, crazy, crazy girl!"

"You sure are!" She picked Vanessa up and spun her around the room. "Come on, little love. You're stalling. You don't want to be late."

Vanessa stopped giggling, her expression serious. "No. I'll get my coat, Momma."

An alert chimed from her laptop. It was Janna. Ally put Vanessa down.

> jannasbananas: *Al, are you there?*
> ally1234: *On my way out. I have to drop Vanessa off at school. BRB in 15.*
> jannasbananas: *Can't wait. I'll call you on your cell, K?*
> ally1234: *All right. Give me two minutes to get into the car.*

Once they were safely buttoned up in the SUV, Ally shivered in her light jacket. She should have chosen her parka. In two short days, the weather had taken a 180 degree turn from unseasonably warm to right back into the Deep Freeze. She loved winter and was glad for the change of season. It meant the Three S's – skating, snowmobiles, and skiing. Like Greg, Ally was the outdoorsy type. They enjoyed the harsh Minnesota winters as much as they did the humid summers.

After strapping Vanessa into her car seat, Ally dialed Janna on her hands free. Janna answered before the first ring sounded.

"Al, that was quick."

"I've got to get Vanessa to school. We're running a little late. Fruit Loop Wednesday, you know."

"Got-cha. Well, what do you think?"

Ally looked in her rearview to check Vanessa. She was occupied with singing songs to Garcia, the tie-died Beanie Baby. The VMs had long ago given up hunting for Beanies. The arsenal of the small, plush toys came in handy for keeping the little girl busy. Ally thought her heart would drop out of her chest the first time Baby Vanessa sucked off the pristine ear tag of Erin the Irish bear. The panic subsided a little at a time each time she gave a new beanbag toy to Vanessa. Now seeing her once-prized possessions turning into beloved playthings didn't hurt at all.

"What do I think about what?"

"About Ashe, what do you think I'm talking about?"

"I don't know. Seems nice."

"Did you read her blog?"

Ally maneuvered around a school bus that was crowding most of narrow 34th Avenue. "I scanned it. I've been busy with Vanessa."

"Hi, Nessy! It's your Aunt Janna!" Janna called out through the car's speakers.

"Janna, Janna, Janna," Vanessa sang from the backseat.

"Thanks a bunch, Janna; I'd quieted her down enough so she wouldn't be bouncing off the walls at school."

"Oh, snap! Sorry. Be a good girl at school, Nessy."

"O-*kay*..." Vanessa sang from the back seat.

"Janna, I think I'll be shipping you a tiny package in the next day or so. Something small with lots of curly hair." Ally laughed. She heard "Oh, no, Momma!" and "Go ahead!" chorus at the same time.

"So back to Ashe... What do you think?" Janna was persistent.

"I don't know. What am I supposed to think?"

"Well... Ashe is so lonely. Skye's so lonely. They might be perfect for each other."

"You little vixen. Matchmaking again?"

"What can I say? It's in my blood. It was my Mimi's career, you know, back in the old country."

Ally laughed out loud. "So you inherited the busybody gene from your grandmother?"

"Sha. I've always been more successful mixing it up for other people."

"You'd find true love for yourself if you weren't so discriminating."

"Are you kidding? I lowered my standards and ended up with Dennis."

"Yes, but look what you got out of that. Tell me you'd give up Mandy and Rachel."

52

"You're right about that, Al," Janna admitted. "So what about Ashe? Think Skye will go for it?

"Does Skye *know*?"

"Heavens, no. Ashe is clueless, too. I thought since Skye is single again, and Ashe likes girls…"

"She does? Wait. Where does it say that in the blog?"

"It doesn't. She let it slip."

"Do you know her that well? Where you can suggest a hook up?"

"I've known her for a year."

"Have you met her in person? Have you talked to her over the phone?"

"Not yet. That's the easy stuff. All that can be arranged. The hard part will be putting my plan into action and making it seem like I had nothing to do with it," Janna laughed.

Snow began to fall, coating the pavement enough to make driving treacherous. Ally slid to a stop at Lake Street. "I'm *so* glad we're on the same side. You can be one scary woman, Janna Abraham."

"Aunt Janna is scary?" Vanessa piped up from the back seat.

"In a fun way," Ally answered into her rear view. "In a devilishly, girly fun way."

"That's right, Nessy. You could learn a lot from me."

"Oh, great. Corrupt my child."

"Think of it as preparing her for the world."

***

"Ty, son. What are you up to? Dinner's getting cold."

Asheley MacDaniel eyed the dining room table where recently broiled hamburgers held their position on a lazy Susan. Attention darted between the computer screen and the enormous jowls of Jim Bob. The dining room table was hardly an effective barrier. If the blue tick hound were hungry enough, he would scale a mountain to get at food.

Tyler appeared, one tiny fist clutching a piece of paper, the other a fat pencil, its lead ground to a flat stump. "I'm doing homework."

"Homework? You're in kindergarten. You're not up to algebra already, are you? Driver's ed? Creative writing?" Ashe smiled.

Tyler slid into his chair and giggled. He flattened the paper on the table. "Al-ge-who? Cree-te bite? No, silly. It's my A's and B's. See?"

Ashe's computer chimed. An IM from Janna! "Impressive. Here's your supper, small fry. Want some chips?"

"Yay! Chips!"

Ashe fished a handful from a bag and placed them on Tyler's plate before turning attention to the computer.

jannasbananas: *Yo, Ashe. You busy?*

AsheMacD: *No, Ma'am. Nourishing the youngster, then back to work.*

jannasbananas: *How's it going? Get any more feedback from my mommies?*

AsheMacD: *I have! The ice has broken.*

jannasbananas: *Good, good. I told you so. Who's melted?*

AsheMacD: *Ally's been so helpful. We've been comparing notes on five-year-olds.*

AsheMacD: *Missy is sweet, and Laurel seems stressed out but she's friendly. Celia? I don't know yet.*

jannasbananas: *What about Skye?*

AsheMacD: *Very nice.*

AsheMacD: *You're right. I love all your friends.*

jannasbananas: *OUR friends. You're a VM now. We're a fab bunch, all right.*

jannasbananas: *I'm on the run.*

AsheMacD: *I've gotta run too. Jim Bob is threatening a grab for my dinner. TTYL.*

***

Soft, butterfly kisses brushed against Ally's eyes and a warm hand cradled her hip. She yawned and turned into her afghan, moaning as she pulled the wool to her chin. Two seconds later, she threw off the covers and jumped from the couch. The family room was dark.

"Oh, my God, no! What time is it?"

Greg looked up, bemused at her response. "Six o'clock. Why?"

"Where's Vanessa?" Ally's heart churned with panic and alarm.

Greg grabbed her arm and grinned. "Settle down, woman. She's upstairs in her room. Reading. Or plotting world domination, I can never tell."

Ally sank into the couch. "I'm such a horrible mother."

"You're a wonderful mother. The best. Both kids say so." Greg's big arms surrounded Ally and she leaned back exhausted.

"I can't believe I fell asleep like that. I didn't mean to zonk out. I sat down for a second… and now dinner's not made." She rubbed at her eyes and patted her cheeks, hoping to draw blood flow and life back into her head.

"Calm down, Al. You were busy with Monster Nessy. Let's go out tonight. I'm feeling like Chinese anyway."

"Wing Hong! Let's go, Daddy!" Vanessa appeared in the doorway bundled in her snowsuit.

"Someone's ready to go. I guess I'm outnumbered." Ally was too drained for a night out and too tired to argue.

At the restaurant, Ally picked at her almond chicken. "Janna should leave those two alone." She had felt ravenous when Greg first mentioned Chinese food at the house. Once the dish was before her, her appetite waned. Vanessa abandoned her sweet and sour chicken and was across the room playing with the Hong children. Wing Hong prided itself as being the only Chinese restaurant in Minnesota with a play area that rivaled the largest McDonald's. Complete with ball pit, slides, games, and enough distraction to turn any child's frown upside down, Wing Hong was a favorite among families with small children. "If Ashe and Skye were meant to be together, they'll get together without any help from us."

Greg snickered as he balanced his Mongolian beef on chopsticks. "You have a short memory."

She returned a perplexed frown. "What?"

"If it weren't for Janna, *we* would have never gotten together."

Ally shook her head. "That's different."

"How so?"

55

"Number 1, we lived in the same town. Number 2, I introduced myself to you in person. Janna didn't know you, so it wasn't really a blind date situation. It was more…a *dare*." Ally laughed at her twisted logic. "Okay, okay. I agree. Our story sounds equally ridiculous. It's different online. Just saying. Those two don't know each other. It's weird. Don't look at me like that. I'm shutting up now. I don't know what I'm talking about."

"Don't you want to see Skye happy?"

Ally reached across the table to find Greg's hand. The VMs were closer than sisters. Of course, she wanted the best for them. "Sure, I do. She should find her own happiness like I found mine. Janna didn't ask you out for me. I asked you out – for me."

Greg kissed the back of Ally's hand. "A little nudging in the right direction never hurt. Just saying."

Ally looked into Greg's dark eyes and saw in them Vanessa's kindness and empathy. Ten years brought many things, including wrinkles, gray hair, and a slight beer pouch, yet he still looked fabulous. She leaned across the table. "Have I told you lately how handsome you are, Mr. Smith? And how much I love you?"

Greg winked and he drew his head closer to Ally's. "As a matter of fact, you did. This morning. Seems like a hundred years ago, though." He glanced across the room where Vanessa was attempting the Guinness World Record for number of consecutive slides in a Chinese restaurant play area. "Let's collect the young one and go home. I hear Round Two calling."

***

Laurel attached a stamp to the final thank you note. An old-fashioned girl, she believed in manners and etiquette. She had thanked the Virtual Moms for the 'surprise' online birthday party both in the chat room and through email. Proper etiquette required hand-written notes. She lined up the cards, addressed in her best penmanship, and paper clipped them together. "Don't let me forget these tomorrow," she told herself. The days since the party were crammed full – work, Marcus's hockey, Marcus, Joe. She felt guilty for waiting so long to write although this was the only day of the week she found a break in the schedule.

The party was great fun and completely unexpected. It was also too much. Presents were unnecessary; she was happy for the

56

attention from her long-time friends. While she appreciated the goodies and goodwill, she fretted about the possibility of having to reciprocate in the future. Finances were tight. Laurel wasn't sure how they'd pull off Christmas this year. She would die of embarrassment if the other VMs sent gifts. She'd thought of forgoing Christmas cards to save money. Sending cards through snail mail was quaint, old-fashioned, and expensive, if you included every person that crossed your path.

The ringing of the telephone shook her out of her daydream. She tucked the thank you cards into her purse and answered the phone.

"Hello?"

"Laurel! You're still up."

"Celia. It's good to hear from you." Laurel sank into the couch. Of all the Virtual Moms, she was most comfortable with Celia. Janna was a whirlwind; Skye seemed preoccupied, Ally was older, and Missy was too beautiful and out of her league. "What's up?"

"I know you're busy during the week and you haven't been online much. I wanted to find out how your birthday went."

"Great minds think alike. I'm preparing my thank you notes."

"No need."

Laurel twirled the phone cord around her fingers. "Sorry. I have to."

"What did Joe get you? Did you go out to dinner? Did he give you something pretty?"

Laurel gulped. She couldn't reveal what happened on her birthday night: that Marcus was clueless, that Joe had spaced out her birthday and only realized his error when he arrived home to find Janna calling and the online party in full swing. "It was nice," she lied, "We went out to dinner. It was only Applebee's. At least it was out. He gave me a pretty bracelet. Nothing much, a little trinket." Laurel hoped Celia wouldn't press for details. She couldn't remember the last time she was in Applebee's and was unfamiliar with the current menu, and she certainly didn't know the latest trends in the fashion world.

"I'm glad you had a good time. That was the intention."

"It was great. Fun time is over now. I've been running around like a headless chicken since then. How are you?"

"Great! Got a good review at work. Kimber's fantastic, as usual. The reason I called is I wanted to find out if you were coming down for the holidays to visit your dad."

Laurel bit her lip. *Not unless I hit the lottery,* she thought. "I'm not sure yet. It depends on Joe's schedule. He has some leads on a few houses..."

"Let me know," Celia said cheerfully. "It's been forever since you've been here."

"Sure will. Say, what do you think about the newbie?" It was best to steer the conversation away from the Extons. Ashe made a perfect deflector.

Celia groaned. "Ugh, Ashe. I suppose you're in love with her too?"

"It's nothing like that. She seems nice."

"Yeah, well, Ted Bundy was blessed with good looks and charisma and he was a no-good, raping serial killer."

Laurel gasped. "You don't think..."

"We don't know her, Laurel. That's all I'm saying. It's nice to be friendly. It doesn't hurt to be cautious, especially with someone we've never heard of before last week."

"She hasn't done anything yet to cause me to doubt her."

"That's the operative word. YET."

"Okay."

"I'm older than you, Laurel. I've lived through bad times you can only imagine."

Laurel shook her head. If only Celia knew. "I'll let you know about our holiday plans. Right now I have some grading to finish before tomorrow. I'll talk to you later."

"I have to run too. See you online sometime."

***

Vanessa, lapsed into a peaceful coma the moment the car exited the Wing Hong parking lot, remained asleep. Greg carried her limp body up a flight of stairs. Ally removed layers of snowsuit, sweaters and tee shirts, and tucked her into bed in her long underwear. Vanessa instinctively reached for her child-sized teddy and turned into its fur, her lithe body spooning the bear. Ally stood at the door smiling. Sometimes it was impossible to tear herself away from her daughter.

"You coming, Hon?" Greg's hand lingered on Ally's shoulder. He drew close, pushed her hair back and blew into her ear while cupping his hand against the seat of her jeans.

She giggled, turned out the light and whispered. "In a minute, Fabio. I want to check email. No need to get up early if tomorrow is a snow day." School closings were not only broadcast on the news; those with Internet access received a warning email.

Greg gave her backside a hearty slap before heading to the bedroom. "You know where to find me, Doll."

Ally scrolled her email inbox. Along with pre-Thanksgiving missives from department stores, joke forwards from Mike, a few VM responses, and the usual Nigerian dead uncle promising twenty million dollars. No messages from school. It would take more than frigid temperatures and a few inches of snow to warrant a shut down.

Before she logged off for the night, her inbox chimed once more. The subject line read "Miss Ally." She opened the email.

To: Ally1234
From: AsheMacD
Subject: Miss Ally

I haven't had a chance to personally thank you for allowing me into the Virtual Moms. In the last year, Janna has shared so many wonderful stories about all of you. She's so good at storytelling, I feel as though I've known all of you forever. Janna's a special woman. Through her, I finally was able to come out of my grief and depression.

That's not to say I'm taking her away from you all. I want to add something positive to her circle of friends – now mine – much as she has added so much to my life.

Plus, it's nice to know someone with a five-year-old! As you might have been able to tell by the number of questions I've pounded you with in the last couple of days, I am without a sounding board here. What a relief to know my child is normal. ☺ If not, in the normal range.

Thanks again for the vote of confidence.

59

Peace out,
Ashe

"Oh, Ashe honey," Ally said out loud as she powered off her computer. She smiled. "You don't know the half of it."

Chapter Six

The New Normal
Dear Mac

    I've been trying my best to keep things status quo. It's not easy.

    There's the empty chair at the table. Tyler won't let anyone else sit in your spot. He keeps a setting, complete with place mat, glass, a dinner plate and silverware (in the correct order – Miss Manners and his grandmamma would be proud), for 'just in case.' He wants you to see he's a grown boy now, not a baby.

    There's a spare spot in the driveway. Tyler runs to the window when he hears the crunch of gravel, thinking it's you coming home from work. Sometimes it's a deliveryman; sometimes it's the postal carrier. Most times it's a replay of memories of when you were here. He doesn't understand you are too far away to come home each night.

    He chases Jim Bob from your favorite chair. (You'd like that. No hair. No drool.) Sometimes he sits on the floor in front of the recliner. He'll lay his hand on the seat and stroke the velour, push his head into the fabric and rub his face into it.

    The biggest hole is the empty space in my bed and the times when I miss you most is when the house is buttoned up tight and asleep. I'll admit it; Tyler's not the only one missing you. It's easier to maintain in the light of day when twenty million catastrophes are going off at the same time. Who has time to think then? When I reach over late at night, expecting a warm body and pull up air, I want to kill someone.

    OK, Mac, so I did the bad thing, I caved and I did it right away. I let Tyler take up that space, though all the parenting books say children his age should stay in their own beds. It's the only way either of us could get to sleep.

    I'm looking at him right now, watching his shallow breathing. His mouth is slightly parted; his eyes are rolled back into his head.

He's our cutest, clueless little angel. I wish you could see…
or can you?

***

Manhattan, Upper East Side

Janna Abraham awoke with a knot in her neck. It was no wonder, what with Mandy hogging a third of the queen bed and Oskar, the morbidly obese orange cat taking up the middle. Janna was allotted a six-inch swath, barely enough room to stretch out, much less get a restful sleep.

Mandy, a senior at Penn State, had been sent home the week before with the flu. Turned out it was H1N1. The outbreak felled her roommate and half the dorm. Mandy suffered a fever and was delirious the first few days. With days of rest, lots of Grandma Mimi's famous chicken soup recipe and plenty of fluids, she conquered the virus. She would go back to campus today.

Janna had been in Paris when she got the call from Penn. Dispatched by her parents for a reconnaissance mission in search of a Louis IV armoire, she had been taking in the sights and indulging in rich French cooking. Once notified, she took the first plane back to New York to tend to her daughter.

As she gazed at Mandy's sleeping form, a lump formed in Janna's throat. Mandy looked as angelic as she had as a young girl. She was so grown up in so many ways. For one, she earned money to help pay her way toward school. She didn't have to. The Abraham Trust would see to that. Janna's great-grandfather, Morrie Abraham, came from the old country and made a killing in the garment district. He was frugal and wise with his wealth, building it into a considerable sum. Despite the money the trust could provide, Mandy had worked part time at Macy's, hoping to gain insight in the retail business before graduating in the spring with her marketing degree. She aspired to become a fashion buyer. Janna was blessed in that both her girls had turned into responsible young adults. Her oldest child, Rachel, graduated from NYU *magna cum laude* and landed a job as a weather personality in a small market in upstate New York. Rachel, a stunning beauty and smart to boot, had her own blog and a throng of loyal fans.

62

Leaving Mandy and Oskar undisturbed, Janna slid out of bed and proceeded to the kitchen to make coffee. She turned on her computer to check her email as the coffee brewed.

"Jannasbananas." Janna took her screen name from the nickname her grandfather Abraham had given to her as a small child. Of course, Janna grew into the title. As a young girl, she was impetuous and quick to find trouble. As a teenager, she was wild and uninhibited. Though Janna graduated with a prestigious business degree from the University of Michigan, she spent her summers away from school as an amateur groupie. She picked up the AC/DC tour a week after Aerosmith called it quits, and traveled with Foghat and REO Speedwagon. After snagging her degree, Janna was back at home on the Upper East Side, between boyfriends and bands, not ready to find a job. It was club time in the '80s.

In a trendy coffee shop in Soho, she met Dennis Zee and it was love at first sight. Not only handsome, he was artistic, well-read *and* well-bred, and best of all – as far as her mother was concerned – he was Jewish. They shared so many likes and dislikes, Janna thought that their souls face-to-face was like staring into a mirror.

Like Janna, Dennis was into nightlife. Unlike Janna, he succumbed to the pressures of the party life, frequently indulged in substances both legal and not, and ended up addicted to cocaine. She was unaware of the severity of his problem until Mandy was born, at which point she made the difficult decision to make a break. It was too arduous a chore to handle two small children and Dennis's growing addiction.

Thanks to her diploma and some family contacts, Janna landed a job as a stockbroker. She climbed the corporate ladder and in no time was successfully providing for both her girls. Her dreams were realized – nice car, beautiful apartment appointed with sumptuous furnishings, high fashion clothes, trips to Europe, cruises in the Mediterranean – everything was looking up. Her income so flush, *she* ended up paying Dennis spousal support.

September 11, 2001 changed her life. Janna was late leaving her uptown apartment that morning because, once again, Mandy was sick. In the end, it was Mandy's illness that saved her life. The second hijacked airliner tore through the part of the building that had once been her office. Both she and Mandy watched in horror as the World Trade Center buildings disintegrated right before their eyes on national television. They took turns emailing and IM'ing their friends and relatives who couldn't get through by phone. Janna lost many of her colleagues that day, and it left her in shock.

It took several months. Once she recovered, she realized she couldn't go back to how life was before. She continued day trading at home, yet abandoned the brokerage to watch her daughters finish growing up. As she did so, she realized how much of their childhood she had missed because of her commitment to work. Every day was a blessing, and both Rachel and Mandy realized it too. They could have been left orphans that day.

Janna poured a big mug of coffee as she opened her inbox.

To: jannasbananas
From: AsheMacD
Subject: Good Morning!

Miss Janna, for the first time in a long time, I'm actually looking forward to beginning each new day, and it's all because of you. You dragged me out of my depressing cave and right on time. The Virtual Moms are a frenetic blast of sunshine and light. I can't thank you enough for bringing me back to life.
Virtually yours,
Ashe

Janna smiled and put her coffee mug down before she excitedly pushed the 'Reply' button.

To: AsheMacD
From: jannasbananas
Subject: RE: Good Morning!

Sha, Ashe, no need to thank me! I'm glad you're in the group, and everyone else is excited about getting to know you. I told you they are a great group of girls. We help each other as much as we help ourselves. The VMs were a godsend after Evie died. I'd still be in a mental dungeon without them.

64

Janna glanced at a photo framed in silver hung above her monitor – she and younger sister, Evie side by side in a formal portrait, toddlers dressed in identical flouncy lilac dresses and sweaters trimmed with collars of rabbit fur. Those carefree days were a lifetime away. Although Janna tried to protect her, Evie struggled with her demons for years. Depression, drug abuse, self-destructive behavior. Was it a year ago that she took her life when the world proved a burden too much?

Janna had wandered into an online grief forum where Ashe's four word post caught her eye. "New Here, Need Help." Newbie meets newbie while sorting out death; it was a perfect match up. The forum posts exploring loss and sorrow turned into casual email exchanges, then frequent friendly IMs and text messages. She was already sharing her life with Ashe; the news on the kids, the updates on her life. She had asked Ashe's opinion on the striking good looks or lack thereof of each potential suitor lucky enough to make it into Janna's *Dating Game*. Ashe had been noncommittal, instead raving about this movie starlet or that female country singer. It was obvious Ashe possessed a fine eye and appreciation of the female form, leading Janna to believe she was a woman who could swing two ways. The two exchanged photographs, Ashe's pastoral country scenes and Janna's urban landscapes. It had been a waste of time to write two separate emails – one to Ashe and one to the group. Inviting Ashe into the VMs made sense.

As she came to know Ashe, Janna's matchmaking gears greased into action and began to spin. Skye was getting over her bad break up with Trina, and here was Ashe grieving alone for a year in a community where she knew no one. The more she thought about it, the more Janna realized her plan was foolproof. Janna knew both women intimately and felt the hookup was perfect in every way. In order for her plan to work, she would have to fuel the flames between the unsuspecting East Coast and the clueless West Coast. This hookup might be harder to accomplish than it sounded.

The thought of a VM matchup instigated by Janna made her smile. *No doubt about it, I am a genius!* She turned her attention back to her email.

Say Ashe, I was wondering, can you send us your physical address and phone number? We normally communicate online through email or IMs. It's nice to have the phone number in case of an emergency. We often exchange gifts for birthdays and Christmas – Hanukkah in my case – so we would need your address. Besides, I have something I want to talk to you about. In person would be better than an email for this.

Take your time with it. I know you have your hands full with your deadline and taking care of Tyler.

J

As she pressed the 'Send' button, Mandy appeared at the door, rubbing her brown eyes with her fists. Her bright pink hair spiked straight out from her head. She was wearing the same plaid flannel pajamas she went to bed in five days before.

Janna smiled as she greeted her. "Hey, baby. Up so early?"

"I feel like I've slept for days."

"You have."

Mandy plopped down on the chair beside her. "How are the Virtual Moms?"

"Fine. Celia and Ally wanted to know if you've recovered yet. Missy, too. Kara's going back to school this week.

"I hope you told them I lived!"

"Yes, I gave them the good news. So, you think you're ready to go back to school?"

Mandy yawned and wrapped her arms around Janna's neck to give her a quick hug. "Why? Are you trying to get rid of me, Mom?"

"Not me."

"Sure? Rach thought you might be hiding a boyfriend somewhere. I told her I've looked around. No evidence as far as I can tell. You might have had a secret room built into the living room wall. We'd never know. We don't live here anymore."

"Not me. I'm done with men," Janna fibbed. She wasn't swearing men off permanently, only taking a short breather after a whirlwind round of suitors provided by Dating.com proved borderline disastrous. After almost twenty years of the singles' scene, she knew it was better to stand back when the pickings were few.

"That'll be the day."

"Feeling better?"

"Yeah. I'd go back to school even if I was still sick. I'm so far behind! If I want to graduate in May, I can't miss any more time."

"Get dressed. I'll drop you at the station. Or do you want me to drive you? I have nothing else going on today. Yes, let me take you."

"Don't worry, Mom. I can take the train."

"Oh, no. I saved you from the dreaded *swine* flu, the least you can do is humor your old lady. It's a long three weeks between now and Thanksgiving. We'll use the drive to dish."

***

To: ally1234
From: AsheMacD
Subject: Miss Ally

Ally, I want to thank you for allowing me into the group. What a joy it is to be able to share my pitiful childrearing techniques with someone who has experience with tiny people. I've been disengaged from the "real" world wallowing in self-pity for so long…you don't know what a godsend you ladies are.

Greg sounds like a wonderful person and Vanessa's a doll. A perfect family.

Thanks for the tips on getting vegetables into my fussy eater. A blender, huh? Mash everything up and hide it in a hamburger? It's genius! Why didn't I think of that before? Of course, now I will have to buy a blender. (I know. I'm hopeless.)

Hope to see you around and that we'll get to know each other better.

Peace out,
Ashe

To: AsheMacD
From: ally1234
Subject: RE: Thanks Ally

No problem, Ashe. That's what we're here for – to support each other through bad times and celebrate the good.

Don't worry. I know you've suffered a loss. Someday you'll see through to the other side.

As for recipes, I have several generations' worth of hearty Scandinavian dishes etched in my brain. I can pretty up anything that's 'good for you' and make it appealing to fussy eaters. Let me know when you're ready to tackle hot dish.

Sincerely,
Ally

To: ally1234
From: AsheMacD
Subject: RE: RE: Thanks Ally

Hot dish!? Sounds demanding. I'll pass, for now.

It's late, got to see Ty to bed. I'll catch you online sometime.

Peace out,
Ashe

***

Missy stood before her closet, contemplating the choices. A perfect dress would be necessary for dinner tonight, something stunning yet not too sexy. She chose a black silk cocktail dress with tight bodice and a short, full skirt. "Very Marilyn Monroe," she said aloud, "I like it." She slipped into it, zipped up the side, and twirled in front of the full-length mirror. Thanks to regular yoga and spinning classes, she was still a size 4. Her hair, newly colored and styled, cascaded in heavy blonde waves. She completed the ensemble with tall, strappy sandals and nodded approval to herself.

Tonight she had to be a vision of feminine loveliness. She not only wanted to look desirable, she needed to wow Earl. For this Date Night, she'd made a reservation at a tiny French restaurant, dark and romantic. She had scoped the place out in advance and it was perfect – booth seating, candlelit, discreet, and the food was out of this world. Missy had visions of bouts of friskiness between courses, something along the lines of their college days, when petting in restaurants often morphed into risqué adventures. She needed the trip down memory lane, only this time it would be *she* who would make the advances. *Poor Earl, he won't know what hit him.* She giggled, the anticipation rising.

Her cell phone rang and Missy picked up. "Hi, honey, I'm ready..." Missy looked in the mirror and watched as the joyous expectation on her face melted away. She tried to keep her tone upbeat. "Yeah. I understand... Sure. No. Don't worry about it. I'll see you when you get home."

She kicked her shoes off at the mirror. "Missy, you're a fool," she said. She tried to smile at herself while blinking back tears.

It's hard to be happy when you're being stood up.

***

It was early evening as Janna motored her way back from Penn State. The monotony of the moment was disturbed when her Blackberry chimed. She glanced at the number. It was Skye returning her message.

"Skye! I'm glad you called back. How's it going?" Janna's voice rang with enthusiasm. This virtual pairing was genius and promised to be a grand project. She hadn't had this much fun since organizing the surprise VM baby shower for Ally.

"You know the time difference. It was the middle of the night when you called." Skye yawned. "Where are you? Working?"

Janna laughed. The only 'work' she did these days involved teaching a few art classes when asked by the local crafts store or alternative school. "Driving back from Penn State. I dropped Mandy back at school this afternoon. She's risen from the dead."

"Good. Glad to hear it. So what's up, virtual Sister?"

"I was wondering if you've heard from our latest mommy." Janna fished, barely able to contain giggles. "What do you think?"

"Tyler is adorable. Reminds me of Rob at that age. I admit, the woman can write. No kidding, I emptied an entire box of Kleenex. Makes you reconsider your own life when you read about how bad others have it."

"I thought you two might hit it off." Janna was glad she was without dash cam in her car. She couldn't stop smiling.

"How's that?"

"You're both widows."

"Us and millions of other women."

"You both have boys…"

"What's the alternative?"

"Sha. You're not being helpful at all. Has she emailed you? I mean personally?"

"A note to thank me. Why?"

"Oh, no reason…" Janna's voice betrayed the fact that a universe of deliciously naughty reasons orbited in her head.

"Janna… I can hear the gears in your brain churning from here. Whatever you're up to, stop it."

"*Mais moi? Je ne le pense pas! Je suis innocent.*"

"Whatever."

"Don't pout. Girls just wanna have fun."

"At whose expense?"

"Honest, no one is going to get hurt." A warning flash pulsed on her dashboard. Empty? Already? Janna looked for the next exit. "Hey, Skye, I have to pull over for gas. Will you be online later?"

"Like when?"

"Sixish is dinner time for you, right? I'll be back at the apartment by then, and we can IM a little more."

"OK." Her voice betrayed 'I don't get it, but I will.' Janna would have to divulge the next part of her plan to keep Skye hooked.

Then there was Ashe to consider.

Chapter Seven

One Step Forward, Twenty-nine Steps Back

So Mac, I think you'd hate me today.

Let's see, first Tyler had another bedtime accident...again.
It wouldn't be so bad, except it's the fourth one this week and Ty's
been sleeping in our bed. There's nothing like the cold, wet,
pungent odor of urine to greet you in the morning. I had to make a
special trip to Wal-Mart to load up on sheets. The washer has been
going nonstop and now it's making that 'creekety-creekety' noise
you hate so much.

I can't get him to eat anything green. Not that I'm a fan of
green (or purple, blue, yellow or red). I figured I'd do my best to
showcase some of our local farmers' market harvest on the dinner
table. You know, mix a lesson on sustainability with the four food
groups. I think Tyler is down to one food group – peanut butter
and jelly. (Or is that two?) That was yesterday. Today he's only
eating the crusts off the bread.

Remember that separation anxiety we thought Tyler had
gotten over? It has returned, with a vengeance only a hurricane
can top. I can't go to the mailbox by myself. Heck, I can't walk
across the room without him tangled up in my legs. We go to the
bathroom together, whether I like it or not. The only good thing
about it is taking a shower together. I suppose I'm saving money
on the water.

He wants me to hold him all the time. I could do it at first. I
needed his touch and his smell to reassure me that life is something
close to normal. Our boy went through one heck of a growth spurt,
Mac. He's a heavy kid and not a baby anymore. I get busy with
work and he's right under my nose. I push him away – gently, of
course – and he'll stay curled up under my desk like a cat,
listening to the tapping of my keyboard, his hand on my foot to
make certain I won't get away.

Poor kid forgot how to play. I wish I had more time to
devote to him. I know his psyche is damaged. I want to fix it, or at

least cover it up. Other times I want to run away. I want to take him by the shoulders and shake some sense into him. I've got to make a living for both of us; can't he see that? I need time; I need space. I want to scream.

No, I don't. I feel fine. FINE. I've bottled it up and fermented it. I smile; I hold it in. Life's a peach and a couple of pears. This can't be happening to me.

I see you on your heavenly cloud wagging your finger at me.

Damn it.

***

St. Louis, Missouri

"What a day!" Eight o'clock – she had been on the run since five a.m. Laurel Exton threw her keys on the kitchen counter and slumped into the nearest chair. Marcus followed behind her, shedding his jacket, a backpack, hockey stick, and an enormous athletic bag in the doorway before he peered under the lid of a steaming pot. Laurel was surprised to see her husband Joe manning the stove, outfitted in a ridiculous apron that featured naked man-boobs airbrushed in front. "What are you doing home? Didn't you have a late showing tonight?"

"I decided to ditch that appointment and make dinner. I knew you would have major running around to do today. Don't worry. I've got water going and the spaghetti will be done in ten minutes, tops." Joe winked at her. To Marcus, he said, "How was hockey, Squirt?"

"Good. I don't know if I'm going to make the cut to the traveling league though." Marcus picked up an end piece of Italian bread and picked the soft, doughy center away from the crust.

"Not before dinner, young man," Joe said. "Better go wash up. It's tee minus eight minutes and counting."

"'K." Marcus picked up his backpack on the way to his room.

"So, how was work today, hon?" Joe asked as he stirred the pasta.

"Busy. Who would have thought teaching third graders would be so exhausting? With the lower grades, you're trying to

72

instill some discipline and rules and they're willing to pay attention. You'd think by the time a kid was eight, they'd start listening."

"I don't remember Marcus listening at that age."

"You don't remember what happened yesterday!" Laurel teased back. She should have replied jokingly yet she couldn't rein in the steely edge to her voice. She caught it and lowered her tone a notch. "Anyway, Marcus was different. He was good."

Joe released a hearty laugh. "Boy, your memory isn't exactly crystal clear."

"What do you mean?"

"I remember him being a little demanding, that's all. Whiny. Clingy. That's why I thought hockey might be the answer. I thought a sport would help him man up."

Laurel tried to recall back to that time. Had it been four years since he was that age? It seemed like a hundred years ago. "Hockey helps. Anyway, I disagree. He was an angel compared to this crew. How was your day? Get any leads?"

"Not bad, not bad at all. How was the hockey, *really*?" Joe deftly changed the subject. It was only recently that he declined talking about his job. Years before, he would regale the family with hilarious stories of this person or that. His real estate office and his wacky clients were a gold mine of material for the one-time English and philosophy major. Now in a recession, houses weren't selling and most were foreclosures fetching pennies on the dollar. These days, the job – or lack of – was a sore spot between the two.

Laurel let Joe's quick-change go. She was dead tired and in no mood to argue. "I can't tell, Joe. I know nothing about hockey. The coach seems to like him. I don't know what we'll do if Marcus ends up in the traveling league though. It's a terrible commitment of time and money. I don't have enough hours in the day as it is." Marcus loved skating, yet Laurel could tell her son was uncomfortable with squalls and checking the other players. Joe had enrolled Marcus in hockey camp when he was a chubby five-year-old. He hoped it might improve his coordination and give him a sense of independence, and at first Marcus was enthusiastic. Since then, Marcus had grown into a slender, small adolescent – hardly hockey material.

Although complacent in previous years, tryouts this year were different. Marcus had to be coaxed into playing again. Cajoled. *Bribed*. In a secret deal, Joe offered him a new Xbox if he would stick it out until Christmas. Laurel found out about the arrangement two weeks before, and when she did, she was livid. She was the one who shuttled Marcus around to school, doctor appointments and practices although the school where she taught was on the other side of town. In contrast, Joe worked his real estate job part time, if at all, and seldom helped out. There was also the matter of money. Times were tough and getting tougher. She was horrified to learn he had let two mortgage payments go unpaid over the summer, and was humiliated when the bank called her at school. She had done her best to cut down on movies, trips, and new clothes. She clipped coupons and bought store brand to save money. She learned to make a cheap cut of meat last for two or three meals. The Extons would never experience that new car smell again. Hockey and Xboxes were expensive and unnecessary hobbies. Thinking about her situation made Laurel's blood pressure rise.

She took off her shoes and rubbed her feet. "How soon until dinner?"

"Five minutes."

"I'm going to check my email. Call me when it's ready."

She was sure of tons of email from the Virtual Moms. Laurel could not access her personal account at work, and the loop was buzzing with constant updates between the newbie, Ashe, and the rest of the group. She typed in her screen name, *laurelextonsbunch*, thinking how inappropriate the name was these days. They weren't a bunch anymore, as much as three separate persons living in the same house. Marcus could be a sweetheart; he was also in the throes of puberty and could be secretive and moody. The older girls in the group explained it was growing pains and he would emerge from it someday. "Girls take longer," Janna warned, "Be thankful you have a boy."

Then there was Joe, who for all his cheerfulness had become a major disappointment. He was lackadaisical about making money. Laurel *had* to take the teaching position otherwise they would be homeless. She couldn't remember the last time Joe actually sold a house, and wasn't sure if he had any listings. He wouldn't find any part time work doing something else, since it was 'beneath' him. She tried pleading. "Anything? Please?"

"I'm not flipping burgers for minimum wage, if that's what you want," he fired back.

The past year had been one of uneasy truce. He knew she was angry, and she realized he wasn't about to change. If Laurel hadn't had the Virtual Moms, she didn't know what she would do. Tonight she needed to send out an SOS.

To: missymom, jannasbananas, celiasunshine, AsheMacD, ally1234, shootingskye
From: laurelextonsbunch
Subject: HELP ME!

Girls… just returned from hockey practice after working across town, driving all afternoon. The traffic…you don't want to know. I'm beat! I'm not sure how much more I can take. Please, someone. Adopt me. Send me a plane ticket. Get me the heck out of here!

She pressed the 'Send' button and released the message into cyberspace. Laurel slumped back, overcome by immediate guilt for complaining. Things could be worse. The Exton bunch had their health. She was blessed with a great kid and a terminally cheerful husband. The house, though far from extravagant was nice enough. Best of all, it was still theirs, for now. Sure, they couldn't afford frills these days. Maybe someday the bills would be caught up and Joe's business would catch fire.

Or maybe they were teetering on the precipice, mere seconds from total calamity…

The phone rang, and Laurel picked up. "Hello." She sounded as tired and small as she felt.

"Girl, what in God's name is the matter?"

Laurel smiled. It was Ally. Hearing a compassionate friend on the line improved her mood in seconds. "It's nothing. Just…*life.*"

"I could tell. I got your email." Ally's voice rose.

"Don't listen to me. I'm being a big crybaby," Laurel whispered.

"Is it Joe?"

"Laurel, Marcus! Dinner's ready!" Joe's voice boomed from the kitchen.

"I have to go. I'll write you later. Or we can IM after Joe goes to bed."

"Or you can *call* me. Promise?"

"Sure."

***

missymom: *What the hell is going on?*

celiasunshine: *?*

missymom: *Laurel, duh.*

celiasunshine: *What else? It's Joe. I can tell by the panic.*

missymom: *Aw…I feel badly for her.*

celiasunshine: **Men**!

missymom: *Come on Celia. You don't mean that.*

celiasunshine: *Ha!*

missymom: *You'll find someone someday and then you'll feel differently.*

celiasunshine: *Not me. They're all flawed, imperfect. Scoundrels.*

celiasunshine: *You can't live with them and damned if you live without them.*

missymom: *What's that supposed to mean? I happen to* like *being married!*

celiasunshine: *Oh, yeah? Where's* your *husband tonight?*

celiasunshine: *Or have you turned that rough cut into a diamond?*

missymom: ☹ *Not fair, Celia. You know Earl has to work.*

celiasunshine: *No one works that hard.*

celiasunshine: *Missy?*

celiasunshine: *Missy? You there?*

***

Dinner wasn't a total fiasco. So the noodles were gummy, the Italian toast was scorched, and the spaghetti sauce carried the piquant aftertaste of burned tomato paste. At least the salad was crisp. Marcus wolfed down his meal in less than two minutes and excused himself from the table. "Marcus," Joe called after him. "I haven't seen you all day. Don't you want to talk about hockey?"

"Homework, Dad." Marcus dug a handful of cookies out of the cabinet and stuck one in his mouth. "Term paper," he said through his cookie.

"Tomorrow's Saturday."

"Wah, wah," Marcus replied through his cookie.

Their son's departure left the two of them alone to stare at each other in uncomfortable silence. Laurel separated a tomato chunk cinder from the rest of her plate and rolled her coagulated noodles into a starchy ball.

"Who called?" Right on cue, Joe would try to make up for his shortcomings by being personable and charming.

"Huh?" Although Joe was talented in the charisma department, his boyish appeal had long worn off where Laurel was concerned. She was deep in thought.

"I said who called before?"

"Oh. It was Ally."

"How's she doing?" The Extons had met the Smiths during a trip to Minnesota five years before. Joe and Greg hit it off right away. They were outdoorsmen and had shared a mutual disdain for the Green Bay Packers.

"Good."

"What about the other mothers?"

"Busy. We're all busy, Joe."

He lay down his fork with enough force to knock the breadbasket to the floor. "Meaning what?"

"I didn't mean anything…"

"Meaning *I'm* not busy?"

"Joe. It's late; it's been a long day. I'm dead tired. I don't want to fight."

"Screw it. I had dinner waiting for you. What you expect from me? What more do you want?" Joe picked up his jacket and headed for the door.

"Joe. Where are you going?"

"Out." The door slammed shut.

***

To: laurelextonsbunch
From: AsheMacD
Subject: RE: HELP ME!

77

Laurel, sorry to hear about your troubles. I can certainly relate to being overwhelmed.

I don't know the history behind your family, only from what I've read in the loop so far. You might not want to hear my opinion. I'm going to give it to you anyway.

It's a bad economy, sure. Still, no man wants to acknowledge he can't provide for his family. Men are crazy creatures. They are hard wired to view their jobs as their entire lives, where women live through their families. Maybe it's foolish; maybe it's a genetic defect.

If you and Joe still love each other, you have to be prepared for give and take. Let go of your disappointment. You'll be surprised what comes back to you.

If you want to tell me to go jump in a lake, I will. I don't want to butt in, and I don't want to tell you what to do. Only you and Joe and figure that out for yourselves. If you want to talk, the door is always open.

Peace out,
Ashe

***

After cleaning the kitchen, which included heavy-duty elbow grease applied to blackened pots, Laurel turned the lights down and went back into the family room to get online. It was after ten and Joe hadn't returned yet. *Where did he go?* She suppressed an urge to dial his cell. Perhaps they should be apart for now. It would give both a chance to cool off.

Her inbox had been jammed with messages from the Girls. Her plea for help resulted in invitations from Janna and Skye to come out for a visit. Laurel wished she could pick up and get away on a whim. Both San Francisco and New York City would be fabulous places to see. She had never been to either city. With their finances in shambles, pleasure trips were out of the question. She wasn't the type to run from her problems. Besides, she couldn't afford the plane fare. She couldn't afford the gas either, and her ancient minivan was too shaky to make a trip across the river to Illinois much less across the country. She was trapped.

Celia offered to come and kick his ass. Laurel smiled to herself. Anytime a VM was in trouble, Celia *always* offered to come and kick butt or break an appendage. Damn, that Mafia blood. Missy commiserated in her email. She was a stay-at-home mom, yet rarely saw her husband due to his busy schedule, so it was like the Extons but in reverse. Laurel chatted for a while with Ally online.

> laurelextonsbunch: *Thank goodness tomorrow's Saturday.*
> ally1234: *You and me both sister.*
> laurelextonsbunch: *This week should have ended Monday.*
> ally1234: *You okay now?*
> laurelextonsbunch: *Yeah, go to bed. Don't worry about*
me.☺

At midnight, Laurel yawned. Joe had not returned. Angered, she wasn't going to wait for him.

Hours later, she lay in bed, alone, shivering. She glanced at the nightstand clock. Two a.m. She sighed and rolled over.

She couldn't sleep without Joe. She needed him. On the infrequent occasions when he went out of town, Laurel suffered insomnia. She and Missy went around and around trying to outdo each other in late night chats. It wasn't only his warm body spooned next to hers; she needed the husband she thought she had married. Not just the happy guy who was funny and carefree. What about the one who was serious and wanted to take responsibility for providing for his family? Did it matter? No matter how disenchanted she became or how irritated she was with Joe, she still loved him.

Headlights illuminated the inside of the bedroom. She heard the roar of a car engine sputter to a stop. "Joe." Fifteen minutes passed before she heard the car door slam. Her anger bubbled to the surface. "Damn him. What was he waiting for?" Laurel gathered her blanket around her and rolled into a tight ball. She was still angry and tears flooded her eyes. She turned toward the wall and hoped Joe would get a clue. If there were ever a time for it, this was the night the couch would have a neon "Vacancy" sign shining over it.

Laurel's mind raced from her long day of driving, her ultra-tiny bank balance, and her no-account husband. He could help her instead of adding to her stress. She'd accumulated plenty of fuel for the fire in her head.

Joe surprised her when he slipped into bed and gently grabbed her around her waist. Her back to him, she twisted away, her tears released and slid down her cheek to puddle on her pillow. He moved his body closer to hers, his skin touching hers from head to toe. He was as warm as a furnace to the touch, and she felt an instant charge of fire from deep inside her.

"Laurel, Laurel honey, you awake?"

She closed her eyes tighter and pretended to be asleep. She was a terrible actor. Joe knew she couldn't sleep without him; she was so angry, she was shaking.

Joe wrapped both his arms around her and squeezed tight. "Laurel, about tonight. I'm so sorry about the fight. I drove and drove until I was almost to Kansas." He drew her closer. "You're my hero, Laurel. You're the whole reason this family survives. I know I should do better. I can't lose you. Please forgive me?"

Laurel sniffed. Was Joe crying?

She shrugged her shoulder and snapped the blanket from him.

Chapter Eight

Saturday, November 7
Bonnie Doone, North Carolina

The bed was a tangle of bodies. It hadn't started out that way ten hours before. A congested snore hung in the air; the owner of the raspy cacophony curled up cat-like halfway down the bed and to the right. Hot canine breath laced with a case of halitosis and accompanied by a long glob of drool brought up the left flank. Jim Bob the hound needed a serious dental work over, in addition to a round of animal therapy to adjust his species identity crisis.

Ashe elbowed Jim Bob in the doggie ribs and was in the process of loosening Tyler's death grip as the back door slammed shut. An effeminate voice echoed through the quiet house. "Ashe? Ashe, honey? You up yet?"

Damn. Was it Saturday already? Ashe was ill-prepared for a brotherly onslaught, especially after a late night tending a sick child. As luck would have it, with Tyler coughing, feverish, and full of runny boogers, Jim Bob chose that precise moment for a bout of diarrhea. The dog's iron-clad stomach could tolerate almost everything except honey buns and barbecue sauce. Jim Bob chose the most inopportune occasion – last night – to consume both. Ashe decided looking after the child was more important than the dog's malaise. As a result, the house was a total wreck.

God bless him, Rhett was as reliable as a timepiece, arriving promptly at nine. He drove in from Charlotte each Saturday to spend time with Ashe and Tyler, his ministrations meant to lessen their collective grief. The weekly visits soon became habit and not charity. Although the siblings had shared a close relationship before, Ashe had to admit the extra attention felt pretty damned good.

"Ashe! Don't let me find you in bed. Don't tell me you're letting this fine fall day go to waste." Rhett's voice grew louder as he approached and his light footfall tapped on the oak stair steps. Tyler stirred from his Children's Nyquil-induced slumber.

The bedroom door flung wide open. Rhett stood in the doorway, his hand on his hip. His tall slender frame – minus skinny tie, pencil-tight jeans, and flamboyant purple vest – so resembled the posture of their dearly departed father it was frightening. A ray of sunlight bounced off spiky dark locks tipped with blond. Still half asleep, Ashe couldn't make out anything else in the blinding light. "Asheley Wilkes MacDaniel! You don't plan on sleeping all day, do you?"

Ashe's face burned, hearing a name so hated and rarely used. Their mother had been an ardent *Gone With the Wind* fan, determined to bless (or burden) her children with their ridiculous monikers. The childhood teasing had been so relentless Ashe dropped mention of the dreaded middle name. In college, it was easier to be known as 'Ashe' although 'hey you' was perfectly acceptable. "I'm not sleeping, *Rhett Butler* MacDaniel."

Rhett huffed and targeted a pillow for the bed. "Ashe, you best hush your mouth. Mama's probably spinning in her grave. Too bad she's not around to give you a case of what for." Unlike Ashe, Rhett gloried in his name.

Ashe ducked the downy missile. "I don't plan on sleeping all day. If you must know, Tyler was sick all night. I didn't crawl into bed until after five."

"Honey child." Rhett rushed to Tyler and sat at the edge of the bed. He pressed the back of his hand against the child's forehead. "You sure he's sick? He doesn't appear to have a fever."

"It's down now," Ashe replied. "I think it's a bad cold, not the flu. His head is congested big time."

"Hi, Uncle Rhett," Tyler said, sniffling and rubbing his eyes. "Are we going to the nature center today?"

"I don't know, Ty-Ty. I think we'd better lay low if you're sick."

"Aw... I never get to have fun."

"You poor, abused boy! Now, Tyler, I'm concerned about you. We don't want your congestion to go from here," Rhett touched the top of Tyler's head, "to down here," motioning to his chest. He shot Ashe a stern look. "That would be no fun at all. Besides, going to the nature center isn't up to me."

Tyler displayed his best hang-dog pout.

"We'll see, shrimp," Ashe said. Saying 'no' to Tyler proved a difficult transaction; these days refusing him anything was nearly impossible.

Rhett jumped up. "Now that you're up, you two get dressed. I'll go down and make some coffee and get some breakfast going. You hungry, Ty?"

"Pancakes!"

"I'll see what's around for provisions, though I bet nothing healthy is in the cupboard."

Ashe frowned.

Rhett noticed the scowl and continued his lecture. "Cheerios, pork rinds, and faux mac and cheese – that's not healthy. You do realize someone in this house would need GPS to get around a Piggly Wiggly, don't you?" Rhett winked at Tyler. "By the way, what the hell happened last night? The place is an absolute pigsty. Completely appalling. Did Godzilla meet the *Exorcist* child and have a party?"

Ashe pointed to the hound. The dog looked up at Rhett with mournful eyes.

Tyler patted the loose skin around the Jim Bob's massive face. "Jim Bob was sick, too, Uncle Rhett."

"Oh. *Great.*" He mouthed the words "why don't you get rid of that horse" as he closed the door.

***

celiasunshine: *Laurel! You're home on a Saturday morning?*

laurelextonsbunch: *Marcus's team has a bye this week. Practice tonight.*

celiasunshine: *What time?*

laurelextonsbunch: *Late. 11 p.m. It's going to be a late night.*

celiasunshine: *I feel for you. The best thing to happen to me was Kimber getting her driver's license.*

celiasunshine: *Gives you new worries. At least I don't have to run all over like a madwoman.*

celiasunshine: *Can't Joe take him?*

laurelextonsbunch: *I guess not.*☹

celiasunshine: *How's it looking for a trip during Christmas? It's been so long since I've seen you. You guys can stay here if you want to save on the hotel expense.*

laurelextonsbunch: *I'd love to. Everything is so up in the air right now. Maybe we'll figure it out closer to Thanksgiving. Believe me, I'd go if I could.*

celiasunshine: *Winter! Yuck. Don't miss it at all.*

laurelextonsbunch: *I gotta run. I've got to get some housework done. And catch a nap before tonight. I don't want to fall asleep on the way to the rink.*

celiasunshine: *Sure, no prob. Keep a Gulf Coast Christmas in mind, will ya?*

laurelextonsbunch: *Always, Celia. And thanks...*

***

"Tyler must be feeling better. He ate three whole pancakes and a half side of bacon," Rhett remarked as he cleared the table. A fastidious man, Rhett was quick on the draw. He managed to clean up after the dog and straightened the rest of the mess accumulated from the past week before Ashe and Tyler had finished dressing. Jim Bob performed his after-breakfast sweep of the kitchen floor with his thick, slobbery tongue, searching for wayward crumbs and maple syrup drippings. Rhett piled the dishes into the sink. He poured Ashe another cup of coffee.

Ashe's head was buried deep in the morning paper. War. Pestilence. Unemployment. It was the usual pap. "Tyler didn't have much to eat the last few days, so he's got to be starving. I think last night was the worst of it. Hey, Rhett... can I ask a favor?"

"Sure, Ashe. Whatever." He snatched the editorial section from Ashe's hands.

"Can you take Tyler out for the afternoon? If he's not up for the nature center, can you take him somewhere else? The mall? Can you take him overnight? I have to pound out an edit by Monday and I'm so far behind I'll have to work two days straight to catch up. With Tyler being out sick since Wednesday, I haven't had a chance to write."

"You working on the blog?" It had been Rhett who encouraged Ashe to blog about the many feelings experienced losing Mac. The blog started out as an anonymous online venture, a way to iron out the kinks of the soul.

Ashe's heart skipped a beat. It had been a year since Captain Mackenzie "Mac" MacDaniel was caught in a bomb blast

84

in Iraq. Some days of the last year stretched into a never-ending eternity, while others were painfully brief.

Rhett reached across the table. "Ashe. We will *always* miss Mac."

"I know."

Rhett's somber mood lightened. "So what are you working on? What new project do you have going? Still hoping to be the next Karen McCullough? Or are you channeling Pat Conroy these days?"

Ashe would more likely meet the legendary author, Pat Conroy, in the local Starbucks than to receive galley proofs from Any Big Publishing House. The current work in progress – a romance titled *Love and Laughter in Bonnie Doone* – had been eight years in the making. Based in part on life with Mac, the initial draft making the rounds was a historical romance drawing on Ashe's Scottish heritage. When Mac was first deployed to Iraq, Ashe spent many sleepless nights rewriting the story with a modern twist.

No matter what was done to the piece, including edits, alternate points of view, great chunks of cut and paste, and gender swaps, *Bonnie Doone* couldn't find any takers. Rejection letters and email numbered in the hundreds; enough to wallpaper the entire inside of the house. Ashe's work had been politely declined by both the best in New York *and* most of the small presses. No longer personally assaulted after receiving the "thanks, but it's not what we're looking for" letters, Ashe took to dispatching query letters as a sporting event these days. He could only endure a certain amount of revisions. Ambition waned after attempting a fifth rewrite – one that involved younger characters and a vampire storyline. Ashe made a living now by editing other people's manuscripts. "I have this book edit. I also want to catch up with these people I met online…"

Rhett's eyes narrowed. "People? Online? What kind of people?"

"Virtual Moms."

Rhett put down his coffee mug. "Virtual *whats*?"

"Moms. You know. Women with children."

Rhett punched Ashe hard in the arm. "I know what moms are, you moron. What's the story?"

"There is no story. About a year ago, I met this woman in a grief chat room. She was easy to talk with and I liked her. Her kids are older and she had answers to my child rearing questions. She introduced me to her friends last week. It's pretty cool. They've been in this Virtual Moms loop for thirteen years or so. It's like a neighborhood coffee klatch with gossip and tips. Instead of meeting at someone's house we're all over the country. Don't worry, Rhett. They're all nice. I don't think there's a serial killer in the bunch." Ashe headed for the coffeepot.

Rhett shook his head in disbelief. "Ashe MacDaniel, as I live and breathe. You mean to tell me you've joined a virtual *moms* group? Online? Are you nuts?"

"It was a nice gesture that they invited me."

"Do they know about you?"

"Well…" Ashe couldn't admit the true reasons for accepting the invitation

"Well, what? You're leading these women on?"

"Not really. I'll tell them someday."

"*Someday?*" Rhett trailed after Ashe. He caught up and pointed a long fingertip into Ashe's chest. "Listen, fruitcake, I wouldn't appreciate it if you came in under some kind of anonymous cover and infiltrated *my* group of friends. Have you lost your cotton-picking mind? You've gone and stepped off the deep end right into the abyss. Mama and Daddy are doing the Charleston in their graves right this minute." It was a dressing down reminiscent of their mother's lectures extolling the virtues of respectable Southern ladies and gentlemen. Of course, Mama and Daddy lacked the luxury of modern technology.

"Rhett, aren't you being a touch melodramatic? You don't get it. You have a real job in an office where you deal with real people on a day-to-day basis. I work from home, in the house all day. Except for Tyler, I'm lucky if I see another human being. When I catch the mailman, it's a Kodak moment worthy of a ticker tape parade and a glass of champagne. Look at it from my perspective. I need adult interaction and adult conversation. It's the 21st Century, Rhett MacDaniel. This is how I – no – how millions of people socialize."

Rhett shook his head. "Lordy. Are we truly related? Was one of us switched at birth? You're one whack-a-doodle, Ashe."

"You mean you just noticed? What about the last thirty-five years?"

Rhett pinched Ashe's arm before he left to find his nephew. "I still think you're making a huge mistake. You wouldn't have this problem if you got out once in a while. Instead, you stay cooped up in here like an old bear. You better watch your hermit ways." He stopped in his tracks and waved a finger at Ashe. "You'll end up the Southern version of an old lady with a house full of…" Rhett glanced around the room. He spotted an indifferent Jim Bob and frustrated, looked back at Ashe. "…*Cats*."

"I'm a fully formed adult."

"That could be debated."

Ashe scowled. "I can run my own life. Anyway, I'm a dog person. I'd never cross to the Dark Side and get a cat. I have to think about Tyler."

"Oh, my God, please. Stop it, Ashe. Tyler's in school now during the day. As for the other times, do you know how many young women around here are looking for babysitting jobs? You don't need to look for friendship online. Do you know how many of my friends ask about you? For some ungodly reason, they believe you're a catch, despite your stupid real name."

"Thanks, Rhett *Butler*…" Rhett succumbed to an urge to pinch his sibling's arm. Ashe let out a wild scream. "Ouch! Uncle!"

"You'd better say 'uncle.' Now you get on to work, while Tyler and I find some trouble we can get into." He turned to face Ashe. "And stay out of trouble yourself."

***

shootingskye: *Are you busy?*

AsheMacD: *I wish I could get busy. I can't concentrate.*

shootingskye: *?*

AsheMacD: *Too much on my mind. What's up?*

shootingskye: *Can you think of a nice way to tell someone to lay off? With some force though…*

AsheMacD: *Who's giving you trouble?*

shootingskye: *Who else? Janna. She's trying to match me with someone. I can feel it.*

AsheMacD: *It's nice to be wanted, isn't it? In a relationship. Feels good.*

87

shootingskye: *I'm not saying I'm forever out of the picture. I'd like to find someone someday. I want to get my head on straight before I start dating again. Besides, I'm not over Trina.*

AsheMacD: *Takes time, doesn't it? I didn't think I'd ever get over Mac.*

shootingskye: *Are you? I mean, over Mac?*

AsheMacD: *I never thought I'd ever admit this. Mac and I shared something huge. It was a love you can never get over. I'm surprised to find it's getting easier every day. Time doesn't heal all. It does soften the hurt. You'll see. It's like swimming in a flooded creek. You have to hold your breath to get to the other side.*

shootingskye: *I think it's better to breathe.*

AsheMacD: *Maybe so.*

***

Ashe stared at the computer screen, trying to make sense of the words. Out of a thousand ways to procrastinate, Ashe was proficient in every one of them. One thing could be said about the job editing manuscripts for a print-on-demand publisher, the reading was never boring. Whoever this Parker Thornton was, he was a real piece of work, turning out writing like this and thinking it was art. Dysfunctional and myopic art, perhaps? The storyline was bobbing and weaving like a drunken college student on a bender, leaving Ashe wondering what the hell was happening. Worse yet, the author couldn't spell and had tense trouble. First, third, heck, throw the in entire third grade English grammar workbook. *Charlie's Problem* was a problem, all right. The man couldn't string two coherent sentences together if his life depended on it. Ashe paused mid-complaint to ponder the situation. One positive thing about Parker Thornton; he had money, enough to print his own book, enough to give Ashe a job.

Ashe rubbed at tired eyes and decided to step away from this literary challenge. *I have to, before I'll be pronounced irreversibly blind and dumb.* AOL was always left open in case Janna wanted to chat. There was no virtual door creak signaling her entrance today. It was Saturday. She was likely busy with Mandy. It had to be terrifying to have a child come home with the swine flu, especially if you were in a foreign country at the time.

Thank God Tyler was right here when he was pronounced sick with the common cold.

Ashe smiled at the thought of Janna. What a gift! One dark day, late last October, they found themselves in the same grief chat room, Janna looking for answers after her sister committed suicide and Ashe... Ashe barely managing to hold it together. The grief after Mac died consumed every waking moment. Then concern ran in the extreme opposite direction. Ashe didn't want to feel numb; it would be better to embrace the sorrow.

Janna was smart and easy to talk with. Her bravado and sass was uplifting. She was verbal about her grief – angry, sad, and frustrated. Listening to her was a relief for Ashe. Janna's daughters were adults and her parental experience, although with girls not boys, far outweighed Ashe's. Before Mac deployed to Iraq, Ashe was the typical spouse. The job teaching creative writing at the local college, the dreams about expanding the family, of watching Tyler grow. Mac was the dynamo who powered the MacDaniel family. After the loss, Ashe was a soul in free-fall. Janna filled in the blanks, with advice for Tyler's separation anxiety and his fussiness when it came to mealtime. It wasn't long after their online meeting that they were exchanging photographs of their kids.

Ashe was honored to have been asked to join the Virtual Moms. *Rhett is wrong about them.* The email exchanges of the past week proved all of them likeable and interesting. The camaraderie was infectious and Ashe felt comfortable chiming in with insights. "I'm a butt-insky," Ashe muttered, "albeit a humorously witty one." For a random online mix, the VMs were an impressive bunch, considering most had been together for at least a decade.

Janna asked for Ashe's information, name and address to add to their directory. The thought of sending the home phone number gnawed at Ashe's gut. Maybe someday, when the truth could be told? Ashe mulled the request over, weighing trust against caution, and decided, "What the hell?"

"I should get Janna a gift," Ashe said aloud. "Or maybe I should get them all a little something." Greasing the wheels might make the truth easier to swallow. Ashe opened the VM address list and printed it. What a brilliant idea! Each of Virtual Mom would receive something sweet as a thank you.

Chapter Nine

Sunday, November 8

Christmas Alone

This is the time of year when I don't know what to do. I do know this: I have two options.

Option One: Behave as though nothing has changed. Put up a tree. Sneak out and buy presents. Send out Christmas cards. Visit Santa at the mall. Toss a wreath on the door. Buy some sugar cookies and eggnog.

Option Two: Hide under a rock. Deny that Christmas is a pervasive holiday. Forget you're not coming home. Pretend like it's another day. Cry.

Were it not for Tyler, I think I'd be deep into Option Two. When children are involved... I don't have the luxury of burrowing into a cave for the duration. Tyler is a constant reminder that the world is still rotating, although time has stopped for me.

Although I have tried to keep it casual, it's not the same. Tyler isn't anticipating the holiday like I know I did at the same age. The gleeful expectation is absent. He's quiet, pensive. I feel him studying me, gauging me for a reaction before he opens his mouth. My little boy has become a little man. He's taking care of me now, and that's scary.

Mac, I'm going to let it ride like this for a while. I'm too tired to straighten it out. I need to save my strength for Christmas shopping and Santa Claus.

Thanks for leaving me with this.

Sarasota, Florida

Celia loved Sundays. It was her only day off from the hospital and she seized every second of it to catch up on housework, laundry, and shopping. This day off was different. Kimber surprised her bright and early – albeit not too early – with breakfast in bed, a huge bouquet of flowers, and a cute card. "I'm taking care of you today, Mom," she announced proudly. "I've got the day off from the store and I'm going to do the housework and laundry. *You* are going to sit poolside or in the lanai and put your feet up!"

Celia rubbed her eyes, caught unawares. "What is it? It's not my birthday. It's too soon for Christmas."

"You do everything for me. Now I'm going to do something for you. It's only one day out of the year. You deserve it."

"What about groceries?"

"Brandon's coming over later and we'll take care of it. I know what to get. Your list is on the fridge. You're going to spend the next twenty-four hours chillin'."

Celia eyed her suspiciously. "You didn't do anything wrong, did you? Crack up the car? Fail a class? Oh, no. *You're not pregnant, are you?*"

"Mother! Brandon and I aren't doing anything!" Celia wasn't sure she could believe her, yet Kimber was a good girl. They were also close. She would tell Celia if and when the relationship progressed to the next level. As she turned to leave the room, Kimber teased, "I'm only assembling the ingredients. The cake's not in the oven yet. We haven't mixed it up." Girlish giggles floated in the air behind her.

Celia looked for something handy to throw. A tray bearing scrambled eggs and hot coffee was the barrier separating her from her daughter. Celia wasn't about to sacrifice a breakfast in bed she didn't have to inspire or beg for.

After her tasty breakfast, Celia decided on a bubble bath and leisurely soak. She lit candles and plucked a novel off the neglected pile of books she had no time to read and settled in for a half hour of sheer laziness.

Dressed in a robe and her hair wrapped in a towel turban, her next stop was the computer. She carried her laptop to a poolside lounge chair and fired off a quick email.

To: jannasbananas, AsheMacD, laurelextonsbunch, ally1234, missymom, shootingskye
From: celiasunshine
Subject: I have the best daughter!

91

Girls, Kimber decided to surprise me today by taking over all the chores! I got breakfast in bed, flowers, a card, a long bubble bath, and now I'm going to sit at the pool and play online all day. If any of you want to join me, the weather here is 85 and sunny. I'll make a pitcher of margaritas! Come on down!

How's your Sunday? ☺

An immediate response came from Ally. "Bee-yotch! Don't dangle your sunshine and margaritas in my face! It's 20 degrees and snowing like a bitch here in the Tundra! I might have to break out Vanessa's skates! :-P – P.S. Your daughter IS the best!" Celia chuckled. She knew all about winter, having left chilly Ohio behind forever when she divorced Marvin Davis. She loved poking fun at Ally. Ally's dream was to move their brood south. With the economy in the toilet, no way Greg would be able to find another job. They were stuck in Minnesota, at least for now.

She noticed Janna online, so she IM'ed her.

celiasunshine: *Nice day up where you are?*
jannasbananas: *Warm for now. Tell Kimber she's a doll.*
celiasunshine: *I will. What are you doing today?*
jannasbananas: *Bead show. Like I need any more hobbies.*
LOL.
celiasunshine: *Tell me about it.*

Celia loved knitting. She could keep her hands busy while waiting for Kimber back in the days of running her around from one activity to another. Since her promotion and the increased work hours associated with it, she no longer had the time to work with yarn. She missed the calm rhythmic clicking of the needles, the fashioning of homemade sweaters and scarves from a single strand of wool.

jannasbananas: *What do you think about Ashe?*

Janna's words burned a hole in the screen.

What did she think? She didn't know. Celia remained the only group member with reservations about the newbie. Although she was polite, she'd given Ashe a cool reception. Celia read the blog and was impressed. She had cried like the rest of them. However, something about the writing set off alarm bells. Something was wrong, something she couldn't put her finger on. Every chance she got, she went back to the blog and read the words over, looking for a clue. Celia was doubly annoyed that Ashe kept forgetting to send a photo of herself. All the VMs did in the beginning, as a frame of reference. It was nice to have a face to match with the online personality. And what was with the 'peace out' ending to each email? So 1980s! How could she reply without revealing her guard was up?

> celiasunshine: *Seems nice. Why?*
> jannasbananas: *I think she might be perfect for Skye.*

Skye! *Skye?*

> celiasunshine: *Skye? What do you mean?*
> jannasbananas: *Nothing. <g>Only that I smell a romance!*

Janna's glee came over loud and clear.

Celia scratched her head. It didn't make any sense. She knew Skye had been married before, met Trina and hooked up, so she supposed it could happen. Could it happen so easily?

> celiasunshine: *?*
> jannasbananas: *I thought they would make a good match.*
> *What do you think?*
> celiasunshine: *Match?*
> jannasbananas: *Yes, silly. As in* love. *Why not?*
> celiasunshine: *I'm... I'm not sure.*

She wasn't lying. She wasn't sure.

***

The setting was gorgeous: old stone winery tucked into a valley protected by redwoods, surrounded with ancient grape vines and a garden of roses and cork trees. Napa Valley was experiencing an exceptional fall due to a late frost, and the hillsides were ablaze in varying shades of gold and red. Skye inhaled deeply, savoring the scent of evergreen and fallen leaves, the last of the roses, and the unmistakable aroma of suckling piglet roasting somewhere nearby.

The wedding had been a small one: bride, groom, parents and relatives, and a few friends, fifty people at the most. Skye had been asked – no, begged – by the sister of the bride, who was an old college buddy. "I'll pay you double," Stacy had implored, "and don't forget the free food! It's going to fab. Kris is having a fantastic chef do the meal. Bring Rob, too."

Skye didn't know how she'd tolerate being so near the happiness of newly minted wedded bliss. One thing was sure: she couldn't say no to the money *or* to Stacy's pouting. Rob declined the invitation as she knew he would.

She had to admit, the ceremony was sweet. The groom stumbled over his vows, the bride, Kris suffered a round of unstoppable hiccoughs, and a giant crow interrupted the proceedings by flying onto the gazebo and angrily screeching at the minister. Those in attendance cried, laughed and giggled – even Skye.

After the ceremony, Skye started with group photos and then to the couple. Not only were they unable take their eyes off each other, the newlyweds were constantly touching: his hand on the small of her back, her fingers brushing away his rumpled hair, his stroke of her cheek, their heads together in conspiratorial whispers. Skye winced at the memory of her own lost love. *It's a job, only a job,* she told herself. *Do it, and get out of here.*

While the guests ate, partied and laughed, Skye slumped on a stone bench, too exhausted to put her equipment away. She wondered about the traffic on the 101 and was trying to gauge a good time to leave when a man came up to her with a plate in hand.

"You look like you could use some nourishment," he said.

Skye looked up. The man seemed familiar; he was older, gray hair in a long ponytail, dancing blue eyes. She shook him off. "I'm fine, thanks. I think I'll leave. The party's almost over."

"Friend of the bride?" The man sat next to her.

"Friend of the sister of the bride. Doubling as designated photographer. How about you?"

"Hired gun, like you, I'm supposing. I'm the chef." He smiled. "Sure you won't have some? You won't find better in Napa, or the City, for that matter."

The offering looked and smelled heavenly, and Skye's stomach growled in response. "Sure, why not?" She grinned as she removed her belongings to make room for the plate. By the time she looked up, the mystery chef had vanished.

***

Celia put her glass of ice tea down and clicked on the bookmark for "Missing Mac." Tyler's photo beamed back at her. "Missing Mac" could be about anyone. Ashe hadn't used her last name, for reasons of anonymity. That made sense. Internet personalities were often far from real and some of the people behind the façade could be dangerous. Most of the VMs didn't use their real names in chat rooms in order to weed out the crazies. Celia reread the first blog post. It was filled with sorrow and laced with rage. As she navigated the pages, she noticed a curious thing she hadn't noted before. Except for the one photo of Tyler, there were no other photographs – none at all. No photos of Mac or Asheley MacDaniel, either separately or as a couple.

"Why would Ashe have only one picture of Tyler, when he's such a cute little boy? A mother would be proud of such a handsome kid," she mused out loud, remembering the shoe boxes of snapshots she'd taken of Kimber at the same age. "Why not a picture of the parents?"

Kimber appeared in the doorway. "What are you talking about?"

Celia folded her laptop closed. "Nothing. It's a Virtual Mom thing."

"You and your mommies! What happened to real life?"

"This *is* my real life. Like you don't have Facebook friends?"

"Sure, but we're kids. Middle-aged mothers shouldn't troll the web for friends. Hey. Nearly forgot, some guy's at the door. He's with the pool company."

"What does he want?"

"He said something about a complaint you made against Carlos. Mom, you didn't rat him out, did you?" Kimber struck a chastising pose with her hand on her hip. She liked Carlos a lot.

Celia rose from her lounge chair. "It's not personal, Kimber. I pay for a service. I expect to get what I pay for."

"Blah, blah, blah. I'm leaving with Brandon to get the week's groceries. Where's the debit card?"

"Here." Celia grabbed her purse from the inside of the lanai and handed Kimber the card.

"Be back in a bit."

"Okay. Drive safely."

"Oh, sure." Kimber turned and left through the back gate.

Celia approached the open front door and was stopped dead by a vision. Instead of Carlos, a tall, nicely tanned man with bulging muscles and a careless mass of blond hair – highlighted perhaps? – stood facing the street. His back was broad and tapered to the tiniest waistline she could imagine. He was wearing board shorts, and she noted sinewy calves, small feet, and perfectly shaped toes peeking out from leather flip-flops. *The dream?* His back was to her, and as she neared the doorway she realized he was checking out Kimber's swishy sashay to her Ford Focus.

Celia coughed. Men! They're all animals; they just come in different disgusting packages. "She's only 16, you know."

The stranger swung around, startled. A blush rose through the tan of his pretty neck straight up to his chiseled face. It gave her great satisfaction to feel him sweating. "Oh! Sorry, ma'am. I'm Doug. Doug Taylor. From Taylor Pool. You know, your pool guy?" He pointed to a van emblazoned with the name and an 800 number. Kimber backed up her car and nearly hit the van's front fender. Celia jumped and cringed, partly because of Kimber's reckless driving and partly because she had been "ma'am-ed." She made a mental note to keep her eye on this one.

"How can I help you?" Celia was still frosty from the horn dog's attention to Kimber. What nerve. The guy was old enough to be her father.

"The office said you had trouble with Carlos not showing up some days and doing a bad job when he managed to get her. He… um, how can I put this?" Doug leaned into the door and lowered his voice. "It appears Carlos had a little trouble with his… papers. You'll be happy to know he's completely out of the picture now."

96

Celia crossed her arms and glared. "Right. Is that supposed to excuse the lack of a clean pool?"

"Heck no. I thought I'd come by to let you know I'd be taking care of it myself. Same time, Saturday mornings. You didn't notice it was better yesterday afternoon?"

Yesterday?

"Here, allow me to show you." Doug Taylor entered the house, took Celia by the elbow, and led her to the backyard. She shook off his hand. *How dare this man act so familiar? And how would he know the way through my house?*

"I'm sorry about the trouble with Carlos," Doug added once they were on the lanai. "I took his word that he was in the country legally. I guess I should have checked more thoroughly."

Celia frowned. "Humph… I guess you should have." *What else did he let slide? Taxes? Insurance? Safe chemicals?*

"That's what happens when your business grows too quickly. I used to do all the maintenance myself. Don't know if you remember. That was a few years ago. All it took was word of mouth and the company took off. Unfortunately, when you have to hire employees, you take your chances."

Celia followed, her arms crossed.

"Look here." Doug pointed to a filter. "I don't know how Carlos was cleaning your pool, but this was completely clogged. I promise it won't happen again. And the pH values were off the charts. Kimber said her eyes were bloodshot and her skin was itchy after being in the pool, and that's the cause. I added the right balance of chemicals. It should be okay to use by now. I informed Kimber yesterday not to go in for twenty-four hours after treatment."

Kimber? He was here with my baby? Celia could feel the veins bulge in her neck. "Oh?"

"Nice girl, your daughter. Intelligent, too. She explained the law of supply and demand and Keynesian economics as it relates to the pool cleaning business." Doug laughed. "Didn't know they taught that in high school. Huh. Made perfect sense to me."

"My daughter is sixteen," Celia repeated, her breath icy.

"I know! You've got to be proud to have a genius for a kid."

97

"She has a boyfriend."

"How could she not? She's quite the looker." Doug winked. "Looks like her mom."

Celia blushed and rushed to compose herself. "Mr. Taylor, are we finished with the pool now? My time is valuable and I have a lot of things to do." She backed away, headed for the safety of the lanai.

Doug winked again. "A clean pool is a healthy pool."

"So I gather. Thank you for your attention. Now if you don't mind…" Celia kept her cool; inside she was raging. *I'll drain the freaking pool and fill it with dirt,* she thought, *if it would get Doug Taylor out of here.*

***

The short, friendly diversion with the handsome Doug ended and Celia shooed him out of the neighborhood before Kimber returned. She gave the pool a quick glance; it was spotless, pristine, wonderful – end of story. She couldn't see a reason to subject her daughter to a predator like Doug Taylor. Celia was happy to see his van pull away. "Now, where was I? Back to Ashe, back to Ashe…" This online situation needed further investigation, and if anyone was going to get to the bottom of this puzzle, it would be Celia Davis.

Celia opened up the VM address list and stared at the North Carolina number. She disliked intrusion. Celia was a private person herself, and email was less expensive. She had to know. She picked up her cell phone and dialed.

A male voice dripping wet with an enchanting Southern drawl answered. "Hello?"

Celia pulled the phone away from her ear and looked down. Sure enough, she had dialed the correct number. A man, in Ashe's house? Was she hiding a boyfriend? She swallowed hard, made a quick recovery, and plunged on. She had to do it for Janna and Skye. Heck, she had to do it for all the VMs. "Hi. May I speak to Asheley? Ashe MacDaniel?"

A sputtering cough erupted on the other end of the line. "May I ask who is calling?" choked out.

"It's Celia Davis, from Florida. One of the Virtual Moms?" Did Ashe tell this unknown man who the VMs were? The hacking continued; a crash of glassware, the howling of a hound, and something that sounded like 'damn it to hell.' "Excuse me? What's going on there? Are you all right?"

"Nothing. Please hold." Although the sounds were muffled, Celia could make out yelling, doors slamming and the clatter of dishes. A few seconds passed. "Ashe isn't available at the moment. You've called at a bad time. May I take a message?"

"Can you tell her I called? I'm sorry, your name is?"

A moment of awkward silence passed. "I'm…the sitter."

Ashe has a male sitter? That's a novel idea. "Oh, yes?"

"I'm visiting."

The phone shook in Celia's hand. She had to get to the bottom of this for the good of the group. "Are you living with Ashe?" she ventured, "She never said…"

"No, I'm here for the afternoon. I'm sorry. I have to go. I'm watching little Tyler and he's a handful. I'll tell her you called." The phone line went dead.

Celia stared at her phone. *What the hell?* "That was the most unpleasant, unusual phone call ever," she muttered.

One thing was for sure. Celia's bloodhound nose had been aroused. This puzzle was going to be solved one way or another. She would make certain of that.

Chapter Ten

Monday, November 9

A letter came yesterday, a letter in your hand. The postmark was six months ago, September. I ripped open the envelope, and my eyes clouded over. I couldn't read the words, until I realized the tears were in the way. I took a deep breath and prayed for strength.

It was one of the most astonishing letters I'd ever received:

Dear Ashe
I know I've been putting on a brave face, but I have to confess something to you, and an email doesn't seem appropriate.

My darling, I'm scared. Please don't tell Tyler. I want him to think of me as being brave and invincible. I don't want him to be scared, too.

It's not that I'm afraid of being here and doing the job. You know I'm more than capable. Since I've been away I've realized how precious you and Ty are to me and what a great life we have in the United States. Remember how I used to complain about every little thing? I can't do that anymore. I've come to appreciate the bounty we have, it's much more than many people elsewhere could dream of.

Dearest Ashe, you've been the love of my life since our first days in college. I want you to know how much I love you and always will.

I would say "Take care of our little boy." I don't need to. I know you are.

Staying safe.
Love, Mac

***

San Francisco, California

"Why are Mondays such a disaster?" Skye asked herself aloud. The debacle of a day was the continuation of a weekend that flew by too quickly. Skye was late returning from a late shoot at the Farmer's Market Sunday night because the N-Judah had broken down, underground no less, which resulted in a claustrophobic bout of hyperventilation. The passengers had to walk out of the Sunset tunnel. Cell phones were useless; she had no way to call Rob. By the time she emerged from her subterranean hell, she had no time to buy decent take out or to do laundry.

Rob slept past his alarm and was running forty-five minutes late for school. She offered to drive to make up for lost time. While retrieving the car – plastered with an exorbitant parking ticket thanks to the street cleaning Gestapo – Skye spilled coffee on her new cashmere sweater and had to resort to wearing something soiled because, of course, last week she had no time to run her dry cleaning in.

"Rob, you ready? We've got to leave *now*," she yelled. "I could sure use a maid," she said to herself.

"I heard that. You could use a husband. Or a wife." Rob winked as he appeared from his bedroom, his hair uncombed, his shirttail out, and his backpack slung over his shoulder.

"Very funny." Skye had to admit he was right. She'd inherited the disorganization gene along with ADD. It was Lee, and later Trina, who kept the household running smoothly. Much as she would love one, she couldn't afford a maid, not even once a month, not after six months of depression and dipping into what little savings she had. She would have to work her butt off for the next year to come out in the black.

The outlook for a mate looked equally bleak. Bless his heart; Rob wanted nothing more than to see his mother happy. He'd been less than thrilled with Trina, yet he gave her a chance. Skye imagined their bickering was friendly banter. Rob had a wry, cutting sense of humor. Skye appreciated it; Trina was put off. The tension between the two wasn't the only thing causing the split. Trina claimed Skye was needy and too dependent for her. She had to wait three years to say such hurtful things? Their last conversation still stung each time Skye replayed it in her mind.

After the dumpage, Skye found herself uninterested in anyone, male *or* female. Being cooped up in self-imposed house arrest didn't help. Her release back into the real world was slow and methodical. She would have no time for romance, and would instead concentrate on Rob and getting her backload of bills paid down.

The traffic on Oak Street was in full rush hour madness. The lanes were narrow and the drivers perilously quick. By the time she made it to Gough, her nerves were shot. Bicyclists whizzed down the Oak Street hill faster than the cars they passed with mere inches to spare. Hitting a car or bike was a constant possibility. Skye preferred to take the MUNI, driving only when it was necessary or when she wanted to get out of town.

"Don't forget, Mom; I'll be late today," Rob said.

"Huh?" Skye's full attention was on defensive driving.

"Remember? I have a play rehearsal. I don't want you to freak out if I walk into the house late."

"Okay." She pulled up to the school drop-off lane and Rob collected his backpack and got out. "I suppose it wouldn't be right to ask for a kiss?" she hinted. Rob was so far past the goodbye kiss stage she'd forgotten what it felt like.

He leaned into the window. "I love you, Mom. But, *no*." He smiled and waved. A surge of emotion tugged at her heart, interrupted by a noisy round of car horns urging her to move on.

***

Monday was the day Skye worked on her photos from home, retouching and color correcting with Photoshop. The week had been a busy one, with magazine shoots for the culinary academy and for a vineyard in Sonoma. It was back up to Napa Valley the next day for the wedding. Event photography was one thing; food shots were her bread and butter. After the delicious meal she had sampled, thanks to the unnamed chef, she had hunted him down without luck to take photos of the food and the wedding cake.

As she opened the folder containing the photos of beaming bride, handsome groom, and an eclectic collection of guests she didn't know, Skye was filled with longing. Her wedding to Lee was magical and perfect; performed at sunset on the beach in Malibu. It was the happiest she'd ever been. Everything that came after paled in comparison. After Lee died, the world lost a little of its color. Trina was a welcome change of scenery, a new diversion taking the concept of love into another direction. It was thrilling, or

102

so she believed. Looking back, signs were the relationship was tenuous at best.

Skye loved working at home; stillness broken into seconds ticking on her grandfather clock. She stored her photos online after adjusting them, and stayed logged on to AOL for those moments when one of the Virtual Moms wanted to chat. Janna worked from home too, so they were most likely to see each other during the day. With the addition of Ashe, who also worked from home as an editor, she had a new friend to talk to. The three-hour time difference wasn't much of a problem since Skye often got up in the middle of the night and Ashe worked late.

They had so much in common: being widows, having sons, working from home, working in the arts. Ashe was sympathetic and kind and she lost her husband only last year! Her daunting life experiences resonated with Skye. By the end of the week, after hours of IMs and hundreds of email exchanges, Skye felt an affinity with her new friend. Ashe was interested in the most intimate details about her life with Trina.

Skye took a break from her work to check her email. She noticed had Ashe logged on.

shootingskye: *Hey! Are you busy?*

No reply. Skye knew Ashe had her hands full with a job and a young son. She flipped back to Photoshop and organized the Farmers' Market photographs. All sorts of lettuces and greens, oranges, strawberries, and persimmons filled the bins, and the bright explosion of contrasting hues made interesting photographs.

A chime pinged and a small pop-up window opened. Skye was excited to see it was Ashe.

AsheMacD: *Hi. Sorry I didn't see you before. I had to meet Tyler at the bus stop.*
shootingskye: *How are you?*
AsheMacD: *Busy. I finally finished that edit. Took me until five a.m. What about you?*
shootingskye: *The usual Chinese fire drill this morning. I wish I were more organized. Rob overslept! Weekend was crazy. I'm getting caught up.*

AsheMacD: *How was Napa?*

shootingskye: *Beautiful. It's always beautiful, no matter the season. You should visit sometime. Bring Tyler. He'd love it. All boys love the ocean, and we moms could do a wine tour. You can stay with me and Rob.*

AsheMacD: *Maybe.*

Maybe? What a noncommittal answer! The one thing tying all of the VMs together was the desire to meet every last mom. After sharing all the facets of your life including every secret, the next logical step would be a final face-to-face encounter. It wasn't a race to see who would be the first. It was understood that the goal was the same for all of them. Ashe was enthusiastic about it days ago, mentioning how much she wanted to visit California. She was an East Coast kind of girl and had never ventured west of the Mississippi.

Several minutes elapsed. Skye went back to work. An hour went by and her IM screen chimed again. Thrilled to be speaking to Ashe again, Skye was annoyed to find it was Celia.

Celia rarely IM'ed her. Celia was closer to Laurel and Missy and was friends with Janna. It seemed she only tolerated her and Ally. Celia's coolness intensified after Skye announced Trina as a partner. Skye knew some people could never warm to the idea of two women sharing a commitment. The other girls congratulated her when the two hooked up; Celia had not. Despite her prickliness, Skye refused to let Celia ruin their friendship. She was cordial to everyone, especially to Celia, who could be abrasive, opinionated, and hardheaded. The core of the group was that their friendship would transcend differences while celebrating common interests.

celiasunshine: *Skye, are you there?*

shootingskye: *Yes. Isn't it late for you?*

celiasunshine: *Just got home from work. I wanted to ask you something.*

shootingskye: *Sure. Shoot.*

celiasunshine: *What do you think of Ashe?*

Ashe? It would be like her to pick on the newbie. Celia was no shrinking violet, full of robust opinions. Bitchy, even. Ashe might be a newbie, yet she held her own. Skye couldn't lie.

shootingskye: *She's cool. I like her. Why do you ask?*
celiasunshine: *I'm wondering. We don't really know her.*
shootingskye: *Janna does. I feel like I do too.*
celiasunshine: *Do you? Does she?*
celiasunshine: *Has Janna met her?*
celiasunshine: *Has Ashe sent a photo of herself?*
celiasunshine: *Have either of you spoken to her on the* phone?

Skye shifted in her chair, uncomfortable with the rapid fire remarks. A wave of protective loyalty for her new friend washed over her.

shootingskye: *I haven't yet, but I don't expect it. We're on* different time zones. *I'm sure a phone call will happen in time.*
celiasunshine: *What do we know about her family?*
celiasunshine: *Did she mention any relatives?*
celiasunshine: *Parents…sisters…*brothers*, perhaps?*
celiasunshine: Boyfriend, *maybe?*

Skye thought hard. In their many hours of conversation, they only talked about the boys and lost spouses. Skye was guilty of talking about herself. *Damn that Celia's typing speed.* She couldn't match it, although she had to try.

shootingskye: *No, but it's not unusual. She's only been in* the loop for a week.
shootingskye: *What's the problem?*
shootingskye: *You don't have to meet a person or hear* their voice to know they're real.
shootingskye: *Look at all of us. We're real.*
celiasunshine: *We're* different.
shootingskye: *Why? Because we've known each other for a* decade?

Skye sighed, exasperated. She rooted around for her cell phone. Speaking to Celia directly was the only way to deal with her, but her cell was a room away, tethered to a charger in the kitchen.

shootingskye: *That's not fair, Celia.*
shootingskye: *You have to start somewhere in a relationship.*
celiasunshine: *There are lots of nut jobs on the Internet. Just saying.*
shootingskye: *Janna's known her forever. Hasn't she spoken to Ashe?*
celiasunshine: *That's the thing. She hasn't.*

Celia planted it – an uncomfortable seed of doubt. The recent hours of late night and early morning chatting with Ashe flowed through Skye's mind. She had shared everything about herself in the space of a week. *Everything.* Her address, her innermost thoughts, the name of Rob's school. What if Ashe was a psychotic cyber stalker? What if she meant harm to one of them? *Calm down, Skye, it can't be. Celia's only being her normal paranoid cynical self.* What purpose would it serve for a person to crash the Virtual Moms group? Back then it was to scam Beanie Babies, and now? It had been years since the heyday of trades or buys; the group was now about friendship, affection, and understanding. Celia's theory lacked a motive.

shootingskye: *What are you implying? That Ashe is dangerous?*
celiasunshine: *I don't know. Something doesn't ring true about her, that's all.*
shootingskye: *Like what?*
celiasunshine: *If I knew, I wouldn't ask for your opinion.*
celiasunshine: *Sorry to bother you.*

As quickly as she had appeared, Celia logged off AOL and disappeared from her buddy list. Her abrupt departure was like Celia, only this time Skye could feel panic rising. *What was Celia seeing that I can't see?* Skye closed the IM box and opened her

106

email inbox, filtering the list to Ashe's mail. She opened and reread each one in her search for clues. Something had to be between the lines, the red flags Celia was seeing.

As for danger signs, they were invisible to Skye.

***

"Girly, what's shaking?"

Janna. Skye noticed her caller ID and answered on the first ring. She needed positive reinforcement after her odd IM with Celia.

"You sound winded," Skye noted. "You're not… with someone, are you?"

"Holy hell, no. I'm on the treadmill. It's been raining for two days and I haven't been able to walk in the park. Plus it's cold. Yuck." Janna's tip-top shape meant she could hold a conversation while working out. Skye needed an hour's recovery.

"Shouldn't you be tucked into bed by now?"

"Bed! I might be old but I'm not dead yet! Besides, I'm thinking it's almost time to start the man search again. Have to look my best."

"Like you need it. You're model pretty, you be-yotch. I'm so glad you're a night owl."

"Heh. We should rename the loop the 'Virtual Insomniac Moms Ex-Beanie Fanatics.' Hey, hey, the VIM-ex-BFs…One or all of us are up half the night. What's the problem? It can't be Rob. You've been blessed with the nicest kid on the planet."

"You're right about that. It's not Rob. Something weird happened now. I got a strange IM from Celia."

"Celia can be that way." Skye smiled at Janna's observation. Celia's rigid character had been the topic of conversation between the two on many occasions.

"She *never* IMs me."

"It's rare when I get one. What's her problem now?"

"She wanted my opinion on Ashe."

"And?"

"I told her I liked her. What's not to like?"

"Good, good!" Skye could hear Janna's hands clapping.

"She brought up some good points, though. I mean, on why she doesn't trust her. How well do you know Ashe?"

107

"I know her enough to recommend her to the group. Wait a minute. Has Ashe done something to you or Celia? Or to anyone else?"

Skye thought about it. Ashe had been outgoing and compassionate. She fit in so perfectly, it was as if she had been with the group from the beginning. Ashe's warmth made instant camaraderie possible. "No."

"I told you she was a great gal, didn't I? I'm an excellent judge of character. I picked all of you. I kept you all, too." Janna laughed.

"I trust your judgment, it's that…"

"It's Celia. We all know our Celia. She has to pick at everything and everyone. She did it to all of us. Once she dissects Ashe and is finally satisfied, she'll move on to the next thing. I hope it's a man, because she sorely needs one."

Skye giggled. "Maybe a little bedroom action would soften her rough edges."

"Sex? The girl needs to make it past first base before she can bring it home! Anyway, I knew what was coming. I warned Ashe before I offered the invitation. Celia's a tough nut. You have to admit, once you pass the smell test, she's a great friend."

"I agree."

"Feel better?"

"Definitely."

"I wish Ashe would send us her pic, don't you? Don't you wonder if she's attractive? She has to be, Tyler is a doll baby."

"She's a delightful woman. She doesn't have to be attractive. We can't have too many beauty queens in the mix. I'll get a complex. Besides, I'm afraid there's no room for another princess in this group. That title belongs to you alone."

Janna's cackle cracked the receiver. "You never know. So, what do you think? Is Ashe a good match for you?"

"She's fitting in with the group."

"I asked for *you* specifically."

Skye lowered the phone and looked at the screen. What was Janna getting at? Skye had seen her in action. Janna's pitch was squeaky, indicating her excitement. "Is something going on I don't know about?" Skye ventured.

"Never mind," Janna teased.

Chapter Eleven

Tuesday, November 10

Another news item on TV about a local boy meeting his Maker in the war zone. This latest one was 21, a Duke grad, newly married, his wife pregnant with twins. Twins! He looked like he wasn't much older than Tyler. His babies will never know their daddy and it's a crying shame.

I don't know how much more I can take. Every time I think I have this thing licked, every time I think life is getting normal, someone else dies and I'm back to square one. My stomach is churning over the thought of this colossal waste of time, energy, and beautiful human beings.

If Tyler were to enlist, I don't know what I'd do. Cut off his fingers, maybe? Lock him in a closet? Oh, my God. What if the draft came back? I'd be paying for a one-way ticket to Switzerland or marking the road map to Canada.

I hate to say it, on days like today my anger spills over to you, Mac. Promises were made all over creation. A promise to love and cherish, to be here forever. A promise to stay safe. We were going to grow old together, twin rockers on this old wooden porch. Now what do I have? No soul mate and my hands full with Tyler. He doesn't understand any of this.

Thank you, Mr. President, thank you members of Congress and the Joint Chiefs of Staff. Why don't your loved ones go over and pay the price? Thank you all for sending our young men and women to get killed. I know the arguments on the other side – you supplied eloquent debates – some good has been done. Is it worth the price? The truth: the Army sucks, the military sucks, and this country sucks.

***

Las Vegas, Nevada

As Missy opened the door to leave, the phone rang. The phone wouldn't ring for hours, yet it never failed. She would get a call if she was running late. She dropped her keys on the table and ran to answer.

"Hello?" She noted a trip to the gym was in order. Breathless after the short sprint? Her round tummy wasn't going to disappear without it.

"Mrs. Martin? This is Mrs. Proctor, Kassie's principal."

"Mrs. Proctor. Nice to hear from you. Say, can I call you back? I'm heading out the door. I'm late for my appointment and I can't cancel again... It'll be months before I can get another..."

"Mrs. Martin, I'm afraid I need to speak to you. In person, right away. It's Kassie."

Missy put her purse down, various scenarios of illness and misfortune flashing through her head. It was normally Kara who was germy and accident-prone. "What's the matter? Is she sick?"

"Mrs. Martin, I'm afraid it's far more serious than that. It's not something we can discuss over the phone. You should get here right away."

Missy recognized the 'principal' tone. Mrs. Proctor's voice went from cordially blasé to perilously frosty in nanoseconds. Kassie was in some kind of trouble. What could it be? "Is she hurt?"

"It's nothing like that. However, this situation demands your immediate attention."

Missy would have to find another dentist.

"Okay. I'll be there as soon as I can."

***

Not a word was exchanged between the two during the car ride home. Missy kept her eyes trained on the road, too furious to yell. While mentally composing a wise parental lecture, she stole sideways glances at her daughter. Kassie remained slumped in her seat, alternating folding her arms and tugging at the hem of her dress. She picked at the upholstery with black painted fingertips. *When did she paint those? Wait a minute. Where did she get black fingernail polish?* Once in their driveway, Kassie leapt from the passenger seat and ran into the house. Missy assumed her bedroom door would be absorbing the brunt.

Missy remained in the car and dialed Earl's cell phone number. She hated calling him during working hours. His attention was either with clients or on the job site. When he was immersed

110

in a project, he could be brusque and rude, making her calls seem like unwanted intrusions. The phone rang several times before going to voice mail, meaning the ringer was turned off and it was on vibrate. He likely looked at her number and disregarded it. No crisis on the home front would be worth interrupting his day.

She sighed and flipped her phone closed without leaving a message. He wouldn't believe her, not over the phone. Kassie was the perfect angel in their family. As Mrs. Proctor said, this situation had to be dealt with in person.

Missy headed inside after she felt calm enough to begin a discussion with Kassie. She stopped at Kassie's bedroom– door closed, of course, with Emo music blaring from stereo speakers – and tapped lightly. "Kassie? Kass, open up."

The music abruptly stopped and Kassie, sullen with arms crossed, cracked the door an inch. Missy pushed it open and stepped in.

"I suppose you're going to ground me." Her pose was indignant, her chest puffed up like a mad hen.

Missy consciously checked her anger. "I won't do anything until your father gets home. We need to discuss this as a family."

"He never comes home. Why don't you figure it out on your own? Go ahead. Ground me. Don't let me go anywhere until I'm eighteen. I know. Why don't you send me to reform school? I'm sure you'd just *love* that. It doesn't matter; I don't care." Kassie crossed her arms and shot Missy a defiant look.

"Kassie, this problem can be worked out. We'll do it together."

"It's not a problem for me."

Missy shook her head. Kassie had been unrepentant at school. Talking to her now was futile. She turned to leave and stopped. "Can I ask you one thing?" As soon as she asked the question, Missy knew it was a mistake. Kassie's blank look meant that little she said would sink in. "*Why*, Kass? Why would you steal those earrings from that girl? Didn't you know you'd get caught? I don't get it. I need to know why. You have everything you want and more. All you have to do is ask."

Kassie put in ear buds, cranked the stereo on high, and flopped on her bed.

Missy retreated, at a loss as to her next step.

**

To: AsheMacD
From: shootingskye
Subject: Do you ever feel something is going on?

I'm getting odd vibes from Janna, aren't you?

To: shootingskye
From: AsheMacD
Subject: RE: Do you ever feel something is going on?

Skye, when *isn't* Janna planning something? I get the impression she's immersed in a dozen projects at once. I wouldn't worry about it.
Peace out, Ashe

**

Missy shot a nervous glance at the kitchen clock while she tried to keep her head. The second hand dragged from marker to marker, taking its sweet time. *Where the hell was he?* It was later than late, 10:30. Earl's many construction projects meant the occasions when he missed a meal were commonplace. He had never been this late before. Before the call from the principal, she had planned an exceptional feast for a Tuesday: prime rib roast and twice-baked potatoes, his favorite. She kept the roast warm for as long as she could, but Kara and Kassie were hungry. Missy broke open a bottle of wine, unusual for a weeknight, and poured a generous glass as she served dinner.

Annoyed yet not wanting to act like a possessive wife, Missy began calling him in earnest during the afternoon. He didn't respond and the calls went straight to voicemail. Each time she hung up without leaving a message. After dinner, she busied herself by tidying the kitchen, scrubbing the counters with enough force to dull the granite finish. Kassie and Kara finished their homework and went to bed.

By the time 9:30 arrived, her annoyance morphed to anger. She dialed Earl's number again. Properly inebriated with a half bottle of Santa Barbara's best pinot noir, she left a terse message. "Earl, this is Missy. Missy *Martin*. Remember me? Your wife? Kara really needed your help with math tonight, and Kassie has had some trouble in school today. Remember them? Or did you forget your daughters? Do we need to make an appointment? Anyway, it's late and I'm wondering if I should hold dinner for you, although it's burned to crispy crap by now." She slammed the receiver down hard and missed the cradle. It left an indentation on the table's mahogany surface.

She called every fifteen minutes after that, and was dumped into voicemail hell each time. By 10:30, her anger developed into fear. *What if Earl was in an accident?* She would never forgive herself if he were dying in a ditch somewhere. Maybe he was bleeding. Car jacked? Mugged? Anything could happen in Vegas, especially in the back alleys along the Strip. Missy searched for the phone book to ring the local hospitals when her husband staggered into the house. He was glassy-eyed, his tie was loosened, his shirttail out.

"Earl! Are you all right? I was worried sick!" Missy's concern faded to relief and then ignited into rage when she realized he had been drinking. Not only did he reek of alcohol, he was plastered. "Earl Martin. Where have you been?"

"Missy, you have to sit down. We have to talk." His words slurred together into one long, rambling noise.

"We're not talking until you sober up." She crossed her arms into a tight bow.

"I've been drinking but I'm not drunk. See?" Earl bowed, drew an imaginary line on the kitchen floor, and walked straight down. When he reached the dining room table, he pulled out a chair and motioned for Missy to follow. Still skeptical, Missy obeyed and took a seat. Earl joined her across the table.

"What's up with the Joe College imitation?" Missy asked.

"Sorry. The time got away from me," Earl answered.

Missy exploded. "The time? Come on, Earl. Where *were* you? Why didn't you call? Don't you know how worried I was?" She reached across the table and grabbed his arm. "Earl, you're a married man with two kids. It's bad enough you work long hours and you're away from home so much. You can't act like you're single."

"I'm sorry, Missy." Missy looked into his eyes and realized Earl was as somber and serious as she had ever seen him. His eyes were misty.

She was afraid to continue the conversation although she had to. "Sorry for what?" she asked in a quiet voice.

"I… I can't do this anymore…"

"You can't do what anymore?" Missy was perplexed.

Earl extended his arms, a huge circle that quickly collapsed. "*This!* This house. This car, these kids. This life. You. *All* of this. I don't know how to tell you. I can't keep this charade going any longer."

"Earl, what are you talking about?" Before her was a mad man, someone who'd lost his marbles. He was obviously suffering a nervous breakdown.

Earl rose. "I only came back tonight to pick up my things. I'm leaving you, Missy. I don't love you anymore."

He turned and wove a crooked path down the hallway toward the master bedroom, leaving Missy in shock, staring at the empty space behind him.

She could have cried. What good would it have done? Missy sat at the table for a good, long time replaying Earl's arrival. *He came home, he was drunk. He said he can't take it anymore. He's leaving.* The last fifteen minutes appeared straightforward; it still made no sense. They had been married fifteen years and were successful and happy. They never fought. They agreed on everything: the house, the yard, and childrearing. They liked the same food, music, and sports. They went to church every Sunday. This had to be a very cruel practical joke. How could he *not* be happy?

Missy followed Earl into the bedroom. If he were joking, she couldn't tell. Two suitcases lay open on the bed. One was half full of underwear and tee shirts, the other contained a tangle of dress shirts and pants. Poor Earl. He couldn't figure out how to make the optimum use of space. Missy always prepared for his business trips. She had a system of rolling up clothing before packing. More items could be packed with her method and everything would be wrinkle-free by journey's end. She suppressed an urge to help him. *Wait a minute!* What was she thinking? Help *him*?

"Earl? What are you doing?"

"Packing." He slammed the top down on one bag, zipped it up and swung it to the floor.

"Don't you think I deserve an explanation? How can you love me one day and not the next?"

Earl made a show of zipping up the second bag, busying himself to avoid eye contact. "It's complicated." His job finished, he rolled both bags toward the hallway. "I hate doing this, Missy. I have no other choice." His eyes darted down, catching the sight of a wastebasket. They lingered there.

Missy bit her tongue. She wanted to know, yet the question hung heavy in her mind and lodged in her throat. Before she could talk herself out of it, a challenge gurgled out. "Wait a minute. Do you have…someone else?"

"I'll be at the La Quinta Inn off the highway, in case you need me. It had better be a *real* problem if you call," he announced. "And yes, there is someone else."

***

A swift, hard kick in the stomach would have been easier to take. Once she'd gotten her bearings back, numbness replaced the pain. She could shed tears, but she didn't know what she did wrong. Her eyes were dry. Earl's leaving was surreal. This was someone else's life, not hers.

Kassie. In all the commotion, she had forgotten Kassie's in-school suspension for attempted theft. She would need help in dealing with this. "Earl, wait…What about the girls? Kassie…" She jumped from the bed and ran to the front door. She only caught her husband's tail lights as they disappeared into the night.

Missy wandered the house, now cavernous and quiet. She stopped at the girls' room. The hall light illuminated their innocent faces. With their bedroom on the second floor, they had slept through their father's homecoming and leaving. She didn't see the need to wake them with such harsh news. She brushed their hair away from their eyes and gazed into their faces. Both Kara and Kassie were angelic when asleep, like china dolls. Yes, Kassie, who could be less than an angel these days. Missy sighed. They would have questions tomorrow. Lots of them. She would have to figure out answers, all alone with no road map and no dress rehearsal. It would be impossible, since she couldn't figure out the reason herself. 'Someone else' Earl had said. Missy couldn't tell her daughters that. She couldn't break their hearts that way. She lingered at each bedside, pulling up the blankets, making certain

115

their water glasses were full, as if her attention would keep all things bad away from her angels.

The mystery woman – who could it be? Missy recalled the business card she found in Earl's pocket. Would that be the home-wrecking slut? What was her name? Marisa? Marcia? Missy headed to the bedroom. The card was on the dresser right where she placed it a week before. *Marcella Bainbridge.*

Her eyes burning, she focused at the card. She picked up the phone, stared at the numbers on the receiver and then at Marcella's number. The indignant wife in her rose to the surface. This could be the tramp that stole her husband out from under her nose. The sensible Missy came to the card's defense. *What if she's a business contact? I'll look like a psycho jealous wife if I call this woman in the middle of the night.* Earl had lost contracts on far less than an angry spouse suffering from rash conclusion jumping.

Missy flopped on the bed. She knew she wouldn't find sleep tonight. She grabbed her laptop and signed on to AOL. If anyone needed the support only a Virtual Mom could provide, Missy's situation would put her right at the top of the list.

To: jannasbananas, AsheMacD, laurelextonsbunch, shootingskye, celiasunshine, ally1234
From: missymom
Subject: An awful day.

Kassie was suspended. Earl left me.

Missy looked at her short note. Six meaningless words. No one would believe it. Everyone thought her girls were flawless. Celia and Kimber loved Earl. Janna and her girls thought he was funny. If Missy's situation wasn't real to her, how could she explain it to her friends? Missy had been smug in the past, rubbing her so-called perfect marriage into all their faces, especially the single gals. She would be embarrassed to admit her marriage suffered from flaws. Big, honking flaws, the kind that would make her look foolish and stupid.

Missy deleted the email.

It was late. With the possible exception of Janna, the East Coast moms would be asleep. Missy noticed Skye online and sent

116

her a smiley face. She certainly couldn't send an unhappy one. Skye responded right away.

> shootingskye: *What's up?*
> missymom: *Can't sleep.*
> shootingskye: *Me neither. Maybe wine would help?*☺
> missymom: *I've had my limit.*

Good thing too, Missy thought. *She couldn't take this without alcohol.*

> shootingskye: *Ah, ha! Drunk typing!*
> missymom: *Not really. Hey. Can I ask you about Trina?*
> shootingskye: *Sure.*
> missymom: *Was it a surprise? When she found someone else? Or did you expect it?*
> shootingskye: *That's an odd question.*
> missymom: *Is it?*
> shootingskye: *I guess I was surprised. At first. Looking back I see Trina was waving a warning flag at me for at least a year. Why?*

Missy bit her lip and stared at the glowing screen. She was afraid Skye would say that. Had she dismissed her own warning signs?

> missymom: *No reason.*
> shootingskye: *Has Celia asked you about Ashe?*
> missymom: *No. Why?*
> shootingskye: *She doesn't like her.*
> missymom: *Celia's a tough cookie. And smart.*
> shootingskye: *She thinks Ashe is up to something. Or is some kind of cyber weirdo.*
> shootingskye: *It got me thinking and I talked to Ashe about it today.*
> missymom: *You came right out and asked her? You called her?*
> missymom: *What does she sound like?*

117

Missy imagined Ashe's voice as a stereotypical Southern belle along the lines of Scarlett O'Hara, coquettish, and dripping with Tupelo honey.

shootingskye: *No, silly. Email. IM.*
missymom: *What did she say?*
shootingskye: *She appreciates Celia's caution. Said if she was too much of a distraction, she would leave the group.*
missymom: *No!*

Missy had her own doubts a week before, yet she'd gotten over them. Ashe had a fun, helpful personality, easy to like.

shootingskye: *I told her I'd still be her friend if she dropped.*
missymom: *I'm with you.*
shootingskye: *The way she writes about loss – it's uncanny. I found myself relating Lee's death and my break up with Trina with her loss of Mac.*

Had Skye picked up on her vibes? Did she sense Earl's leaving? Missy now had recent first-hand knowledge of heartbreak. Wallowing in other people's trials might take the edge off. She clicked on the *Missing Mac* bookmark, although Missy hadn't lost her husband to war, only to some unnamed floozy. Her eyes filled with tears.

missymom: *I'm there now.*
shootingskye: *Missy, you all right?*
missymom: *Yeah. Why?*
shootingskye: *You don't seem yourself.*
missymom: *It's been a killer day. I'm exhausted. Maybe I should go to bed.*
shootingskye: *Write to Ashe. Or call me. I'll be around all night.*

Chapter Twelve

Take a look at this face; I took this photo a half hour ago. You tell me. Is this kid one bit nervous?

Monday is the first day of school and Tyler is wound tighter than a cyclone. He's been dancing around like a dervish since we checked out the school, the little orange bus, the teacher, and the lunch menu. He picked out his own school wardrobe thanks to a quick trip to Sears. We scoured the aisles at Staples looking for the perfect pencils, markers, crayons, and notebooks. Let's not forget the backpack; its construction is better suited for a month in the Arctic, not a daily trip to kindergarten. I'm still checking out all the pockets in my search for any contraband Army men, while Ty knows where every item is and should be.

And me? I'm a basket case.

While it's nice to see our little boy grow into a little man, I have some misgivings, seeing my only child take a step out of the door and into another life passage. Raising a child on my own has been harrowing although it was nice to have him here, under my wing for the last eleven months. We've commiserated and mourned. We've missed you. We figured it out. Tyler and I have become close – I'm closer to him than I was to either of my parents.

I've found – amazingly so – that I can do Life on my own. Without you? It's a scary thought. I know you'd want to be here to see the transformation. We miss you as much now as we did a year ago. With time, the jagged edges have been filed down.

Am I going to cry when Tyler jumps on the little bus for the first time?

You betcha.

For you.

***

Minneapolis, Minnesota

Snow fell steadily, huge white flakes unaided by wind, descending like parachutes from the sky. The pastoral scene was straight out of Currier and Ives, yet Ally was too absorbed to notice. She sat at her kitchen table with a steaming cup of coffee, attempting to navigate both eBay and Etsy at the same time. She'd spent a busy week of cleaning out the basement in advance of Thanksgiving. This year she would be hosting the family celebration and needed the space downstairs to contain the young children who would no doubt be bouncing off the walls. What used to be a rec room had turned into a 'wreck' room – a depository for things unwanted and forgotten.

Her excavation unearthed many items Ally thought were ancient history. Old books, knickknacks, family heirlooms, baby clothes from both Vanessa *and* Mike. She'd discovered a box of Mike's old Halloween costumes and carefully stowed school papers. Ally opened a dozen boxes of Greg's belongings, moved in after the wedding yet untouched after a decade. She located a box of pottery, some wire and forged jewelry and other arty-facts from her brief college stint at the U of M.

Then the mother lode of all forgotten treasures – a huge plastic tub of Beanie Babies buried beneath the rubble. She'd thought Vanessa had them all. Ally considered keeping them as souvenirs or presents for Vanessa's children, or to hold them as an investment. In the end, she'd decided against it. The beanies were on a one-way trip out the door. She spent a weekend photographing and cataloging. It was going online, up for sale to the highest bidder. She didn't need junk cluttering up her house. And with Christmas right around the corner, she could use the extra cash.

Ally left her AOL window open to chat with whoever was available. Celia and Laurel would be absent; they were working. She could count on the schedules of Skye, Janna, and Ashe to be mildly chaotic. Only Missy was a stay-at-home mom, although she was active in the girls' school. Except for obligations as a room mother, reading assistant, and domestic goddess, Missy was always online.

Ally reflected on the past week. Along with the waning interested in beanies, the Virtual Moms loop had undergone a subtle yet distinct change. In the span of a few days, the dynamic of the group shifted. It was Ashe or Skye who started most of the week's email, and the replies were dominated by Ashe, Skye, and Janna. The tone between the three was chummy yet strange, as though they were in on a joke to which the rest of the girls weren't privy to. Janna led an interesting life in New York, so it wasn't unusual for her to have interesting anecdotes to share every day. She rubbed elbows with politicians and rock stars and bumped into movie stars and Tony Award-winning Broadway actors on her way to getting coffee or groceries. Such hobnobbing was mundane for Janna.

Celia's silence since Ashe's induction was curious. Celia, so Internet savvy, opinionated and smart had no problem expressing herself among friends. It was Celia who clucked over everyone like a mother hen, although Ally was four years older. Missy, Laurel and Skye were never big contributors to the email group before, and Ally knew the three had teenagers. She knew from experience living with adolescents could be a psychically, brain-sucking venture.

Ally finished listing a hand-dyed batik sarong, a relic from her post-hippy days, when her desktop chimed.

jannasbananas: *Al, U busy?*
ally1234: *No. Miss Vanessa's in school, so I'm making use of the time to post stuff for sale.*
jannasbananas: *Ebay or Etsy?*
ally1234: *Both.*

Ally laughed aloud. Both women were artistic and dabbled in Internet commerce. She should put it all up for sale. Cataloging their possessions would take years. Over the course of her marriage, the family amassed a huge collection of toys, books, and sporting equipment. Every square inch of their foursquare two-story Craftsman house was jammed.

ally1234: *What's up?*
jannasbananas: *Have you heard from Celia?*
ally1234: *Jinx. GMTA.*
jannasbananas: *She upset Skye the other night. She* IM'ed *her. She never IMs her.*

ally1234: *?*

jannasbananas: *She wants Ashe out of the group. Doesn't like her. Told Skye she thought Ashe was some sort of Internet stalker or a nut job. Do you know why she'd think so?*

ally1234: *Beats me. I've got nothing against Ashe. You know Celia. She's not afraid to speak her mind.*

As far as Ally could tell, Ashe was pleasant. She was a mom like the rest of them. She saw no reason to distrust or dislike her.

ally1234: *Celia hasn't said a word to me. I noticed she hasn't responded much to the email chatter. It could be...*

jannasbananas: *What?*

ally1234: *Nothing.*

jannasbananas: *Must be something. Spill.*

ally1234: *It's... You and Ashe and Skye. Seems like you're breaking off into your own group.*

jannasbananas: *Not true! You know I'm trying to fix up Ashe and Skye! The two of them are in the dark but the rest of you know what's going on.*

ally1234: *I know. It seems like a three-way conversation sometimes.*

jannasbananas: *You can chime in any time.*

ally1234: *I know. The other girls are busy with their lives and don't have the time to jump into the conversations. It doesn't mean we're going to break up the group.*

jannasbananas: *:-/*

ally1234: *It's my opinion. It's how it appears to me.*

jannasbananas: *Okay.*

Ally ticked off several minutes of silence. *Oh, my God, I don't want to start a war.* Why hadn't Janna phoned? Playful tones could be lost on IMs, while benign words could appear pointed and harsh.

ally1234: *Don't be mad, Janna. I don't mean anything by it.*

jannasbananas: *I know.*

122

ally1234: *BFFs?*
ally1234: *Sweetie-pie?*
ally1234: *Honey bun?*
jannasbananas: ☺*Don't make me laugh, Al. You know I can't stay mad at you for long!*

Ally smiled as her fingers flew across the keyboard.

ally1234: *You know I love you...*
ally1234: *BFFs?*☺
jannasbananas: *Forever and always...*
ally1234: *Good. Got to run and pick up Vanessa from school. TTYL, Okay?*

***

To: laurelextonsbunch
From: celiasunshine
Subject: Newbie

Laurel, we're the closest out of the VMs and I trust you to be frank. It's been a few weeks. Don't you think something's a little weird about our newbie?

Call me a skeptic, call me extra careful, call me a nagging bitch. Something's off-kilter here. Don't you think she's a little different? I'm reading the blog…I'll admit parts of it are powerful. Maybe it's the words? Maybe it's something else.

Tell me I'm not going crazy. And let's keep this discussion to ourselves, okay?

Celia

P.S. Have you made any decisions about spending Christmas in Florida? I miss you!

To: celiasunshine
From: laurelextonsbunch
Subject: RE: Newbie

I don't know, Celia. Maybe you're jumpy because of the past. I'm not seeing what you are…of course I've got barely enough 'me' time to clear my email, so I haven't paid much attention to Ashe's blog. I wish I could support your instinct, but I don't see it. You're going to have to count me out if you want me to help you analyze Ashe.

Don't worry. Your email is safe with me. ☺

Laurel

P.S. I don't yet know about Christmas. Wish I could be more positive. I'll run it by Joe tonight.

***

An easy dinner of tuna hot dish was simmering in the oven by the time Ally made it out of the '70s and into the disco era. Neatly folded and labeled items were stacked on the dining room table. Vanessa grabbed a sequined dress adorned with peacock feathers and slipped into it, before stepping into heels, spiked sky-high, the burgundy satin straps dry and crackling after barely surviving two decades of time travel. "Mommy, look at me!" Vanessa located a pink boa and wrapped it around her neck, a perfect accessory to complete her fashion statement. She twirled around the room.

"Oh, Nessy! You're a vision. I don't remember looking that good when I last wore it."

"I'm a princess! Can I keep this, Mommy? Please?" Vanessa pleaded, her eyes begging.

Ally was stuck. She fingered the slinky polyester and fluffed up the feathers. The last time she wore the dress was on her twenty-first birthday. Her girlfriends had kidnapped her to a one-night-only show of the Chippendales. It was her first trip to a bar, the first time she had ventured from the rolling farmland of southwestern Minnesota to visit downtown Minneapolis, and the first time she'd witnessed a male strip show. The memory seemed both crystal-clear fresh and horribly stale – stale enough to bury it in the past where it belonged, where no one else could find it. She smiled. "I ought to say no, Nessy. I need to get organized and the only way to do this…" Vanessa's eyes pooled and her lower lip extended. Ally relented. "Okay, Punkin', maybe we'll keep this for a little while longer."

"Yay! Thanks, Momma." Vanessa floated across the room.

Ally's computer chimed with an incoming IM from Ashe.

AsheMacD: *Ally, you there?*
ally1234: *Yup.*

124

AsheMacD: *You're not busy?*

ally1234: *Long day winding down. Dinner's on. We're going quick and easy tonight. Tuna casserole.*

AsheMacD: *Sounds great.*

ally1234: *It's a no-brainer. Simple's the best.*

AsheMacD: *You'll have to email the recipe.*

ally1234: *Recipe?*

Ally smiled at the absurdity of the thought.

ally1234: *I'm ashamed to admit it's stupidly easy. Involves opening cans.*

AsheMacD: *I could handle that.*

ally1234: *You working?*

Ally conjured up an image of Ashe bent over her computer, stacks of papers surrounding her. The newbie was long overdue in sending a photo of herself.

AsheMacD: *Taking a break. How about you?*

ally1234: *I was online all day, listing my junk for sale. Hopefully what P. T. Barnum said was true. I could use a couple hundred suckers born a minute apart right about now. If they've all signed up for eBay, so much the better. What's up?*

AsheMacD: *I was wondering. What's wrong with Missy? Do you know?*

ally1234: *?*

Missy? Ally thought to herself; why would Ashe bring up Missy?

AsheMacD: *You haven't noticed?*

ally1234: *Noticed?*

AsheMacD: *She hasn't responded to any email today. None.*

AsheMacD: *She hasn't logged on at all. It's like she fell off the face of the earth.*

Ally had been so busy straightening out her own life she hadn't noticed Missy's absence.

ally1234: *Maybe she's busy. Parenthood is time consuming, you know that. Even when they're perfect. Her girls are angels, but they're rounding the bend to the teenage years.*
AsheMacD: *OMG. I'm so not looking forward to that age. I'm reveling in the fact that Tyler has successfully conquered toilet training.*
ally1234: *Ha! Wait 'til he gets his permit. Oh, and when the girls call. That's when the real fun begins.*

Ally placed a stack of books under the table. With Greg coming home, she needed to reclaim her dining room for its intended use. He might be easy-going, yet he insisted his dinner served on a table.

AsheMacD: *I'm really concerned about Missy.*☹

Ally bent over between loads of books and quickly typed.

ally1234: *Not Celia?*

With Celia causing problems with her inter-VM gossip, she would have thought Ashe would have more concern with the human hurricane coming out of central Florida.

AsheMacD: *Celia? She's remote. I get it. I'm the newbie. Celia doesn't bother me.*

Ally nodded although she knew Ashe couldn't see her.

ally1234: *Stick it out. She'll come around. She did with the rest of us.*
AsheMacD: *Skye mentioned a strange conversation with Missy late last night.*
ally1234: *Those two. They're incurable insomniacs.*
AsheMacD: *I know. Skye said her tone was sad.*
ally1234: *Call her.*

AsheMacD: *??? Who? Skye?*
ally1234: *No, silly. Missy. Or I can call her.*

Several minutes passed, enough time for Ally to set the table and pour water. She kept her eye on the monitor for a response. None came.

Ally heard Greg's car pulling into the driveway. Her computer chimed once more. Ashe had added to the IM box.

AsheMacD: *Sorry, Ally. Tyler troubles. Maybe you should call Missy. You know her better. I think I'll email her.*

Ally had no time to type, "Great! I'll call," before Ashe had disappeared.

***

To: shootingskye, jannasbananas, laurelextonsbunch, missymom, celiasunshine, AsheMacD
From: Ally1234
Subject: Ashe/Celia

I heard some of us have been talking about Ashe. Do some of us have doubts? Is something brewing? What's the scoop?

If anyone has reservations, it should come out in the open and we should all discuss the topic like rational human beings. Girls?

***

"Honey, you coming to bed? It's late." Greg came from behind and wrapped his muscular arms around Ally, giving her a firm squeeze. He nuzzled his nose deep into her neck, his moist breath tickling her right ear. *Oooo la-la.* Her man was frisky tonight.

She turned away from the computer, took his head in her hands, and kissed him. "Damn, Sam. You're one hot husband," she sighed. Greg was toned and athletic, with enough BMI for a tiny pot belly and accompanying love handle-ettes. Like a fine cabernet, the years intensified the depth and complexity of the man she fell in love with. What few facial wrinkles he had earned and his graying temples lent a distinguished look to her hunky husband, leaving a full-bodied, velvety rich profile, dry finish and

127

tingly tannins. Or was that the wine? Enjoying a half glass with dinner helped ignite the fire in her core. "Let me check my Mommy Mail one last time. I'm concerned. It won't take a minute."

Greg growled his disapproval and nipped at her left ear. She shivered with delight.

"You and your Virtual Moms."

"Now, Greg. They're my best friends. I promise, no more than five minutes. Ten, tops."

"Remember this, sweetie. I don't know how long I'll be sizzling." Greg licked his finger and touched his rear end with it, as he produced a hissing sound like he was on fire. He smiled and threw Ally a kiss.

"One minute! I swear!" Ally couldn't ignore this invitation. They took advantage of every opportunity for amorous encounters, difficult to achieve with a five-year-old in the house.

"I'll be *naked*," Greg teased as he mounted the stairs.

"I'm sure you will be."

Ally turned her attention back to her email. After Janna's IM, she decided to email Skye privately to ask her about Celia's doubts. She also emailed Celia and Ashe. If trouble was brewing, she wanted to contain it. The Virtual Moms had been friends too long for a troublemaker to splinter the group.

In her inbox was a message from Skye, Ashe and Celia.

To: Ally1234
From: shootingskye
Subject: RE: Ashe/Celia

Ally, thanks for writing. I don't know what's going on with Celia. I happen to like Ashe, a lot. She's already informed me that she'll drop out of the loop if Celia wants her to. If that happens, Ashe and I will remain friends. I'm sure she and Janna will still be friends, too. I like her, and she's been helpful to me and I'm not giving up her friendship. I hope Ashe doesn't bother you as much as she bothers her. I'd hate to see thirteen years of friendship go down in flames over this.

S.

To: Ally1234
From: AsheMacD
Subject: RE: Celia

If Celia doesn't want me in the group, I'll drop out. I've already informed Janna and Skye. Thanks for your time. I like and admire every one of you. You're all strong, beautiful women.
Peace out,
Ashe

To: Ally1234
From: celiasunshine
Subject: RE: Ashe/Skye

I only have one thing to say on the subject.
Beware of wolves in Asheley clothing.

Chapter Thirteen

Thursday, November 12

Dear Mac,

Update: As a single parent, I'm getting more organized. We actually attempt three of the four food groups during our meals, and some of the time the food is actually unprocessed. I figured out that I didn't break the washing machine (or dryer) and I now vacuum before I find enough dog hair on the floor to knit a sweater. I feel I'm making progress as a good parent, compared with the lack-luster, negligent bad parent I was a few months before.

Part of the reason is due to the friends I've made at an online grief forum. I've bounced back and forth between a dozen or more. I've always returned to Beyond Grief. It's not only for people who have lost military loved ones; it's for anyone who is suffering a loss. At first, I listened (or read) and didn't participate. The stalking, no talking was helpful. The first few weeks without you left me isolated, feeling odd and disconnected from the rest of the world. So many of us that need support. Now I know I'm not alone.

I still miss you, but when the going gets tough, I have somewhere I can go for consolation and virtual hugs.

New York City

"Maybe I'm too old for dating. I should give up and become a nun – the first Jewish nun in history!" Janna sighed as she opened her latest matches on JAPMatch.com. It shouldn't have been possible. The month's pickings for *this* Jewish American Princess were considerably slimmer than the month before, only five potential hook-ups.

Her exasperation increased with each opened email. The assault was on, with photos of smiling older men with a noticeable lack of style *and* of hair. One enclosed five photographs. Janna could see his age-progression right before her eyes, and it wasn't a pretty slideshow. *Why is this so hard? This should be a piece of cake.* Janna might be forty-nine, but she didn't feel it. She occasionally hit the nightclubs with Mandy and Rachel, although it had been a long time since the three of them had been in New York at the same time. Janna didn't want much – only an understanding man, someone with a youthful soul and a handsome, well-preserved body, someone successful, artistic, kind – someone like *her*.

She sent emails containing the photos and profiles for the Virtual Moms to critique, hoping to get feedback or insight. A little validation. *Something.*

Laurel responded first. "Aren't you being a tad picky? I don't see anything wrong with any of them! Well, maybe the underwear salesman…what's up with that? What kind of guy sells bras and panties for a living?"

Celia was next. Janna could count on her skepticism. "Have you Googled them to see if they're solid? If you don't feel comfortable, don't respond. There are too many fish in the sea." Spoken by the woman who had sworn to terminal singleness. Celia hadn't had a date in a decade, and it wasn't because she couldn't get one. She didn't want one.

Missy was in Laurel's camp. "The bald one is a doctor. He'd make a great catch." Doctor? What about the fact that the man lived in Brooklyn and had no car? He was a global warming nut who believed mass transit would save the world. Maybe not the whole world – at least the five boroughs. If he were that environmentally conscious, he could have done his part for the Big Blue Ball by tooling around in a Lexus hybrid. That would have snagged Janna's heart in an instant. Good God. A Prius-driving man would hold some allure!

Ally suggested Janna shake up her profile and add a few things that 'weren't exactly true.' "A white lie doesn't hurt anyone. You can see by your results that these guys have stretched the truth a little." *A little, Ally? Do you think?* The bald, aging, car-less doctor proclaimed himself 'extremely' attractive. Janna wondered what his idea of 'ugly' entailed. If her father weren't still alive, she could toss that one off to her mother. He was too grandfatherly for her. And weird.

131

"You should widen your search, Janna," Skye suggested in an early morning phone call. "How about Lithuanians? Lutherans?"

A coffee spray spewed through Janna's nose. *No* way. "Are you kidding? My parents would disown me! No thanks."

"Would it matter? Wouldn't your parents want to see you happy?"

"Happily married to a Jew!"

"Sorry. It was only a suggestion."

"You could pass the word around in San Francisco."

"I'm two years ahead of you. It's mostly agnostics or atheists here."

"Great."

"I could widen the search and include some ladies I know."

"Thanks. Not to insult you, I haven't given up on men yet."

"Have it your way."

The only person who hadn't responded back was Ashe. Janna glanced at her buddy list. Ashe was presently online yet she was silent. Janna didn't mind. The two of them had this same conversation at least a half dozen times in the last year. Every so often, Janna's interests in finding her One True Love would spike and she would jump back into the dating pool, enthusiastic and vowing to swim for the gold. In discussing her outcomes, Ashe developed an interest in Janna's forays into dating web sites. She asked probing, provocative questions and Janna was more than happy to share her knowledge and delve into the gritty details. After all, it was a new dating world, especially with technology. Match.com, eharmony.com, NYCsingles.com, even Alt-Ctrl-Del.com for those enjoying indeterminate lifestyles – no one found a date the old-fashioned way anymore.

The days of meeting someone in a restaurant, a club, in a synagogue or church or with friends and relatives were over, kaput, gone, along with orchid corsages, white gloves and walking in the safety of the inside of the sidewalk. Everyone was wired up. Mandy and Rachel text messaged each other when they were in the same room. She and Ashe had shared raucous IMs on the subject.

jannasbananas: *One of these days you'll have to make the leap. When you're ready to date, that is. I don't know how deep the*

132

waters are in North Carolina, but honey, I'm living in one of the biggest, glitziest cities in the world filled to the rafters with millions of men and I'm still without Mr. Right.

AsheMacD: *I'll never be ready.*

jannasbananas: *If you do, let me know. I should write a book.*

AsheMacD: *Hey! I'm the writer.*

jannasbananas: *I have a million and one rules for online dating. First, no touching, not a handshake, unless you're armed to the gills with Purell. And for God's sake, don't let the guy kiss you on the first date. It's disgusting! You don't know where that horn dog has been.*

It had been one of her many fun conversations with Ashe, something she missed in the past week rife with group intrigue. Perhaps Ashe's silence was because of the trouble brewing with Celia. She and Skye emailed Ashe, begging her to give Celia a chance to chill. Ashe countered by saying she would drop off the loop. The whole thing was silly. Of course, they could *all* trust Ashe. *She* did. Why should she leave since Celia hadn't asked her to leave – at least, not directly.

Ashe appeared to be off the grid. Janna knew she'd taken another book to edit and was busy. Celia's caution never bothered her like it did other women. She wasn't really a bitch – she only possessed a healthy distrust of everyone and everything. When Celia took hold of an idea, she wouldn't let go until she was convinced everything was perfect.

Email was the only way to go.

To: AsheMacD
From: jannasbananas
Subject: Opinion, please…

Did you get my email regarding my new dating lineup? What? No comment? This bachelorette needs some feedback, sister. Spill.

To: jannasbananas

From: AsheMacD
RE: Opinion, please…

Yes, I read it. Where's the freaking fire? I thought you were taking the next round slower and more cautiously. Tick tock. You can't be listening to your biological clock, can you?
Virtually yours,
Ashe

To: AsheMacD
From: jannasbananas
RE: RE: Opinion, please…

Did someone wake up and find her panties in a twist? Are you out of coffee? Is it that time of the month for you? OMLady GaGa. You know me, Ashe. When I'm ready to go, I'm ready to *go*. Today I'm so totally ready, I can't stand it. Don't you ever get *lonely*? Listen, I'm not asking for an analytical thesis on each potential date. Could you be a pal and tell me which of these lovelies you like best? I honestly want your opinion. I value it. I crave it. It's important to me.

To: jannasbananas
From: AsheMacD
RE: RE: RE: Opinion, please…

Does it matter which one I like best? What if none of them tickles my fancy? What if I think they're a motley crew of carpet bagging liars? What if I wouldn't trust any of those horny perverts in a convent full of saints trussed up in chastity belts? What if I tell you to pass on these yahoos and wait for a better guy? You're not that desperate, are you? Are you *that* lonely?
BTW, I don't wear panties to bed, I've had two pots of coffee so far this morning (thank you for asking), and it's not *that* time of the month for me. What about you? What's your problem?
Virtually yours,
Ashe

To: AsheMacD
From: jannasbananas
RE: RE: RE: RE: Opinion, please…

First of all on the panties: TMI. And the rest? Be-yotch. Desperate? Who said anything about desperate? I'm trying to make a decision here. A *serious* decision. I respect your opinion. A thoughtful one would be most appreciated.

I don't have any problems. It appears you do.

To: jannasbananas
From: AsheMacD
RE: RE: RE: RE: RE: Opinion, please…

Okay. You asked for it.
[Scroll down.]
Ta-da! I like the bald tree-hugging doctor.
Tell him I said 'hi' y'all.
Virtually yours,
Ashe

"Yuck. All that back and forth and she picks the bald guy."
Why is Ashe being such a bitch?

Janna took another look at her dating options for the week. Out of the five possible candidates, Ashe's favorite, Dr. Bald, was a definite non-contender. Or was Ashe being facetious? She threw Mr. Age Progression into the mental circular file. If the guy aged that quickly in five photos, he was probably a shriveled up, skeletal mass by now. She considered Barry – smoker, drinker, God knows what else – nope; and Thom, the underwear salesman who might have been a stellar nice guy, except Janna couldn't get over the thick black glasses and the thicker fuzzy caterpillar eyebrows. If his eyebrows were that dense, it meant he had a forest of hair growing out of his collar, out of his back, out of his *ears*. Ick! Mammals in the Bronx Zoo had less hair. That left Juan Bernstein,

135

a half-Jew, half-Puerto Rican real estate agent who bore a striking resemblance to Geraldo Rivera.

"Well, Juan Baby," Janna said to herself. She opened up a clean message to introduce herself to him. "Congratulations, Juan! It's your lucky day. You've hit the Janna Banana jackpot."

***

AsheMacD: *What are you doing home?*

shootingskye: *I got a late start on my run. Forgot to set my alarm. Good thing not much going on today. You?*

AsheMacD: *Tyler's in school. Some days I'm relieved when he gets on the bus. It's tough to work at home with him here.*

shootingskye: *I hear that.*

AsheMacD: *Other days I miss him following me around. I guess today's one of those.*

shootingskye: *I've got bills to get out today…thrilling. Not!*

AsheMacD: *I did want to ask you something…*

AsheMacD: *personal…*

AsheMacD: *You can tell me to bug off any time…*

shootingskye: *?*

AsheMacD: *It's that…*

shootingskye: *Yes? You've got me worried now…*

AsheMacD: *Oh, don't. Janna told me a while back that you don't…well, that you're challenged when it comes to the kitchen.*

shootingskye: *LOL. I suppose she told you about the time I burned a pot of water.*

shootingskye: *It wasn't my shining moment. I'm great taking photos of food, I just can't make any. That's edible, I mean!*☺

AsheMacD: *That's my problem, too! I was spoiled. Mac did all of the cooking.*

AsheMacD: *I'm tired of eating fast food, frozen junk, and boxed dinners.*

shootingskye: *Honey, you're way ahead of me. I wish I could get to that point! If there weren't literally thousands of restaurants in San Francisco, I'd be seriously malnourished.*

AsheMacD: *I was thinking…I'm ready to stretch my wings a bit in the kitchen. Besides, I think my microwave is about to give out.*

AsheMacD: *I'd like to see if the stove works.*☺

136

shootingskye: *I use my oven to store my bills.*

AsheMacD: *I use mine to hide the Krispy Kremes. Jim Bob knows how the clear the table. He hasn't figured out how to open the oven door. Yet.*

shootingskye: *Funny!*

AsheMacD: *So, Ally gave me some recipes she thought would be easy. I was wondering if maybe we could try them out together, maybe? Then compare notes?*

shootingskye: *You're braver than I am. The last time I spent more than a minute in the kitchen, we had a visit from the fire department.*

AsheMacD: *Come on. Think of it as an adventure.*

AsheMacD: *You'll probably do better than I will.*

AsheMacD: *I've got pathetic tied up.*

AsheMacD: *Please?*

AsheMacD: *Pretty please?*

shootingskye: *Okay, you twisted my arm. On two conditions.*

AsheMacD: *Of course.*

shootingskye: *One – it better be a fool-proof recipe a dope like me could figure out.*

AsheMacD: *I'm not beginning my cooking career with chi-chi French cuisine.*

shootingskye: *Good. And #2 – if I end up homeless from a scorched kitchen, you're going to find a couple of refugees on your doorstep.*

***

The sidewalks were packed with people making their escape from work. Janna hurried to her favorite coffee shop for her first rendezvous with Juan, all the while wondering how she could convince her folks he was Jewish. Perhaps a late afternoon meeting was a bad idea. She had barely enough time to get read. She'd sent a quick email, a briefer phone call, and their first 'date' was set for a bistro in Soho.

Once the date was set, Janna called Skye. "He sounds nice. He was the most handsome one of the bunch for this week."

"Good. I was pulling for him."

"I figured so. He was the half-Puerto Rican."

"I know! Hunky! He's half-Jewish so your parents won't disown you."

"They'll half-disown me. I hope he's not some weirdo."

"You're meeting in a public place, right? What could happen?"

"I don't know. Ask Celia. According to her, a serial killing rapist wearing a tin foil hat lurks behind every grassy knoll."

Skye laughed. "You're too funny, Janna."

"You're doing better?"

"Not perfect, on the way up. Call me later and let me know how it went."

"Will do. Hey, do you suppose he celebrates both Christmas and Hanukkah? Does he have his turkey with a side of latkes?"

"Only one way to find out. Ask him! Then let me know."

At least one of the VMs was happy for her. After Celia's comments and the exchange with Ashe, Janna was starting to question her own motives. She felt refreshed and buoyed by Skye's enthusiasm.

Janna looked at the face of her Blackberry. If she didn't literally run the next five blocks, she would be at least fifteen minutes late. She was about to dial Juan's number to warn him when her phone rang.

It was Missy. "Yell-ow," Janna said.

"Janna. I didn't know who to call. Since I know you best…" Missy sounded lost and soggy. She'd been crying.

Janna stopped dead in her tracks. A man behind her typing on a smart phone neglected to notice and he collided into her. "Sorry," she said to the man as he scowled. "Missy? Is that you? What's the matter?"

"It's… Earl," she sniffled. "And Kassie."

"Oh, honey. Are they all right? Were they in an accident?"

"No. He… he… he left me! Kassie… she's impossible." Once she got the words out, Missy began to sob.

Janna put her hand to her head and spun around. After knowing the Martins for ten years, she wasn't surprised by the announcement. Earl Martin was a detached, soulless man, not at all like Missy. He was decent enough, a good provider – so Missy said – but not boisterous and sociable like Missy. Janna rarely saw him on her visits, and when he was around, he was reticent and unfriendly. Janna's considerable charms had never melted Earl's stodgy exterior. Janna's eyes drifted to a clock in a store window. Precious minutes were ticking away, and with every second she was becoming later and later. *Not now, not now. Missy, please. Don't you know tonight is Date Night?* She hurried into a crosswalk seconds before the light turned red. A cab, horn blasting, came within inches before she retreated to the safety of the curb.

"Missy, this is terrible news. We need to speak at length, so you can give me the skinny. I'm late for an appointment. I'll call you as soon as I can, in about two hours."

"I need someone now!" Missy wailed.

"I know, honey, but…" Janna combed her vocabulary for sympathetic words to offset the Juan Baby bubbles popping over her head. "I really want to talk to you, you know that, right? In the meantime, you can email the VMs. You can IM Ashe. She works from home and never goes anywhere. Or you can call her." The light turned green and Janna charged ahead of the crowd.

"I don't want to! She's a virtual stranger," Missy whimpered.

"Believe me when I tell you she knows all of us through my stories. She won't mind."

"I haven't talked to her yet, have you?"

Janna cocked her head and thought about it. No, she hadn't spoken yet to Ashe and it had been a year. She often imagined what their conversations would be like, especially after the spirited email exchanges. The times when Janna tried, the call went straight to a generic answering machine. "No. Go ahead and try. You need to email the details to everyone for sure."

"I don't want *everyone* to know. I'm so ashamed."

"Listen, Missy. We are all friends. We're not judgmental. Email the Moms and we'll figure it out. After my meeting, I'll call you, okay?"

Missy sniffed. "Okay."

"Take care of the girls."

"Okay."

"I mean it. You will – WE will – get through this together. Promise."

Missy disconnected the call.

"Just my luck," Janna grumbled. She dialed Juan's number as she attempted a clumsy sprint in Louboutin heels. "What do you want to bet Juan Baby is the One? And I'm late."

Chapter Fourteen

Friday, November 13

Some Habits Die Hard

I thought about you today and a thought came to me: the MacDaniel Family is like a three-legged stool.

Three-legged stools are only stable when all three legs are in place. We're missing an appendage here. (Hello? Mac?) The stool can't stand without all three right where they belong.

The MacDaniel stool keeps tipping over.

I try to remember your schedule, how you do things. I try to remember your recipes, your favorite laundry detergent. Most of all I try to remember your gentle calmness. I try to remember your smile, so I end up smiling. If I didn't, my frown would be permanently imbedded into my forehead.

I have no patience. I used to march Tyler up to his room for naps – no nonsense, all business – no wonder he preferred you to me. You treated him to a happy ritual every day. You'd tickle him, throw him up into the air, and get him to squeal like an intoxicated pig. Then a quick story, a run-down of the alphabet, counting to a hundred, a flip of the blanket, and it was all over.

I'm a curmudgeon by comparison. I've got a puny fuse. I work from home. I'm busy. I don't have time for whining or stalling or silly rituals. My time is valuable.

Or so I thought. Now I have too much time.

Today I thought I would copy your naptime style. It beats yelling at the kid. I threw Ty up into the air. It was easy to do; he's so tiny and light. His screams weren't hysterical giggles though; they were frightened cries. I read a story, it's not the same. It appears I don't change my voice properly with each character. I'm told my Thing One sounds exactly like Thing Two, a no-no.

I also found out the ABCs and counting to one hundred was so last year.

The stool toppled over again.

Ty was gracious though. As my face was getting redder and the veins pulsed an impending explosion in my neck, he patted my arm as he said, "It's okay. You'll get better as you go along."

Somewhere outside St. Louis, Missouri

Superstition was never part of Laurel Exton's makeup. She came from sensible stock, people who worked hard and didn't believe in other worldly phenomena or intangible ideas. Black cats were nothing special; neither were rabbits' feet, full moons, or finger crossing. On her way out of the house with a half-sleepy Marcus in tow, Laurel noted on the calendar the day – Friday the Thirteenth. Although she didn't believe in superstitions, she wouldn't tempt the Fates. She would be extra cautious today.

Her plan came to an abrupt end after dropping Marcus off. The freeway was jammed with orange barrels and narrowing lanes. She'd come to a dead halt in front of a flagman when the driver behind her slammed into the backside of her minivan. The impact was jarring. She exited the car shaking. To her relief, both bumpers suffered only minor scratches. Considering the state of her antiqued minivan, the new dent would join the other hits and nicks the car endured over the past ten years. Laurel waved the driver off and she was back on her way.

With the traffic and the accident, Laurel was five minutes late for school. In that short span, the class had broken out in total chaos. She entered her classroom where her gang of hyperactive boys had tried their hand at interior design – sheaves of construction paper flung over everything. The culprits chased each other through the mess.

"Students! Let's get organized!" Laurel clapped her hands and cast a glance at her student teacher, a mousy young college student named Penny. Her nose in a book, she was oblivious to the mayhem. By the looks of the half-dressed hunk smiling from the book's cover, Penny was engrossed in a romance novel. Penny was supposed be her assistant and step in whenever Laurel left the room. Two and a half months into the term, Laurel could see Penny would have a short shelf life as a teacher unless she grew some balls. "Penny, didn't you get my text? I told you I was going to be running a few minutes late," Laurel huffed as she shed her coat and book bag. "Couldn't you have started them on a worksheet?"

Penny shrugged and went back to reading her novel. Laurel had her hands too full to deal with her student teacher. She'd need a quiet moment to discuss attitude. Penny didn't care. It wasn't *her* class. As long as she could stick out the next six months, she'd have her teaching certificate.

The day progressed from bad to worse. It took an hour to calm down her charges. Laurel imagined they all had enjoyed bowls of sugar topped with caffeine for breakfast. The minutes ticked with painful slowness toward noon, when Laurel could then unwind in relative peace and quiet for half an hour before returning to the lions' den once more. It was not to be. As Laurel retrieved her lunch from the microwave, she turned abruptly. Principal Cottingham, right behind her, knocked the Tupperware container into her chest. Chicken soup splattered everywhere, with her blouse bearing most of the brunt. Mr. Cottingham was aghast; lucky for her, none of it ended up on his spotless blue suit.

"Excuse me, Mrs. Exton," he apologized, "I'm so sorry!" He grabbed a paper towel and began a futile dabbing at her blouse.

"Never mind; I'll take care of it." Laurel threw her lunch container in the trashcan and ran humiliated to the teachers' rest room. Once inside, she was horrified at the woman staring back at her: eyes red, hair mussed, wet-plastered with homemade broth, and tipped with a couple of errant noodles. "Oh, my God!" Tears burst forth. She'd dammed them for so long, the torrent felt like sweet relief.

As her watery display was grinding into third gear, the door opened. Tammy Kirk, the school secretary, came in gripping a Lincoln Elementary sweatshirt in hand. "Jesus God, Laurel, I saw what happened. Here, take off your blouse and wear this."

Laurel did as she was told, and when she did, she poured out her now uncontrollable frustration. "Leaving home late, getting rear-ended, my class out of control, and now this," she sobbed as Tammy pulled the sweatshirt over her head. A youth size large, the bright purple cover-up emblazoned with the school's white shark mascot was too small for Laurel. The ribbing was tourniquet tight around her forearms and waist.

143

"Another normal day at Lincoln El," Tammy responded in a supportive yet pragmatic tone as she corralled wayward noodles from the sink and flung them into the trash.

"It's not just school. My whole life is like this. I can't keep up with the house, with the bills, with my car breaking down every other day. Then Marcus and all the running around I have to do with him. And now I feel like my classroom is slipping away, too. I can't do anything right!" Laurel sat down on the toilet, her head in her hands.

"Tell me about it. You're juggling so many balls, it's making *me* dizzy."

"And Joe…"

"He's not helping, is he?" Tammy patted Laurel's shoulder in sympathy.

"No," Laurel sniffed. "He couldn't catch a hint if one broadsided him on the head."

"Poor thing. Why don't you go home?" Tammy urged. "I'll find you a sub, or I'll have one of the paras take over for the rest of the afternoon."

"I can't," Laurel wailed as she looked up. "Penny isn't exactly…"

"Competent?"

"I was thinking of a kinder adjective."

"Now, now. If I can't find a replacement, Mr. Cottingham is so embarrassed he'll take your place."

"He said that?" Laurel snorted and blew her nose.

"He's standing right outside this door." Laurel looked up, hopeful. "Mr. Cottingham may never again be as mortified as he is this minute. If I were you, I'd take advantage of his offer." Tammy stood back and took a look. She tried to suppress a giggle, but couldn't. "Go right home and change into something decent. Don't stop and pick up a few things at the store, and for God's sake don't acknowledge your neighbors when you drive by. Honey, I wouldn't be caught dead in that outfit."

Laurel smiled. "Thanks, Tammy. I needed a laugh, even if the joke's on me."

***

To: ally1234, shootingskye, jannasbananas, AsheMacD, celiasunshine, laurelextonsbunch

From: missymom
Subject: Earl

Janna knows this, for those of you who haven't heard, Earl left me a few days ago. He's not far, but he's not talking. I don't want to whine. I can't stand keeping this to myself any longer. The girls don't know and I'd appreciate it if you didn't tell your own kids. That is all.

P.S. No it's not. Kassie was suspended.

Day Three and counting since Earl left the house, and each minute dragged in unbelievable slow motion. At first Missy denied his absence. The girls were neither that young nor that stupid. After much whining and prodding from Kara – and looks that could kill from Kassie – she gave the girls a lame story about Earl having to go out of town to oversee another construction project. Earl was a partner and hadn't had to travel for work since arriving in Las Vegas. When Kara asked for how long, Missy returned a brusque yet open-ended reply. "He's not sure," she lied. "It's a special project." Missy reasoned she would be covered whether he came back the next day or not at all.

"Where is he?" Kara could be persistent. "Can we go visit him?"

"He's in Alaska." Missy replied quickly. She noticed Kassie behind her sister rolling her eyes. *So shoot me*, Missy thought. Alaska was the first place she thought of that was far enough away to be reasonable. It would be stretching the truth into a horrible pretzel-shaped lie if she'd told them he'd gone to Dubai or the Ukraine. Missy hugged Kara as she busied herself in the kitchen. "He's so far into the woods it wouldn't be practical to visit him, honey. Let's wait until he comes home, okay?"

When Earl first left, Missy wallowed in a state of shock. She told herself he would return, if not in the next five minutes, then in the next thirty minutes. Time dragged on from minutes to hours, then days. He, of course, did not return. Missy shook off the last vestiges of her denial after the first twenty-four hours. Earl was never coming home. This was awful, not an awful joke. After realization hit her, every action she took involved a Herculean amount of energy, and she performed her day-to-day tasks without feeling. In between hiding her feelings from her daughters and trying to keep up pretenses, as though nothing had happened, Missy phoned Earl, rang the office, called the worksite. She emailed his personal account. With no response, she switched to the business account where he continued to ignore her. 'Her' messages came from the girls, like "Earl, Kassie needs to talk to you about a Christmas trip," or "Earl, Kara wants help on her math, and that's not my area." Missy found each message becoming more plaintive and clingy than the one before. The last one: "Earl, the girls need you. Don't you care about them anymore?"

After a few days of weathering her rejection alone, Missy was ready to burst. Thank goodness for the Virtual Moms. The news was embarrassing to admit to *anyone*. At least they would understand. She certainly couldn't go to *her* family. Missy's parents had never liked Earl. Her mom thought he was aloof and far too stuffy. Missy wouldn't survive the tsunami of "I told you so" she knew she would have to face. After fifteen years, Earl's parents hadn't warmed up to her, although they were attentive grandparents. She imagined the elder Martins doing a jig atop the newly dug grave of her marriage.

Missy didn't share all the gruesome details, yet the return overtures were warm and supportive. Missy was overwhelmed. Leave it to the VMs to come through in a crisis. Flowers from Skye arrived the next day. Ally forwarded so many jokes and cartoons that Missy's face and stomach muscles were sore. Precious part-Sicilian Celia called and offered to come to Vegas and break his legs. "I can fix him so he won't know what happened to him," she offered.

"I don't think going to jail will help," Missy answered.

Janna informed her she was coming to Vegas to spend Christmas with her parents. "You and I are going out for a Day of Beau-tay once I get to town," she promised. "Manicure, pedicure, facial, massage, the works!"

"I can't." Missy protested. She wasn't sure what was left in the bank account or where their separation was going. She could easily find herself homeless tomorrow.

"Don't worry about it; it's on me," Janna replied. "The girls should come, too. My treat."

The pain still stung, but life was so much better with her posse backing her.

***

Laurel stayed off the interstate and took the scenic route home, passing through the familiar neighborhood she had lived in as a child. It wasn't a conscious decision to detour along Memory Lane. Remembering what was still there and what had changed had a calming effect. It was a long journey from poverty to hardscrabble middle class. Although some might describe her younger years as being deprived, Laurel always felt her childhood was a happy one. Things looked up after her father had landed the sanitation department job with the city. Now decades later, her father was retired with a small, comfortable pension in Florida. And she? Their life was paycheck to paycheck.

She made an effort not to drive by Joe's real estate office to see if his car was in front of it. Of course, his car was never there. She wasn't sure what he was doing with his time. Whatever it was, he brought no money into the household. Her anger flared at the thought of her lonely struggle.

As Laurel turned into her subdivision, she wondered what she would do with her two hours and fifteen minutes of free time. Maybe she would prepare dinner and put it in the oven on a timer so that she would have one less thing to do after running Marcus from school to hockey practice. She could throw another load of laundry in the washer, or take a look at her bills. Then she remembered Tammy's admonishment. "Put your feet up and enjoy yourself. You won't get this chance again, at least, not until the day after Thanksgiving." Tammy was right. The next two weeks would be more hectic than the last two. Maybe she would pour herself a cup of tea and check her email. It had been years since she had been a stay-at-home mom with the luxury of chatting online in the middle of the day during toddler naptime.

Thank God for the Virtual Moms. She didn't know what she would do if she didn't have her tight network of friends. Their only flaw was that they lived all over the country and not next door. The newbie, Ashe, seemed especially kind and thoughtful. Too bad the moms were all too far away to be a real comfort.

Laurel exited her car and checked the mailbox on her way in. She retrieved a stack of catalogs, junk mail, the handful of bills, and a small package. The box was addressed to her, with an unrecognizable North Carolina return address. She fumbled with the mail, her book bag, and the keys when the front door opened.

Joe's face was lined with concern. "What happened? Tammy called me from school and said you were coming home. Are you okay?"

"I'm fine. I was having a rough day. A *really* rough day."

"She said you were in an accident."

"Which one? I was rear-ended on the freeway and side-wiped in the teachers' lounge. See?" Laurel lowered the mail and displayed her blouse, ruined by a chicken soup bath.

"My God. The car?" Joe looked past her into the driveway.

"It's nothing. A scratch. Some guy on his cell phone wasn't paying attention and rear-ended me. The dent will feel right at home with the other dings on the bumper."

"You sure you're okay?" Joe scanned her from top to bottom, looking for a non-existent injury.

"Yeah. See?" Laurel pirouetted in two complete circles. "No whiplash, not a bruise. I'm going to change my clothes, check my email, and pick up Marcus on time for a change."

"Don't worry. I'll get Marcus. You stay here and relax."

"He has hockey…"

"I know. Let me do it today."

"Okay…" Laurel looked hard at Joe as he took the soiled blouse from her hands and headed for the laundry room. Who was this guy, and what did he do with the *real* Joe? She kicked off her shoes. The package she received in the mail came into her line of view. "What the heck?"

The tiny box was plastered with package tape, the seams obliterated by multiple layers of 3M's finest. *This could survive a nuclear blast,* she thought. With a pair of scissors, Laurel freed the contents. A small crystal angel adorned with gold wings nestled in a wad of shredded newspaper – sans note. Hung with a pink satin ribbon, Laurel raised it to the window, where rays of sunlight reflected from the glass. She strained to see the engraving etched on the bottom.

"Mom, Angel, Friend."

***

jannasbananas: *AL-LEEE!*

ally1234: *What's up, j?*

jannasbananas: *I received a special present in the mail today!*

ally1234: *Not so fast, youngster. You're not that special.*

jannasbananas: *?*

ally1234: *Did your little trinket come with shiny wings?*

ally1234: *Was it crystal?*

ally1234: *About three inches tall?*

ally1234: *Hung on pink satin?*

ally1234: *Postmarked Bonnie Doone, North Carolina?*

jannasbananas: *ASHE!*

jannasbananas: *Wait a minute. You got one, too?*

ally1234: *From what I gather, we'll all be opening a little surprise.* ☺

jannasbananas: *Oh, pooh. I thought I was special.*

ally1234: *Now, now. We're all special, J.*

jannasbananas: *You're right!*

jannasbananas: *What did I tell you?*

ally1234: *?*

jannasbananas: *This proves my point. Ashe is okay.*

***

After a quick shower, Laurel jumped into sweats and bee-lined for her computer where she could savor her alone time. Without her boys, the house was quiet and dark. She noticed Missy online and hurried to IM her. Laurel already received confirmation from Janna and Ally on their packages. If their angels came from North Carolina, they had to be from Ashe.

laurelextonsbunch: *Hey, are you around? Did you get anything in the mail today?*

missymom: *?*

laurelextonsbunch: *Look in your mail, Missy.*

Laurel's angel hung from a southern window in their family room to the left of her monitor. She touched it with her fingertip and it spun in a slow circle.

missymom: *I checked. Nothing. Why?*

laurelextonsbunch: *No reason. I thought you might have received a surprise, that's all.*

missymom: *You sent me something? Oh, Laurel. I could sure use…* something.

Laurel winced. After receiving Missy's frantic email regarding that dirty dog Earl leaving her, Laurel called right away to find her friend fluctuating between sorrow and numbness. Missy's problems far exceeded hers. The Extons may be broke, tip-toeing the high wire over bankruptcy, but at least Joe was loyal. Marcus was no scholar or athlete, and he managed to stay out of the principal's office. For once 'average' looked pretty good.

'Below average' appeared to have definite perks as well.

laurelextonsbunch: *It's not from me.*
missymom: *No?*

Laurel made a note to organize the other girls into care-package mode. The other girls had already begun a flurry of gifts and well wishes. Laurel couldn't afford to send much; she knew a simple greeting card would go a long way. VM bombardment was always a good thing. *Maybe homemade cookies?*

laurelextonsbunch: *Keep your eyes open. Maybe it'll come tomorrow.*
missymom: *'K.*
laurelextonsbunch: *How are you?*
missymom: *sigh* *I'm fine. No I'm not. Who am I kidding? My life is over.* ☹
laurelextonsbunch: *Have you heard from him?*
missymom: *No, and I'm afraid to call him now. I feel like I've called too much. I get so angry I can't call him because I'm afraid I'll start screaming. I don't want to see him because I might kill him.*
laurelextonsbunch: *Missy. {{{hugs}}}*
missymom: *I'll live.*
laurelextonsbunch: *How's Kassie?*

Kids were hard. Kimber cracked up her car two days after getting her license, Ally's son was ADHD, Mandy contracted mono and every other germ on a regular basis, and Rob was bullied during his elementary years. Kassie was the first VM kid to be suspended from school, and for theft. It wasn't only her friend's diamond earrings. Missy had found a treasure trove of stolen items under Kassie's bed, from gel pens and Jonas Brothers' notebooks, to Tampax and expired Hostess snack pies. Who would think a nice girl from a well-to-do family would plunder her classmates' lockers?

missymom: *She hates me. She hasn't said two words since I grounded her.*
laurelextonsbunch: *You* had *to ground her.*
missymom: *I know. It's tough because Earl's not here, not that he'd be a help anyway.*
laurelextonsbunch: *You mean he won't show up for this? What a nimrod!*
missymom: *I didn't tell him.*
laurelextonsbunch: *Why?*
missymom: *I told the girls he was out of town on business. He can't show up now.*
laurelextonsbunch: *You're not making sense.*
missymom: *I know. Wah! Gotta run. Kids.*

Missy disappeared from the Buddy List. Laurel knew what that meant. Communicating by email or IM was easier before the kids could spell. Now they had to guard against risqué jokes, nude forwards, and inter-mom bad language.

"A thank you! I have to do this before I forget!" Laurel said out loud.

To: AsheMacD
From: laurelextonsbunch

Ashe, I received the angel today and it's beautiful! Thank you so much. It arrived when it was most needed. Today was the absolute pits. To find this treasure in my mailbox made me forget about my horrible day. (Okay, I didn't forget. It's becoming a distant memory.)

Sorry I haven't been more welcoming, but as you might have noticed, my Real Life takes up most of my time these days. Can I say this? I think you write beautifully. Tyler is so darned cute! He reminds me of Marcus at the same age – inquisitive, boisterous, and charming.

Your story is so sad. What I can do? I know I'm late in offering. I'm not very smart, I can't volunteer much when it comes to money or advice. If you need moral support and a friend's ear, I will always be here for you. That's what we do; we encourage each other and help when we can.

Thanks again. Laurel

Chapter Fifteen

Saturday, November 14
Bonnie Doone, North Carolina

"Get up! Get up!" Tyler, in Sponge Bob pajamas and socks, gave the mattress a rigorous trampoline workout. Ashe's head absorbed the recoil. In the distance Jim Bob's hound dog wail echoed through the house.

Ashe glanced to the window and determined a noticeable lack of sunlight. The spotlight atop the neighbor's garage punched illumination through the dark. Ashe turned toward the clock and groaned while Tyler bounced. Mac was missed most during times like these. Not that Tyler could be traded for all the gold in the world. Ashe may never pen the perfect breakout novel, never find fame, or experience true love again, but thanks to Mac here was Tyler – a sole perfect creation.

Having Tyler didn't change the fact that single parenthood was absolute hell. The past year taught Ashe a valuable lesson. Any parent, even a super-parent, needs another pair of hands at times. Ashe's natural clock was that of a night owl's. He preferred to be roused closer to noon. His most prolific work flowed when the house was dark and quiet. Mac, on the other hand, had been an early riser, springing up before the crack of dawn and ready to take on the world in seconds. Tyler obviously had inherited Mac's sleep patterns. Ashe rubbed at tired eyes and sank back. "Son, it's only six o'clock. Come back in an hour."

"But... It's *Saturday!*"

"I know." Ashe wished for half Tyler's energy. If only one could tap into a small part of it, it would be possible to pump out three *New York Times* bestsellers in a year. Perhaps then Asheley MacDaniel would be able to leave the editorial world once and for all instead of only aspiring to be a literary giant.

Tyler cannon-balled his last jump, came to rest, and crawled into bed. Jim Bob ambled into the room, sensing the commotion would lead someone to the back door. The dog rested his enormous brown head nearby. "Uncle Rhett is coming," Tyler announced.

"I know." Thank goodness for Rhett. Ashe quickly computed the previous night's sleep. Two? Two and a half hours, maybe? If Rhett took Tyler for the afternoon, Ashe might be able to squeeze in a nap before tackling the next assignment. If the first three pages of the new client's manuscript were any indication, *The Arsonist's Handbook* would be as painful an edit as the last job, where the tool of choice should have been a book of matches instead of a red pen.

"I already ate," Tyler said.

"No kidding, bud?" Ashe opened one eye and tried to focus.

"I had chocolate donuts for breakfast." Ah. The hyperactivity explained, along with the frosting lipstick. Ashe made a mental note to hide the next batch of Krispy Kreme leftovers in an overhead cache, preferably in a locked and secure cabinet.

"Son, did you let Jim Bob out yet?"

"I'm not supposed to open the door unless you're awake," he said soberly.

"Come on, Ty," Ashe said. "Might as well get up and get the dog fed."

***

Skye jogged along the water's edge, her feet thumping the surface mere inches away from the chill of the Pacific's icy waves. The fog had started to lift, and the skies had begun to color – a watercolor palate of pink, red, turquoise, and persimmon. It was the start of a promising day. More had to follow. She had a great son, enough work to keep her from eviction, and a great group of friends. Ashe, two steps from being a total stranger, was a thoughtful new addition. A tiny crystal angel via U. S. Postal Service was a reminder of how good humankind could be.

Skye pulled out her cell phone and looked at it to time her run today. Over past two few weeks, she had managed to shave off several minutes each day. Her breathing was less labored. She felt her calves begin to tighten, not muscle-bound yet nicely toned. Running had an invigorating effect on Skye's entire life. It had been hard to drag herself out of the house the first few days. Now she looked forward to the alarm at 6:30. She experienced a surge of energy and felt good. Rob noticed her humming and renewed vigor and asked if she were happy. *Happy?* She thought about it. She was something, yet she didn't know if she could go *that* far. Whatever it was, she knew she was heading in the right direction.

That 'direction' was the ability to put Trina behind her. *Finally.* Skye had been surprised when she had gone an hour without thinking about her, then astounded when she realized she had gone a day without ruminating over the break-up. Keeping busy helped. The ache in her heart was constant. At least the pain was subsiding – from gut-twisting anguish to a twinge not quite so severe.

Maybe tomorrow I'll start running all the way down to Sloat and back. She had barely been able to walk the distance only two weeks before. "No, that's crazy," she said out loud. "I *am* crazy! Why put off for tomorrow what you can do today?" Skye took off jogging, heading for the southern end of the beach, screams of "Whoo-eee!" behind her.

***

Ashe and Tyler curled up on the family room couch under a heavy blanket. They'd been watching cartoons when Rhett appeared. Dressed in a parka and hiking boots, the ensemble topped with a pink cowboy hat, Rhett lowered a bag of groceries to the floor. He removed his jacket to reveal a pink, plaid flannel work shirt covered by a black leather vest. Skinny jeans completed the ensemble. Rhett tossed his hat on the nearby dining room table. "Why pinch me! What are my MacDaniels doing up so early on a weekend?"

"Dressing down today, Rhett?" Ashe yawned.

"Ashe, dear, these are my kicking back clothes for outdoor fun. You know that." Rhett emptied his eco-bag, folded it carefully, and opened the door to the fridge to put away fresh peanut butter and hummus.

"Tyler's excited to see you today," Ashe said.

"I'm guessing he's all over his illness then?" Rhett bent over to brush a quick kiss on the top of Ashe's head before picking up Tyler. He threw the child into the air and gave his nephew a hard squeeze.

"Uncle Rhett! You're choking the life out of me!" Tyler chortled.

Rhett loosened his grip. "It's the World Famous MacDaniel love squeeze. Pay close attention to my form, Ty-Ty. You're going to need the love squeeze when you have kids of your own." Rhett plopped on the couch and attempted to grab the remote. Ashe beat him to it and stuffed it into Tyler's pocket. "What's up for today? Not cartoons, I hope?"

"Sleep would be heaven," Ashe said. "This little monster woke up at six. I've had a pot of coffee. Must be decaf. It's not working."

"Is that a hint you'd like me to take him somewhere?" Rhett winked at Tyler.

"Nature Center!" Tyler shouted. He jumped up and down.

"You didn't take him last week," Ashe reminded.

"All right. I'm no dummy. I can tell when I'm outnumbered." To Tyler, Rhett said, "Go on, now. Get dressed. Put on something warm. I feel a chill coming down. It's those damned snow birds bringing their foul weather with them." Tyler sprang up and ran for his room, trailed by Jim Bob. "And don't forget your hiking boots!" Rhett called after him.

"Thanks, Bro."

"No problem. I hope you don't mind if I make another pot of coffee," Rhett asked. "I haven't had any yet and I'm going to need jet fuel to keep up with Ty today." He moved to the sink and rinsed out the pot. "So what's new on the Virtual Mom front? Have you come clean yet?"

Ashe's face burned scarlet. Trouble was brewing with the VMs. Celia's unexpected phone call last week was followed by calls from Skye, Ally, and Janna. Ashe couldn't afford to be found out – not yet, anyway – and began to use the answering machine to screen incoming calls. Skye and Ally left 'thank you' messages for the angels. Laurel emailed her surprise and thanks. Missy was still waiting for hers.

It was a perfect gift for the VMs. Mac always said, "All good women are angels." It was true; these were good women.

It was late Friday when Janna left a lengthy voicemail regarding her recent date with Juan Bernstein, after the exchange of belligerent emails regarding her current picks. Although annoyed, Ashe couldn't stay mad at Janna for long. The sassy sound of her voice with its brash New York accent was appealing.

156

Although she nagged like a persistent mother hen, Janna exuded a certain youthfulness Ashe found endearing. Her thoughts were quick and scattered, making her sentences run together in an exuberant hodgepodge, much like her wisecracking emails. Whatever she experienced, she felt it deeply. How appropriate that Janna's voice matched her photograph. She was slim, blond, and looked too young to have twenty-something daughters. The past year found Ashe appreciating Janna not only as a human being, but as something more.

"It's not so easy, Rhett. I can't email them all and say, 'Hey, love all y'all, and oh, by the way, I'm not who you think I am.' I have to figure out a better way."

Rhett dropped the coffee carafe in the sink and spun around to face Ashe. "*What?* Do I hear you right? You're still haven't come clean? Are you completely bonkers?"

"I *like* these women. All of them. Besides, Missy needs me right now. Her husband left her for no reason and she's a wreck."

Rhett shook his head. "You're making a huge mistake."

"I don't know how to correct the situation without sounding like an ass."

"If you don't stop this charade soon, you *will* be an ass in their eyes. Good Lord, this would have never happened if Mama were still alive. She would have kept you on an honest path." Rhett punched at Ashe's arm. "See what deception gets you? If you'd been honest, you wouldn't be in a pickle like this."

"It was unintended. How did I know what was going to happen? I rolled with the response." Ashe sighed. "I wasn't purposely deceitful. Who could have predicted the sympathy and page hits on the blog? How was I supposed to know I'd meet Janna in the grief forum? How could I predict we'd hit it off like we did? Anyway, it's too late now."

Rhett clucked his tongue, crossed his arms, and shot Ashe an angry scowl. "It's never too late. If you actually care about these women and want to be a true friend, you would stop this farce before things get worse."

Ashe shrugged. "How could it get worse? What could happen? They all live hundreds of miles away from here. It's not like they can drop in for an afternoon of tea and an exchange of

Southern Living recipes. Besides, since last week's phone call, I'm laying low when it comes to the group."

"Someone called here?"

Ashe detected Rhett's worry. "Celia."

"What happened?"

"Not much."

"And so?"

"She spoke to Tyler's babysitter."

"Sitter? You're not making sense."

Ashe maintained a calm exterior in the face of Rhett's rising hysteria. "Tyler has a sitter. That's the story, in case you're here and find a burning compulsion to answer the phone and someone asks you. These women are smart. Celia especially has the mind of an investigative journalist."

Rhett thumped Ashe's head with a bony knuckle. "Great. Thanks for the warning. I'm not answering any calls here. I never thought I'd say this, but you're a certified idiot, Asheley Wilkes MacDaniel. Are we truly related, or was one of us switched at birth?"

"Why?" Ashe deadpanned. "What's the big worry? The whole thing is harmless. My intentions are pure. I'm not hurting anyone."

"You might not be hurting anyone – yet. You have to know that the average woman isn't stupid."

"These aren't average women, they're exceptional."

"Don't lay the sugar on *me*, Ashe MacDaniel. I'm your brother and I know better. Women have the one thing in their arsenal that the mortal man can only *dream* of possessing, and that jewel of a skill is a woman's intuition. Mark my words, one of these ladies will find you out and then you'd better watch it. The wrath of a woman scorned and all that – it's nothing to be messed with. Oh, Lord. Times six? They'll gang up on you. You wouldn't survive the fallout. They'll never forgive you."

"Forgive what? Did I do something wrong?" Tyler appeared in the doorway, dressed in survival gear of long pants, heavy sweater, down jacket, and wool hat.

"Never mind, Ty," Rhett answered as he grabbed his coat and hat. "Remember that honesty is *always* the best policy. You tell the truth *always* and you'll never be in trouble."

Ashe looked down. Although Rhett was addressing Tyler, the true target was elsewhere.

***

Epilogue

The sun had begun to set, the horizon tinged with watercolor hues of yellow and orange. A gentle wind blew in from the south, causing the long grass on the dunes to sway. He spotted the group on the beach. His eyes riveted to the gorgeous blond in the center. Her hair was swept up, individual strands adorned with small white orchids. The diaphanous fabric of her long, white dress swirled in the wind.

As he approached, her face lit up, radiating like a perfect, pale sun. Who was this goddess waiting for him on the beach? Was this vision actually going to marry him? The woman extended her hand. He took the slender fingers and kissed them. She smiled serenely, with her eyes, her body.

"Will you take this woman," a man's voice said, "to be your lawfully wedded wife?"

He looked into eyes of blue. It was like staring into the abyss, a pool so deep and alluring, it frightened him. He stood at the edge, toes in, heels out. If he fell in, he would be lost in her eyes forever.

***

Ashe awoke with a start. Janna. Was it a dream? Or was it the end of the novel? Ashe often used dreams to populate the writing – art imitated life – or was it the other way around? *It was only a dream. It means nothing.* Sure. Ashe and Janna were "friends," end of sentence, period, add the quotation marks and save file. Maybe they were 'good' friends, or 'close' friends, nothing more. Ashe felt guilty and uncomfortable. Mac's passing was only twelve short months before. Thinking about Janna in this way was wrong. It was too soon and it wasn't right.

On the other hand, Ashe was only human, one alive and with certain needs and urges. How could anyone *not* fall in love with Janna? Everyone loved her. She made it so easy. She was beautiful, intelligent, and funny. The trifecta of a perfect mate. Mac had those qualities, too. Ashe had gotten the better of the deal with Mac, everyone knew that. Surely Ashe could find another mate with the same traits, yet the likelihood of finding two in a lifetime? It would be like hitting the lottery.

Ashe ran sweaty hands through bed-head and headed for the computer to check email. It was impossible not to zero in on Janna's email.

To: AsheMacD, missymom, ally1234, celiasunshine, laurelextonsbunch, shootingskye
From: jannasbananas
Subject: Last date

Girls, you wouldn't believe this, I think my search is over! Not only did I enjoy a wonderful dinner with Juan last night, he was a perfect gentleman. He didn't manhandle me like so many first dates have. He didn't rush in to kiss me, either. He's not only handsome and mature, he's also fun. He laughs at my silly jokes and compliments me constantly.

OMG, eyelashes out to HERE. Much better looking in real life than in that crummy pic. When he gazes into my eyes, I know I'm the only woman on the planet. Oh, and the man is a workout fanatic. I haven't touched them yet. I've got it on good authority that he's got abs of steel (and buns of steel and back of steel and legs of steel and, well, you get the picture). LOL, let's hope another appendage is made of steel, too. ☺

We've got a date set up for next Friday. OMG! We're going to the flower show. THE FLOWER SHOW! Can you imagine? A perfect specimen who shares my interests! Girls, I have hit the trifecta.

Ugh. The dreaded 'trifecta.' Ashe closed the email without replying. The room began a slow spin that gained in intensity. Dread washed over, a trickle into a wave into a tsunami. Nausea? Migraine? Earthquake? Impending doom?

Whatever it was, Ashe didn't like it.

***

After dinner, Rhett found a place on the front porch. Bundled in a Duke University blanket, he cradled a mug of hot cocoa and watched as Tyler dug into the front lawn with a trowel. Ashe joined him on the bench, armed with an old plastic sippy cup filled with a double shot of Glenfidditch. Another Saturday was coming to a close, yet rather a feeling a sense of accomplishment, Ashe felt the whole day had been wasted. Unable to focus, and therefore incapable of a single line edit, Ashe spent the afternoon cyber stalking Janna. She was absent as Ashe knew she would be. Stopping wasn't in the cards. Any hope of concentration was interrupted by thoughts of a blissfully happy Janna and imagining a laundry list of dishonorable intentions by that dirty dog Juan Bernstein. Ashe squinted into the yard. "What's Ty doing?"

Rhett blew into his cocoa, separating floating marshmallows. "Hell if I know. I've been watching him for fifteen minutes and I still can't figure it out. It's all about the dirt for him today. He dug up half the nature center. The park patrol came and threatened to confiscate his little shovel."

"No jail time, huh?"

"Not yet. This one is smart as a whip and a budding ladies' man, so we're going to have to watch him close. After he was nabbed red-handed with red clay all over his shovel and his shoes, he began reciting random facts about cicadas and cattails. Officer Jill was eating out of his hands in minutes. A ladies' man in the making. Taking after his father, I'm guessing."

Ashe took a swig and felt the warm surge of scotch bathe a parched throat. All that was needed now was for the alcohol to blaze a trail straight to the brain and put Ashe out of misery once and for all. "Shoot me now."

"Excuse me?"

Ashe directed attention to the conversation at hand. "Please. He's way too young."

Rhett pulled his legs up into the blanket. "When they're as cute as Ty, they're never too young. I don't get it. I'm beat and Tyler has enough energy to light up Fayetteville with some to spare." He slurped his cocoa before continuing. "So, let's be honest. What's the real story behind these virtual women?"

"What do you mean?" Ashe hoped for a blank slate for a facial expression, something devoid of emotion.

"I was thinking about it on the trail. It's easy to do when Tyler's blabbing a mile a minute. Love the little guy, but after a while, you zone out."

"Uh, huh."

"I was thinking about this cockamamie situation of yours. Surely must be a reason for it somewhere. Although I've looked at it from every angle, I can't figure out what on earth it could be."

"You're nuts." Ignorant denial was the best tack. "I don't have any idea what you're talking about."

"I get the blog, though I don't quite understand the whys or wherefores. Personally speaking, I think it would have gotten more attention had you been truthful from the beginning."

"I had to do it this way. I wanted to maximize my page views. Remember, I got a little income from it."

"Was it money enough to sell your soul to the Devil?"

Ashe ignored him and continued. "You know I couldn't use my real name, what with all the horrible things I said about the Army. It's amazing how the Department of Defense frowns on negative portrayals by milspouses. I'd have had Mac's CO on me and been blasted by Internet trolls. Plus, I don't want people to know 'Asheley MacDaniel,' is the same as the aspiring romance writer, Asheley MacDaniel. I'd be labeled a mother's milk-sucking pansy ass by everyone I've ever had the privilege to meet. That's most of the Carolinas, Rhett."

"Whatever." Rhett dismissed the comment with a wave of his hand. "I get your friendship with Janna. You were both hurting and it was therapy to find each other when you did. That makes sense. What I don't get is why you let the friendship go as long and as far as you did without telling her. Unless…"

With eyes closed, Ashe downed the rest of the Glenfidditch, and waited for the unveiling of Rhett's theory. Tyler wasn't the only smart MacDaniel and Ashe was a terrible liar.

"Something else is going on, right? Oh, Ashe, no!" Rhett bounded off the bench, the remains of his cocoa flying from his mug.

"Hey! This is a brand new sweater!"

"Don't tell me you have *feelings* for this woman?"

Ashe feigned shock and ignorance. "Which woman?"

"Oh, *my* God. You do! It's more than friendship. You got that same look in your eyes that you had the first time you brought Mac home for dinner to meet the folks."

"Rhett, calm down. Nothing is going on, except mutual respect and friendship. Maybe I made a mistake with the Virtual Moms. I'm going to fix it."

"Oh, yeah?" Rhett's face clouded with doubt.

"I'm working on it right now. Honest. I just have to figure out how."

Chapter Sixteen

Sunday, November 15
Sarasota, Florida

Paper mounded over the kitchen table – bills, mostly – and Celia set about on her one day off to throw her creditors enough of a bone so that she could rest easy for another month. Thanks to being blessed with eel-like slipperiness, her ex, Melvin Davis, hadn't contributed a dime toward child support in the last twelve years. Before that time, the pittance of an award from the court – $75 a week – was sporadic if he made payments at all. Moving from Ohio to Florida ten years before made it all too easy for the man to slink into the shadows and disappear altogether.

Not that she missed him at all. When Celia reflected on her early adulthood and the choices she made, she would be the first to admit that marrying Melvin was a monumental mistake. He was a pleasant fellow, charismatic and friendly. She was blind to his slacker lifestyle. Celia, in her past life a chunky teenager, was starved for attention and love. He provided it. He was the first man to call her 'beautiful' and the look in his eyes told her he meant it.

Unfortunately, a smooth temperament and a man's love won't pay the bills. Melvin loathed working. Jobs gave him hives. In the beginning, he tried various positions, mostly to please Celia. The longest lasted two months, lawn care at a golf course in suburban Cincinnati. Winter approached, he was laid off, and neglected to return the following year after the snow melted. Most of the time Melvin lay around the house, watching TV and smoking weed. After she became pregnant with Kimber, Celia put her foot down once and for all. "We're going to be parents now. Get a job or get out."

The coward left in the dark of night while Celia slept. He took his clothes, the TV, and all the cash he could find in Celia's purse ($15.92).

Celia stuck it out in southern Ohio for a few years, hoping Kimber's birth would ignite a spark of maturity in her husband. After two years of waiting, Celia deduced Melvin was less than a stellar father figure. She moved south with her mother after Mom retired from the phone company.

Melvin's convenient absence wasn't without positives. Celia would never have to explain him to Kimber. Celia worried her daughter might want to look up her errant father and his backwoods family. It was an unnecessary concern. Kimber knew enough back story to extinguish any urge to look up her father. Every so often, Celia mentioned it and Kimber would rise indignant each time. "Why should I look him up? He hasn't cared enough to look for me!"

The failed marriage to Melvin intensified Celia's distrust of relationships in general and men in particular. Her lofty standards were the reason why her dating dance card was absent a few names. She was thankful that Kimber put her boyfriends under the same rigorous relationship tests that Celia adhered to. Kimber had her head on straight, choosing an academic track that would lead to her goal of veterinary school. School, sports, and church came first. Brandon hung around for six months pining for Kimber before she made a commitment, and her choice was based on the logic that she *might* have extra time for him.

The subject of the newbie Virtual Mom, Ashe, weighed heavily on her. Celia was the only original Virtual Mom left. She had a sharp eye and impeccable instincts when it came to people, and she was choosy. The others in the group were latecomers and not as discriminating when it came to discerning integrity. They allowed anyone and everyone entrance into Virtual Moms. It took many years before she felt completely comfortable with the final composition of the group. Ashe MacDaniel reminded her of some in the original Virtual Mom group, an interloper with no background or history. This woman came in on Janna's recommendation and nothing more.

She would be more understanding, but Ashe was an enigma. The phone call of the previous Sunday stunned her. Ashe had given Janna the impression she was alone and had no nearby relatives, much less a brother. Celia tried calling Ashe several times during the week and the most she got was the answering machine. Instead of calling back, Ashe would email back. *Weird.*

The girls still didn't know what Ashe looked like, because after two weeks in the group, she had yet to send a photo of

165

herself. All Celia had to judge her by was her blog. *Missing Mac* was emotional, yes. Something about the words activated Celia's radar. Sarasota wasn't that far away from North Carolina; perhaps a weekend road trip should be planned. "Damn it," she cursed under her breath. Her 'weekends' consisted of a mere 24 hours, and she wasn't going to expend the time, money, and energy on her one day off to follow a hunch.

Perhaps Celia was wrong, as Janna suggested. Maybe she *was* picking on Ashe for no good reason. Her informal poll of the other girls indicated they all liked her. None of them shared the nagging doubts that lingered in her mind. Celia periodically asked Kimber what she thought. She listened intently before answering. "I know what you mean. They can't *all* be wrong, Mom."

Maybe.

Celia Googled Asheley MacDaniel, finding little –the *Missing Mac* blog, an email address, and a white pages listing with the same North Carolina info Ashe had shared. An Asheley MacDaniel had placed in writing contests under the "romance" genre – that matched up with the editing job. True the name was common; in this day and age, most people had thick online dossiers. Celia dove into Facebook, MySpace, and LinkedIn searching for Ashe MacDaniel and surfaced empty. The woman had a sparse online persona, another oddity. Supposedly she was a writer. Except for the blog and the romance stories, she could find nothing else from Miss Asheley MacDaniel. "Pen name, maybe?" she asked aloud, stymied. Celia then Googled Tyler MacDaniel, North Carolina. More nothing. Searching for Ashe was like looking for one speck of dust in the Milky Way.

A vibration in her pocket interrupted her thoughts. Celia looked at the caller ID – Laurel. "Celia. Are you busy?" Her voice was shaky.

"Not at all. I'm paying bills."

"Something awful has happened!"

"To Marcus? To Joe?"

"No, no, they're fine. It's my dad. He's in the hospital."

"No, Laurel. Is he all right?" Celia tamped down her concern.

"I don't know. He's had a heart attack. I'm flying down tonight."

"Honey, I'm so sorry."

"I hate to ask you this, but can you come to Orlando? I'll be flying down alone. We can't afford for all of us to go. Celia, I don't think I can handle this by myself."

"Of course, I'll pick you up! Which airline? What flight number?"

Laurel burst into tears. Celia could hear the rustling of paper and drawers being slammed. "It's here somewhere. I know it is. Joe?"

"Don't worry about it. Take a breath, Laurel. I'm sure your dad is in good hands. If you want, I'll call over and make sure he is." Celia modulated her voice to bedside manner. If Laurel was a basket case, she didn't want to be responsible for tipping it over.

"Oh, God…what am I…"

"I'll be there. Call me before you take off so I'll know when to meet you."

***

The sound of raucous singing coming from her backyard caught Celia's attention. Not Kimber, not Brandon, but a man's deep voice bellowing an *a cappella* version of "My Girl." The pained rendition sounded more like a bull moose floundering in agony on his deathbed. On her way out of the lanai to investigate, Celia looked for a makeshift weapon. Lacking serious armament, she grabbed Kimber's South American rain stick for protection, being careful not to upend and shift the seeds. Stealth was a necessary component for defense against the home invader. She tightened her grip on the rattle. For all she knew, her intruder could be homeless and hopped up on drugs. Or worse, mentally ill and drunk.

She dropped the stick as she entered the backyard. It clattered on the pool deck and rolled away. The unexpected crooner was no B&E man; it was Doug Taylor, who was cleaning her pool complete with headphones, iPod, and pathetic singing voice. His back to the house, he was absorbed in the task at hand and didn't notice her approach.

Celia smiled at the hilarious sight. Doug's tight rear end – clothed in thin shorts – swayed to the rhythm of Motown. The hem of his gaudy Hawaiian print shirt followed close behind. She allowed Doug to make it to the chorus "I *guess* you'll say, what can make me feel this *waaay*?" before she poked him in the back.

Doug teetered and nearly fell into the pool. "Hey!" He pulled off his headphones and flashed a killer smile. His eyes twinkled.

Celia crossed her arms and tapped her foot. She wasn't *that* amused. "My service is a day late."

He leaned in close and whispered. "I *know*."

Celia observed curly, thick eyelashes – ones she would kill for. Doug's wrinkles were grinning at her, damn it. She noticed that for a working man, Doug smelled heavenly, a mix of musk, sweat, and sandalwood. She took a protective step back, outside the aura of his influence. No flash in the pan man was going to make a lust zombie out of her.

Doug waved his hand at the pool. "I'm doing a kick-ass job, though, don't you think?"

Celia blushed. "You're not serious, are you? You're really taking over for Carlos?"

"Have to. I'm missing a man and haven't been able to replace him. Too busy with snow birds coming down for the winter to run employment ads. Everyone wants maintenance done in November. I'm booked solid. You don't mind being serviced by the owner of the company, do you?" Doug winked again. *Serviced*? His eyes danced off random points on Celia's body; her ears, her hair, her breasts and calves, before settling in on her eyes.

The usually unflappable Celia felt her locomotive knocked off track. "I don't care who does it. I want a clean pool." She backed away, tripped over the rain stick, and stumbled through a maze of lounge chairs on her escape to the safety of her house.

Had she looked back, she might have noticed the pool man smiling as he gave her a hearty thumbs' up.

***

To: AsheMacD
From: missymom
Subject: Thank you!

I opened my mailbox today to find the sweetest surprise! Since I don't know anyone else from North Carolina, I'm assuming you sent the angel.

168

Sorry if I've been out of the loop lately. I've got lots to think about, serious stuff. If you read the latest, you know about Earl. I can't eat, I can't sleep, I can't concentrate. I've had to face things I thought I'd never have to – you know?

I'm looking at this angel and thinking how perfect they are. What if it were all a cover? What if devils hide under the wings of beautiful angels? What if the exterior was one big, fat, ugly lie? If what was underneath was dark and scary?

Sorry to depress you.

Missy ←Mystified

***

Doug disappeared without a word as mysteriously as he arrived. No matter. Celia had bigger problems than an overgrown, horny pool boy to attend to. After an afternoon of hurried phone calls between her, Laurel, and Janna, Celia sat down at the computer again and checked her email. Ashe was conspicuously absent, having replied to only one group message. "Curious," she said out loud. "Why would she hang back when she was so vocal the first week?"

"Talking to yourself again, Mom?" Kimber broke the spell of her preoccupation. An overflowing basket of dirty clothes perched on her hip. "You know that's the first sign of senior citizenship. After that, it's downhill all the way." Her right hand arced from shoulder height to below her waist. "Zoom!"

Celia smiled. "I'm thinking."

"Are you still worried about Ashe?" Celia knew Kimber's thoughts. She'd been intrigued by the Virtual Moms, those magic ladies who could find special Beanie Babies when the local stores had none. Now with this question mark…

"Yes. I can't put my finger on it. I definitely feel something is wrong."

"Why don't you Google her?"

"I have. I wish I could find something. It's a clean slate."

Kimber leaned in and peered over Celia's shoulder. Her fingers flew over the keyboard. "What about different spellings? Did you try Bing? Facebook? If she's old-fashioned like you, she still might be on MySpace."

Celia brushed her daughter's hands away. "So MySpace is now 'old-fashioned'? Har-dee-har. I remember when it was the be-all and end-all for you."

Kimber stuck out her tongue. "MySpace is so last decade, Mom. Get current, will you? How about email addresses? IP searches?"

"My dear, I have worn a path all around the information super-highway and back. I'm still stumped."

Kimber folded her arms and leaned against the doorframe. Celia stared at the screen, her mind blank. Kimber jumped up and chirped, "What about professional help?"

"What do you mean?"

"Why not hire an investigator?"

"You mean a private eye? That's going to cost money. I don't exactly have a lot of disposable income, thanks to a certain sixteen-year-old I know. One who likes to eat, wear clothes, and plans to go to college." She winked at Kimber.

"Har-dee-har back," Kimber retorted. "Think about it. What would it hurt to check it out? Call a few people. See what it costs. I bet it's less than you think."

A private investigator, huh? The gears began grinding in Celia's head.

Chapter Seventeen

Monday, November 16
San Francisco, California

Skye Murray's phone rang as her left foot reached the front porch. Running late as per usual, she berated herself for not starting her day out earlier. Rob had left an hour before. A date with a classmate regarding a play both were in. Skye fished for the cell in her backpack, hoping to answer before it went into voice mail. She'd expected another job offer from *Sunset* and couldn't afford to miss the call. The magazine had been impressed with her culinary school photographs and wanted her to shoot more food pictures, maybe in restaurants in Napa Valley or Mendocino. A quick response would prove her eagerness.

Lost in a jumble of lenses, notebooks, makeup, and keys, Skye could hear her phone yet couldn't locate it. She hit her head with the heel of her palm. Of course, the phone was in the front pocket of her jeans.

"Good morning. Murray Studio," she answered brightly without looking at the caller ID. Between 8 a.m. and 6 p.m., she was Murray Studio. After that, she could be plain, old Skye.

"It's me, Janna."

"What's up?" She relaxed, locked the door behind her, and trudged through the foggy mist toward the MUNI stop.

"A couple of things. I wanted to give you an update on the Juan Adventure."

"You mean the *Don* Juan adventure?" Skye smiled. Everyday life for Janna was a historic exploit. She didn't need a hunky heartthrob to spice up her existence; Janna's life was quite sensational without a man in the mix. A dating Janna added infinitely more plot twists.

"You wouldn't believe it," Janna sighed. "He's such a dreamboat! So kind, so generous. Friendly, not pushy. The one thing I can't stand is instant intimacy. Just because our profiles match doesn't mean it's a sure thing and I should call the caterer. A couple needs to grow into a relationship slowly. You know?"

"You missed the best part, Bananas."

"Yeah?"

"He's not bad on the eyes, either!"

Janna released a hearty laugh. "True. I wonder how my parents will react. They're so old school."

"He's Jewish! Sort of. They should love him!" Skye panted as she ran to the MUNI stop. A train screeched toward her from Ocean Beach. She made it to the corner before it took off. She boarded the N-Judah and flashed her MUNI card, taking a seat in the back.

"They should *adore* him, he's so perfect. Hey, what are you doing? You sound like you're working out. You're not *with* someone, are you? I mean doing the naughty-naughty?"

"I know what you mean and I have two words for you: As if. I ran to catch the train."

"Sha, girly. You need to stick a toe into the dating pool."

"I think not. I give up on romance. Too messy and I always get hurt. I can do without the drama. I'm starting to think the old maid option is workable. Except for this Juan dude, we could be old maids in tandem. Coast to Coast Old Maids' Society." Skye referenced the 'Coast to Coast Beanie Loving Moms,' their old moniker, when the VMs had taken the Beanie Baby hunt more seriously.

"Sure. Think of the fun we'll have. We could take in stray cats and pick up recyclables with stolen shopping carts. Not! So what's on the agenda for today?"

"Parent-teacher conferences first. Then hoping, cross your fingers, a job."

"Don't worry, Skye. Someday you'll find someone for you somewhere, maybe sometime soon. Love springs eternal and all that."

"What do you mean?" Skye could read Janna's mischief from three thousand miles away. While Janna was perennially cheerful; in the last few weeks, she had been downright giddy.

"I'm thinking out loud." Janna answered coyly. "That's the other thing I called about. What's your opinion of Ashe?"

"Ashe? You keep asking. She's nice enough. She's easy to talk to. You know that for yourself. We've had some pretty deep conversations in the last couple of weeks. Life, death, that kind of thing. Actually, she's a lot like you."

172

"*Moi*? No thanks, friend. I don't swing that way."

Skye stumbled into Janna's line of thought. "What are you saying?"

"Nothing. Ashe *does*."

Skye made a quick computation of the many references Janna had made about Ashe in the past two weeks. Had she become a pawn in another Janna-Banana plot? "Janna, please. Don't tell me the whole Ashe thing was a set up? You're kidding, *right*?"

"I'm serious. She has a significant appreciation of women. And I figured, she's a good match as a Virtual Mom, she might be a good match for you. I'm surprised you didn't figure it out before."

Skye smiled. Janna's brain contained more cogs and mesh than a nickelodeon at the Musée Méchanique. "Why would I figure it out? I'm not looking. I told you, I've sworn off relationships for a while. A good, long while, if I have anything to say about it."

"No, Skye. Boo. It's not right to be alone. Solitary confinement isn't healthy!"

"Being set up isn't either. One of us might kill you." Skye flashed a smile at an older gentleman as he eavesdropped. He smiled back. Long gray hair pulled back into a ponytail, he looked familiar. She turned away and lowered her voice. "Does Ashe know?"

"Not yet. I'm thinking of dropping the bomb today. I've added the ingredients and stirred up the bowl a bit. It's time to throw this cake into the oven!"

"You might be dead wrong. I like Ashe fine. *Not* in that way. I think she feels the same."

"Come on, don't be a sourpuss. Play along. I'm happy. I want you to be happy, too."

"So you think Juan Baby is a sure thing? It's only been a few days."

"I can tell. It's as sure as anything could be. He says he likes the idea of Mandy and Rachel as stepdaughters! How perfect is that?"

How indeed, Skye thought.

"Janna, we're going into a tunnel and I'm going to lose you. Let me say that with my horrible track record, I should check into a con…"

Too late. The phone went dead.

***

Celia threw her car keys on the kitchen table and kicked off her shoes. Work today was more gruesome than ever, what with skyrocketing costs, the nurses' union threatening a walk-out, and all of it covered by the local news. Despite the bickering and misinformation, Sarasota General had seen hard times before. Celia was confident that adjustments could be made. "They'll all have to give a little, that's all," she said as she slumped into a chair. She put her feet up on another kitchen chair.

Kimber was gone – probably at work at the sandwich shop. Her backpack was on the table along with a stack of mail. On top of the bills and circulars was a small box addressed to Celia. Curious, she turned it around, noting a package heavily mummified in tape, the postmark blurred, and sporting no return address. She picked at the box with her fingernails and finally walked to the kitchen drawer that held shears. "Jesus Jimmy! It's only mail, not something that needs to be wrapped up this tight."

With a little work, the package was untangled. Celia tore into the inner box and pulled away the bubble wrap. "What?" She pulled on a string, bringing to light a tiny crystal angel with the engraving "Mom, Angel, Friend."

***

Skye left Rob's school light and happy, although the fog had turned into a drizzle. She opened her umbrella and beamed. The parent-teacher conferences went better than expected. Rob's academics put him at the top of his class, he was helpful and kind, participated in a variety of extra-curricular activities, and was a joy to have in class. During the conference, her phone rang and she took the call. This time, it was a job offer, not from *Sunset*, but from a friend of a friend for a wedding. Yippee! More income! Who needed love? She had a great kid, her work life was shaping up, and her flabby thighs were shrinking. At this rate, her debt would be discharged around the time of the Marathon. Perfect timing.

174

As she walked to the library, Skye thought more about her conversation with Janna. She loved Janna for being a staunch friend. She was funny and her heart was huge. Janna was front and center anytime trouble blew up. She was the problem solver. Janna was the starlet of the Virtual Moms, a hopeless romantic. No matter how much she appreciated and loved her friend, no way would she and Ashe would hook up. "It doesn't work that way," Skye said to herself as she shook the raindrops from her umbrella in the library entrance. Love would come where it's least expected. It can't be forced.

Skye's thoughts drifted to the two big loves in her life. Her marriage to Lee Murray found their friends' jaws literally dragged on the ground. The two started platonic friends, unlikely lovers as oil and water. Lee was thoughtful and serious, while Skye was hyperactive, sometimes manic, and hopelessly disorganized. Somehow, the two opposites made a life together. As for Trina, it was another unlikely match up. As with Lee, it started with genuine friendship. She had been impressed with Trina's work as a chef, with her enthusiasm for organic food, and her athleticism. Deeper feelings developed from that point, a natural progression. It didn't matter that her love was directed to a woman.

Skye found a vacant computer terminal and sat down. Her intent was to research the Napa winery where her newest wedding job was to take place. First, she checked on her email. A brief message from Janna sent from her Blackberry, a "na-nee-na-nee-na-nee" message. "I'm right about you and Ashe. You'll see."

Skye responded with one sentence. "I'll bet you Rob's college tuition you're wrong." She laughed out loud as she clicked the 'Send' button. "No way, Jose," she said to herself, "or should I say, no way, *Juan*."

She opened a private message from Ashe. They'd exchanged a great deal of information in the last two weeks. At first, Ashe had questions regarding Tyler. "It's not easy raising a boy," Skye had written. "According to the moms of girls in this group, it's better than having daughters." She and Ashe also discussed Skye's relationship with Trina at length. Ashe took an interest in learning the details of their failed partnership. Skye found it easy to tell Ashe things, some of them things she hadn't shared with the other VMs. After finding out Janna's intentions, it made sense. Maybe it was more than friendship with her. Maybe Ashe keyed in to her loneliness and wanted to find a way into her heart. She shook her head. *No, that's nuts.*

Skye opened Ashe's email.

To: shootingskye
From: AsheMacD
Subject: RE: Finding my way

Going with a girl isn't much different than having a boyfriend or being married to a man, is it? A relationship is two people, committed to each other, ready and able to sacrifice anything and everything to be together. From what you've told me, if you and Trina were meant to be, she would be there for you – as much as you are for her. Think about it. It was easy for her to walk away with no concern for you or for Rob. Although it hurts to lose someone, you have to remember one thing. When one door closes, another one opens. You have to realize pain happens for a reason. You can't experience happiness without it.

Hey! I guess I should have figured that out myself, huh?

Skye, I want to thank you for your friendship. I appreciate it more than you know. I wanted to tell you I will be 'off the grid' so to speak for the next week. I have a lot of thinking to do. It concerns my future. Tyler's too. I'll miss your witty emails, but I think I'll get more accomplished if I weren't online.

Peace out,
Ashe

Her reply:
Dear Ashe,

I don't know if you've spoken to Janna yet. The wench has an evil plan for us, one I had nothing to do with, mind you. I like you a lot, you've been a fantastic friend to me. I'm not looking for a relationship.

Skye stared at the words. "This is silly," she said out loud. Whatever happens, happens. What did Trina say? It's karma. She wouldn't fight it, and she wouldn't encourage it either.

She deleted the message.

176

Skye was so wrapped up in her email she did not notice the man sitting across the bank of computers from her. An older gentleman, maybe in his late fifties, his pony-tailed hair escaped from the back of a black beret. She noticed eyes an odd shade of blue, bright and sparkly as though he were wearing colored contacts. The man's face was lined with wrinkles – friendly wrinkles, not stress lines – and he smiled at her. Skye felt her face redden. He nodded his head in acknowledgement before getting up to approach Skye. He bent over to whisper into her ear.

"Excuse me, and don't think I'm some sort of pervert. Do I know you from somewhere?"

Skye studied his face. He *did* look familiar, although she couldn't put her finger on it. San Francisco was full of aging hippies. They all looked alike to her. "I don't think so. Maybe you've seen me here before. I come here a lot. My son's school is a few blocks away, so…"

"I don't think so." The man turned to walk away, but returned. "Say, perhaps you wouldn't mind sharing a cup of coffee with me. I know a place on the other side of Van Ness. The coffee is super-charged and free trade. Best coffee outside of Seattle. The place is tucked in an alleyway and used to be someone's garage…"

"The Blue Bottle! I know that place, too! You're right. The coffee is like jet fuel. And the croissants are to die for."

The man extended his hand. "Well?"

Well, well, indeed.

***

Celia finally motored into the arrival area at the Orlando airport, after a trip that included a drenching thunderstorm, re-routes through road construction, and a three-car pile-up that knotted the freeway for hours. The sun had begun to wane. She'd hoped to pick up Laurel hours ago. She slowed and peered into the crowds waiting for rides from relatives, taxis, and rental car vans. "Door 5" Laurel had said in her last phone call.

"There she is," Celia said to herself. Laurel sat on a cement bench, a little paisley valise by her side. Her head was in her hands. She looked drained. Celia pulled up and opened the trunk, before she leapt from the car. "Laurel!"

Laurel looked up as if in a daze. "Celia?"

177

Celia decided to turn on her Cheery-It's-Okay voice. She'd mastered it after years of overseeing inter-hospital political squabbles. Celia's ability to arbitrate and coddle warring factions ranked beside any doctor's best bedside manner. Besides, she had some good news to report. On the way to Orlando, she had contacted Orlando Regional and learned that Laurel's father was weak yet resting comfortably. They were running tests to determine the next step. Celia hugged Laurel and smiled. "I'm so sorry I'm late. There was mad traffic coming from Sarasota, tons of rain. Drivers here act like they've never seen it before."

Laurel looked at Celia. Worry framed Laurel's teary eyes, her mouth was drawn into a tense line, and her face was pasty gray. "Celia, he's the only parent I have left. What am I going to…" she began as tears flowed anew.

Celia picked up Laurel's suitcase. "There, there. He's going to be fine. I called the hospital. They're waiting for you to arrive. He's not in grave danger." She smiled. "Come on, honey. Let's go and see what kind of trouble the old man is up to."

***

He'd introduced himself as the 'Dude,' real name Corbin Strait. He'd been given many names over the years, starting with Chili. That name stuck after he'd learned to make five-alarm chili during his Army mess hall gig. "Dude is easy to remember," he said. "And it beats the hell out of some of the names I've been called."

After paying for twin double espressos and a bag of croissants, Skye and her companion took seats at a microscopic bistro table. The 'sidewalk' was a narrow slab, a perilous, uneven afterthought, and part of the table jutted into the alley. "We've met somewhere before, haven't we?" Skye tilted her head as she studied the stranger's face. In the hurricane that was her everyday life as a struggling single parent, she'd become accustomed to tuning out the noise of the rest of the world. She had to, for sanity's sake. The photographer in her was intrigued. While he was older, the kind wrinkles lining his face curled up and reminded her of Santa Claus. She wondered what he looked like minus a few years and a few pounds. She stirred her coffee while she thought. "I know! You're on television!"

178

He laughed; a huge roaring noise that caused Skye to startle and the barista to stop making foam for a moment while both gained their composure. "Television? I don't think so." He winked. "Think harder."

Skye leaned forward and stared hard. "News? Movies? *Woodstock*?"

"You're a little too young to remember Woodstock."

"I'm not that young. I love that era. The music, the clothes, the peace marches. It's the reason I live here. Once I came to San Francisco, I couldn't live anywhere else. The city has such a rich past, and I love history. I think the '60s was one of the most important times."

"It can be a great city. It can also be not so great."

"What do you mean?" In Skye's mind, everything about San Francisco was wonderful.

Without a word, he took his cup and one of the croissants and walked down the alley. Two buildings down, he turned into a doorway and bent over. Skye strained to see what he was doing. A few minutes passed, and Dude turned and walked toward her, without the coffee or pastry.

"What?" Skye mouthed the word; he answered before it sounded.

"I know a guy who lives in that alcove. Homeless guy. When I can I bring him something to eat." His shook his head toward the alley. "It's hard for him to get around. His leg's messed up. A car hit him a year ago. Yeah, he was drunk, still… It's kind of hard to heal on the streets. I know he'd rather have booze. A guy's got to eat something."

"Oh." Skye looked into her cup of creamy foam and covered her pastry, embarrassed to have so much when a few yards away another had so little.

"He's too proud to beg. That, and he's mental." He laughed and shook his head.

"How do you know him?" Skye was curious. The homeless were invisible to her, a social problem she easily ignored. If people lived on the streets, she never noticed them.

"He's a buddy of mine from 'Nam. His head's been messed up since he got back, and that was forty years ago. He never *really* came back, you know?" His blue eyes clouded as they searched for something. His gaze shifted far down the alley, far past the point of the homeless man, or maybe he was trying to dredge up a more intangible target.

An uncomfortable silence hung over them. Skye flushed with embarrassment. She considered herself a compassionate person yet her virtue paled in comparison to what she had witnessed.

"What a kind gesture." Skye didn't know what to say.

"You don't understand. I have to give back." He shifted in his chair. "See, two years ago. That man was me."

Chapter Eighteen

Tuesday, November 17
Las Vegas, Nevada

Missy burst into her daughter's room cheerfully bearing a tray of eggs, toast and orange juice, a card, and a small box wrapped in pink and purple paper. She'd decided to put Kassie's suspension and subsequent grounding on the back burner. The day before, Kassie had expressed her regret to Missy. The unasked for written apologies to the principal and the classmates she stole from were appropriate remorseful touches. The box on the tray contained a pair of diamond stud earrings. "Happy birthday! My baby's finally a teenager!"

Kassie rubbed at her eyes as she sat up. "I am *not* a baby."

"Yes, honey, I know. You're a teenager." Missy winced and tried to keep a cool head. On what day did Kassie become so contrary? Did it happen all at once, or had she missed a gradual shift in her attitude, one that became apparent only in the last few weeks?

"Where's Dad?" Kassie scowled.

Missy placed the tray on the bed and arranged the single rose bud vase to complete the perfect picture. She took back her wish that Kassie was turning three, not thirteen. She loathed reminiscing. Kassie was so *good* back then, a joy to be around. Mom and daughter were joined at the hip – Missy Mom and MiniMissy. What happened to her baby? "You know where he is. He's away on a job." Missy straightened Kassie's coverlet and opened the blinds. Her eyes focused on a palm tree outside the bedroom window.

"You mean he's not coming home for my birthday? Why?" Kassie frowned and shot her best hostile glance.

"He sends his regards. He'll call you after school. Open your present. It's what you wanted. I hope it's the right shape."

Kassie threw the velvet box across the room. She knocked the glass of juice down as she extricated herself from the tray. Orange juice pulp spilled over the eggs and blanket. "I don't want it. It's not right, Dad not being here. What did you do to him?"

Missy attended to the mess and tried to maintain cheer. "Why, nothing, Kass. You know he's working. Kassie, come back."

It was too late. Kassie had already stomped away and slammed the bathroom door.

***

"Hey! Hi! Didn't think I'd see you here!"

Celia spun around in surprise, nearly knocking a nurse in the stomach with her bag. As soon as she heard the chipper, upbeat and positive voice, the hair on her neck stood straight out.

"Do-, I mean, Mr. Taylor. Good afternoon. Are you here to have some work done?" Celia asked. She hoped that SNIDE had been blasted loud and clear, albeit with a touch of forced courtesy.

Celia turned and walked away, with Doug following close behind. "I've dropped off my grandma for her physical. Gramps doesn't drive anymore. She's a sweet old bird. She's getting a little rickety, if you catch my drift." He winked. "So, what are you in for?"

Celia stopped abruptly in mid-stride and stared up at Doug. Was he smiling, or was it an annoying smirk? She inhaled his now familiar musky scent and took a cautious step backward. "I'm not *in* for anything," she answered tartly, "I *work* here."

"Oh, yes. I think Kimber mentioned it. Funny, I always imagined you were a nurse."

A rage quickly shot from her stomach to her head. She could feel blood boiling. If Doug Taylor didn't disappear and soon, the top of her head would blow off. "No, Mr. Taylor, I am *not* a nurse, I'm an administrator." Celia pointed to her door.

Doug smiled, completely oblivious to Celia's terse tone. "I suppose we all end up where we should be."

Celia frowned. "If you'll excuse me, I'm very busy, Mr. Taylor. Shouldn't *you* be working, too? I'm sure you have more than enough pools in Sarasota to keep you busy."

"Grandma, remember?"

The nerve of this Neanderthal! His eyes were laughing at her – every cell in his body was amused. Celia, of course, was not.

Celia huffed, entered her office, and slammed the door with the gusto Kimber reserved for their kitchen door.

***

182

"Did Dad call?" A breathless Kassie sounded like she ran the two miles from school, not the two hundred feet from the bus stop. Kara trailed behind, her angelic face colored with a dark frown.

Missy turned from the computer. "He hasn't yet."

"You're lying. He knows what time I get home. He wouldn't forget my birthday. Not *this* birthday. It's a special one. He has to come home. He promised we were going to do something together. Alone. He *promised*." Tears began to pool in her eyes.

"Kassie, I'm telling you the truth. I'd tell you if he called. Listen, call him yourself if you don't believe me. I'm sure he'd love to hear from you. He can take a minute out for you." Missy offered her the phone. Kassie stared at it.

"What did you do to him? You're such a b…"

"Kassie!" Missy didn't know whether to be angry with Kassie's outburst, or sad because her daughter felt she was a bitch.

"It's *your* fault he's not here! This is the worst birthday ever!" Kassie stomped off to her room, on the way knocking Kara into the wall. Kara's eyes filled with tears.

Missy sighed. She wanted to cry, too. Holding the family together was proving to too difficult to do alone. She wished she could be truthful; she couldn't. She would never portray Earl as less than a perfect father.

"Is Daddy ever coming home?" Kara whimpered.

"Sweetie, of course he is!" Missy ran to Kara and wrapped her arms around her. "He's so busy with a special project right now. He still loves you. I do, too. Don't worry, sweetheart, please, don't worry. Everything will be fine soon, you'll see."

Missy mouthed the words for her youngest because she needed to hear them aloud, too.

***

Dinner was a disaster. Kara picked at her food, rolling peas around her plate as though they were running a race. Kassie refused to come out of her room. Missy couldn't blame the girls for the lack of interest. Kass was right – this was the worst birthday ever. The pink and purple frosted birthday cake sat on the counter untouched, a monument to Missy's failure as wife and mother.

Missy was so distraught she put Kara to bed right after dinner, leaving the plates and food on the table. Kara didn't object, and put on her pajamas with a sadness that Missy found heart-wrenching. *It's my fault,* she thought. Although she spent her life skirting hoops of fire, she couldn't make anyone happy; not Earl, not Kassie.

She found her way to the computer and logged on. How she wished she could be a traveler on the real information superhighway. A tiny bit, a miniscule blip on the radar, pinging from site to site, anonymous, and one of the crowd. If only...

A familiar IM chime rang. Ashe. Social small talk was the farthest thing on her mind, yet she answered anyway.

> AsheMacD: *Missy, are you okay?*
> missymom: *I'm still breathing. I'm not sure that's a plus. :-/*
>
> AsheMacD: *It's awfully late. Midnight?*
> missymom: *Late for you, too.*
> AsheMacD: *I'll be getting up soon.*
> AsheMacD: *Have you heard from Earl?*
> missymom: *Not lately. I give up.*
> AsheMacD: *?*
> missymom: *I don't like the way I'm sounding, and if I don't like it, what must Earl think?*
> AsheMacD: *I'll admit I've never been in your situation...*
> missymom: I *wish there were some way...*
> AsheMacD: *What do* you *want?*
> missymom: *I want things back! The way they were.*
> AsheMacD: *You can't go back to what was. You can only forge forward.*
> missymom: *My life is over!*
> AsheMacD: **Don't** *say that! It's never over until you kiss this sweet earth goodbye.*
> AsheMacD: *Believe me, I know. I thought it was over for me once too.*
> missymom: *I'm sorry! I know. It had to be harder for you.*
> AsheMacD: *Grief is what happens when you lose someone. Doesn't matter how it happens; it's still hard. You'll find your way back.*

missymom: *Even me?*
AsheMacD: *Lord, yes. If I can do it, you can too.*

After several hours of hashing and rehashing her story to Ashe, of reliving her mistakes and missing the cues of Earl's unhappiness, Missy paused. Ashe had stopped typing. It was 2 a.m. Pacific time, 5 on the East Coast where Ashe lived. Missy thought she had fallen asleep.

missymom: *Ashe. You there?*
AsheMacD: *Thinking.*
missymom: *Sorry for my verbal diarrhea.*
AsheMacD: *It's okay.*

Missy sat back. The house was quiet and dark except for the glow from the computer screen. Several minutes passed with Missy staring at the screen. She watched the minutes tick by on her desktop's clock.

AsheMacD: *Is there someone else?*
missymom: *I'd never cheat on Earl!*
AsheMacD: *LOL… not you, silly. Do you think Earl found someone else?*

Missy looked at the words and thought hard about them. Admitting she had been replaced by this year's model would be difficult to do, even via IM. Why was it easier to tell Ashe than the others? She shared a long history with the VMs; they all knew Earl. Ashe was new, a clean slate. Missy gathered her courage to type.

missymom: *He said there was someone. I didn't ask him about the particulars.*
AsheMacD: *I don't want to hurt you, but you should think about it now.*
missymom: *I didn't want to believe he could do that to me.*
AsheMacD: *I know. Unfortunately, the best of them have been known to stray.*
AsheMacD: *Do you still love him?*

185

missymom: *YES! OF COURSE!*

AsheMacD: *That's what I thought. That's our starting point.*

***

A Confession

Dear Mac,

I haven't been here in a couple of days. Instead, I've ignored the black and white of my words. I feel embarrassed and ashamed, Mac, and so my absence. If I keep away from that which is deep in my heart, maybe you won't see. You won't know what a terrible person I have become.

I have a confession to make and it won't be easy.

It's this: there are times when I forget about missing you.

At first it was a few minutes out of the day. I would be busy dressing Tyler, getting his breakfast, running him to the dentist or making a pit stop at the store and I would suddenly realize I hadn't thought of you at all. Then it would be a few hours, usually while I was working.

Last weekend, an entire Saturday afternoon went by without a thought of you.

Have I been perpetrating a lie? Were we really that much in love? Did I genuinely miss you as much as my first posts have indicated? Or is it all 'out of sight, out of mind'?

After thirteen years together, I can't believe I could forget you so easily. We promised to love each other forever. Then I think, would you do the same if the roles were reversed?

Friends say it's the natural progression of things. I'm up to acceptance now. It's normal.

If it's so 'normal,' why do I feel so badly?

***

The next thing she knew, it was almost seven.

missymom: *OMG! I have to run, Ashe. Look at the time!*

missymom: *The girls aren't up yet. They need to get ready for school.*

AsheMacD: *No problem. Remember what I told you.*

186

AsheMacD: *Want me to email you with notes?*
missymom: *No thanks. I've got it.*
AsheMacD: *Don't forget the steps you need to take. Fight fire with more fire.*
missymom: ☺

Missy closed the IM box, the smile on her face matching her last comment. Although she hadn't slept in two days, Missy felt calm, composed and energized. The difference between now and then?

Now she had a plan.

First things first. Once the girls were off to school, Missy dialed the familiar number and sat back. A young woman with a distinctly British accent answered, "Matsumora and Martin, how may I direct your call?"

Missy wondered if the receptionist's voice laced in acid and bile belonged to the tart that clawed into her husband. She chased that demon thought from her head. What a mistake it had been to allow Earl his space! She should have taken an interest in his work and visited his office on occasion, instead of letting him go off leash. Missy tamped down her hurt and anger and put on her smoothest business voice. Her assignment: make an appointment with Henry Matsumora. Her long-dusty architectural degree from the University of Indiana had to be worth something to someone. "I would like an appointment with Mr. Matusmora, please."

"May I ask who is calling?" *Young, smart-assed and full of herself*, Missy thought.

"Melissa. Melissa… Crenwinkle." Crenwinkle was her mother's maiden name. The testy receptionist wouldn't know it. Missy doubted Earl knew it. He hardly recalled his own mother's maiden name. She had never met Henry Matsumora and *he* certainly wouldn't know it.

With the appointment on the schedule, Missy had much to do. She had to find documents, make copies, and prepare for her debut. On her way to the bedroom, Missy noticed the kitchen. It was a total disaster, a scene out of hoarder reality TV. Missy hadn't cooked or cleaned in days, preferring instead to eat take out and fast food. Wrappers, pizza boxes, super-sized cups and straws were everywhere. The girls were too happy to be off a strict

187

balanced diet to complain. Missy grabbed a garbage bag and tossed everything in. She set the dishwasher and mopped down the counter. *What was I thinking? He'd never come back if he saw this!*

She next treated herself to a long soak in the tub and dressed in her best business attire, a simple wool suit and matching black pumps. As she looked in the mirror, Missy saw herself, impeccably dressed yet disgustingly frumpy – almost *old*. Where had the runner-up to Miss Indiana gone? Missy peeled off the suit. Under the black blazer, she decided to wear a form fitting, red dress, a hot number she bought for a Christmas party in 1990. It was simple, not too low cut, yet left plenty to the imagination, and the firehouse color played off the staid black jacket to perfection. She kicked off the sensible pumps and excavated a pair of sky-high stilettos that hadn't seen the light of day since she was pregnant with Kara. "Not bad," she said out loud as she surveyed the new Missy. "Not bad at all."

Chapter Nineteen

Wednesday, November 18
Minneapolis, Minnesota

Greg returned the milk back to the refrigerator and brought the last of the dirty bowls to Ally. He nuzzled close to her and buried his head in her long hair. Large hands gripped her from behind. They traveled from her waistline to her breasts, cupping them over her robe. Ally took the dishes and submerged them into warm sudsy water before twisting away. "Hon, Vanessa's in the next room," she whispered.

"That's okay, I'm watching cartoons," Vanessa called from the family room.

"That one has the ears of a hawk," Ally said. "*And* she can see us."

"Snow days make me horny," Greg whispered. An early winter blizzard had deposited eighteen inches of the white stuff over most of Minnesota. It was still coming down. Weathercasters had predicted a mere ten to fifteen inches. They erred on the low side. Not only did Vanessa get a day off from school, Greg's plant called and told him to stay put.

Ally surveyed the winter wonderland from her kitchen window. "Snow days worry me. I hope Mike didn't have to go out in this. Or Mike Junior. Not until they get the snowplows out, anyway."

"They'll be fine." Greg's hands were at her waist again, and he swayed back and forth. "We men know what to do in a blizzard. Grrr-OWL!" Greg pecked at her neck.

Ally took a clean spatula and waved it at her husband, causing a spray. "And women *don't?* I'm the one who was born and raised here, Mr. Big Stuff."

"Truce, truce!" Greg waved a white dishcloth in defeat.

"Look at you, screaming like a little girl." Ally chased him around the counter. Vanessa turned her attention to her parents. She squealed with glee. Greg let Ally catch him. Ally allowed her hand to slip from her hip. "Fine. I'm too old to chase you down."

"Honey, you're not too old for anything." Greg grinned.

"Ow. Oh." Ally doubled over and grasped her left side.

"What's wrong, Babe?" Greg worried. He pulled her up.

Ally waved him off. "It's nothing. A twinge. I'm a little dizzy."

"You sure?"

Ally nodded and straightened up. "See? Perfect." She pirouetted in front of him.

"Okay, if you're sure. Hey, I was thinking of taking Vanessa out for a romp in the snow. Want to come with?"

"No thanks. I don't feel up to it. I think I'll take the opportunity of an empty house to check up on the Girls. Seems like everyone's suffering a crisis these days. It makes me feel guilty for leading such a charmed life. I've been too wrapped up with Vanessa to keep up with the VMs." The great thing about being in Virtual Moms was the easy camaraderie. If Real Life proved too much for a member, she could slip off into the shadows until the crisis was over. Sometimes the absence could be measured in days or weeks; sometimes it could extend into months. The wayward VM always came back. Ally could pop in and out as easily as if they all lived on the same block.

"What's up? Does Janna have too many choices for potential suitors?"

Ally gave Greg the Cliff Notes version of the current Mama Drama. "Janna's great. She's narrowed it down to one guy. This week, anyway. You know how long that's going to last. Her standards are so high I'm surprised anyone can survive the first date. I'm so worried about Missy and her girls. She hasn't told them about the separation and Earl is being a butthead. And Laurel, she's in Florida with her dad in the cardiac unit. What a scare. Celia, of course, is the same Iron Maiden we all know and love. And Ashe and Skye..." Ally let her voice fade away. "No hook up there."

"Sounds like the same old same old to me," Greg laughed.

"Greg, honey, they're my best friends." It no longer seemed strange to refer to the VMs as her best friends, despite the fact she had not met Ashe, Celia, or Missy. Her concern for them was valid. She wished they all lived closer.

190

"Mine too. I love your Moms." It was true. Greg loved everything about them. "I'll get the munchkin ready for sledding in the park."

"You won't drive?"

"No. It's close enough to walk. Besides, Vanessa and I have to burn off our breakfast." He leaned in and whispered. "And maybe I'll get her so tired she'll take a nap this afternoon. And then…" Greg gave Ally's rear end a little tap, "when the cat's asleep the mice can party hearty."

***

Ally's email box was jammed with incoming messages. The VMs were concerned about the onslaught of winter weather. Celia and Skye wanted to know if a snow day was called – both Kimber and Rob would jealous. Schools in Florida would close for hurricanes and in California maybe for the occasional earthquake, otherwise it was a straight shot of 180 school days with hardly a wrinkle in the schedule. Janna fretted over the enormous weather pattern that was leaving the Twin Cities and heading her way. "I hope it poops out before it gets here," she wrote. "The girls are coming home this weekend in advance of Thanksgiving. I don't need them driving off the road trying to get here."

Laurel checked in from Florida, using Celia's laptop. "Celia's such a good friend," she wrote, "she's right here in the waiting room with me. And Kimber's been the sweetest. I saw her for a bit. She went back to Sarasota. She wants to keep up with her schoolwork. Dad is doing better. Girls, he gave me such a scare! He looked so pale and weak when I saw him. The doctor is going to put stents into some of his arteries tomorrow. I think after a few days' rest, they'll release him. They're very hopeful. Oh, and thanks to all of you for the flowers you sent. They are beautiful!" The VMs got together to pitch in for a handsome bouquet for Laurel's dad, with enough left over for a restaurant gift certificate for Laurel.

As Ally read her mail, she realized that both Ashe and Missy were absent from the replies. Over fifty messages sent back and forth in the past twenty-four hours and neither one had a word to say? *Very strange.* Maybe the kids were sick again. Not only did the moms have the regular flu to worry about, they also had the H1N1 swine flu to worry about. "I should call Missy later," Ally

191

said to herself. The last email she'd received from Missy sounded depressed and negative, not like the Missy she knew. Ally fretted over her, wondering if she was eating right and if the girls were okay.

Ally glanced outside and watched the snow as it piled up against the birdfeeder in the back yard. "Ashe? Yes, I should call her, too."

Ally scrolled through her address list and found Ashe's address and phone number. "Ashe MacDaniel. Bonnie Doone, North Carolina." What a charming name for a town! Why hadn't Ally called her before? *How rude of me! My life's not that busy.* Ashe had been a VM for almost three weeks. She'd sent a present, an adorable crystal angel to put on their Christmas tree. Ally hadn't had time for a proper introduction or a gracious thank you. She could always blame her neglect on Real Life. "Nope, not using that old excuse." She punched in Ashe's number. "Now is as good a time as any."

The phone rang once, twice, and a third time before someone answered. "Hel-lo?" It was a child's voice and a sweet one at that, tentative with a hint of a Southern drawl. Ally guessed it might be Tyler, although what he was doing home in the middle of a school day was a mystery. She doubted the schools would call a snow day due to a blizzard in North Carolina, though stranger things have happened. She computed the time change difference in her head and decided it was possible Tyler could be home from school in mid-afternoon.

"Hi, honey. May I speak to your mother?"

She heard a gasp and the sound of crashing, most likely the phone as it hit the floor. A dog howled in the background, a low moaning more than a bark. Ally strained to hear more. "Daddy, Daddy!" The little boy cried.

After two minutes of the commotion of the child screaming and doors slamming, Ally heard a few seconds of silence before someone picked up the phone. "Hello?" It was a male voice, forceful and mature, yet as sweet as the child's. Ally was perplexed. She'd expected something along the lines of Scarlett O'Hara. Who could it be?

"Hello? May I speak to Ashe MacDaniel?"

"May I ask who's calling?"

192

"It's Allyson Smith, a friend of hers. One of the Virtual Moms. I'm from Minneapolis. I don't know if Ashe told you... I'm sorry, I didn't get your name." Ally wondered if she had misdialed the number. Perhaps this was a total stranger's house. If it were she would be beyond embarrassed.

"I'm...the sitter." The voice was low, a whispery growl. Ally detected an odd quality in the voice. Anger? Fear? "Ashe isn't here now. May I take a message?"

"No thanks. I'll call back later." Ally clicked the phone off and stared out of the window again.

Wait a minute. Sitter?

Hold the phone.

Daddy?

***

Ally absent-mindedly stirred a pot of hot chocolate. The phone rang. "Damn," she said as she wiped her hands on a dishtowel. "Greg, can you get that?" While it was late, she was expecting a return call from Ashe.

Greg appeared at the doorway. "It's for you, Al."

"Is it Ashe?"

"Nope. It's Celia. Hey, let me grab that for you." Greg took the wooden spoon and kept stirring while Ally took the receiver.

"Okay, only five mini-marshmallows for Vanessa, okay? I want her to go to sleep tonight. I'm sure she'll have school tomorrow."

Greg gave her a military salute. "Will do, captain."

Ally took the cordless phone into the formal living area. Why they didn't fill the space with something other than couches – like a pool table or a hot tub – was beyond her. She couldn't get anyone to *live* in the living room. In their house, people gravitated toward the kitchen or attached family room. She joked if entertainment were a focus of the room, people might use it. She sank into a seldom-used chair. "Celia, what's up?"

"Hi, Ally. I'm calling because... well, I noticed in your last email that you said you tried to call Ashe." Celia sounded breathless and excited.

"Yes. I didn't connect with her. I'm still waiting for her call."

"Did the answering machine come on?"

193

"No, it didn't."

"Did Ashe answer the phone?"

"I think little Tyler answered the phone. Celia, he's got the cutest little voice. Reminded me of Mike Junior's before he went to school and matured into a seven-year-old. Tyler must be a fragile kid, what with losing his dad. I think I scared him. He ran away crying." Ally omitted what she believed was Tyler's cry of "Daddy" – no need to stir up gossip or give Celia an excuse to pry into the newbie's life.

"Did you hang up after that?"

"Actually, no. Someone else picked up the phone. Said he was the sitter."

"Oh."

"Why, Celia? What's up?"

"Don't you think it's odd? A male sitter for a little boy?"

"It's not that unusual. Mike Junior used to babysit."

"He was a teenager at the time, not a grown man." Ally detected a noticeable sneer in Celia's voice.

"Celia, what are you getting at?"

"Nothing. At least I don't think it's anything. Maybe I'm paranoid. I don't know."

Ally was confused. "So?"

"I'll keep you posted. I promise."

***

"What? No late night rendezvous with the VMs? No reading frenzy with the latest romance novel? I can't believe you're sacked out already. Is something wrong, honey?"

Ally stirred, drawing the fluffy soft flannel sheet under her chin. "Huh?"

Greg sat on the edge of the bed and stroked Ally's hip. "You must be beat, having both me and Vanessa to keep up with all day. It's not 8:30 and you're already asleep? You don't know how unappealing that can make a guy feel."

Ally struggled to sit up. "It's not because you're a slouch."

Greg grinned. "I'm trying, Hon, I'm trying."

"I'm sorry. I don't know where my energy has gone the last couple of days. I'm so sluggish and sleepy. Maybe I'm coming down with something." She reached out and grabbed a love handle before settling into bed. "Can I get a rain check, my darling stud muffin?"

Greg pulled off his shirt revealing a taut chest. What a pleasant sight to doze off to. "Done, my love. It had better be an extra special romp."

Ally smiled. "So worth the wait."

Chapter Twenty

Thursday, November 19
Lower East Side, Manhattan

Janna yawned and turned over, her hand hitting the backside of a massive mountain of manhood. "Mmm…" she purred, and slipped her fingers down the warm slope of hip. The hand traveled from back to front, tracing a rolling trail over exquisitely scented skin. It was smooth, save a forest of prickly hair right where expected. Her journey ended at the waist. She snuggled close to the sleeping form, her lips brushing Juan's shoulder blades. "Wake up, baby. I want some more of this." Janna reached downward and gently moved the body toward her.
  She recoiled in shock.
  Her bedmate wasn't Juan. It was a woman.
  It was Ashe.

***

Janna woke with a start, soaked in sweat and gasping for air. "What the hell?" She pounded the bed around her. Empty. "I have to stop eating Thai food before bedtime," she said out loud. Pad Prik Gow was a five-alarm gastronomical thrill ride, plenty of crisp veggies, noodles, peppers, and a sauce to die for. For her fearless venture into the tasty dish, she would have to pay for walking the high-wire of culinary exploration. The price included stomach cramps and restless sleep. A burp bubbled up; she let it escape with a blast as she slipped back onto downy pillows. Janna couldn't fall asleep. No way would she could surrender into unconsciousness and be subjected to the possibility of *that* dream.
  It wasn't the first time she'd dreamed of Ashe.
  At first, the dreams were innocent. Most focused on meeting Tyler and she used what she knew of his features to imagine what Ashe might look like. It was only in the last month where the dreams took her to meetings with Ashe. They had progressed from casual conversations in the park to this. She and Ashe… in *bed*? A most disturbing thought. Although she knew her share of homosexuals and was intrigued by her lesbian friends, Janna was most decidedly straight. She wouldn't deny that she and

196

Ashe shared a special friendship, perhaps the deepest and most complete of any of the other Virtual Moms.

Janna recalled the last twenty-four hours. Her mid-week date with Juan Bernstein a few hours before had been magical. He arrived on time, rang her doorbell, limo waiting at the curb. Promptness was one of the top ten virtues Janna looked for in a potential mate. She opened the door to the sight of her hunky date impeccably dressed with single red rose in hand. Dreamboat looks and a sense of style were also requirements, and roses are a plus. That put three solid marks in Juan's column.

Their date began at a charity benefit at a chic gallery in lower Manhattan. All proceeds were intended for a struggling arts school. A sense of civic duty was admirable. *Numero Quatro*. Juan introduced her to artists and real estate moguls amidst bottles of fine French bubbly, towering trays of imported cheese and golf-ball sized hydroponic strawberries. A decent social standing was a necessity, and that rounded out number five. Juan was suave and smooth, and the best part was that he knew to give her the right amount of attention. Knowing when *not* to smother was a gift – number six. He drifted away when she was deep in conversation with the famous painter, Noel Masters, and was at her side when she felt lost and needed him as an anchor. Knowing when she needed rescue was number seven.

After the benefit, they headed for a late-night dinner at the microscopic Peep Pad Thai, a tiny hideaway tucked away in a corner of the Village. They laughed and talked for hours, eventually shooed out the door way by the annoyed owner. It was way past closing time and even with the language barrier, Janna could tell he wanted to lock up. On the way back to her apartment, Janna and Juan canoodled in the back seat of his limo. Kissing Juan was the ultimate nirvana. He smelled heavenly, deep, sweet musk and manly leather, and the kisses were expert, warm yet not sloppy. He used his hands with confidence, yet he was gentle, loving, and respectful. Janna could have easily flung her inhibitions and caution overboard, he was that lovely. Limo sex was the best car sex of all. Instead, she applied the brakes. She'd only known him a week and she wasn't ready. Not yet. Juan backed up, not angry or insulted, yet somewhat amused. Sex would happen; it would have to be in the right place at the right time.

"Eight, nine and ten," Janna counted off. Unusual Boho restaurant serving great food, world class kisser, and respects a girl for saying 'not yet.' No doubt about it. Juan was the perfect man.

The first thing Janna did when she returned to the apartment was email the VMs to report back on her outing. The last week was like living on a cloud where she and her Dream Date ruled over the masses. She was a goddess and Juan was her Greek – well, Puerto Rican and Jewish – god. "Keep your fingers crossed, girls," she wrote. "This one could be *the* one!"

Before she had a chance to log off, she noticed a personal message from Ashe in her inbox.

To: jannasbananas
From: AsheMacD
Subject: RE: Perfect Adam
Janna, I hope you take what I'm going to say as a friend and nothing more. I know you're over the moon about Juan. What do you know anything about this guy? He sounds like a slick operator to me and he's moving way too fast. Remember your last boyfriend a few months ago? The one you said was the 'forever' guy? Remember how he threw you over for a younger woman? I believe she was a young model. You were so heartbroken, you cried over him for a week.
I don't want to see you hurt that's all.
Virtually yours,
Ashe

Janna's brows furrowed with annoyance. Yes, she remembered Bert, Bart, Bob or whatever his name was. True, she had fallen head over heels in love with the loser. How dare Ashe cast doubt on über-consummate Juan? Ashe's words glared at her from the monitor, the letters an obvious stabbing attempt at her dream balloon, a fervent effort to deflate her stunner of a find. Perhaps Ashe was jealous. Ashe was alone; Janna was not. Ashe had no prospects; Janna had a world of them. Ashe was stuck in dumpy, backwoods North Carolina; Janna was living the high life in glamorous NYC. Ashe's negativity was a new and unforeseen wrinkle in their relationship. Maybe Celia was right in sounding alarm bells over the newbie. What did any of them know about Ashe MacDaniel?

Janna's response to Ashe was complete in four words: "You sound like Celia." She thought of meaner, choicer words before deciding against starting VM War II. Janna turned off her computer and went to bed.

"No wonder I was dreaming of Juan and Ashe," she muttered as she slipped out of bed. "I've got both my boyfriend *and* my BFF on the brain."

***

Rudimentary Metals, a class Janna had volunteered to teach at the local alternative school, was wrapping to a close when her phone rang. The class was her offbeat contribution to bringing art into the world. Each Thursday she traveled downtown to work with disadvantaged teenagers. Most hadn't received any exposure to the fine arts. Sometimes they worked in 'studio' while other times Janna would take them on field trips to galleries and museums.

Today's class must have forgotten to take their Ritalin. They were bouncing off the walls and the listening quotient was nil. Janna glanced at her phone and hoped it was Juan. "Put your supplies away," she sang out.

"That's cool, Ms. Abraham," answered one thin boy. She couldn't remember his name. He was quiet, respectful, and hung on her every word – a keeper. He began gathering pliers and files as the rest of his class fled.

"Yell-o," she answered.

"Janna, Laurel here. I wanted to thank you for the flowers you sent. My dad loves them!"

"I'm so glad! How is he doing, Doll?"

"Better. They'll release him in a few days. Scared the crap out of me for a while. I'm so relieved he's getting better."

"Did you read my email from last night?" Except for Ashe, not one response came from any of the VMs regarding her momentous dream date with Juan. Janna made it a point to linger in the apartment until the very last minute before taking off for school for the express purpose of bathing in her radiant glory, for nothing. She scanned her Blackberry every thirty seconds for the thumbs' up response. The spontaneous absence of five females

199

exclaiming their mass approval both baffled and annoyed her. Janna knew how Ashe felt. She needed confirmation, damn it. Unless… unless they all had reservations like Ashe? *No, couldn't be.* All six of them couldn't be wrong.

"Sorry, I didn't get a chance. In my rush to get here, I forgot my laptop. My dad is severely computer challenged. If he had one, it would end up an expensive paperweight. I can't get online from the hospital. Why? Anything juicy happen?"

Janna sighed. "Only the most exquisite date sent from heaven, that's all. But it can wait." Laurel had an excuse. *Her* father was on his deathbed after all. This didn't explain the inaction of the other four. Where was her rousing rendition of the *Hallelujah Chorus* when she needed it? What were they waiting for? Christmas? Hanukkah?

"I don't want to bother you. I know it's your class day. I wanted to let you know how Dad was doing and that he got the flowers. The arrangement is so beautiful. It brightens up his room. Can you let the others know?"

"Sure. I'll be your human telegraph, your connection to the VMs." Janna hoped she hadn't sounded bitchy. She hadn't meant to.

"Thanks, Janna. *You're* the doll."

Oh, sure.

***

Juggling three paper bags, her art supply tote, and her purse, Janna departed the elevator and promptly dropped everything. One of the grocery bags broke. An orange rolled down the hall, coming to rest against an urn holding a large, silk ficus tree. "My luck," she muttered.

Her day had started out with a hot, sweaty and completely uncalled for girl dream, her class had been unusually demanding, and the applause from the VMs over the Juan catch was decidedly lacking.

Seconds before, she'd paid for and was collecting her purchases from the checkout lane at the market. She'd spent a fortune on groceries expecting to prepare a gourmet dinner for her new beau, when his text appeared begging off. Something about a late showing in Brooklyn, tricky commercial property, multi-million dollar deal, blah, blah, blah.

200

"Come later anyway," she texted back, "We'll have a late dinner."

He responded, "Can't. Call you tomorrow."

She blinked at the screen, her exasperation growing exponentially. "Call me tomorrow? What the hell does that mean?" she complained out loud. All persons within earshot perked up at her outburst. Her terse tone garnered attention from everyone in the line.

Now she was stuck with a choice piece of expensive ahi tuna too big for one. It would likely not survive twenty-four hours until tomorrow's dinnertime, and Janna only felt like sushi for breakfast in Tokyo. Oh, well. She would chase after her fruit and wallow in *both* the pre-made baby crème brulees she had snagged as their intended dessert. *Juan's the big loser here,* she told herself as she corralled the errant citrus.

She'd finished putting her groceries away when her phone rang. "Yell-O!" she panted as she shoved a bag of sushi rice into a high cabinet.

"Janna, it's Skye."

"Girlfriend, what's up?"

"I got your email and I had to call to say... way to go, girl!" Skye giggled.

"Don't break out the Dom Perignon yet. He blew me off tonight."

"He *what*?"

"Told me to take a hike." Janna unwrapped her dessert. She stuck her index finger through the caramel crust deep, licked the creamy custard off her finger, and attacked the other with gusto. The gorged cups looked as though they suffered a stabbing, but they *were* most delicious victims.

"He did not. Why would he do such a thing when you had such a great time last night?"

"Work. Showing a listing. So he says." Oskar made an appearance, his back hugging the refrigerator. Janna rolled the orange toward him and he sidestepped it.

"Don't be down. Maybe he really *is* showing some property. A man's got to work, and he's in real estate. Look at Joe. That's a brutal gig, especially these days."

201

"Yeah, I know. I'm being a baby. I was hoping to bask in some Juan loving, you know."

"You don't think he's lying, do you?"

"It's a possibility, isn't it? According to Ashe, I don't know everything about him." Janna spat the words out. As much as she loathed admitting it, Ashe's words stung.

"Oh, Ashe. Who knows anything about everything? We're all stupidly flawed, if you ask me."

"I guess." Janna fidgeted. "Hey, can I ask you a personal question?"

"Sure. Shoot."

"Do you know of any straight women who have dreams about women?"

Janna heard Skye's transcontinental choking. "Whoa. Where the hell did that come from?"

"Nowhere," Janna lied, "I'm curious."

"Why? A friend of yours? It's not Mandy or Rachel, is it?"

"Just a friend of a friend." If there were ever a reason to be glad videophones weren't common, now would be the time. Janna could see by her reflection in her stainless steel refrigerator that she was beet red. "I mean, how'd the whole Trina thing happen for you?"

"You know how it happened for me. I didn't dream about her in advance, if that's what you mean. I don't know how you approach people. My relationships are seldom about the sex. It's about the connection between two souls. To me, Trina was more than a sex object. I loved her totally and the physical part came later. Much later, as I recall."

"Was it weird?"

"No, seemed natural at the time. Hey, what's with the twenty questions?"

"I'm wondering. I was afraid you would say that about your relationship."

"Say what?"

"The connection thing. That's what I'm most afraid of."

Chapter Twenty-one

Friday, November 20
Orlando Regional Hospital

The first thing Laurel saw when she exited the elevator was her father toddling down the hall, supported by a nurse on one side and an IV pole on the other. "Dad!" she cried, "Should you be up and walking around so soon?"

"I couldn't stand to lie in that bed a minute longer." The minute Sam Johnson woke up in the cardiac unit, he strained to get mobile. Five days confined to a hospital bed and his cabin fever burned red hot. Moving from the room to the hallway meant he was one step closer to putting the hospital in the rearview mirror.

"Your father's doing fine, Mrs. Exton. He's hell bent on going home, but he has to be ambulatory before that happens." Although all of the staff had been helpful and kind, Cindy was the best. She was short and stocky, with a pie-shaped face and twinkling eyes. She was knowledgeable, genuinely compassionate, and kind. Cindy took special interest in Laurel's father, possibly because they shared the same wry humor.

"I'm ready to run a race." Mr. Johnson smiled broadly and released his grasp on Cindy's arm to beat at his chest. "They cleaned out the plumbing and now I'm feeling like a million bucks and ready to go!"

"Don't beat on your scar, Dad. You should take it easy. One day at a time." Laurel chewed on her lip. Her father was the only parent she had. If she had anything to say about it, he would live a very long time.

"They say I can go home tomorrow."

"If the doctor gives the okay," Cindy interrupted, "and it looks like it's a go. Mrs. Exton, your father has made a remarkable recovery. As long as he keeps his diet clean and starts to exercise a little every day, he should do fine. We may never have to see his sour puss in these halls again." She patted his back. Laurel could tell Cindy was joking.

"All I know is I have to get out of here. Simon misses me." Simon was Sam Johnson's pet dachshund, old, fat, and blind in one eye.

"Dad, Simon's fine. He needed a vacation from your spoiling." Laurel had been staying at her father's apartment and used his truck to get around. It made sense. She couldn't afford a motel room or a rental car.

"If you guys are going to be a while, I'm going to call home." Laurel glanced at the clock above the nurses' station. Marcus was at school. She wanted to catch Joe before he left to do God-only-knows-what. It was certain he wouldn't be at the office working.

"Sure. We'll get him back in his room and you two can have a nice visit."

"Ah, come on. One more lap around the ward?" Mr. Johnson turned on the charm. "You told me I need all the exercise I can get."

"Don't overdo," Laurel warned. It felt strange; their roles reversed.

Cindy laughed as she patted Laurel's arm. "Don't worry. I'll keep Tiger on a short leash."

Laurel took the elevator up to the top floor, where the hospital had installed a rooftop garden. Part of it was surrounded in glass, like a greenhouse. The rest was landscaped with paths and trees. Potted flowers, grasses, and plenty of benches lined the walkway. It was a serene, peaceful place.

She found a vacant corner, took her cell phone out, and dialed her home number. Several rings later, the voicemail came on. Where was Joe? "Hi, Marcus. It's your mom. Grandpa is doing better. He may come home tomorrow. Call me when you get home from school, okay? Love you."

Laurel had directed her message to her son. She couldn't say a thing to her husband. Who was she kidding? It had been that way for quite some time. She used to want to know everything about Joe, until he mistook her concern for nagging. It reached a point where she was afraid to open her mouth. Laurel shook her head. Her marriage was teetering; how did it get that way? Once she thought Joe as an unrivaled complement to her many character quirks. He was her foil to the dry humor she'd inherited from her father. All that seemed so far away in the time warp of last week. Her father's heart attack seemed like it happened both yesterday and two years ago.

When they learned of her dad being hospitalized, she thought Joe was amazingly supportive, until she realized Joe's relationship to her father was closer than the one she'd had with either. Her dad regarded Joe as the son he never had. The respect was mutual. Joe wouldn't make the trip to Florida. There was no credit left on the MasterCard to buy a pack of gum, much less purchase an unexpected plane ticket to Orlando. Joe saved the day, getting the money for her ticket with a quick pawn of a hunting rifle. Laurel protested; hunting and fishing were his favorite pastimes.

Joe was adamant. "You've got to get to Florida, and soon. You'd never forgive yourself if you don't go and God forbid something happens."

He was right.

When she first saw her father, she was frightened by the severity of his illness. Thank goodness she had Celia at her side for moral support. Celia had collected her from the airport and drove straight to the hospital. Hooked up to tubes and machines, Laurel's dad was a ghostly shade of gray. His skin was so transparent she could see the blood pulsing through spidery veins. Her father aged fifteen years since she last saw him.

That first visit was a haunting look into the future. Someday her dad would be gone and then what would she have left? Her son? Her work? The Virtual Moms? Her husband? With all the drama, the fights, and the hurt feelings, it seemed unlikely she and Joe would last beyond the end of the year. Their marriage had started out with such high hopes, too. She could see herself growing old with him. Laurel's parents had celebrated twenty years together when her mom died of breast cancer. Two decades was a long time, and her parents made it seem so easy. As for Joe… he made so much of the last fourteen years difficult. *Very* difficult.

Something nagged at the back of her mind. Where was Joe?

Laurel had been in Florida since Monday. She hadn't spoken to either Marcus or Joe since Wednesday; instead they played phone tag for two and a half days. As much as she loved her father with all her heart, Laurel felt a pang of homesickness. She was a devoted daughter and loved Florida yet she missed her son. She missed her hectic schedule and her upside down life. She missed the annoying and familiar rhythms of her husband, as lackadaisical as he was.

Laurel felt a tear rise and she brushed it away. She'd cried way too much in the last week – heck, in the last year. She needed to go downstairs and tend to her dad. Later she would have all the time in the world to feel sorry for herself.

***

Laurel took a deserted stairway down to the fifth floor. Walking gave her a chance to compose herself. Heaven forbid if anyone should see her start crying again. Crying was a constant pastime *du jour* and she was sick of it. Life wasn't always this difficult. Somewhere in her past, she had laughed, although these days she could hardly recall a memory of it.

Laurel wished she had inherited the stoic and strong nature of her father or could shake off worries and approach life happy and positive like Joe. Once on the cardiac floor, Laurel took her time on her way to her father's room, taking notice of the patients, accompanied bedside by concerned relatives. It was an easy task to separate the ones who'd heard good news from the ones who were marking time until the very end. Laurel felt a sudden urge to take her dad away from this place of both hope and death. He was getting the best of care, although she understood why he disliked it so.

The door to Room 531 was closed. Perhaps the doctor was examining him. Laurel hesitated for a moment before she tapped at the door. "Dad? Can I come in?"

The door opened with a doctor's hand firmly on the doorknob. He led her into the hallway. "Mrs. Exton. Good news. Your father can go home tomorrow."

Laurel felt the tight band around her own heart loosening. "Dr. Thomas, are you sure? He's going to be all right?"

"He's weak. That's to be expected. The stents are doing the job. He'll have to change his diet, quit smoking, and exercise. I think he's ready. He's had quite a scare."

Laurel exhaled, releasing a flood of emotion. "We all have. Thank you so much, Doctor. You don't know what a relief it is…"

"You're welcome. I think I do know. Go on, now." Smiling, he grasped the door and gave it a shove. "Have a nice visit."

Laurel pushed the door open the rest of the way. She blinked once, then again to be sure. Her eyes were not playing tricks on her.

It was her turn to have heart failure.

To her surprise, both Marcus and Joe were sitting in her father's hospital room, and all three were grinning.

***

Skye stood before the array of fruits and vegetables displayed on the sidewalk in front of the China Market. Some was familiar – oranges, strawberries, onions, and mushrooms – while other items looked exotic. The sight of wild tubers, greens she had never seen before, fruits in odd shapes and sizes confounded her. She clutched an ingredient list in her hand and wondered if she would be better served at Safeway, in the safety of brightly lit aisles lined with cans and boxes. As shoppers hurried past her on their way to somewhere else, others inspected the produce. One woman thumped on cantaloupes for five full minutes until she located the perfect one far at the bottom of the bin. Skye could only wish she knew what to look for when it came to choosing fresh food. She shook her head, regretting that she should have paid more attention to Trina during the three years her girlfriend was in her kitchen cooking.

"It's not going to bite you."

Skye jumped. She had not seen Dude approach. Under a black beret, his hair was pulled back, and he wore a corduroy jacket, and blue jeans. He clutched a walking stick fashioned from driftwood. "You scared me!" she exclaimed, her face flushed.

"It's only food. It's not going to hurt you." Dude said, smiling.

"I know. It's a little intimidating. No, it's more than that. It's scary. I told you, I'm not much of a cook."

"Here to shop?"

Skye shook her head. "Actually, I'm here to dream."

"Oh?"

"Someday I might get up enough nerve to buy something here. Once I know what to do with it, that is." Skye smiled shyly.

"When you're ready, this is the right place. Great selection, reasonably priced." He picked up something that looked like it was part of a cow's diet and sniffed it. Skye looked at him quizzically. "Lemon grass. Used in Asian cuisine. Want some?" Dude extended it toward Skye.

She shook her head. "I'm not ready for the advanced class yet. I think I'll start with something simple."

"Why try? You're in a city full of restaurants." Dude's bemused look told her he was laughing at her.

"I don't know why. Maybe because it's the adult thing to do?" Skye blushed. "I'm learning with a friend. Someone who's as pitiful in the kitchen as I am, if you can believe that. A mutual friend of ours gave us what she thinks is an easy recipe, and our assignment is to follow it and see what happens."

Dude took the ingredient list and smiled. "Now this *is* basic, isn't it?"

Skye nodded.

"All of these items are right here. And cheap." He pushed her toward the door. "Go on. You'll do fine." He studied her panicked face, pulled out a pen, and began to scribble. "I don't normally do this. Here's my number, in case you get hung up. Don't call unless you're in trouble."

Skye took the slip of paper. Before she could thank him, he had disappeared into the crowd.

***

This had been a good visit – no, a *great* visit – with her dad. With Nurse Cindy popping in on occasion to monitor her patient, the four of them relived past family get-togethers, Christmases, Marcus's birth, and his tempestuous toddler years. Jovial Joe was in his element, regaling all of them with long-forgotten side stories. Marcus hung on his grandfather's every word. Laurel sat back. She noticed a rosy glow return to her father's face. He was going to be all right after all.

"What do you say we pick up a bag of burgers? Or a pizza?" Joe suggested on the way to the parking lot.

"Burgers!" Marcus excitedly answered.

"Joe, I don't think so." Laurel mentally computed how many dollars she had left. A casual fast food meal had to be carefully plotted into the budget.

"Don't worry. I've got it covered," Joe responded.

"One thing. How did you two get here so fast?" Laurel asked as she took the freeway entrance headed toward her father's apartment. Joe and Marcus were squashed in the front seat next to her. The tiny foreign pick-up left little room to breathe.

Joe smiled. "Let's just say you have an amazing group of friends."

"The Virtual Moms?" Laurel veered into the rough shoulder before regaining control of the truck and coming back to pavement.

"Celia called the house Monday after she picked you up from the airport. She said your dad was in rough shape and you were in worse. I explained the situation to Marcus. He really wanted to see his grandpa." Laurel glanced over to see her son smiling as he looked out the window. "I thought we might drive down. My car is in the shop. Catalytic converter went out, that's another story. And yours is, how can I put this kindly? It's a hunk of junk. I couldn't chance the minivan breaking down on the way here. She must have called or emailed everyone. It took a couple of days. Finally, we got the tickets to get down here and back, with a little left over for incidentals. What a great group of friends."

"Why, those little…" Laurel was amazed at the gesture and thankful, yet she was pinged by a twinge of embarrassment. "God, Joe. How are we ever going to pay them back?"

"The tickets came without strings, Laurel."

"I know, I feel so… awful." Laurel felt tears welling in her eyes. She blinked hard to stop them, but only succeeded in blinding her vision with a wave of blubbering. She pulled over to the freeway shoulder as quickly as she could and opened the door. Nauseous and gasping for air, she ran to the back of the truck and bent over.

Although traffic whizzed dangerously close by, Joe followed Laurel and grabbed her arm. He pulled her to the far edge of the freeway shoulder. "Laurel, what's the matter?"

Laurel collapsed into his arms. "It's too much."

Joe frowned. "What's too much?"

"Everything. I can't take it anymore."

"Honey, your dad is going to be fine. Sure, he'll need a little tending. The doctor said he could outlive all of us."

Laurel blinked back tears. "It's not only my dad, Joe. It's you and Marcus. It's the car, the house, school. My life is an unmitigated disaster."

Joe shook her, concern lining his face. "No, it's not. Don't say that, Laurel. Please don't."

"I give up. I don't have the energy anymore." Laurel's stomach lurched, and she tamped down an urge to vomit.

Joe shook her hard. "Come on, Laurel. You can do it. We can fix this. You being gone this week made me think. About you, me, Marcus. It's the most thinking I've done in years."

"My dad…He has no one to help him and we're so much in the hole. How are we ever going to recover?"

"Laurel, I love you," Joe whispered as he squeezed Laurel tight. Her body shook with sobs. "Please don't. Please don't say that we can't work our way out of this. I need you to believe…"

"You don't understand. Everything's a mess!"

"Let's talk about this later. Let's get back to your dad's house and get some dinner and get Marcus settled in. Because Laurel," Joe raised her head by the chin and looked into her eyes, "I have a plan."

"But…" Laurel gave him a wary look. Who was this Joe? Kind, caring, supposedly with a plan?

As a semi roared by, the driver blew his horn. Joe smiled. "Have faith, Laurel."

***

ally1234: *Ashe! Ashe, are you available?*

AsheMacD: *I only have a minute. Tyler's taking a nap.*

ally1234: *Okay, I won't bother you. I was wondering… Have you heard from Laurel?*

AsheMacD: *Not yet.*

ally1234: *Was wondering her reaction. You know?*☺

AsheMacD: *I hope she'll be pleased!*

ally1234: *You know it! What a great idea you had.*

AsheMacD: *It was Celia's idea.*

ally1234: *Yes, but you're the one who circled the wagons. Good going, Ashe!*

ally1234: *Way to be a Virtual Mom!*

AsheMacD: *I think your props are going to the wrong person…*

ally1234: *I disagree. Thanks for chipping in on Skye's part.*

AsheMacD: *No prob. She's still cash strapped. She can pay me back whenever. Or not.*

ally1234: *I think Janna was right about you.*☺

AsheMacD: *Gotta run. I hear Tyler.*

***

The rest of the ride was spent in a stony silence. After picking up and devouring a sack of burgers, Marcus laid claim to the couch, happily channel surfing until he fell asleep, remote control clutched in his hand. Both Laurel and Joe picked at their food. Joe was strangely quiet, having run out of one-liners and funny stories after his day at the hospital. He left Laurel at the table and retired to the bedroom, wiped out from jet lag and charged emotions.

Laurel sat alone in the kitchen, nursing several cups of tea from scalding hot to ice cold without taking a sip. She tried to catch up on her email. Thank goodness Marcus remembered to bring the laptop. It was her lifeline to the outside world and the Virtual Moms. She needed them now more than ever.

She opened dozens of sympathetic messages from fellow teachers, parents and students, and the VMs. It took two hours to clear her inbox. By the end of it, she was physically and emotionally drained.

Laurel saved an update for the VMs moments before logging off.

To: AsheMacD, jannasbananas, celiasunshine, ally1234, shootingskye, missymom

From: laurelextonsbunch

Girls.

I don't know what to say. You are all angels (dirty, rotten, scheming angels!), and I'm blown away by your generosity. Thank you all so much! You don't know how happy my dad was to see both Joe and Marcus. They needed to see him, too. I don't know how I'll repay you, I promise... I'll make it up to all of you someday.

Dad is fine. We are fine. He's going to be released tomorrow. Joe says to 'have faith.' Maybe things may work out. *Finally*. More later.

Chapter Twenty-two

Saturday, November 21
Bonnie Doone, North Carolina

"This is one Saturday where having an annoying kid brother is going to pay off in spades," Ashe thought. The minutes dragged to Rhett's arrival. Ashe need back up, although the arrival of the cavalry was days late. After Tyler picked up Ally's telephone call Wednesday afternoon, it took monumental efforts to calm him down. Forgetting to turn off the ringer was a horrendous mistake Ashe would not repeat. Neglecting to turn on the answering machine was another. One moment's inattention and Tyler ran for the phone. And why not? An inquisitive child Tyler's age would *want* to answer the phone. Ashe winced at the thought. *Stupid, stupid, stupid!*

"May I speak with your mother?" Six innocent words that set the fragile Tyler into a tailspin. "Where's Mommy? Where's Mommy?" Good Lord, the crying went on for hours and then days, at an intensity that far exceeded what happened after the funeral. Tyler was inconsolable; he couldn't go to school. Rather, he *wouldn't* go, no doubt thinking his brief school time absence would cause the rest of his world to evaporate.

"I'm not going anywhere, Ty," Ashe repeated again and again. Tyler's stricken expression, told Ashe the little boy couldn't believe.

What have I done? Pursuing a relationship with the Virtual Moms? For what – out of loneliness? Tyler's delicate world turned upside-down for Ashe's selfishness?

The hardest part was that Ashe couldn't share this problem with any of the Virtual Moms. Their advice was sorely needed. These were strong, sensible, sagacious women with plenty of sense. With Tyler's heightened anxiety of the past few days, Ashe had little time for work, much less time to come up with a successful ruse as to why the advice was needed in the first place. Friend of a friend, perhaps? Celia's radar would blast off the charts.

Ashe couldn't forget Janna…and Janna's goo-goo-eyed bliss over finding supposed soul mate, Juan Bernstein. It wouldn't be half bad if she gave a dispassionate synopsis, but no, Janna wrote excited rambling emails outlining every minute detail of their date nights. It was painful to read the original posts. Ashe couldn't bear to read the 'Reply All,' where the VMs asked more in-depth questions and received all the gory details in response. Kissing, touching, hands here and there. *Juan Bernstein's hands.* The damned Yankee had money, too, and he was handsome to boot. Flash and cash. Thinking about Juan was enough to make Ashe gag. After reading the first few messages, the rest were deleted unopened. An array of emotion washed over Ashe: panic, worry, jealousy. Love sickness. "No!" Ashe slammed a cup of coffee into the counter. *Keep your head.*

The past few brutal days found Ashe rethinking the decision to join the Virtual Moms. Rhett was right, as usual. Damn the page views and the Google income. Ashe should have been honest with the VMs; if not with the whole group, at least with Janna. Had the truth been told, the last year might have ended differently. At first, the idea of being included in the group was campy and fun, an inside track to the hearts and minds of six beautiful women. Now Ashe was stuck. With the lies gaining, Ashe backed away from communicating with most of them. *Not yet. Not until I can figure out a good way.* Ashe worried about the flip side of the equation – the side that concerning Missy and Laurel. In a very short time, with the possible exception of Celia, all of them had become close friends.

"Dear MacDaniel sib, what are you doing up?" Ashe jumped, his full mug of coffee spilled on the table. Rhett wasn't always loud and flamboyant; he could slink in on cat's paws if he wanted to.

"Rhett. Long night," Ashe replied with an expression of exhaustion.

"Ty isn't sick again is he? Where is my little urchin?" Rhett removed a pea coat and bright orange scarf and threw them on the chair, along with an over-sized man bag. He pointed to the coffee. "I'll have some of that, if you don't mind."

"Help yourself. Tyler's asleep. He was up all night crying. I finally got him to nod off around four. He won't be up for another

214

hour or so." Rhett opened his mouth to inquire; Ashe cut him off. "No, he's not sick. Not physically, anyway. He's been missing Mac the last couple of days. Missing Mac *badly*."

From the cupboard, Rhett picked out a bright yellow happy face mug matching his sunny disposition and poured a generous cup. "That's to be expected, isn't it? It's only been a year. A child so young losing a parent is a sad state of affairs. Especially if he's left with the worse half for the surviving parent." He punched Ashe in the arm.

"You don't understand, Rhett. Something happened. Something not so good." Ashe looked at the floor. Whoever said confession was good for the soul probably meant the end result of absolution and not the painful revelation.

Rhett noticed the somber response. His reply was firm and serious. "Asheley MacDaniel. What have you done now?"

"It wasn't on purpose." Words. Slippery, slimy little boogers. Here was Ashe, a professional wordsmith suddenly lacking a string of coherent syllables, not to mention the right ones. The only way to start was at the beginning. "Last week, I... I forgot to turn the ringer off on the phone. Or maybe Tyler turned it off."

"So?"

"Tyler answered when the phone rang…"

"Yes?"

"It was Ally…"

"Ally?" Rhett's face scrunched up in confusion. "Who is she? Tell me she's a telemarketer or the lady at the gas company? Tell me she's a new neighbor. An old student, perhaps?"

Ashe swallowed hard and whispered. "No. Ally's a Virtual Mom. From Minneapolis."

Rhett spewed coffee across the counter. His words spat forth as quickly. "Virtual Mom? What did I tell you, Asheley Wilkes MacDaniel? What did I say right here in this kitchen…last week? I told you your lying trickery was going to come back to bite you right on the butt." Suddenly aware that Tyler might be in earshot, Rhett dropped his voice to a near-whisper, sat next to Ashe, and grabbed the nearest arm. "Please, Ashe. Please do not tell me my little Ty spoke to one of those women."

"She's a nice woman," Ashe protested. "Absolutely. She has a daughter Tyler's age."

"If she and the rest of them are so damned sainted, what's the problem?" Ashe could see Rhett unable to connect the dots.

"When Tyler answered... She asked Tyler... if she could speak with his *mother*."

"Oh, my God." Rhett's face drained.

"Of course, he reacted badly. He was confused and scared. He thought Mac was alive and coming home. He remembers the funeral. He thought I was going to leave him like his mama did. He cried for *days*, Rhett. He was too upset to go to school. I couldn't very well force him to. He thought if he left for school, he'd have no parent to come home to." Ashe put his head into his hands.

"You didn't call me." Rhett's accusing look brimmed with hurt.

"I couldn't. How could I?"

"You know I would have raced down from Charlotte in a heartbeat if you'd have told me. You know I'd do anything for that little boy."

Ashe gave his brother a hang-dog look that rivaled Jim Bob's most pathetic stare. "I felt so bad. I was humiliated. Embarrassed I could be such a selfish ass. Scared for my little boy. The only thing I could do was give him all my attention so he'd know I'd always be here. I couldn't think to do anything else."

"You've finally come to your senses, Asheley Wilkes MacDaniel," Rhett said. He traced a finger on the rim of the ridiculous happy face mug. "And now?"

Ashe sighed. "I'm not sure what to do. I think he'll be okay by Monday, if we both spend a lot of time with him this weekend."

"Of course, I'll do whatever is necessary to help him. I love the little cub, too, you know." Rhett squeezed Ashe's arm. "You have to promise me, Ashe. You have to come clean to these women. You have to explain who you really are. You have to apologize and leave the group. Ashe? Are you listening to me?"

Ashe ignored Rhett's pleas. His eyes were fixed on a faraway place, somewhere deep inside his heart and soul. If Ashe were to turn a leaf from the dark side to honesty, he might as well start with his brother. "Wait a minute, Rhett."

Rhett got up and crossed his arms. "Good God, no. There's more?"

"You were right. I think I'm in love."

***

Vanessa had constructed a blanket castle between two chairs and a coffee table. From her place on the couch, Ally could hear her chatter, content under cover with a half dozen Barbies and their assorted accessories. She smiled as she overheard Vanessa act out *The Next Runway Model* between the dolls. "Now, Darling, you look like a deer in headlights! Where's the shine? Where's the sparkle? Do you want to *win* this competition, or do you want to go back to your little hick town and work at McDonalds for the rest of your life?"

Ally found it hard to suppress a giggle and concentrate on her long-neglected novel.

The phone rang, and Ally picked up. "Hello?"

"Al, it's me, Janna. You busy?"

"Where have you been? My Juan update is seriously late!" Ally chided.

"Yeah, well…I've had my hands full." Ally could detect a note of mischief in her friend's voice.

"Haven't we all? Have you heard from anyone? It's been all quiet on the VM front the last few days."

"Only Laurel. She's doing so much better. She was so surprised when Joe and Marcus showed up! I hope someone caught it on camera."

"I'm glad. As much negative you can say about Joe, he *does* love her."

"Have you heard from Ashe?"

"A brief IM yesterday. Tyler was home, taking a nap. I think the poor thing is sick again."

"Hmm…" Ally knew Janna was thinking, trying to deduce the Ashe absence.

"I know what you're thinking. It's been a while. She did such a stand-up job getting the money together for Joe and Marcus's plane tickets. Don't take it personally. Skye's busy with work, Laurel's been worried about her father, Celia's been driving back and forth, and Ashe has her hands full, too. Let's not forget

217

our Jewish American Princess, who's been taken with one hunky Juan dude."

"Sha on the Juan dude. He's been fun but he'll never take the place of a Virtual Mom. It's just…I miss that first week Ashe was here. All the email back and forth. It was almost like the good old days, you know?"

Ally smiled. "You know this group ebbs and flows. Once things are settled, we'll go back to entertaining each other."

"Yeah. I hope so."

***

Thank goodness for Rhett and his imagination, Ashe thought, as he found a place to sit. He allowed Rhett to take the lead on this problem. Rhett raced through the house and gathered up several photo albums. He rooted through the slim pickings in the refrigerator, assembling cheese, sausage, grapes, olives, and carrots for an eclectic lunch basket. He rummaged through cabinets, finding crackers and cookies. In a far nook, he dug out a familiar box. "Moon Pies, Ashe? Damn, boy. No wonder your spare tire is overinflated. How old are these?" he muttered. Satisfied with the expiration date, he threw them in the bag. By the time Tyler woke up, Rhett had the car packed and ready to go.

The three headed for the Outer Banks, to the beaches where Mackenzie loved to visit, and spent the afternoon walking the sand. It was a perfect fall day for it – cool breeze, skies bright, and sun shining. Tyler grabbed Ashe's hand and held on with a death grip. Tyler's usual beach activities included running into the water and digging for shells. Today he stayed close. Rhett took his tiny hand and swung him high into the air. His goal was to elicit giggles. The most Tyler gave him was a wan smile.

Ashe viewed Tyler as his little man, a roommate and buddy. Nurturing was something he was uncomfortable with, although after Mac died, Ashe tried to fill in the gaps. The father-son relationship was light, fun, and physical. Ally's call upset the balance. Ashe hated seeing his son depressed.

Tyler was calmer in Rhett's care and always had been. He was far from the boisterous, happy child he could be, but at least this afternoon was a step toward the right direction. Perhaps it was a nurturing touch that Tyler craved – Ashe knew it was the one thing *he* could use. In that area, he was deficient. He would never be able to give Tyler his mother's touch…or his mother.

They enjoyed a late lunch. "Remind me to hit up the Piggly Wiggly before we get home, Bro. You need a refresher in the four food groups and a primer in Organics 101."

Ashe shrugged. "Be my guest."

As Ashe cleared the remains of their meal, Rhett brought the albums out from his bag. He made a great show of arranging them just so on the beach blanket. "Ty-Ty. Come here. Want to see what I have?" He extended the mismatched and worn albums in front of him.

"What is it?" Tyler asked, curious yet cautious.

"Come see," Rhett offered. Tyler approached and sat near his uncle. "I found these in the den. Have you ever seen them before?"

Tyler's eyes grew big and dark. "No. I'm not supposed to go in the den. That's Daddy's office."

"I got a special dispensation to let you see these." He winked at Ashe.

"A dispa-sensation?" Tyler quizzed.

"Yup." Rhett smiled and opened the first one, a worn and yellowing Hallmark bridal album covered in ivory satin and lace. "Do you know what this is?"

Tyler cuddled into Rhett and peered at the cover. "It's a book, right?"

"This, my man, is the story of your mommy and daddy's wedding. See, here is the invitation. Someday you'll get married, so you pay attention."

"Not me, Rhett." Ashe smiled as he deposited debris into a nearby trashcan. It was a smile that masked lingering pain.

"You never know. You might change your mind."

"Can I marry Daddy? Or you? You're pretty."

Rhett laughed out loud. "Why thank you, Mr. MacDaniel, that's the nicest thing anyone has said to me in years. I'm afraid that's problematic. You see, I'm much too old for you, Ty. And someday you might prefer someone like your Mama. Now…let me see. Look here. Here's a photo of your dad when he had long hair! And here. Look at your Mama. What a beautiful mother you had, don't you think?"

Ashe flashed back to the day. Mackenzie, the antebellum princess, stunningly gorgeous in yards of lace and tulle. Ty's tiny fingers traced each image. Rhett moved from the wedding folio to albums with Mackenzie pregnant and beaming, to ones that featured newborn Tyler surrounded by his happy parents.

"Uncle Rhett, these pictures are my Mama, right?"

"Yes."

"Where is my Mama?"

"She's in heaven, darling." Rhett answered quickly.

"Oh." Tyler pulled his legs up and anchored his chin on them, lost in thought. "She can't come back?"

Rhett shook his head sadly. "I'm afraid not, Ty."

"So I'll never see her again?" Tyler asked plaintively. Ashe looked up, reining in an urge to burst into tears.

"Not until we leave this earth."

"So we'll die, too?" Tyler asked the question without fear.

"Now, Ty. Everything dies. You had a hamster that died, didn't you? And every fall the trees lose their leaves and the flowers die down. Someday Jim Bob will grow old and his body will give out someday. It's life, Tyler."

"If you and Daddy die, I'll be alone."

"Nope. We'll always be around to protect you. You'll always have us to hold in your heart."

"So Mama's in here?" Tyler pointed to his chest.

"Forever and always. She's in heaven with your Grandmamma and Grandpapa, and they're in my heart, too."

"I thought she left me because she didn't love me anymore."

Rhett gave him a firm hug and pressed his head into Tyler's. "Oh, no, honey. Your Mama loved you to pieces. She wouldn't leave you if she didn't have to. She went to heaven protecting this country."

"From the bad guys?"

"That's right. You remember, don't you?"

"Yes," Tyler said with conviction.

"It's hard sometimes, because we don't want to forget. As time passes, you might think her memory will fade, but it won't. If you think it will, you ask your daddy to see these photographs. He'll let you. Your mama will always have a special place in our hearts." Rhett took Tyler's small hand and placed it from the boy's chest to his own. "There. Right there."

"I miss my momma." Tyler said the words plainly, without tears. It was a simple fact of life.

"I know, honey. I miss her, too. She was a good friend to me and a special friend for your daddy." He gave Tyler another big hug. Ashe thought he would break down and blubber. Instead, he turned toward the ocean and watched the waves as they crashed to shore.

***

With a long day of driving and the beach behind him, Ashe was exhausted and should have crashed; he had too many things on his mind. After returning home, Rhett and Tyler popped in a *The Sound of Music* DVD. Both ended up asleep before Maria left the convent. Jim Bob took up his position with his head on Tyler's lap. Ashe pulled a throw over all of them, curled up and cozy on the couch. With his brother and son out for the night, he decided to get caught up on work. Ashe grabbed a bottle of water and headed for his den. Maybe reading someone else's fantasy world could clear his head.

The monitor turned from full screen to black; that was how long Ashe stared at it – long enough for the screen saver to come on, for the machine to go into sleep mode, and for it to finally shut down. This was a hell of a time to have writer's block. He opened the desk drawer and took out a pad and pen. It had been a long time since he'd written in this archaic way, with his hands, like they did in the Ice Age before technology turned calligraphy into a lost art and the Post Office into a monolithic dinosaur. His words must be carefully crafted. This one piece of writing had to be perfectly executed, and one could only achieve that through painstaking deliberation and the manual movements of the tip of a pen.

Email was easy. Stupidly easy. The simplicity of the Internet is what got him into trouble. It wasn't only the anonymity of it all. It was quicker to type, to jot ideas down straight off the top of his head, to send it along its way without deeper consideration about the words or their implications. Words were tricky little devils; words could be taken many ways, in many contexts. Ashe was smart enough. He should have predicted the end game to his situation. He hadn't. Perhaps he didn't want to.

He sighed. This was going to be tough. He looked at the notepad. Was there enough paper on the planet to say what he wanted to say? He could go on and on to eternity. If he had only one sheet to explain, it would force him to be succinct. *That's it*, he thought.

At the top of the page, he wrote "Dear Janna."

At the bottom of the page, he signed it, "Virtually yours, Ashe."

Now all he had to do was round up those pesky words in between and assemble them into cohesiveness.

He had to dig deep into his heart to find them.

Chapter Twenty-three

Sunday, November 22
Sarasota, Florida

The thick dossier arrived by Express Mail the day before, and Celia spent a full twenty-four hours staring at it. She knew where it had come from – Spark Investigations – yet she was far from sure about opening the package. She and Kimber found the Tampa-based detective agency online, and Celia used part of her Christmas 'fun' money, the funds she saved all year to splurge on herself, to pay for it.

It had been Alabaster Spark himself, the president and CEO of the agency, not John, the investigative geek she initially spoke to, who called her late Thursday night. He wouldn't say exactly what he had learned, yet did a fine job of teasing his findings. "Ms. Davis, I'm afraid your intuition was correct. Your friends are not in physical peril. As far as I can tell, the subject is not a criminal. However, I've located some inaccuracies with, *ahem… Ms.* MacDaniel. I'll send out our findings tomorrow. Thank you for your business. Please call again should you need my services."

The suspense was killing her, although a part of Celia didn't want to know the truth. All Friday, she fingered the package, wondering what horrors might lurk inside. Kimber noticed her pensive mood as she and Brandon inhaled the leftover pepperoni pizza from the night before. "What's with the package, Mom?"

"Spark Investigations." Celia answered without thinking. "It's the findings on Ashe MacDaniel."

"Oh!"

Kimber bounded from the couch, dragging a tail of melted mozzarella from the pizza box behind her. "Hey, hey!" Brandon yelled.

"Oh, Mom, it came? What are you waiting for? Why don't you open it?" Celia could count on her daughter's enthusiasm. She'd shared all her doubts and suspicions about the mysterious Ashe MacDaniel. It was Kimber who Googled and found Spark Investigations.

"I feel kind of weird about it," Celia replied. "Like it's personal, private material. I'm not sure what we did is legal."

"Of course, it's legal. Otherwise the guy wouldn't be in business. Let me see." Kimber enjoyed a good, strong case of drama. She shoved what was left of her pizza slice into her mouth and jockeyed for the envelope with both hands.

Celia pulled it away, stashing it behind her back. "No! Not yet."

Kimber's words were muddled by a mouthful of her pizza. She chewed and swallowed in a hurry. "Come on, Mom. What are you waiting for?"

"I don't know. Divine intervention?"

"What if the Virtual Moms are in danger? What if *you're* in danger? You can't keep the information to yourself."

"Spark said we're not in danger. Only that my instincts were correct. As usual."

"That's crazy, Mom. Anyway, what does *that* mean? Why waste the money and go through with a private eye if you won't bother to read the information? Aren't you curious at all?" Kimber turned to her boyfriend for backup. "What do you think?"

"I think we should get another pizza," Brandon said as he brought the empty box to the kitchen. "I'm still hungry."

Kimber gave Brandon a friendly slap on the backside and shook her head. "Boys. They're so predictable, especially when it comes to boy food."

"Don't worry about it. I *will* open it." Celia placed the envelope high atop the refrigerator, behind extra canisters and a potted plant.

"When?" Kimber hopped impatiently from one foot to the other.

"Maybe later today," Celia sighed. "You don't understand, Kimber. This envelope isn't a joke; it's serious business. Depending on what is learned about Ashe MacDaniel, the information in here could affect the VMs. It could tear us apart, maybe forever. As much as I like being right, I'm not looking forward to proving that I am. Plus it could backfire all over me."

"What about the truth, Mom? What if this woman is some kind of whack-job?"

"I don't think that's the case. Spark would have warned me if she was."

"Mom, are you telling me you're having second thoughts?"

"No, honey. I'm preparing myself for what might be inside the envelope."

***

The heavy thump-thump-thump of bass reverberated through the house. Kara tried to finish her spelling words. There wasn't an inch in the house quiet enough to concentrate. The last straw was reached after the volume was kicked up higher. Any louder and the roof would blow off. A crash of glass came from the upstairs bathroom. Kara winced and put her pencil on the kitchen table. "Mom…I can't think. It's so *loud*."

Missy kept her cool façade, although inside she was seething. Kassie had been less than a comfort to her the last few days. Instead, she displayed a surly attitude headlined with one-word responses and plenty of mumbling. She slipped out of the house each day before Missy could perform the before-school inspection and returned in the afternoon a stranger. Her eyes were made up with too much black liner, making her skin appear paler than it was. "You've got to ignore her," Janna had told her. "Mandy went through the same rebellious stage at almost the same age. She's dying for attention and doesn't care if it's because she's good or bad."

"I can't," Missy wailed. "It's too hard."

"Remember, if you react, she'll know she's got you right where she wants you, yanking your chain. Try it, what can it hurt?"

Missy gave it her best attempt, smiling serenely when Kassie was nearby. She thought of Kassie as an invisible entity, although she glared daggers right under Missy's nose. She could ignore some behavior, not all. The foul language barely whispered, the plastering of makeup, the sudden animosity toward Kara – Missy could almost dismiss that as acting out because of absent Earl. The passive-aggressive tactic with her stereo system had gone too far. Missy had had enough. Without a word to Kara, she rose from her seat.

On her way up to Kassie's room, she plucked a photo from the floor. It had been decibel-bounced from the wall. It was a picture of Earl, the glass shattered in a spidery web. Missy sighed and put the photograph in a drawer and summoned up her reserve. She wasn't sure what she would say. She hoped it wouldn't be something she'd regret as soon as the words left her lips.

She opened the door to Kassie's room without knocking, wordlessly went straight for the iPod stereo set up, and wrenched the plug from the wall. Missy picked up the docking system and headed for the door. "Mom!" Kassie screamed. "What are you doing? You can't take that! It's mine. Dad gave it to me."

Missy kept her eyes trained for the door. Her first impulse was to rush to her daughter, put her arms around her, and tell her everything was going to be all right. *You can do this, Missy. Ignore her. Don't cave.*

"Gawd! No wonder Dad left you."

"Kassie!"

"I hate you! You're such a bitch."

Missy turned back to look at her daughter. In a balanced voice she said, "I don't know about that, Kassandra Lynn Martin. You want to see what a world class bitch looks like, take a look in the mirror."

***

Kimber and Brandon were frolicking in the pool when Doug Taylor stopped by for the weekly cleaning and treatment. Celia sat safely in the lanai, folding sheets and pillowcases, with a sharp eye the infamous Mr. Taylor. No way would she go poolside until the cleaning job was finished and Doug was safely in another zip code. She would avoid contact with the pool man, no matter how treacherously good-looking he was.

At his arrival, both Kimber and Brandon hopped out and grabbed towels. They shadowed Doug as he swept for debris, the three of them laughing and joking. Celia strained to hear the conversation. Their voices were decibels below earshot. She noticed Doug's eyes wandering in appreciation of her daughter's form. The lecherous lout! Celia's mama bear instinct flashed. With a huff, she put down the sheet she was folding and poked her head out the door.

"Kimber! Kimber! Can you come here, please?" Kimber smiled, innocently releasing her towel to reveal ample perky breasts in a tiny pink bikini. She waved at Celia.

Oh, my God, she's practically naked, and in front of that maniac. "Kimber!" Celia screamed, this time making certain her voice was as loud, obnoxious and commanding as she could get without having the neighbors calling 911. *Bitchy. I can do that. He would be making a huge mistake messing with me.*

Kimber picked up her towel, threw it around her shoulders, and sprinted to the lanai, a mass of lanky legs and wet hair. Brandon stayed with Doug. Both of them looked at Celia as though she had pointy ears, was newly landed from outer space, and speaking Vulcan. "Mom. What is it? You don't have to scream. I'm right here."

"Come in. I want you to…" Celia's voice faltered. She looked around for a worthy excuse. "I need you to help me with this." She pointed to the sheet at the top of the laundry basket.

Kimber rolled her eyes. "O-*kay*, Mom. That's real special. We were only talking to Doug."

"You know who he is?" Celia's jaw dropped.

"Sure. Doug Taylor. He owns the pool company. He does everyone's pool. Brandon's. Alyssa's. He's a nice guy. He's been here lots of times before. What's the beef?"

"I want you to stay away from him, that's all."

"Mom, he's totally harmless. By the way, don't you think he's dreamy?"

Celia blushed and turned away before Kimber could notice the rosy shade of scarlet coloring her cheeks. "His face is so-so. Nothing I'd write home about. He's rather stuck on himself."

"Doug? No way. He's the nicest guy I know. Totally cool and with it." Kimber extended her arms to shake out wrinkles in the bed sheet. She lowered her voice. "You know, Mom, he's single, too."

"What a surprise. He acts it." Celia wanted to add, *he acts like a horse's ass.*

"I think he *likes* you," Kimber teased.

"What's that supposed to mean?" Celia snapped as she threw a corner of the sheet to Kimber.

"He asks about you all the time."

"Does not!"

"Hey, I'm not lying. Whoa, look at you blush. Don't tell me you like him, too?"

Celia put down her end of the sheet and glared. "He's not my type."

"You seem to be his."

227

"I have no time or patience for romance, Kimber. I've got my hands full with work, a house payment, Virtual Moms, and seeing you into adulthood." Celia hoped her voice was forceful and serious, yet she heard a crack she hoped Kimber might have missed.

"Oh, come on, *Mother*. He's totally hot and you're not dead yet. I would *so* give him a spin if I were you."

"Kimber!"

"Only if I were much older and not already spoken for." She winked. "You need to mix it up a little. Have some fun. Don't you think it's time?" Kimber gave an exaggerated sad look.

"No thanks."

"Besides, I think he really likes you. He really, really likes you." Kimber sang.

Celia huffed and dropped her end of the sheet in frustration. "I'm going inside for some lemonade. Would you and Brandon like some?" She opened the door to the kitchen to make her escape.

"Don't get mad at me… It was a thought, Mom. Doug might be the thing you need to even out those rough edges."

"Rough edges?" Celia sputtered. "Young lady, if I have any edges at all I'll decide when and how I'm going to even them out. Stay away from that guy. I don't like him." Celia didn't mean to, but she slammed the door behind her.

***

It took a half hour of cajoling. After Doug had performed his weekly duty, Celia finally convinced Brandon and Kimber to leave the house. She needed dead calm to think, so she funded an outing for the two to see the recent *Twilight* movie. While Brandon groaned his disapproval, Kimber was excited enough to drop the touchy subject of Doug Taylor and start chattering about dreamboat vampires.

In their absence, Celia paced the floor, the burden of her secret weighing heavy on her soul. As much as she wanted to learn the truth, the desire now felt awkward and unseemly. She reminded herself that people use private detectives all the time. Kimber was right, if it wasn't legal they wouldn't be in business. Employers did routine background checks. Certainly for $250, she was only going to get the bare minimum of information. She checked her email once again to see if she could glean any information from Ashe's initial responses.

Unfortunately, she had few responses from Ashe to study. It was as though Ashe MacDaniel dropped off the face of the earth as quickly as she had appeared. Celia went through her old mail in an attempt to construct a timeline. Ashe hadn't responded to any mail since sending out well wishes to Laurel and her father. The last Ashe email was written Wednesday, when the Virtual Moms got together to pay for plane tickets to bring Joe and Marcus to Orlando. They were to chip in whatever they could afford, and most donated $150. According to Janna who arranged for the flights, Ashe wrote a check for the lion's share of the tickets. Janna sent on the extra funds to the Extons. They were going to need it with Laurel being away from her job for a week.

Celia noticed Janna online. She'd get to the bottom of this somehow.

celiasunshine: *Janna, are you there?*

jannasbananas: *I've got a second. I'm on my way out. Meeting Juan in the Park.*

celiasunshine: *So you're hot and heavy with him again?*

jannasbananas: *Sure. We're back on track. I was feeling needy that one night.*

celiasunshine: *Good. Don't mean to intrude or keep you.*

celiasunshine: *I'm wondering. What's up with Ashe?*

jannasbananas: *You're not still harping on her, are you?*

jannasbananas: *It's getting old.* Really *old.*

celiasunshine: *It's not like that, Janna.*

jannasbananas: *So? What do you mean?*

celiasunshine: *I noticed she hasn't been around for a few days. I was wondering if you'd heard from her.*

jannasbananas: *Tyler stayed home from school Thursday and Friday. I don't know if he's sick again or what. She didn't say and she hasn't been online, from what I can tell.*

celiasunshine: *Did you call?*

Celia hoped *someone* had spoken to her. It would alleviate a lot of her doubt if she knew one of them could corroborate a real voice for Ashe MacDaniel.

jannasbananas: *I left a message. Ally spoke to someone there. Wednesday, I think it was. Tyler answered the phone.*

Celia's interest perked up. Was this a new phone call?

celiasunshine: *Tyler the little boy or someone else? The sitter?*

jannasbananas: *Both I guess. Listen, gotta run or I'll be late. I'll shout out to you later.*

celiasunshine: *'K. Have a nice time.*

Celia's face fell and the balloon bubble of excitement burst. She'd get no choice nuggets of insight from Janna.

***

True to habit, Kimber slammed the door on her way in. "My God, you scared me!" Celia exclaimed. "I didn't hear you drive up." Celia had been deep under a kitchen cabinet looking for a box of Rice a Roni she knew was there but had kept eluding her.

"I parked the car on the street."

"Did you enjoy the movie?"

"*I* loved it! Brandon snored." Kimber bent over her mother and kissed the top of her head. "Thanks for paying. Brandon won't get his paycheck until Friday and we know I don't have any money."

"You're welcome."

"So, got any news to report?" Kimber reached for the top of the refrigerator to retrieve the Spark Investigation report. She frowned when her reward was a handful of dust bunnies. "Eww...gross." She ran for the sink. "Did you open the package?"

"Not yet." Celia noticed the grab. "If you're that interested in the top for the fridge, you could get up there with some Mr. Clean and a dust cloth."

"No thanks, Mom. Honestly, how can you sit so calm without opening the envelope? Isn't the suspense killing you?" Celia smiled. Kimber was the type who would pick the tape off Christmas presents and would scour the house for weeks in advance of her birthday.

"Patience, Kimber. I'm giving Ashe a chance to redeem herself before I open it."

Kimber grabbed a bag of chips from the counter and plucked a handful out. "What do you mean?"

"Look." Celia pointed to her computer screen. An email sat idle, waiting to be sent.

To: AsheMacD
From: celiasunshine
Subject: The truth shall set you free

Ashe, first of all, I want you to know I have nothing personal against you. However, none of the Virtual Moms, with the exception of Janna, knows you very well. We all – that includes me – are willing to give you a chance to prove yourself. This is a great group of women, and we want to keep it that way. If you and Janna are such good friends, you would know that we have experienced some VMs who haven't worked out for one reason or another over the years. That's the nature of life online. It's also the nature of life.

I also want you to know that I love all the VMs. Most of us have been together for 13 years, some longer. We are more than friends, we are family. In that vein, I recently did something to protect the group. I hired an agency to do a background check on you. I have received the results in yesterday's mail.

However, I have not yet opened the envelope.

I feel weird about doing this at all, Ashe. My intention is not to hurt you. You seem like a caring, warm person. I won't read the contents of the report on one condition, and one condition only. If you have anything you'd like to share with me about you, I'd like to hear it from you. I'm giving you this one chance to tell the truth.

Otherwise, in 48 hours, I WILL open and read the report. And share it with the rest of the group.

Celia

"Do you think it sounds too harsh?" Celia asked.

Kimber sniffed. "I don't know how you can wait two whole days. I don't know what the purpose of the email is. Blackmail?"

"Is that what it sounds like?"

"Mom! This is crazy. *Think* about it."

231

"Think about what?"

"I hope you haven't sent this yet." Kimber frowned.

"No."

"I know I'm not one of the Moms. I'm not sure this is the right approach either. You're either friends or you're not friends. Either you open the letter or you don't. Pick a path and stick to it." Kimber took the bag of chips and headed for her room.

Celia looked after her. "Out of the mouths of babes."

Chapter Twenty-four

Monday, November 23
San Francisco, California

Her morning run complete, Skye trudged toward the sea wall and collapsed, sprawled flat with her arms extended, protected by the safety of a valley between two sand dunes. The wind gently swirled, carrying grains of sand across her body. She watched as some stuck to her skin, while others kept flying toward the City. An hour and a half of constant non-stop sprinting – not bad. She'd pushed herself hard in the last few weeks, running every other day and running until she felt her heart near implosion. The self-imposed house arrest of the past months had left her fat and apathetic. During her depression, she'd forgotten what a high could be had by strenuous exercise. It felt good to stretch her muscles, to run although when the wind whipped mercilessly, and the mist was as thick as. Skye preferred those days over the warm, sunny ones when the sea lapped tranquilly at the beachfront.

Her heart thumped in rhythmic measures, a wild conga drum she could feel in her ears. She closed her eyes and imagined her blood cells rushing out, along her arms and legs to her fingers and toes, and circulating back to her heart. As she slowed her breath, her body cooled under the drizzle. She stared straight up into the gray fog and smiled. Chance of the sun making an appearance was slim and none. Chilled, she arose and shook the sand from her moist body. She could stay all day, lost in her thoughts and the fog. Too bad she had too many things to accomplish.

During the brisk walk home, Skye mused over the past week. Rob's stellar progress report was a highlight in an otherwise stressed time. She sent a card and flowers to Laurel's dad, and a special card to Laurel. Poor woman. Laurel was proof-positive that being in a committed relationship was no guarantee of security or happiness. Thank goodness Celia was close by to lend a hand. Joe would be worthless in a disaster like this. While Good Time Joe was a jovial guy, he lacked the basic ambition to provide for his family. The Extons made the common mistake of living beyond their means and now the bills were stacking up. No wonder Laurel had to go back to work. It had to be a tough confession to make, what with the relative successes of the other VMs. Janna was well-fixed, Celia was strong, independent and was making her own way. Ally had Greg's support. Ashe made her living at home. As for Missy, she *seemed* to have the perfect life.

Missy's problems were devastating. In the same week, the VMs were reminded of another example of a person who couldn't count on her spouse. After reading her email confiding that her husband Earl left her out of the blue, she called Missy right away. As of Saturday, Missy still hadn't told Kara or Kassie the truth. "I can't bear the thought," Missy said. "They love their dad too much. I can't tell them he left me."

"He left both of them, too," Skye reminded her. It was a pointed statement she regretted saying as soon as the words left her lips. Missy was fragile, prone to teary outbursts at random conversations, some having nothing to do with Earl. It wasn't Missy's fault Earl left, and while potentially hurtful, the remark was far less provocative than what she longed to say about the two-timing idiot. Skye's choice of descriptions for the horn dog included 'coward,' 'ass,' and 'stupid bastard,' along with a few others of the bleep-able kind. She couldn't say those words out loud, not to Missy. For some unexplained reason, Missy still *loved* the guy. Skye couldn't understand keeping his exit a secret from the VMs. Thank goodness they knew now, so at least they could pool ideas. It made little sense to keep it from the girls. After Trina left her, Skye couldn't wait to announce her pain and angst to the world. She felt she had to, or she would implode. "Sorry, Missy. I don't mean to…"

"Forget it. You're all right." Missy said. "I should be truthful with them. Ashe gave me an idea. I have to try it before I give up."

Ashe. For some reason, Ashe had been absent the last couple of days, barely online and seldom responding to emails at all. Skye looked for her on her Buddy List, and sure enough she had not signed on, not since Friday. Perhaps Tyler was sick again and her hands were full. Skye would have to send her a personal email today. If she had a problem, Skye would offer her support.

She was thankful for Ashe's friendship and would too happy to help.

As Skye walked back to her house, she thought about Dude, the man she met at the library downtown last week. At first, Skye balked at the invitation. It wasn't often she accepted solicitations from total strangers. In the end, she was glad she did. The impetus for a jet fuel-infused cup of Joe ended up in an afternoon-long discussion of life, especially after the Dude gave food and drink to his homeless friend. Skye was embarrassed for her own ignorance and impressed by his concern.

Dude talked about the military, a failed marriage and kids long lost. He spoke of wild tales of San Francisco in the '70s, parties, pot, and rock and roll. He related earnestly of his slow descent into substance abuse and homelessness. Each enjoyed an inspired passion for food, although Skye confessed her lack of ability while Dude outlined simple pointers. Skye sat rapt, hanging on every word. She had lost track of time, not noticing the sun had set, darkness falling fast, and the alley coffeehouse shuttering its garage doors. Skye arrived home long after Rob returned from school.

Skye hadn't mentioned her coffee date to the VMs, or the brief run-in with the mystery man at the China Market. The chance encounter could have been a fluke; she might never see the Dude again. He had been kind enough to leave his phone number for her foray onto the kitchen stove; certainly no addresses were revealed. Skye chalked it up to a friendly afternoon's diversion in the big city. Plus, Celia would have a field day if she knew. Celia was protective and suspicious, as witnessed by her treatment of Ashe. She would have Dude filleted, drowned in batter, and sautéed in ten minutes. Janna, the hopeless romantic, could blow up an innocent cup of coffee and a chance meeting at the local grocer into a formal wedding. Laurel, Missy, and Ally would think she'd gone crazy.

"I don't have to tell the girls *everything*," she said to herself.

Maybe.

***

With major cajoling and a little bribery, Ashe succeeded in talking Tyler into school. It hadn't cost much; only a promise that

Ashe would be waiting for Tyler after kindergarten and they would spend the afternoon at the park. "Ice cream, too?" Tyler asked.

Ashe knew the little boy was pushing the point and that he shouldn't cave. Ice cream before dinner? *What would Mac do?* He knew the answer. Mac was sensible. She was a great mom; she would hold steady. Maybe it was time for Ashe to be Ashe. No way could Mac be replaced, not by a broken-down spouse who tried his best to imitate her. Perhaps he should come to grips with the man he was, the father he was, and the lot he was dealt with. "Hell," he said aloud, "I'm not Mac, I'm me." A side-trip to Dairy Queen was penciled in.

Once Tyler had safely boarded the bus, Ashe grabbed the keys to the car and headed out. The morning air was brisk; the sun shone with a vengeance. *Was it always this bright at 8 a.m.?* That time of the day usually found Ashe hunkered down in his den, drapes drawn, the only light coming from his computer monitor. Or he would head back to bed and put the covers over his head and try to sleep away the last year. Ashe's eyes burned, he squinted into the road as he fumbled for his sunglasses.

It was a short drive to Sandhills. He'd made the journey so many times in the last year, he knew all the landmarks: the lay of the land, the curve of the pavement, every tree, mailbox, and highway sign – heck, he was probably well-acquainted with every pebble on the shoulder.

Once inside, Ashe took one road that lead to another, and then another. He recalled the first trip he made, right after the cemetery had set Mac's marker. The headstone was bone white, like the thousands of other markers, and dizzying, rows and rows, acres and acres of the same. He thought he could remember where she was, on the outskirts of the fallen, three rows up, five graves in. He was wrong. It was all changed somehow, more graves, more white markers, different season. He wound up driving in circles for an hour and ended up back at the office for a map.

It was a different story now. After making the journey so many times, he knew right where she was.

Ashe parked the car in his usual spot, turned off the car, and sighed. Mowers clipped grass in the distance. Ashe reached for the flowers on the passenger seat; he had picked them that morning, what remained of the rose garden Mac once tended, now horribly neglected. Red roses, one a bud, the other a small bloom stunted by the chilly onset of fall. "She'd kill me if she saw this," he said. "I'm no gardener."

Ashe walked to Mac's plot. In a national cemetery he couldn't leave a huge arrangement. He could get away with the two small roses. He placed them on top of the headstone, his hand lingering on the cold marble. The words stuck in his throat. Other visits would find him telling Mac about Tyler, about his editing job, about the weather, about his sadness. He'd have a thousand things to say, yet today was different. How could he start this conversation? It seemed traitorous to think it. Could he tell Mac that it might be time to move on? Could he admit to her what he could barely admit to himself? That it might be possible he had fallen in love with someone else?

***

"Mom! I'm home!"

A door slammed shut, the thud of a heavy backpack hit the bamboo floors, and Rob shuffled to the kitchen where Skye conducted a symphony of boiling pots and pans. Although Skye couldn't crack an egg and had trouble opening a box of cereal, she decided to experiment with the VM crash cooking school using some of the tips she garnered from Dude.

"Hey, what are you doing?" Rob poked his face into a huge pot of boiling water and opened the lid to another.

"Cooking dinner." Skye carefully measured tomato sauce with a measuring cup and held it up to the light. She hummed as she worked.

"From *scratch*?"

"What does it look like?"

Smiling, Rob returned the lid and took a step back. "Uh, Mom, you don't cook. And while we're at it, you don't *hum*, either."

"It's about time I learned, don't you think? I can't rely on the kindness of partners or San Tung takeout for the rest of my life. What if I never find love again? What if the Tungs retire and close the restaurant? I'm an adult. I *should* learn how to cook. It's not so hard. It can't be. I've taken plenty of photographs of food."

"Taking close up shots of sushi isn't the same."

"I'm not making sushi."

237

"Should I run to Walgreen's for some Prilosec?" Rob teased. "Or would you prefer Pepto?"

"We won't need it. Even Ashe thinks I can learn to cook."

"Maybe Ashe hasn't heard from Janna what a disaster you are." True. Rob was referring to an unfortunate incident during Janna's visit. What started out a mushroom frittata ended up a brittle disc. After that fiasco of a meal, Janna happily paid for three squares a day for the three of them.

"Ashe is learning, too. We're cooking this same dinner at the same time so we can compare notes."

"You mean another Virtual Mom cooks like you do? No way!"

"Nice boy. I'm so glad you're supportive of your dear, old mom," Skye deadpanned. She smiled as she stepped back to rumple his hair, before returning to her pots. "*This* is what I have to look forward to in my old age?"

"Aw, Mom." Rob picked up a raw piece of pasta and popped it into his mouth. "So when is the feast? Do you think I have time for some homework?"

"You can try. I'll call you when I think it's ready."

Dinner was eaten in silence, a rare thing in the Murray household. Skye studied Rob's face. She couldn't gauge his reaction to her ragout. Rob was fastidious about manners and wouldn't wolf down food.

"So what do you think?" Skye leaned forward. From her test-tastes, she knew it wasn't bad enough to make her sick. Skye felt she had reached a culinary milestone and needed validation from her son.

"Well…" Rob began, as he folded his napkin into a neat triangle and placed it on the table, "it's not Trina's cooking, but it's edible."

Skye frowned. "What's wrong with it? Maybe I'll add more garlic next time. Or maybe oregano? What do you think?"

Rob laughed. "I'm kidding, Mom. It was awesome! Totally punk."

"Really?"

"Sure. For you, anyway. Honest!" Rob laughed as he returned dirty dishes to the sink.

"Oh, you. You're a terrible tease." *Like your father*, she thought. It was one of the qualities that drew her to him in high school. She was a mess and Lee Murray was serious with an edgy humor. "For that crack, you should clean up."

"Don't worry. I was planning to. Put your feet up and relax. You're probably whipped."

Her computer registered a familiar chime of an IM. Skye rose from the table and went to check. She was surprised to find it was Ashe.

shootingskye: *Ashe! How did the cooking lesson go?*
AsheMacD: *I wouldn't call it a success. My noodles did something funny.*
shootingskye: *How?*

Skye shook her head. Her noodles had turned out fine.

AsheMacD: *It came out of the pan one big noodle.*
shootingskye: *Eww…*
AsheMacD: *Good thing I've got a frozen pizza in my back pocket.*☺
shootingskye: *Where have you been? I wasn't sure if you remembered the cooking challenge.*
AsheMacD: *I'm up to my eyeballs with problems. It's Tyler.*
shootingskye: *Something serious?*
AsheMacD: *No. Only the kind that takes a lot of time and attention. He was missing… Mac.*
shootingskye: *Poor little guy. A boy needs his dad. Rob missed Lee, especially the first couple of years. Is he okay?*
AsheMacD: *I'm not sure…*
shootingskye: *Can I help?*

Several minutes elapsed before an answer popped into the box.

AsheMacD: *Can I ask you something? It's about one of the VMs.*

239

Skye could only guess whom Ashe was referring to. Celia could be relentlessly brash if she believed her world wasn't rotating correctly. Skye quickly typed back.

shootingskye: *Don't worry about Celia. Underneath all that bluster, she's a nice person. She'll come around.*
AsheMacD: *It's not Celia.*
shootingskye: *No?*

Skye was confused. She couldn't imagine who it could be. The other Virtual Moms liked Ashe.

AsheMacD: *It's Janna. I know you guys talk a lot. I was wondering...*
AsheMacD: *What do you think of this Juan guy she's been dating?*
shootingskye: *Oh, Juan!*

Skye giggled, causing Rob to cast a bemused look from the kitchen.

shootingskye: *She really likes him.*
AsheMacD: *I know. Don't you think they're moving too fast?*
shootingskye: *Maybe. Except for that one night their wires got crossed, they seem to be a good match.*
AsheMacD: *Does she know anything about him?*
shootingskye: *Other than he's a hunk and successful? and half Puerto Rican and half Jewish?*
shootingskye: *What's to know?*
AsheMacD: *Do you think it's...*
shootingskye: *Yes? Ashe? You there?*
AsheMacD: *...serious?*
shootingskye: *I'm not sure. I've known Janna forever. She maintains a set of very high standards. They're so high, I'm not sure they're attainable.*
shootingskye: *She'll bounce guys out if they aren't* perfect. *We all know perfect men are one in a million.*

AsheMacD: *I've only known her for a year and that's what I thought. She must have dated a dozen guys since then. I figured it was normal for life in the big city. I can't put my finger on it. Her mood is different with this one.*

shootingskye: *Great! I'm glad to hear it. If anyone deserves to be happy, it's Janna. I know she's led a charmed life and all. She should settle down. She never remarried after Dennis. It was full-throttle with her career and looking after the girls.*

shootingskye: *Women need more than that. More than a fling, you know? Something deeper, satisfying. Sometimes you* want *to come home to a friendly soul, not just a warm body.*

Skye looked at the words as they disappeared from the top window and ended up on Ashe's half. It was how she felt about Lee, was it how she felt about Trina? She once believed they were soul mates, meant to spend eternity together. Or was Trina the flavor of the week, and Skye the casual romance she'd snagged when trolling for babes?

AsheMacD: *Is that how you feel?*

Oh, no! Skye held her breath. She stared at her monitor. Had Janna's evil plan come to fruition? Was Ashe looking to make a connection? Did Janna or one of the other girls say something to her?

shootingskye: *Um, Ashe, I like you as a person. I'm sure you're a nice girl, but I'm not interested in you...*
AsheMacD: *Me?*
AsheMacD: ***ME?***
AsheMacD: *LOL!*
AsheMacD: *ROFLMAO!*
AsheMacD: *Oh, no!*☺
shootingskye: *?*
AsheMacD: *I'm sorry, Skye. I don't want to disrespect you. I'm sure you're a very nice girl, but I'm not interested in you either!*

241

Skye's emotions ranged from anger to annoyance to disbelief. She was both relieved and insulted.

shootingskye: *I'm glad we got that out of the way. You know the real reason Janna asked you into the group?*
AsheMacD: *No, what was that?*
shootingskye: *It was to hook us up.*
AsheMacD: *No!*
shootingskye: *She sprung it on me after she knew you and I were getting close.*
AsheMacD: *I'll be.*
shootingskye: *Wait a minute. Why the questions about Janna?*

Skye realized the roundabout conversation had less to do with Juan Bernstein and more to do with Janna. *Two could play this game, Ashe.*

shootingskye: *Do I detect an interest on* your *part?*
AsheMacD: *No. Nothing more than friendship.*
shootingskye: *You sure?*
AsheMacD: *I've come to like her, that's all.*
shootingskye: *Like, as in more than just friends?*
AsheMacD: *I don't want to see her hurt.*

Skye heard the slamming of a buddy door. Ashe had logged off AOL before she could answer.

Chapter Twenty-five

Tuesday, November 24
Las Vegas, Nevada

"Bye, kids! Have a good day!" Missy waved. She waited until Kara and Kassie boarded the school bus at the corner before closing the front door. Two days before Thanksgiving and she had much to accomplish before the big day.

She managed to talk her 'new' employer into having her start the Monday after Thanksgiving. She'd been floating on a cloud ever since the interview. Her success buoyed her spirits. The 'old' Missy returned – maybe not the old Missy, but a new and improved Missy, one with confidence *and* employment. Finally, she would have a place to go, a real job to earn real income. In the meantime, she needed a few days to set the next part of her plan in motion.

This Thanksgiving would find the four of them together with an added surprise. Somehow she finagled Earl into accepting her invitation for dinner. Her treatment of her way-ward husband this week was all due to Ashe. Thanks to her bright ideas, Ashe gave Missy a step-by-step plan of attack with several Plan Bs as backups. While Missy was unconvinced at first, she now had to admit The Plan seemed to be working.

Last week was no exception. She arranged to meet Earl at the Denny's near his hotel to have him sign some insurance papers. Over cups of black coffee, Missy concentrated on the lines of her husband's face, the twitch of a mandible and the amount of perspiration on his brow. She looked into his hazel eyes, which he tried to avert, to gauge an insight. Missy hadn't looked at Earl like that in years. She hadn't noticed the wrinkles before or the gray sprouting at his temples. She tried to imagine the college Earl, with his fine chiseled features and what she thought of was his provocative banter. This older Earl's demeanor was a blank slate and she came away with nothing.

She wondered about Earl's change of heart regarding the holiday. The night he walked off, Missy was convinced she'd never see him again. He surely didn't care, or he'd have come back days ago. Maybe the other side of the fence wasn't as green as he'd imagined. Perhaps the home-wrecking and yet unnamed slut he ran away for wasn't an accomplished cook. Maybe the little vixen was married herself! That would explain a hot potato drop during the holiday. Missy hoped at the very least that he missed the girls. Earl asked about them in a perfunctory way, as though he were an uncle or business associate, or a random shopper in line at Safeway. He'd been an absentee dad for so long, it amazed her he even knew their names. She realized in hindsight that he was as detached from them as he was from her.

Martin holidays were traditionally spent back home in Indiana. Both sets of grandparents lived in Indianapolis. Missy considered a girls-only trip, but with the trouble she was having keeping her marriage together, she wouldn't feel comfortable enough to fly to Indiana for the weekend. If Missy left town, Earl would have every right to feel deserted, thus giving him a good reason for hanging out with the Other Woman. Had things been solid, Missy would have loved a girls-only visit. However, if they were to show up without Earl, she'd be bombarded by questions. She would no doubt be the subject of a thorough grilling. She didn't want to deal with it.

Both girls pouted when she gave them the news about Thanksgiving in Vegas. They were close to her parents, Mimi and Granddad, and Earl's parents doted on them since Kara and Kassie were their only grandchildren. She hated using her daughters as a tool in her grand plan. It had to be done for the sake of the family. Kara and Kassie were clueless as to where their father was. Kara was still a child and let her hopes rule her emotions. Kassie, on the other hand, asked more pointed questions, especially after her disappointing thirteenth birthday.

"So, Mom. Where in Alaska is he?" Kassie had been working on her homework, and out of the blue put her pen down and posed the question.

Missy, who was cleaning the kitchen after dinner, was knocked off kilter. "Why do you ask?" she countered and continued scrubbing.

"I'm studying the states in school." A leaden pause separated them. Missy held her breath. "He doesn't call very much. Don't Alaskans have phone? Don't you think it's weird?"

244

"He's busy. The time zone is different." Missy plunged on, taking a clean plate out of the dishwasher and giving it extra attention it didn't need. She struggled to keep the conversation truthful and kept her back to Kassie. She was a terrible liar. "I talk to him in the middle of the day."

"Oh, *really*? A-hem. I thought I saw him the other day."

Oh, dear. That was a possibility Missy hadn't considered. The La Quinta Inn wasn't that far from the school. "I don't think so," she answered. Not a bold-faced lie, but tiptoeing along the edges. "He'll be here for Thanksgiving. He promised."

"Okay, Mom," Kassie answered, unconvinced. "Whatever."

Missy dodged a bullet with that one.

With the kids in school, she had to get busy. Time was precious. A cleaning crew was arriving at 10 a.m., the interior design people at noon, and delivery of flowers and groceries soon after.

This was going to be the best Thanksgiving ever.

***

Ally finished boxing the last of the sugar cookies and sat down with a steaming cup of tea, a contrast to outside where the wind was howling and snow began to swirl. She was exhausted and would need to take a break before tackling the stack of cookie sheets and dirty bowls that begged to be washed. She had put her feet up when the phone rang.

"Hello?"

"Ally, it's Laurel."

"Laurel!" Ally was surprised to hear from her. It was cheaper to email and she knew Laurel's budget was tight. "It's so good to hear from you. How's your dad?"

"Glad to be home."

"He's okay, then?"

"He'll need to adjust his diet. Less cheeseburgers, more vegetables. And he'll have to start exercising. I would say he's much, much better."

"Great!"

"Ally, I don't have a lot of time. I wanted to call you and thank you for what you did."

"You mean with the tickets? It was nothing. I got the email."

"No, this time the VMs' generosity deserves individual phone calls. I know you're busy with your family and I'm busy with mine. I wanted to tell you how much it means to me…" Laurel's voice broke. "You guys are…"

"Janna would say we're 'stupendous' or something equally silly." Ally smiled.

Laurel joined her with a giggle of her own. "Yes, she would. Honestly, I don't know what I would do without all of you. When I think back over the years, all the things we've shared and the stuff we've gone through…"

"It's amazing, isn't it? How friendships can transcend the miles?"

"The Internet helped."

"No doubt." Ally grinned.

"I wanted to tell you personally: Way to come through."

"Honey, that's what friends are for."

***

Missy collapsed into a heap on her bed. What a workout! The marathon session was worth the time and effort. Everything was spotless and impeccable, right out of *Better Homes and Garden,* even the laundry room. The house smelled of cleaning liquid and orchid blossoms. She glanced at the clock on her cell phone. "Oh, my God!" she said aloud. Time's up. She noticed voice and text messages piled up in queue. One was from Kassie. "Hamburgers tonite, plz?" She retrieved her voicemail. Hmm… Three calls from Earl – nothing serious or earth shattering. His voice sounded flat and unaffected in the first two calls, a little panicked in the third.

Missy smiled, but declined to hit redial. Missy Martin would not be speaking to Mr. Earl Martin, not until Thanksgiving Day. She straightened up and went to the den and signed on to AOL.

Missy was glad to notice a quick note from Ashe. She was hoping to hear from her.

To: missymom
From: AsheMacD

Subject: You know?

Sorry I haven't been online much, Missy. Tyler took a turn for the worse over the weekend, so I've only been online for a few minutes at a time. He's fine now. I wanted to check in and see how the plan was going. Is it falling into place? Let me know if you have any questions or need to bounce ideas back and forth. What works for one might not be right for another.

Wishing you the best.
Peace out,
Ashe

Her IM alert chimed. It was Skye.

shootingskye: *Missy, you okay?*
missymom: *Yes, fine.*
shootingskye: *You sure? I haven't seen you online lately.*
missymom: *Of course I'm okay. I've been busy.*
shootingskye: *Have you told the girls yet?*
missymom: *No.*
shootingskye: *Why?! You can't hide it from them forever.*
missymom: *They don't need to know… yet. What if he decides he wants to come home?*
shootingskye: *Is that possible? Have you heard from him?*
missymom: *He's been calling me, if you can believe that.*
shootingskye: *Yeah? That's great. Maybe he's come to his senses.*
missymom: *I don't answer his calls.*
shootingskye: *What? Why not?! Don't you want to get back together?*
missymom: *Sure, but on my terms. I have a plan.*

A few seconds later, Missy's phone rang. She glanced at the caller ID. "Skye."

"What is going on? What plan?" Skye sounded breathless and Missy could hear sirens and yelling in the background.

"Where are you? Why is it so noisy?"

"I'm at the public library."

"It's awful noisy in your library."

247

"Sirens are going off somewhere. I can't tell where it's coming from. Maybe it's an earthquake drill."

"You're having a drill now? Or a *real* earthquake?" Missy fretted. She was deathly afraid of them, which is why she lived in Las Vegas and not in Los Angeles.

"I think it's a drill, or maybe a false alarm. I can't feel anything. Let me go outside where it's quieter. Don't worry about me. What's going on with you? I haven't heard much from you in the last few days."

Missy could hear the noise fade and Skye panting. "Ashe is helping me with a plan. That's all. If it's successful, you'll know about it Thanksgiving night. If not..."

"Sounds like a lot of intrigue to me. Hope it's worth the trouble," Skye replied.

"Oh, pooh. Don't be like Celia. Ashe has some remarkably good ideas."

"Yes, I know. From personal experience."

"Sorry to hear the two of you aren't going to hook up." Missy giggled. Skye's email from the previous night explained the mutual non-romantic link between her and Ashe. Missy thought a bi-coastal match between two people who barely knew each other was a long shot at best.

"Don't be. We're still friends, although I don't know why. It's always a letdown when someone tells you they're just not into you." Skye laughed.

"At least you can laugh about it."

"I have to say it was pretty funny," Skye admitted.

"Anyway, if my plan succeeds, I'll let you all know. Because if it does, it means Ashe is a freaking genius. She should give up writing romance and write a relationship book." Missy sighed. "If it doesn't work, I don't know what I'll do. Slit my wrists, maybe?"

"Don't say that, Missy, not even in jest."

"I wouldn't. My options are limited. If this thing blows up in my face, I could end up in the poor house. Or worse, I could have to move back to the parents' house in Indianapolis. Wouldn't that be ducky? No offense, I'm hoping for Earl's epiphany. I'm not looking forward to single parenthood."

"If he pulls the plug, you'll get a nice settlement. He left you, remember? You'll be fine."

Missy smiled as she mentally clicked off her accomplishments against the tasks she had yet to complete. "I didn't think so before. Now, though... I think you might be right."

***

It was impossible getting Kara to bed. She bounced up and down in perpetual motion, her tiny arms flailing and her long hair following behind. The chattering was incessant. "Mama, is Daddy coming home tomorrow? When will he be here? Are we having pie for Thanksgiving? What kind? Can I have a friend over? Can we put the Christmas tree up while the turkey is cooking? I can't believe we don't have school until Monday! *Monday*."

Missy found it difficult to focus her eye on her youngest, now not much more than a flash of pre-teen energy. The conversation was one-way. Her hyperactive sugar rush must have come courtesy of the school Thanksgiving party, where pumpkin cupcakes reigned supreme. With so much to do at home, Missy begged off her regular room mom duty. Without a motherly eye to monitor her, Kara was left to down all the sweets she could consume. "Kara, honey. I want you to get to bed early. I need both you and Kassie to help me tomorrow. We have to make sure this Thanksgiving is the best ever."

Kassie, who was on her stomach in front of the TV, rolled her eyes. "Why? Thanks to *you*, he's not coming home."

Missy ignored her eldest, choosing instead to dig Kara's flannel pajamas from a drawer. *Why did she have to be so nasty?* "Mama!" Kara yelled.

Missy threw Kassie a poisoned glare as she attended to Kara. "Don't worry, honey. Daddy *is* going to be here Thursday. And yes, it's going to be the best day ever."

It was almost midnight by the time she got the kids to bed. She moved to the computer to check her mail. It was quiet on the VM front, with little email to open or answer.

To: AsheMacD
From: missymom
Subject: The Plan

Ashe,

I want to thank you again for all you've done. You're a lifesaver! Everything is in place. I've followed your directions to the letter and all I can do is wait.

Please tell me again it's going to be all right. Sorry. I need some moral support. I'm not used to this!

As you've pointed out, the next couple of days are going to be tough ones either way. I feel so much better knowing I can count on you (and of course, the other VMs) to see me through.

Have a nice holiday with your little one.

Missy

Chapter Twenty-six

Wednesday, November 25
Minneapolis, Minnesota

The bouquet of freshly brewed Turkish coffee wafted around the corner, its thick, piquant aroma winding up the stairs and into Ally's bedroom. Its fragrance tickled her nose and tugged at her consciousness. Cocooned under layers of flannel and down, she snuggled deeper and reached to her right. The flannel on Greg's side of the bed was cool to the touch. Ally raised an eyelid and peered at the alarm clock. After seven? After *seven*! "Oh, my God, no!" She flung the bedding away and raced downstairs in her thermal underwear, robe less, her bare feet striking icy hardwood stairs.

Greg was stationed at the table, his head behind the morning paper. Vanessa was seated at the kitchen counter with a bowl of Cheerios. The tiny girl was dressed in oversized corduroy overalls and turtleneck sweater, and her curly hair was pulled back into a single neat braid. With spoon suspended in midair, she looked up in surprise. "'Morning, Mama," she said.

"Oh, Greg, you should have woken me up." Ally scrambled around the kitchen, checking the coffee level and the inside of Vanessa's bowl. Next, she peered into Vanessa's lunch box. Yes, the four food groups represented by a turkey sandwich, applesauce and carrot sticks were in place. Ally next inspected her backpack for contraband toys.

Greg lowered the paper. "Oh, Hon, I've got it covered. I thought I'd give you a break. You need your rest. Tomorrow's a big day for you." He wasn't kidding. Thanksgiving dinner would be held at the Smith house this year, complete with a contingent of Greg's siblings and their children, his mother, Ally's parents, and Mike and Mike Jr. Ally spent most of the day before baking pies and cookies and starting food prep so that Turkey Day could commence without a hitch. With early snow on the ground as a bonus, the plan was for late night sledding after watching the Vikings on TV. It promised to be a raucous gathering.

Ally calmed. She wasn't crazy and she wasn't running late after all. She grabbed a mug and poured a cup of coffee. "That's so sweet, Greg, but you didn't have to. I have it covered. By the way, you did a nice job with the hair. Are you going to take Vanessa to school, too?"

"That's the plan. The shop gave me the day off. And," he teased, "I have some *super*-secret running around to do after Vanessa gets to school." Ally knew he was going to do some pre-Black Friday Christmas shopping and was trying to arouse her curiosity. He had been taunting her for weeks about the ultra-secret present he had in mind and how perfect it was, while Ally was unconcerned. She yawned, stretching farther than she needed to. His hints bounced off their intended target.

"That's nice."

"Aren't you wondering what I'll be doing?" Greg's eyes were twinkling as he needled her, his eyebrows raised, the corners of his mouth betraying a tease. *Damn, he's hot.*

"Not at all." Ally feigned disinterest, opened the refrigerator, and tried to locate her Half and Half, which was buried under a bounty of vegetables, hams, yams, and a marinating turkey.

"I'll wonder, Daddy!" She could count on Vanessa to shoehorn her way into the conversation.

"Hush, baby." Greg approached Ally and slipped his arms around her waist. "Aren't you curious at all? I could be doing something you don't like. Something... *forbidden.*" He whispered in her ear.

"That's nice." Ally deadpanned, trying hard to ignore an overwhelming urge to drag him into the bedroom. She knew her apathy would drive him wild.

Greg man-pouted, gave up, and grabbed his parka. "Okay then. I'm going to clear the walk. Be ready in ten minutes, Vanessa."

"Hey, you." Ally grabbed Greg by the collar and drew him close. She gave him a big, sloppy kiss. "I love you, dude."

"Yeah. I know. How could you not?" His voice was monotone. Two could play that game.

"Oh, you!" She slapped him on the backside. Ally took her coffee and headed upstairs. She gave Vanessa a kiss on the head as

252

she passed by. "I'll see you both later. Be a good girl at school, Vanessa. Love you."

"Yes, Mommy. Love you, too."

***

Dear Mac

I went to see you the other day. It was a beautiful day, a nice ride. It may sound stupid, but I find solace being near you. I know I'm talking to marble, which makes me crazy. I believe you can hear me. I have to believe it. I've missed you so much... I need the time with you, and I'll take it however I can get it. I start telling you my day, my concerns, about Tyler, and my head clears and I can see what I can't in the dim of my cave.

The last visit was different.

Part of me thinks you'll be angry with me.

You have to know that things have changed. I don't need to tell you, do I? The last year has been horrendous, and I've dealt with it alone. I've shouldered the burden and carried on. Like a good soldier. I've lived my life through your eyes, with your sensibilities and your memory to guide me. It's been all about you, Mac.

Damn it, Mac, you should be here with me.

The last few weeks have been a revelation to me. I once thought I could never re-enter life as I knew it before. It was so far back in the recesses of history, I was content with where it was. You're the best thing that ever happened to me. I'll love you forever and will never forget you. It's only...now I can see the other side. In a way, it makes me hopeful sometimes, in another way, I feel guilty.

There are regrets: I should have done more with you, for you. I should have appreciated you and shown you how much. I should have been better. I should have been caring, understanding, and gentle, but I'm a grouchy old bear (ask Rhett). I know I did wrong by you just by being me. You know I can't change any of that now. I see that pinpoint of hope in the distance, and it takes my breath away.

Because I know in order to move forward, I have to let go. Of you.

***

After a steamy shower and another cup of coffee, Ally was ready to start her day. She decided to check her email first.

Janna penned a brief note wishing everyone a Happy Thanksgiving. Her plan was to pick up Mandy from the train station and Rachel from the airport which meant she would be running from one end of NYC to the next. Celia chimed in next from Florida. She sent a text from her phone at work. "Laurel and her family are spending Thanksgiving with us. Her father gets out of the hospital today. Will e-you later."

Ally noticed Skye online early so she IM'ed her.

ally1234: *What are you doing up so early?*

shootingskye: *Working. I fell into a job doing a series of spreads for a magazine. It's a great job, too. I might be out of debt sooner than I thought!*

ally1234: *Great news! Good for you. What are you doing tomorrow?*

shootingskye*: It's just Rob and me. We might get dim sum tomorrow for our Thanksgiving dinner.*

ally1234: *Dim sum! Are you nuts? You're not doing turkey? What about a ham?*

shootingskye: *I'm a terrible cook. I'm starting to try it now with limited success.*

ally1234: *What about chicken? That's easy enough.*

Ally believed it was the epitome of pathetic to have to go to a restaurant on Thanksgiving. Such a major holiday should be spent in the company of family and friends, suffering over a hot stove with a Norman Rockwell turkey and oyster dressing at the finish line in the afternoon.

shootingskye: *My dear, I can't boil an egg. It's not so nuts, really. Chinese restaurants are always open and Rob loves dim sum. He has a favorite new place in the Inner Sunset. It'll be a blast. What about you?*

ally1234: *I'm hosting the family this year. It'll be a blast here, too, what with all the relatives. I'm afraid of what will come after the mushroom cloud disintegrates. LOL...*

shootingskye: *Make them pick up.*

ally1234: *I've no problems there. Greg pitches right in. And you know me. I'm not much of a neat freak.*

That was an understatement. While the basics were clean, their house was often an obstacle course with a burgeoning array of clutter covering every surface. Ally would choose happiness over a tidy house any day.

shootingskye: *Heard from Ashe lately?*
ally1234: *Actually, no. I haven't checked all my email yet.*
shootingskye: *I should run. I need to get these photographs downloaded this morning. Happy Thanksgiving. Don't work too hard.*
ally1234: *Happy Thanksgiving. Don't eat too much.*

Ally closed the box and went back to her mail. She opened a short note from Missy. "Wish me luck tomorrow."

"That's all?" Ally wondered out loud. Missy had been cryptic the last ten days or so, popping online only long enough to check her mail. In addition, she was conspicuously absent for late-night IMs and phone calls. After the first hysterical email, Missy had been tight-lipped. Now she shrugged off mention of Earl leaving, refused to talk about her current feelings, what she was doing or how the girls were holding up. Ally sent a private response. "You need to spill the wine, Girl, and it has to be soon. We love you and are worrying. Call anytime you want."

Her final email came from Ashe.

To: Ally1234
From: AsheMacD
Subject: A question

Ally, I know you're going to be busy with your family and your holiday. I'm also busy with my work and with Tyler. However, I have something important to say and I'd rather bounce it off you first than subject the whole group to it at the same time.

I was wondering if I could call you sometime Friday. I realize Vanessa will be home – no school –I need to speak with you and *only* you. It's important. Give me a good time to call where we can chat without the demands of our young children.

Thanks for your friendship.

Peace out,

Ashe

P.S. I would appreciate it if you kept this between us for now.

Ally closed the email. She held her breath. Whatever was on Ashe's mind, it seemed serious, almost ominous. She felt a surge of energy, a snap of electricity in her head, a premonition of something bad coming down. Her heart skipped a beat. In the last three weeks, she had grown to like Ashe very much. It hardly seemed possible – Ally felt as close to Ashe as she did to the other Virtual Moms. Ashe must have felt the same; otherwise, why would she choose her – out of all the VMs – to confide in? Ally wondered what was weighing so heavily on her mind. "I hope she's all right," she said out loud.

* * *

The dining room was clear – finally – the extra chairs unearthed from the clutter and table leaves in place, thanks to Greg. Ally placed a festive orange tablecloth over the massive oak and centered all the Thanksgiving Beanie Babies she could locate in the middle. *I am simply amazing!* She was giving the room one last inspection when her phone rang.

"Hello?"

"Al, it's Janna."

"Hey, you. Happy Thanksgiving. I thought you'd be busy running today."

"I'm in the car as we speak, on my way to JFK."

"Be careful."

"No *problema*. The city's dead. Everyone with sense and moolah left town yesterday."

"Same here. The older I get, the earlier holidays start. So what's up?"

"I wanted to know if you've heard from Ashe."

"Why?" Ally recalled Ashe's cryptic email from a few short hours before. She debated over how much to reveal, since she was sworn to secrecy.

256

"I haven't heard much from her since Juan and I started dating. I was wondering if she was busy, or…if she was mad at me. We had a little bit of a blowout over Juan. She was more suspicious than Celia about him, if you can believe that."

"No, I can't. Celia tops the charts when it comes to being a skeptic."

"Ashe and I have had some disagreements in the last year, the normal stuff. Nothing that would interfere with our friendship. She's not psycho like that."

"Ashe emailed me today."

"Private email? You mean now? Because I don't remember getting a loop email from her today. I haven't checked my Blackberry yet since I'm on Bluetooth now."

Uh-oh. Ally sank into a chair. Getting into the middle of a VM spat, even a minor one was the last thing she wanted. "She wanted to chat."

"About what?"

"Don't know. Wouldn't say. She's going to call me Friday."

"*Call* you? Like on the *phone*? For real? On Friday? I've never spoken to her, and I've known her longest! Why does she want to talk to you?" Ally recognized Janna's nervous sputtering as a sign her emotions were being whipped to agitation. The pitch of her voice had ascended into a higher octave.

"Janna, I don't know why. She won't be available until Friday. She's not online so I can't IM her to ask."

"Humph!" The reaction was followed by a long, awkward silence. Ally rushed to think of a valid reason why Ashe would want to speak with her and not to Janna.

"Maybe it has something to do with Tyler," she offered. "Our kids are the same age. Yours are in their twenties. It may be harder to relate the needs of a five-year-old against adult children. I know she's been experiencing some serious problems with Tyler, although she doesn't go into detail."

Janna's voice softened. "I think I'll email her later, to let her know I'm not mad over what she said about Juan."

"I think you should. She would appreciate it. It has to be hard walk in her shoes." Ally took a deep breath, knowing she had dodged the big one. "Friends?"

"Forever. Happy Thanksgiving, Ally."

***

"Prep work finished for tonight?" It was Greg, peeking into the den.

Ally smiled. "You tell me. I believe it's under control." After a frenzied day of decorating, cooking and cleaning in advance of the holiday, this year's Smith Thanksgiving was as good as it was going to get.

Greg came in and slid into Ally's seat, shoving her rear end a little to the left. His arm wrapped around her and caught her before she toppled over. "You're my human dynamo!" He kissed her. "And I love you."

Ally sighed and pulled the lapel of his flannel shirt. "Big day tomorrow, dude. Relatives coming from all over. I hope you're up to it. It's going to be a nut house. Hey, thanks for tending to Vanessa today. You make me feel like a queen. And I love you, too."

"No problem, your highness." He picked up her hand and kissed it. "Coming to bed?"

"In a minute."

Ally was about to power her computer down when it announced, "You've got mail!" She opened her inbox. "Who would be mailing me so late on Thanksgiving Day eve?"

The message was from Celia.

To: Ally1234, jannasbananas, laurelextonsbunch, shootingskye, missymom
    From: celiasunshine
    Subject: Ashe

I have the goods on Asheley W. MacDaniel. If you are interested in joining me on the path to the truth, email back.
    Celia

"Oh, Celia, really! Grow up, will you?" she said out loud. Ally thought since little mention of the Ashe problem was made in the last couple of weeks, Celia had given up her vendetta. Instead it appeared that she was launching a full scale, Virtual Moms War, where sides were drawn and allegiances tested. Having survived

258

the last skirmish nearly ten years before, Ally couldn't look forward to a repeat of hurled insults and accusations and the resulting hurt feelings.

"I can't deal with this tonight." Ally deleted the message without replying and powered off her computer.

"Honey, you talking to me?" Greg called from the living room.

"Never mind. First one under the covers gets kissed all over."

Chapter Twenty-seven

Thanksgiving Day, November 26
Sarasota, Florida

With the turkey tucked into the oven and two refrigerators filled to the brim with side dishes and desserts, Celia poured two jumbo mugs of coffee. Laurel had awakened at six to help Celia start the Thanksgiving production line, and thanks to extra hands they finished in record time. It was quite a sight: Celia in a Florida Marlins jersey and red and green plaid flannel shorts and Laurel in a borrowed pink fuzzy robe and matching slippers. They would enjoy a brief respite of calm before the rest of Celia's family arrived. The two women enjoyed the quiet while the sun came up.

During the food prep, Laurel listened as Celia outlined her plan regarding Ashe. During the million mile an hour chat, Celia lost her at several turns. Laurel touched the wrinkled Express Mail envelope bearing the return address for Spark Investigations, traced her fingers along the metered postage. and pinched the envelope to gauge how many pieces of paper were in it. Twenty? Thirty? Certainly not one hundred. She pushed it across the table toward Celia. "So what does everyone else think?" she whispered.

The last thing Laurel wanted to do was wake Joe and her father, both still sleeping in the next room. It was nearly midnight when they pulled into Celia's driveway. Although a hundred times better than he was the first day in the hospital, her father was weak from surgery and Joe was exhausted from the drive from Orlando.

They stared at the package between them as though the slightest touch would ignite the supposed bombshell news inside. Celia took a sip from her coffee. "I haven't heard from Skye. It's still night time there. Ally's probably busy with her family today, although I know she at least opened my email last night." AOL notifications made it easy for her to check on the mail's status, whether opened, deleted, or deleted without opening. Celia checked her mail every half hour to find out who read her email. Laurel, who could barely stand the computer, couldn't understand the anal backtracking. "As for Janna, she's out all day too. Her Thanksgiving dinner isn't until later," Celia chattered on.

"Aren't you going to give Ashe a chance to defend herself?" While she felt closest to Celia, Laurel was her opposite in mood and temperament. Laurel was no fan of confrontation and was far less mistrustful. The Virtual Moms had been virtually peaceful for the past ten years. Having a grenade like this one might blow the group up forever.

"If Spark didn't find anything, she has nothing to fear," Celia said with confidence. "It was hard to spend the week looking at this envelope, especially with Kimber nagging me to open it. I'm doing this the sensible way. I'm giving Ashe time to come clean. If she's hiding something, wouldn't you want to know what it is?"

"I don't know…" Laurel pushed the envelope closer to Celia, as if distancing herself from it would remove the doubt in her mind. "Don't we all have *some* secrets? We don't know everything about everyone. Aren't people entitled to *some* privacy?"

"What if one of us was a sex offender, unknown to everyone else?" Celia countered. "Come on, Laurel. We all have children. We have a *right* to know the truth."

Laurel considered her statement. "I don't think that's possible with Ashe. The sex offender thing, I mean."

"What if it were?" Celia pressed. "I could never be a friend to a sex offender. Or someone who robs banks. Or a murderer. Or a low-life – you know, *those* kinds of people."

Laurel winced. Celia was not only a cynic, she could be condescending. As far as Laurel was concerned, *she* could be one of 'those' kinds of people. "What do you mean?"

"You know. People from the other side of the tracks. Ones with no character, ones that might not be honest, or make everything into one huge drama. Someone like the Wizz Moms."

"You think any and all these things are likely?" It was Laurel's turn to feel skeptical.

"We don't know, do we? There has to be something she's hiding. Why would Ashe lie about being so alone on her blog, and then have a male sitter answering the phone? And why doesn't Ashe ever call any of us back? And where's her photo? None of us knows what she looks like. She could knock right on our door or pass us up at the mall and none of us would know. Oh, and she knows what *all* of us look like. It's a little weird and creepy to me, that's all." Celia got up. "Want more coffee?"

"No thanks." Laurel put down her cup and stared into it. She measured her words carefully. "So what you're saying is that you have specific limits as to your friendships? If you tell a white lie or make a mistake or come from the 'wrong side of the tracks,' that person is out of the picture for you?"

Celia returned with her coffee, her voice confident. "I didn't say that a friend has to be perfect. I want to know the truth."

"What if I had some awful secret about myself that you don't know about? What if it were so awful, you would be repulsed? Would our friendship end?"

Celia reached across the table and patted Laurel's arm. "Oh, honey, but I *know* you! We don't know Ashe."

"Do you really know me?" Laurel trembled as she rose from her seat. The color had drained from her face, while Celia's turned beet red. "Are you sure? Do you *really* know any of us?"

"Of course. We've been together for years."

"Oh, yeah?" Laurel challenged, her voice growing louder. "Did you know I grew up poor? I don't mean middle class, I don't mean lower middle class, I mean dirt-freaking poor. So poor we lived in the projects and sometimes went without meals. I don't know how we did it. We didn't have state assistance. We went without. Things got only slightly better when my father got a government job. Did you know my father had to mortgage his life to send me to college? He's still paying it back, bit by bit, and it's been almost twenty years. And although he's retired and living in Florida, he barely has enough of a pension to live on?"

"Oh, Laurel..." Celia's head shook from side to side. She pushed her chair back and began to rise.

"Oh, no, I'm not finished yet." Laurel pushed Celia back. She was on a roll. "That's not the half of it. Did you know Joe and I are right with him? We're not well off like you are, Celia. We don't live in a fabulous gated community and jet off to Vegas or the Bahamas for a quick weekend whenever we feel the urge. Didn't you notice we always drive down to Orlando to visit my dad? Do you know in all the years we've been coming here for visits, we've never been inside Disney World? It's because we can't afford a day at Disney and we can't afford plane trips. We can barely afford camping trips. Joe hasn't sold a house in two years. We're making do on my income alone, and it doesn't go far. Did you know we're behind on our credit cards? That we missed a few house payments? That the bank might foreclose on our house?" Laurel laughed. "Funny. I guess if we're homeless, we can camp out, finally."

Celia's face dropped. She reached for Laurel's arm. "No, I *didn't* know. I wish I had. Why on earth didn't you say something?"

Laurel sighed. "Probably for the same reason Missy didn't email us right away about Earl leaving her. She was totally humiliated about being a failure and an embarrassment." Laurel looked up. Joe was at the doorway, silent, his jaw dropped to the floor. Her feelings exposed and raw, she looked away.

Laurel's father approached from behind Joe and pushed past him. Mr. Johnson was dressed in hospital scrubs and still had the standard issue non-slip socks on his feet. With splayed fingers, he straightened out his grayed bed head and rubbed at his eyes. Mr. Johnson teetered toward the coffeemaker, past the adults who were suspended like statues in awkward tension.

The old man broke the silence. "Now that we've all gotten to know each other better, Happy Thanksgiving."

***

San Francisco, California

According to Rob, the best dim sum on the West Coast was at Princess Sun. He'd become a connoisseur of dim sum dining, thanks to his band of teenage friends who roamed the greater San Francisco area in search of good food. Skye, on the other hand, was clueless. Her palate wasn't as finely tuned as Rob's, and it lagged far behind Trina's. It was Trina who introduced Rob to a myriad of different foods. He was a good student, and as he was a growing young man, he would eat anything.

By the time they reached the restaurant, the line was long and snaked out the door and spilled onto the Irving Street sidewalk. Her son was buoyant and excited at the prospect of perusing a great menu. "You can tell by the line this is a great place!" The wind was brisk and temperatures had dipped into the high 40's. Skye nodded and shivered.

The Princess Sun served cafeteria-style, and by the time they reached the counter, Skye was a block of ice, her blood coursing cold. A warm column of moist air, scented with Asian spices, blew back from behind the counter. Her reflection in a wall mirror showed a woman with wild hair, bundled up like Kenny in *South Park*, complete with rosy cheeks. "You choose for me," she instructed Rob, "Whatever you want. I'm totally lost when it comes to this."

"I'm warning you, I haven't eaten since yesterday. I'm going to town. You'd better have enough cash."

Skye listened as Rob expertly ordered plump bundles of dumplings with strange names, hairy shrimp balls, and pork and shark buns. The restaurant was noisy with diners, crying babies and waiters shouting to each other in Mandarin. By the time Skye and Rob reached the end of the line, she found herself overheated. She took off her jacket as they headed for a tiny vacant table, a dry island in a sea of humanity. It was amazing how many people elected to eat out for Thanksgiving. Most of the clientele was Chinese. The rest were single diners and families like hers – as far from Asian as one could be.

"My, my. Look who's here!"

Skye turned around quickly. She couldn't believe it. Dude stood before them. He was alone, jacket slung over his arm, his graying hair pulled into a ponytail. "Hi," she answered shyly, "What are you doing here?"

Dude pointed at a framed article hanging above their table. It was cut from the *Chronicle* and displayed in a handsome black frame. "'Best Dim Sum in The City – 2008.' I happen to agree. I come here for every major holiday." He smiled at Rob. "And who is your Thanksgiving guest today?"

Skye, knocked off-kilter, forgot her manners and her voice. "This is my son. Rob. I might have mentioned him."

Dude extended his hand. "Pleased to meet you. You can call me Dude. It's not my real name, of course. It suits me best."

Rob grasped the older man's hand and gave it a hearty shake. "Hi. Nice to meet you." He looked Dude over with a discerning eye.

"Won't you join us? This table is small, I could get another chair." Skye blushed and made a feeble attempt to clear the space of soy and hot sauce bottles. The 'table' was the size of a laptop, with barely enough room for a matchbook much less the Emperor's worth of dim sum Rob had ordered and was soon on its way.

"No, thank you. I'll take a rain check. I'm going, not coming." He winked at Skye, who for the sake of Rob was trying to play the scene as nonchalantly as she could. "Have a nice holiday. See you around."

When Dude was on the sidewalk and out of earshot, Rob turned to his mother. "*Who* on earth was that?"

Skye face flushed crimson. "A friend. Just a friend."

A waiter appeared with the first of many baskets and plates of dim sum. "The feast begins!" Rob turned his attention to perilously arranged stacks of food. He popped a stuffed crab claw into his mouth while he separated the food between two plates.

Whew! Skye thought. *Saved by dumplings.*

***

Las Vegas, Nevada

Missy folded and re-folded a starched linen napkin into a crane shape, centering it perfectly on a holiday charger. Somehow during the chaos that was Thanksgiving preparation, the bird had lost its beak and looked droopier than the rest. Everything had to be perfect – the house, the food, Kara and Kassie. So far, with fingers crossed and prayers said in triplicate, the dinner would be on time and perfect. T-minus fourteen minutes before the guests would arrive.

Missy raced from room to room, a maniacal human hummingbird in lace and pearls fluffing up pillows and searching for any dust that might have escaped previous attention. Kassie slumped over a chair in the living room. She was a vision in plaid jumper and black tights, but oh, that unhappy face. "I thought you said Dad was coming home?" she challenged as Missy righted an overturned Hummel on the mantel.

"Three o'clock," Missy answered as she headed to the kitchen to check up on her turkey.

"Why three? Is he making appointments now?" Kassie was no fool, and she was old enough to figure things out. Missy hoped this mess of a marriage would be worked out to her satisfaction before she had to admit that things were less than rosy.

"Plane. Read a book if you're bored." It was all she had time for before slamming the kitchen door.

Kara hovered over a vegetable tray that was in a holding pattern on the kitchen island. Her delicate fingers poised to attack an olive as Missy burst through the door. "Not now," Missy warned, "When your dad arrives. Don't spoil your appetite." Kara pulled her hand back.

The doorbell rang. Kara jumped up and screamed. "I'll get it!"

"Wait a minute." Missy gave her youngest the once over. Kara was dressed in her holiday best, a precious red velvet jumper and black tights. She'd combed her hair and clipped it back with a barrette decorated in sparkles and ribbons. Missy turned her toward the front door with a pat on her rear end. "Okay. Off with you." She lingered behind her.

"What are you so excited about?" Kassie snarled at her little sister. "It's not Dad, you dummy. He wouldn't ring the doorbell. He has a key."

Kara stuck her tongue out in return. She opened the front door.

"Grandma! Grandpa!" Earl's parents were at the door, beaming, their arms laden with wrapped packages. Kara cried out in disbelief. Kassie jumped from her chair and straightened out the wrinkles in her dress. She ran to the door.

"Kara-pie! My, look how tall you are! And look at Kassie! You're almost grown up." Grandma Martin gave each girl a kiss and hug. Grandpa brought up the rear.

"Wait a minute. Aren't we forgetting someone?" Grandma Martin asked. She turned to the street, where Missy's parents were getting out of a car.

"Mimi! Granddad!" Kassie ran to the car to meet them. She threw her arms around both of them and hugged them tight.

The two sets of grandparents were whisked into the house. Multiple conversations overlapped. Kara's voice grew louder to compete with the adults, while Kassie corrected her, "Pipe down, Squirt. Let people finish a sentence, won't you?" Kassie glanced at a silent Missy who was taking it all in. She threw her daughter a wink from across the room. She could have been mistaken. Missy thought she saw tear in Kassie's eyes.

At a quarter after three, Earl let himself into the house. With so much going on, no one noticed his entrance. No one – except Missy. She crossed the room and gently removed his coat.

"Happy Thanksgiving, Earl," she said. "We missed you."

She meant it.

***

Minneapolis, Minnesota

Greg carried a sleeping Vanessa and gently placed her in her princess bed. Ally was right behind, her arms full of jacket, scarf and snow pants. "Look at our little angel," he said as he gently removed her jeans. Ally dropped Vanessa's outerwear into a rocking chair.

She removed the barrettes from Vanessa's hair and combed her fingers through the curly knots. "She had a big day, all right. We all have. I'm surprised we could get her to leave the hill. She looked like she could sled all night!"

Greg nodded in agreement. "What a maniac! She was going full guns until ten. She reminds me of me at that age. I could never sit down for more than five minutes at a time. I had enough energy to light up a city."

Ally tapped him on the shoulder. "Leave her shirt and socks on, Greg. She'll be fine sleeping in them this one time."

Greg pulled the sheets and then a down comforter over Vanessa. "Nighty-night, pumpkin." He kissed her forehead.

Ally kissed her finger and then pressed it to Vanessa's lips. "Sleep tight," she whispered. They quietly shut the door and headed down the hall.

"Going to check in with the Moms?" Greg asked.

Ally slid her arm around his waist. She thought of the cryptic email from Ashe. They had arranged to connect tomorrow by phone at 4 p.m. "I don't think so. I'm beat. Besides, tomorrow is another day."

Chapter Twenty-eight

Friday, November 27
New York City

Heads turned when he entered the room, that's how much charisma the man was oozing. Women of all ages were suspended in a mesmerizing spell; the men looked on, their psyches tinged with jealousy and a fair amount of inadequacy. Little old ladies paused mid-fork to gaze upon his chiseled face. The fine lines, a roadmap of perfection, indicated wearying battles on the field of commerce. The war was a tough one, but from his carriage, Janna knew he rose victorious from every single skirmish.

Dressed in an impeccable black tuxedo heightened the allure. There is nothing more dashing than a man in formal wear, especially if it's Armani. His mane of wavy brown hair flowed from his forehead, held together not by man-made mousse, oh, no, but by the hand of God himself. His piercing dark eyes scanned the room. For her? Why her? He could have anyone here, anyone on the globe.

Her chest heaved in anticipation. A longing gripped her from head to toe, the unmistakable desire to meld her body into his. The need to taste, to savor, to appreciate this fine specimen of masculinity overcame her usual common sense. Her heart skipped more than a couple of beats; it was dancing to a primordial drumming, the ancient mating ritual. He dove into the room, not unlike a swimmer tackling the sea, and headed straight for her table.

Eyes misted, she closed them for a moment, wishing upon a star for this slice of time to be frozen forever.

That moment was forever lost. When she opened her eyes, standing before her were a tow-headed boy and a woman bearing the same face.

***

"Mom, get up! Get up! Get up! We overslept!"

"Wah?" Janna stirred, not only because Mandy was shaking her. Her dream, an enjoyable romp at first, was heading to a naughty place. Part of her wanted to go, and the other part was mortified. Thank goodness, Mandy the human alarm clock burst in, otherwise she wasn't sure where the dream may have lead.

"We're late, Mom. We're going to miss all the deals!" It was an Abraham Girl Tradition to hit the stores on Black Friday. Most years they could be found hanging out in the early morning hours on the sidewalk with other hopefuls. Sure they were Jewish, but Christmas was for everyone. Hanukkah shopping was a must – and a bargain was a bargain. Shopping was all about getting the best price. Janna would pay full freight only on the rarest of occasions. Today wasn't one of them.

"Where's Rachel?" Janna hopped out of bed.

"Getting dressed. Sorry, Mom, we forgot to set the alarm. If it weren't for Rach's cell phone alarm, we'd still be asleep." Mandy headed to her room.

Janna hurried to shower and dress. Her weekend was proving to be a whirlwind affair. After collecting the girls from the airport and train depot, they headed uptown for a fabulous spread at the Ritz. It was crazy to labor over a Thanksgiving dinner when a full upscale buffet could be had, featuring carved fowl and beef, a mountain of huge fresh shrimp, and all the inventive side fixings of New York's top chefs could imagine. Her parents had already taken off to winter in their Vegas area home, so it was just the three of them. Janna and her girls enjoyed a leisurely afternoon, and the best part was she didn't have to worry about clean up or leftovers.

She'd invited Juan to tag along, making the invitation sound as casual as she could while urging for a weak commitment. Janna didn't know if it was the press – she was navigating the thin line between neediness and aggressive behavior – or the fact that her daughters would be in attendance to give him the once-over that sent him running. To Janna's dismay, he'd begged off the invite, using the lame excuse of his own family get-together. Janna then waited for an invitation to *his* holiday, and waited and waited some more. It was obvious that to Juan, Janna hadn't made it to the next level in their relationship, the Meet the Family level. Perhaps she was reading – again, common Janna Banana flaw – more into Juan than she should.

Janna sighed as she pulled her Nike cross-trainers. This was not looking good at all. Yet another hopeful bites the dust.

After a satisfying Thanksgiving dinner, the mom and daughter Abrahams window-shopped, prepping for the power retail experience of the next day. It was late when they returned home for coffee and more pie. Mandy and Rachel compared notes on boyfriends, and they commiserated with Janna on the sorry state of Juan-dom.

"If he's going to be like that, he's not for you," Mandy said.

"Don't worry, Mom," Rachel added, "the right one will come along when you least expect it."

Right. Spoken by the daughter who had been dating a fabulous guy for the past three years, News Anchor Bob. What a catch! Bob offered the perfect combination of independence, support, and love. Rachel had experienced unbridled success in running him on the marriage track. He would be News Anchor Son-in-Law in less than two years. And it didn't hurt that the man was adorable.

Before going to bed, Janna checked her email. The sole message came from Celia regarding the dirt she had on Ashe. Janna couldn't click 'Delete' fast enough.

She padded into the kitchen to get a glass of orange juice and a banana yogurt. Stamina is what one needs on Black Friday. She logged onto AOL to find little VM mail sandwiched in between Black Friday sales flyers. Celia sent her usual long post detailing her raucous Thanksgiving with the Extons and her family. Missy reported that the girls, the grandparents, and Earl had a great holiday. Janna was pleased to find a dearth of response to Celia's cryptic Ashe message from the other Virtual Moms. She preferred to think of Celia as overly cautious and not vindictive and mean. Although just as many times she teetered on the fine line between the two.

The last email was from Ashe. True, Janna had been wrapped up with Juan and was not a regular contributor in the past weeks, yet she'd read every email. In recent days, Ashe made herself scarce from her and more so from the group. Janna missed the closeness they shared before. 'Before' was before she hatched the bright idea to ask the Virtual Moms to allow Ashe into the group. Since then, not only had the dynamic of the group changed, the friendship changed. The easy give and take between Ashe and Janna was gone, replaced by a tense wall.

She sipped her coffee and considered the state of the Virtual Moms. Janna spent most of Thanksgiving thinking about Ashe. What was the problem that was so important she had to talk to Ally about? Why not her? Why was she reacting the way she was? She felt abandoned, left out, almost *jealous*. Janna realized her recent private messages to Ashe had been brittle, leaving her new friend no option than to confer with the other VMs about life's challenges. After the phone call with Ally, she dashed off a quick email to Ashe, a short, cheery note apologizing for her absence. Seeing a return note a few minutes later made her feel better.

To: Jannasbananas
From: AsheMacD
Subject: Great News!

Janna,
You wouldn't believe what came in the mail yesterday. It's fantastic! I don't want you to say anything to the others until I tell you first, so please, do me a favor and keep it a secret.

As you know, I've been sending my book out to agents and publishers for years. I've received so many rejection notices I could wallpaper every room of my house. Probably every room in your house, too. Not anymore! Someone in a big New York house wants to publish *Love and Laughter in Bonnie Doone*. Can you believe it?

Like I said, please don't say anything to the other VMs yet. I want to firm up the deal.
Virtually yours,
Ashe

Could this be the secret she wanted to speak to Ally about? If it were, why was she telling her, too?

"Huh," Janna said out loud, "no wonder I dreamed about Tyler last night."

"Mom? You ready?" Mandy called from her room.

"Yes." Janna powered off her computer, picked up her purse and headed for the door.

***

Sarasota, Florida

Despite the tense moments between Celia and Laurel, Thanksgiving turned out a raucous, wonderful time. Celia apologized to Laurel and she accepted. Celia's strong personality and vigorous opinions were no reason to end a thirteen-year relationship. After the rest of Celia's family arrived, the party wheeled into third gear. Laurel's father found an instant rapport with Celia's mother. They were the same age and shared similar circumstances and stories. Kimber and Marcus were already as close as sister and brother. Brandon became instant friends with Marcus, the other Virtual Kid of the group.

On the other hand, Joe was pensive and not his usual life-of-the-party, boisterous self. Laurel watched him closely. Since coming to Florida, he was a different man. He wasn't as flippant as he could be. Perhaps seeing her father in the hospital and the strain it put on Laurel and Marcus affected him, too. Maybe it was the altercation in Celia's kitchen? She didn't know. Laurel hoped that if the light came on over Joe's head, it would stay on for a good, long time. She loved him, although she was tired of carrying the entire weight of the family on her shoulders.

It was quiet in the house. Except for the ticking of a clock and Laurel's dad watching CSPAN, all was peaceful and serene. Kimber and Marcus were out with Celia catching a few Black Friday sales. And Joe? Who knows where he was, she thought. He had taken the truck first thing in the morning and had not yet returned.

They would be going back to St. Louis the next day, Marcus and Laurel on an early flight with Joe flying out later. Laurel began packing, separating the clean from the dirty clothing. She was amazed at what her husband decided to bring on an extended trip. Just like Joe, he packed too many socks and not enough underwear for Marcus. She thought of the catching up she needed to do once they returned home. She fretted over the bills, over what her substitute teacher did and didn't do, over whether or not Marcus would be cut from the hockey team.

Laurel was so lost in a worried tangle of thought she didn't hear Joe walk into the room. "Honey," he said, touching her arm. Laurel startled.

"Oh, my God, you scared me half to death!"

"Sorry."

"You should give a person warning before you come into a room." Laurel turned away and continued packing.

"I said I was sorry. Can you put that off for a minute? I want to talk to you about something." Joe sat on the bed and patted a spot next to him.

"I'm kind of busy, Joe."

"It's important."

Laurel looked into her husband's face and saw his sincerity. She tossed the shirt into the suitcase and sat down. "Okay?"

"Laurel, I love you."

"Thanks. I love you, too." Laurel spoke mechanically. She *did* love him; she just didn't feel like it *this* second.

"I wanted to make that clear from the beginning. And I know I've been…fiscally negligent when it comes to this family. I don't want to lose you, and I know that's a possibility."

Laurel shifted away from him. It was a relief to know he finally got it, although the admission meant they had moved into an uncomfortable area. She didn't know what to say. "Oh?"

"It's not that I don't want to support us. Things haven't worked out the way I thought they might."

Laurel drew a big breath. "Okay."

"I know your family means the world to you. Your dad, me… Marcus. I know this whole heart attack thing with your dad was scary."

"Yes, it was."

"Laurel, while you and Marcus were at the hospital, I did some checking around. I have a plan. I don't want to proceed unless you're with me on this."

"So?"

"I applied for a job in Orlando, in a real estate office. Of course, it's a ground level job, and I'll have to get my license here. And the economy is bad here, probably worse than it is in St. Louis."

273

"Orlando? Real estate?" Laurel was incredulous. To her knowledge, Joe had sold only one house in his 'career' as a listing agent. He might be jovial, good-time Joe, but he lacked a Midas touch for the business.

"Now, don't blow up on me, hear me out. The guy at the real estate office gave me a lead on another job. It's with a friend of his in construction. I could work that by day and do the real estate thing part time. I really want to make this – us – work. The best part is that we could be closer to your dad. I know you miss him. He's not getting any younger, and I know he would love to see more of Marcus. And Celia would be close by. You could probably get a job here teaching." Joe was rambling now, trying to get all his words out before he lost Laurel's attention.

Laurel's eyes filled with tears. She attempted to process all of Joe's words. Key words floated in and out of her head. Her dad. Orlando. Work. Marcus. None of it made sense. She was left speechless. She had only enough strength for one word. "When?"

"I start on Monday. That is, if you agree."

"Monday? Like this coming Monday?"

"I know it's short notice. Of course, you'll have to go back with Marcus alone. You'll have to do most of the settling of affairs in St. Louis, like selling the house, packing. The house isn't worth much. We might be underwater on it and may not make a penny. Your dad says I can stay with him until you get down here. I want to shoot for the first of the year, so Marcus can switch schools at the end of the semester. If it takes longer than that, like the end of the school year, your dad is fine with that. Marcus, too. I sounded him out yesterday and he's excited. He won't miss hockey, can you believe it?" Joe took Laurel's hand. "I could save up and when you get here, we could start over fresh."

"Oh, Joe."

"I love you and I'm going to prove it to you if it takes the rest of my life." He studied Laurel's eyes, now blurred by a pool of tears. "So, what do you say? Harebrained scheme? Typical Joe?"

A-typical Joe. A genius plan; why hadn't Laurel thought of it before? For once, a crisis worked out in her favor. She wrapped her arms around him and hugged him like she had never done before. For once, she felt one with her husband.

"I love you," she said.

274

The promise of new life was breaking over the horizon. She could hardly wait.

***

Minneapolis, Minnesota

With Vanessa and Greg out playing in snowdrifts under sunny skies, Ally paced the kitchen. She was waiting for her arranged phone call from Ashe. Seeing herself as a mediator between dissenting factions, she was anxious to settle whatever problems the Virtual Moms might have recently developed with each other. Despite the problems Celia seemed to be having with the newbie, the rest of the group did not share her concern. Perhaps this phone call would dispel the distrust Celia had conjured up and they could all go back to being friends.

The minutes ticked off slowly. She'd had no other email from Ashe since late Wednesday. Ally could tell from her Buddy List that she hadn't been online since then. With the holidays, maybe Ashe was busy like the rest of them. It would no doubt be a lonely one without a spouse to share it with. Ally tried to imagine a holiday without Greg. The last ten years had been happy ones. She shuddered and shook off the thought. "No way."

At precisely 4:05, her phone rang. Ally jumped up to get it. Her caller ID showed a mobile number with an unfamiliar area code. "Hello?"

"Hello. May I speak with Ally Smith?" The voice was deep, the timbre rich, and the accent doused with Southern charm.

"Speaking."

"Hi. This is Ashe. Ashe MacDaniel?"

Are you sure? Ally thought. *I'm not going to say anything but she sounds positively manly.*

"Ally? Are you still there?"

"Yes, hi." She struggled to compose herself.

"Listen, I'm on the road so my cell is fading. I'm going to pull over for the signal." Ally heard a few seconds of scuffling in the background. "Better?"

"Oh, yes, much better." Ally took the phone from her ear and stared at it. Either she was dreaming or going crazy. She pinched herself. Nope, not dreaming – definitely crazy.

275

"I know this is a shock to you. By now you've figured out that I'm a man," the voice said. "I hope you hear me out and won't slam the phone in my ear. I chose you to explain this to because you seem the most… I don't know… balanced? Non-judgmental?"

"Uh, huh." *Perhaps the one most likely to say nothing when dumbfounded?*

"I hope you have a lot of time, because this is going to be a long, twisted story."

Chapter Twenty-nine

A blast of warm dog breath laced in salmon kibble and accompanied by a long gluey icicle of drool roused Rhett from his peaceful slumber. Not a gorgeous strapping hunk of a man, not a mediocre man, not a homely, wimpy man. "Eww… Jim Bob! Get off me." He pushed the hound off the bed. "If you lived in my house, you wouldn't be *in* the house. You'd be outside with the varmints and livestock where you belong." Jim Bob looked at him with gigantic brown eyes and spiraled a spot on the floor near the bedroom door before he rolled himself into a dog circle and put his head over his front paws. "Don't look at me like that," Rhett cautioned. "I don't know why Ashe puts up with your huge, lazy, sorry ass. He must have his reasons." He pulled Ashe's robe on over his sweats and headed downstairs.

Tyler was up, eating a bowl of Cheerios at the kitchen table. Rhett glanced around, grateful he hadn't located the Krispy Kremes. "Honey-child, did you make your own breakfast?" he asked as he scrounged the cupboards for coffee.

"I'm a big boy now. I'm almost six. I make breakfast *some*times." Tyler announced his achievement with plenty of sincerity. "I could have made *coffee*, too, but Daddy says I'm not allowed to touch anything hot."

Rhett ruffled his hair. "Don't worry about it. I'll live. Imagine that, making your own breakfast. Why, I can remember when your mama and daddy brought you home from the hospital. You were so tiny and pink, not a hair on your head. One teeny, tiny, screaming, helpless thing in diapers."

Tyler scrunched up his nose. "I'm *not* a baby," he declared.

"I agree. I would have never imagined on that day that you would be making your own breakfast. You sure are growing up, Ty-Ty. Just in time. I need all the help I can get taking care of your daddy. Heaven only knows he needs it." He shook his head and went back to scavenging for a caffeine fix.

"Where did Daddy go?"

"You remember. He said he's going to New York City."

"Why?"

"You know that, too, Ty. He has business to attend to." Rhett smiled. *Both personal and professional*, he thought.

"You mean his book, right? That's the business?" Jim Bob made a lethargic appearance. Tyler slipped him a Cheerio.

"Oh, yes." Rhett agreed, only to a point. He'd been thrilled when he'd heard the news. Heck, most of the county heard the news, what with the yelling and hollering and the champagne toasts going on in the kitchen Wednesday afternoon. *Love and Laughter in Bonnie Doone* was only part of the business. The rest had to do with a beautiful, sassy Jewish girl in midtown Manhattan. Now that the novel was a sure thing, Ashe had to clear up the Virtual Moms' misconception about the real Asheley MacDaniel. As the celebration ebbed, Rhett pointed out to that the Moms would figure it out in no time, what with end covers featuring Ashe's photograph plastered all over every Barnes and Noble from coast to coast. And while in confessional mode, it wouldn't hurt for Ashe to come clean about his feelings for Janna.

"I don't feel anything for Janna except a profound respect and admiration," Ashe announced after he rejoined the humans back on earth. The initial rush of jubilation was a heady drug, but like all drugs, there was a downside. What goes up must come down. His expression was filled with doubt and impending disaster. Ashe wasn't stupid. He knew he was in big trouble with the moms.

"Asheley Wilkes MacDaniel," Rhett had chided. "You've always been a horrible liar and here you are again trying to spin a tale. Who are you trying to convince, you or me? Because you're doing a god-awful job with me."

It took two hours of cajoling and threats before Ashe finally relented. He was going to New York to straighten out this mess and come clean to Janna.

***

Sarasota, Florida

Celia stood at the door and waved goodbye to Laurel and her family. In a few short hours, her friend and Marcus would be heading back to St. Louis, and Joe and Mr. Johnson would be getting to know each other much better. Celia was happy for Laurel. Joe was going to take responsibility for the family – a plus. Laurel would be a short car ride away, another bonus.

She closed the door and looked back into her now-vacant house. Kimber was babysitting at a neighbor's, and her mother and relatives were all back in their own homes. "This is what's left. Me, alone." In two short years, Kimber would be an adult and on her own. Celia couldn't feel sorry for herself. It was the life she chose. If the right one came along, she would be more than happy to join the masses of the connected. Of course, The Right One would be subjected to awfully high standards. *Maybe I should get a cat,* she thought.

Celia padded toward her computer to check her email, cup of coffee in hand. "Back to real life," she told herself. It was nice to have a four-day weekend for a change, although it would all come to a crashing stop once Monday morning rolled around. Then it would be back to a six-day workweek and the hectic business of making a living.

Her email inbox was jammed full. Most of the email came from the VMs in response to hers asking who wanted to know the facts on the 'real' Ashe MacDaniel. Each Mom responded back to her personally; not one selected 'Reply All.' It felt like years since she sent the email detailing her investigative work. As she opened each response, most of the comments tended to slant against her. Skye flatly answered, "You can look if you want to. I'm out. And please, don't tell me what you found out. I don't want to jeopardize my friendship with Ashe."

"Huh," Celia said to the screen, as though Skye were sitting across from her, "You're passing because Ashe was meant to be *your* hook-up." She went on to the next one, this one from Missy.

"Don't we have enough going on in our lives? We have to dig up the dirt on one of our own? I've got to vote against this. Sorry, no thanks." She wrote a PS: "Oh, and Thanksgiving was fabulous! Earl is back, thanks mainly to Ashe."

"Of course *she's* going to side with Ashe," Celia grumbled.

She opened another email, this one from Janna. "You know how I feel about this, Celia. You're on your own."

"That's right," Celia said out loud as she deleted the email with a resounding click, "she was *your* friend to begin with." She had one final opinion to count, and that was Ally's. Surely Ally would want to know the scoop on Ashe.

To: celiasunshine
From: Ally1234
Subject: Ashe

Celia, I'm afraid I have to excuse myself from any VM vote on this particular issue. I'm privy to some information that I can't share now, but I will soon. It will explain everything. So count me out.
Ally

Celia sat for a moment, trying to figure out what had happened. She'd been outvoted by everyone, and she was sitting on a full disclosure on Asheley MacDaniel, a report she had invested $250 of her own money on. "I'll be…" She took the envelope outside, not knowing what to do with it. It had been worn down by days of handling by inquisitive fingers. She'd wondered for weeks what secrets Ashe might have hidden in her life, why she was so private. Celia had gone to extraordinary means to protect both herself and the rest of the VMs, to prove she was right. Here she was, sitting on a goldmine of information, alone. Was the price of knowledge worth the cost of her long-time friends? At first, she had believed so, but now? She didn't know. She picked up the report and headed outside.

"Damn it." Celia gave the envelope another look before tossing it on her grill.

"Saying goodbye to the past?"

Celia whirled around. Doug Taylor stood behind her, flashing perfect teeth and eyes so deep blue she could drown in them. "I…"

"Dear Lady, let me be of assistance." He pulled a lighter from his pocket and flicked it to life.

Celia gasped and pulled at his sleeve to stop him. She looked at the envelope and then at Doug. "Oh, what the hell. Have at it."

It's amazing how quickly an Express Mail envelope can burn to ash.

Las Vegas, Nevada

Unbeknownst to the elderly and the children, the Martin house was in the midst of a truce of sorts. Missy had installed both sets of grandparents on second floor bedrooms with the girls, while she and Earl remained in their first floor master bedroom. However, Earl hadn't wormed his way into Missy's good graces just yet. He alternated sleeping positions between the chair and carpet, not yet ready to make the move into the marital bed.

Earl had been floored when he saw his mother and father on Thanksgiving, and then to see Missy's parents too… this unexpected turn of events forced him to rethink his hotel room. Only Missy knew he left her, and he was too much of a coward to make such an announcement on a major holiday with everyone in attendance and so happy.

He was quiet during dinner, speaking only when asked a direct question. Kassie and Kara were overjoyed seeing the family reunion playing out before them, and they excitedly kept the grandparents busy. Missy was the perfect hostess, serving and cleaning up with a smile. She wouldn't be responsible for betraying Earl's secret. Ashe was right. If divorce were imminent, he would have spilled his guts in front of the family.

Although she was cordial and kind to Earl, the sleeping arrangements on Thanksgiving night proved tenuous. He couldn't very well sleep on the family room couch. Missy was afraid of Earl's reactions once the door was closed. He said only one thing before dragging a comforter and two pillows to the floor. "Missy, I don't know what you're doing. I don't like it."

Missy said nothing, instead smiling serenely.

The next day, Earl took the grandfathers out for a round of golf, while Missy, the girls and grandmothers scoured Black Friday sales. At the end of the activities, they met at a restaurant for an early dinner. Again, Missy was charming, kind and sweet. She laughed and cajoled as though nothing were wrong, lightly touching Earl's arm and winking at his jokes while at the same time longing to belt him. It was an Academy Award performance. Later that Friday night, locked behind the doors of their bedroom,

Earl approached her. She was already in bed reading a book. "Do you think we should talk?" he asked sheepishly.

"Talk about what, dear?" She kept her voice sweet and low, while her heart was thumping in cut time.

"About... you know, our situation."

"And what is that?"

"You know..."

"You mean, your leaving me? That situation? Because you surely can't mean having our parents over for a holiday, *that* situation."

"I've had a lot of time to think it over. And I talked to my dad."

"You told him?" Missy sat up straight. Could Earl be braver than she thought? Could he mean to break up the family for good?

"No, we talked. A lot." Missy sank back into bed and returned to her book. Earl struggled to speak. "I'm torn."

"Oh, really?" Missy replied, emotionless and nonchalant. Could his change of heart be a result of her visit to an attorney's office? She didn't tell him about the appointment; he'd know soon enough when he'd find the retainer on the MasterCard bill. That conclusion could be reached in a heartbeat. Earl was too dense to figure out Missy landed a job, one as an administrative assistant to one of the partners – right under his nose in his own company. Celia wasn't the only VM who could do undercover work. While waiting for her interview, she learned by listening to fifteen minutes of office chatter that Earl's Other Woman was a Strip showgirl. *Typical.*

"I didn't leave you because I love... the other person. I don't. Before I left, I felt trapped. Alone. And she helped me feel not trapped and not alone." He lowered his eyes. "It didn't work. Because I still love you. And I found I missed the girls. When I saw them with the folks last night, I realized how much I missed them. Geez, they're growing up before our eyes."

"So they are." She thought, *You're so clueless, you missed Kassie's birthday, remember?* "They'll be on their way to college before you know it."

"College? Oh..." Missy could almost see wheels spinning in his head. He viewed them as babies, not as emerging adults.

282

"Anyway, I wanted to tell you. I love you. I want to come back. If you'll have me."

Missy looked at him. His face was as contrite as a schoolboy's caught red-handed with a stolen cookie. She placed her book on her lap. "I'll have to think about it. If you do come back, there will be conditions. One, you have to keep more regular hours. I don't mind if you work late on occasion. The family has to be your number one concern."

"Okay."

"Second, we go to couples' therapy. I want to know why this happened, and I want you to know why this happened. If I'm going to stay with you, this will *not* happen again."

"Done."

"Third, you're going to have to somehow prove to me that I can trust you. If I can't trust you, you can't stay. And I want very hard to trust you. Because…" She got up and pulled him to her. "I love you very much. Still do. Always have." She grabbed his face and kissed him good and hard on the mouth. Earl reeled backward when she released him. He was still in shock as she proceeded to make his bed on the floor.

All in all, it was a good holiday.

***

New York City

The buzzer sounded in Janna's apartment. Mandy and Rachel were out clubbing with some of their friends and not expected back until the wee hours of the next morning. Janna was alone, curled up with the latest thriller she started reading months ago when it was still on the bestsellers list. She expected no one, yet she got up to answer the call. Perhaps Juan was her late night visitor. He could have come to his senses and realized the huge error he made letting their dating friendship wither on the vine. If it were, Janna steeled herself to remain frosty. No one forgets Janna Abraham and comes out unscathed.

"Yell-ow," she chirped. It was early by city standards and she was game for companionship. "Who is it, out so late?"

She heard a cough and the sound of feet stomping. "You don't know me. Well, you do but you don't… Oh, damn it to hell."

283

The voice was deep, smooth, Southern, and no doubt laced in testosterone. It sounded both familiar and strange. "Helll-oooo?"

"Janna, I have to talk to you. I don't know how to say this without saying this…" Janna held her breath at the pause. The voice spoke again. "It's me. Ashe MacDaniel."

Chapter Thirty

Few cars were left on the darkened street as Ashe stumbled to his car. The sun was still hours away from illumination, and the city neighborhood dead silent. Ashe ran his hands through his hair. "I've got to get out of here." A sense of dread came over him. "Wrong, this was all wrong." His car, a huge hulk of an old Crown Vic with North Carolina plates, was beyond where he thought he'd left it. The monster machine was parked askew among a neat row of small foreign jobs. "Sore thumb, baby, that's me." He jumped in, grabbed the steering wheel, and battered his head against it a few times.

Six hours. After an all-day drive, he'd spent six hours talking. Ashe was at a loss for words at first. Amazingly, once he got going, the words tumbled out faster and faster. He apologized. He reasoned. He talked about his book. He explained away his boneheaded moves while Janna sat wordless.

It was foolhardy; it was stupid. No. It was *worth* it. The long drive from North Carolina, the humiliation and relief he felt coming clean to Ally, the wrath he would no doubt get from the rest of the Virtual Moms once they found out about his lies – it was all worth it just to meet her.

***

It was almost midnight when Janna opened the door, clad in flannel pajamas. At first, Ashe's eyes focused on the tiny pink flowers and green leaves weaving in and out on the trellises of the soft fabric. The next moment found Ashe coming to his senses, as his eyes fixed on a most adorable woman. Ashe was taken aback. She was far lovelier in person than she appeared in the photos she posted on Facebook or sent by email. Her delicate features were blurred in the online photographs, doing her no justice at all. For all her bluster and moxie, her big New York assertiveness and cool, Janna was a delicate little thing, much like Mackenzie. Her diminutive size and willowy features were a disarming surprise – after a year of Internet correspondence, he imagined her much taller and brasher.

"Ashe? As in Virtual Mom Ashe?" She asked the question in a tentative voice, her blue eyes sparking firelights, her blond hair pulled back into a mess of a ponytail. Lavender and spice wafted from her skin, hanging in the air like contrails. He could almost touch her scent, the essence of her being.

At that point, he felt certain he would pass out. It could have been due to a lack of sleep, hours on the road, or nothing to eat since Thanksgiving, or it could have been Janna. She swung wide the door and motioned him inside a large foyer that opened into a huge living area. Although the building was old, the apartment was a funky mix of eclectic art, modern furniture and Asian antiques – exactly as he imagined it would be. Ashe took two steps in and stopped. "I… I…" If Janna was going to throw a tantrum, a Ming vase, or reach for a pistol, he needed to know now so he could make his escape. "I don't know what to say."

Janna's brows were knit, although the look on her face was of bemusement. "How about start at the beginning? Have a seat." She didn't sound angry, but she definitely wasn't overjoyed. Ashe detected a smile. She motioned to the living room chairs.

Ashe chose the most uncomfortable of the three, a modern wood trapezoid with no cushion. He felt a desire for penance and also wanted to keep his eye on the door. A fat orange cat appeared to investigate the visitor, and Janna scooped it up. "Oskar, right?" Ashe asked, with a nervous laugh.

"Go ahead," Janna urged, as she stroked Oskar. She found a seat on a kidney-shaped sofa. "I'm a little confused now and you really have my interest. See, I thought Ashe MacDaniel was a woman."

"You *assumed* I was female."

"You didn't correct me."

"I know." He tried to maintain calm, although it was difficult to concentrate. Janna was so lovely it was all Ashe could do to keep the conversation going. He longed to take her into his arms and show her what he felt inside. The Southern gentleman in his genes stopped him. Instead, he let whatever honesty he had left rule over his words. "I drove all the way from North Carolina practicing what I would say, and now… Crazy, I'm here and now I can't. Here. This says most of it anyway." He extended a yellow piece of paper folded into a small square.

Janna's eyes could have lasered a hole into his heart. Ashe looked down. He prayed for a lightning bolt to strike him dead. If she was going to scream, he wanted her to do it as quickly as possible so he could get back into the car for the long trip back to Bonnie Doone. He braced himself for the worst.

To his surprise, Janna took the square and carefully unfolded it and began to read out loud.

Dear Janna

If you are reading this letter, you've learned my secret. I'm a man, not a woman. There. It's said. I'm sorry for the deception. I know now I should have fixed it long ago.

These are the facts: My real name is Asheley Wilkes MacDaniel, and I have a real son, Tyler, five and a half. I was married for eight wonderful years to Mackenzie (Mac) MacDaniel, who died last year in Iraq. The grief, that was real, the pain, too. I am a writer – or trying to be – and that's the God's honest truth. In fact, my book is going to be published. The blog, that was real, too. My parents are deceased.

What was not true was that I have no siblings. I have a brother, Rhett Butler MacDaniel. He's – how should I say this? Rather flamboyant. He's also my best friend. Oh, and I have lived in North Carolina all my life.

I don't know why I neglected to correct the lies. I've been thinking about that for weeks. First, I was overcome by your kindness in the grief forum. No one touched me as much as you did. As we got to know each other better, I found I liked you a lot – as a person. I enjoyed the stories about your friends and family, about your life and New York. When you asked me to join the Virtual Moms, I felt honored. How could I say no? After meeting everyone, I felt a bond. A very *real* and strong bond.

This is why I wouldn't send my photo or pick up the phone. Rhett warned me this could be problematic; I didn't listen. Who would have thought that I would come to love all of you so?

Because of this, I had to come clean.

Please accept my deepest apologies. I will understand if you (and the others) choose to cut me out of your life. Janna, you do not know how much I admire and care for you. It's more than I can put into words.

Virtually yours,

Janna glanced up from the page. "I need to know…"
"The rest?"
She nodded.

It was difficult to find words at first. Once he started it was impossible to stop. Ashe began from his earliest memories, worked his way through his tortuous high school years and into college at Duke, and told her how he met Mac. He described years of perfect harmony, of Tyler being born, of Mac's service to her country. He explained his relationship with his only brother, his deeply religious Southern Baptist parents, and how his family relationships came into play in his book.

Janna sat speechless, allowing Ashe to emit every thought he might have had.

At 4 a.m., Mandy and Rachel returned from their night out. The two girls were carbon copies of Janna, slightly taller than their mom, blond and attractive. "Girls, this is Ashe. Ashe MacDaniel." Ashe gave them a sheepish grin. The two exchanged surprised looks and giggled as they shook his hand.

They disappeared and Ashe continued. He finally ran out of words ninety minutes later. They looked at each other in an awkward silence, more pointed and uncomfortable than when she first opened the door. "Janna, I…" He wanted to admit to deep feelings for her except the words were lodged in his throat.

Ashe could say one thing about her: she was gracious. She put her hand up to stop him from speaking. "This is a lot to absorb." He felt his face falling to the same low place his heart was. She noticed and grabbed his wrist. "It's late. Or early, depending on your view. We're both tired. You're staying in the city, right? Come back tomorrow, around noon, okay?"

He thought he nodded. He remembered little of saying goodbye, the elevator ride to street level and the search for his car. Now safe inside, he pulled out his cell phone and texted a message to Janna.

"Thanks for not killing me. I'm going home now."
***
Minneapolis, Minnesota

288

Ally waited until morning to send out her group email regarding Ashe's unveiling. She wanted to give him enough time to speak to Janna in person before a round robin of second opinions circulated around cyberspace.

"I can't believe it." Greg spent most of the night shaking his head. "Do dudes do this on a regular basis? Does Janna?"

Ally shook her head. "We haven't had a new member of the Virtual Moms since... hell, I think Missy was the last one in. It's been years and years. You know us, Greg. We're a tight bunch. We didn't feel a need to expand the group. It's odd, isn't it?"

"What do you mean? That he's a guy? I agree with you on that."

"It's not that, silly. Think about it. Janna asks for us to let Ashe in, right? And she's the one who's always looking for romance, right? And Ashe has feelings for her? Who'd have thought?" Ally's mind wandered and she smiled.

"I think I know who the hopeless romantic is," Greg quipped.

Her smile faded as a wave of nausea gripped Ally. "God, oh God..."

"What's up?" By the time the words left his lips, she was already in the bathroom throwing up.

***

San Francisco, California

Skye took the N-Judah downtown to the end of the line. She'd decided to take a stroll along the Embarcadero, something she hadn't done in ages. She could count on the Bay side of the City to be ten degrees warmer, and it was. Armed with her camera, she hoped to take some good shots of the waterfront. A good, long walk on a pleasant Sunday afternoon would serve to clear her head.

Ashe. At first, she couldn't believe it. Asheley MacDaniel was a man? She called Ally seconds after reading the email. "Asheley *Wilkes* MacDaniel," Ally answered. "His mother was a *Gone With the Wind* buff. He has a brother named Rhett Butler MacDaniel, if you can believe that."

"Why? Why us?" It amazed Skye that any man would want to infiltrate a women-only Internet group. "Why lie?"

"Janna assumed he was a woman when the friendship first started. He didn't know how to correct the situation. In her conversations with him, she told him all about us. When she asked if he wanted to be in the group, he didn't know what to say. I believe him when he says he didn't intend malice. Although he keeps telling me he doesn't, I think he likes Janna. A lot."

"It explains a few things."

"Like what?"

"His advice. His outlook on relationships. It was a little off. Celia is right. She couldn't put her finger on it, and that was why."

"So, does it change anything for you?" Skye could almost hear Ally winking.

She didn't know. She told Ally she would have to think about it.

"A warning," Ally whispered so Greg wouldn't hear. "If you ever get a chance to talk to him, his voice is positively *dreamy*. Smooth, sexy, and we don't know what he looks like! I swear, he could look like Woody Allen, but if he talked to me all day long, I don't think I'd mind one bit."

Skye smiled remembering the conversation.

"We have to stop meeting like this." A deep voice shook her out of her thoughts. Skye whirled around. She found herself in front of Pier 39. Dude smiled at her. She smiled back. He was dressed in jeans and sweatshirt and carried a bag with a loaf of sourdough peeking up from the top. "Are you all right?" he asked.

"Maybe," she answered. She reached out and took one of his hands. It was huge, inviting, warm, yet not sweaty. "Definitely maybe."

***

Sarasota, Florida

After Celia received Ally's email, she was glad she torched the envelope that had been sitting for a week on her kitchen table. Her eyes scanned the message. Asheley Wilkes MacDaniel, male, once married to Lieutenant Mackenzie MacDaniel, now widowed, father of one Tyler MacDaniel... It had to be what Spark Investigation dug up.

"Oh, my God."

290

"Oh, my God what?" Kimber noted her mother's pale expression.

"Ashe."

"Ooo, so you found out? Is Ashe a two-headed, one-eyed, murdering child molester?" Kimber asked.

"Ashe is a man."

"No way!" Kimber shrieked.

"Way."

"You found out from Spark?" Kimber ruffled the newspapers on the kitchen table and scanned the top of the refrigerator.

"Not exactly. He confessed to Ally."

"What about the Spark report?"

"I... I, um had a little bonfire with it yesterday, thanks to Doug."

"Doug Taylor? What? How?"

"Never mind."

"How did you find out about Ashe?"

"Ally emailed us. Ashe called her and spilled his guts. It was yesterday, on his way up to New York to see Janna." She explained Ashe's book being published as a motivating reason for coming clean. "Oh, my God." Celia fought to get out of the haze.

"Mom, get a grip."

"It doesn't bother you that he lied?"

"Please. This is the 21st Century. I think it's pretty cool he thinks he's woman enough to handle the six of you." Kimber laughed.

"Kimber!"

"Honestly, Mom. Did he hurt anyone? No. Did he rob any of you? No. He gave you his real name. All he did was pretend to be a woman, which I guess is easy for him. You should be happy he told the truth. Now you can let it go."

"He can't possibly stay in the group."

"Why not?" Kimber plucked a banana from a bowl and peeled it.

"Virtual *Moms*, duh."

"I guess. If she... he's a good friend, why not keep him?"

Celia had to admit, it was something to consider.

***

291

Las Vegas, Nevada

Missy had finished retrieving her last email. She giggled at several of the VM loop responses. The news about Ashe wasn't surprising at the least. The way Ashe outlined Missy's line of attack on regaining her husband had a man's touch to it. It made sense.

The past few days spent with family was nice, to be sure. It was nicer to take her parents and in-laws back to the airport for their return trip to Indiana. After spending the holiday observing Earl, she decided what her next step would be. Earl wouldn't like it. Kara and Kassie wouldn't either; those were the breaks. If her plan worked out, they'd be a stronger family, and if it didn't, they would be stronger in a different way.

"What's so funny?" It was Earl. He peered at the computer screen from behind her shoulder.

She signed out of AOL and turned to her husband. "Earl. We have to talk. *Now*."

***

St. Louis, Missouri

Laurel opened the front door to a darkened house. A week without family activity left it smelling dank and musty. Marcus dragged a suitcase in behind her. She reached for the light switch. Before leaving for Florida, Joe turned the heat down and the air was chilly. The house seemed oddly empty without him. It had taken a foreign feel, like it wasn't their house anymore, like the four walls knew the Extons would be making their exodus soon.

Marcus ran to the answering machine to retrieve messages. Laurel threw her keys onto the table and took a seat. It had been a long day. Traveling at the end of the Thanksgiving weekend, the airports were crowded and tempers flared. It felt good to be home, to familiar walls, and the comfort of her bed. She kicked off her shoes and wheeled her bag back to her bedroom. "School tomorrow, Marcus!" she called. "Get your homework together and get to bed early!"

As she unpacked her suitcase, she thought about Ashe. Celia had called her and left a manic message while she was in the air between Orlando and Atlanta. During the layover, Laurel called her back to get the details. "Ashe a man!" she said out loud. "Who'da thunk it?" She didn't want Celia to think she didn't care. At the moment, Laurel had more pressing matters to think about. Like listing the house, arranging a move, and single motherhood while Joe was in Florida.

She smiled. Oh, that's right. She'd been there before. At least now she could see a light at the end of that tunnel.

***

New York City

How many minutes are in a morning anyway? Janna felt every second stab her in the heart as she endured the countdown to twelve noon. To her surprise, no call came. She figured the phone would ring as soon as 11:59 turned into the witching hour. She tapped at her watch, checked her Blackberry, she made sure the clock display on the microwave was right.

Noon came. Soon enough it was past noon. And then, *way* past noon.

They had agreed to noon, right?

Exhausted and thinking she would collapse under the crushing weight of mixed emotions, Janna had instructed Ashe to call back at the appointed time. In hindsight, she realized she should never have let him go. She should have questioned him, welcomed him. Something? Once she saw his back disappear into the elevator, she should have rushed down fourteen flights of stairs to beg him to stay. *Oh, my God! What if he hates me?* She paced the floor, running a worried trough into her plush carpet.

Sure she was angry at first, who wouldn't be? Her initial reaction left her feeling like the butt of a very rude joke. Celia was right; not only had she'd been had, all of the Virtual Moms had been betrayed. Yet she saw something in Ashe…and it wasn't only the kind eyes, the smooth skin, the lean body or the voice like melted honey. She couldn't put her finger on it. The more he talked, the higher the sympathy rose. She could tell he was sincere, remorseful, panicked almost. He recounted his life as if knowing the background would help her see why he let the farce go on. Ashe was a lot to digest in a short amount of time, and she had been rendered momentarily – and unusually – speechless. Perhaps it was her blank expression that sent him running for the hills.

293

She fingered the letter he handed her, noted the straight up and down block letters, the impeccable penmanship a result of a brief stint in Catholic school. "We might have been Baptists, but Mama saw the advantages of an early parochial background," Ashe had said. The legal paper had been worn thin; its creases softened by many openings, the ballpoint words faded by days of handling and reflection.

What did she do? She sat there and nodded like a dolt.

Worried, she checked her email – nothing. She checked her house phone voice mail – curiously empty. Finally, she glanced at her Blackberry. There, flashing like a beacon, like a siren, like a wildfire, was a text message alert she hadn't noticed before, from an out-of-state number. Her hands trembling, she rushed to open the message.

"Oh, no!"

She couldn't hit redial fast enough.

One ring, two rings. Janna hopped up and down. "Pick up, pick up! Please pick up."

A sleepy voice answered. "Hello?"

"Ashe! Come back."

Chapter Thirty-one

Monday, November 30
The World Wide Web

To: jannasbananas, ally1234, missymom, laurelextonsbunch, shootingskye, AsheMacD
From: celiasunshine
Subject: Friendship and Apology

Girls, I'm ashamed. I need to apologize. Here goes:

I'm sorry about my attitude toward Ashe. If I've learned one thing over the last month, it's that good friends are hard to find. If you have one (or five or six… LOL), you are truly blessed. Count me among those who are.

Friendship should not be based on how much money one has, your political bent or your age. Gender has nothing to do with it either. A good friend listens and is there when needed, and a good friend lends a hand without asking – or maybe provides a gentle shove. J/K.

Friends aren't perfect. They make mistakes. Let's face it girls, I make mistakes. (Yes, me Celia-Perfect.) A real friend sees past the flaws to the real gem inside. I am thankful to call all of you my friends.

All right, enough of the mush.

Love, Celia

P.S. BTW, I forgot to tell you about this super-hot pool guy… but I'll save that for another day.

***

To: celiasunshine, ally1234, laurelextonsbunch, missymom, jannasbananas, AsheMacD
From: shootingskye
Subject: New Friend… Maybe More?

I've been keeping this from you guys. Since we are baring all today, I thought I'd join the rest of you in taking the plunge toward honesty.

A few weeks ago I met a guy. I know, you're all thinking "I thought she liked girls?" As Celia so aptly put, a good friend is hard to find. May I also add that love and companionship is just as hard to locate in this wild world?

His name is Dude (not his real name, it's what he prefers). He's older – early 60's, I think – and not bad looking. Ponytail, glasses, looks like an old hippie. I kept thinking that I had seen this guy before. Turns out I had, many times. He's currently a student at the Culinary Academy and works part time at the main library, both places I frequent. He was the chef at the Napa wedding I did and lives nearby so we're always on the same MUNI. Yes, it was a 'duh' moment.

I don't know where this will lead. I'll take Ashe's advice and go with the flow. Could be something, and it could be nothing, who knows?

BTW – news flash. Trina called me last night! Said she misses me and wants to get together for dinner.

You'd all be so proud of me.

I politely declined. ☺

Skye

***

To: shootingskye, ally1234, jannasbananas, celiasunshine, laurelextonsbunch, AsheMacD

From: missymom

Subject: Earl

Girls, this will be hard for me to say and harder for you to understand, but I told Earl to hit the bricks.

I know he wants to move back in. After some thought, I decided against it. Oh, I still love him, I always have and always will. I want to be sure about *him*. I told him if he really wants to keep this marriage going, he was going to have to prove to me that he's a changed man. I told him we should separate for a year. (! Can you believe I said that? Gah!) So he's out right now looking at renting a condo down the street from the house.

During that time, he's pledged to become more involved with the girls' activities. He will come home to dinner every night to be with them. And to win me over – get this – he's going to have to date me. I don't mean casual, married people dating I mean *romance*, flowers, wine, and walks in the park, love letters. You know. The whole enchilada.

If he's been a good boy, I'll let him move back in.

Maybe. ☺

Ashe, thank you for your help. I didn't believe your plan would work, but here I am – proof positive.

I'm running late. I've got to get to work. Yup, I got a job too. In Earl's company, and get this, he doesn't know yet. Damn, I wish that man would catch a clue.

See you online sometime.

Missy

***

To: celiasunshine, shootingskye, jannasbananas, ally1234, missymom, AsheMacD

From: laurelextonsbunch

Subject: A New Life

I'm on my way to school so I only have time for a short note. Not sure if Celia filled you in, but we're moving! That's right, to the Orlando area. Celia's probably thinking: 'Oh, no, she's coming back – permanently.' Honestly, I don't know what I would have done the last week without her. Joe's in Florida right now, and get this… he's *working*! He snagged a construction job and will stay with my dad. It's nice to have Joe around to keep an eye on Dad until we move down.

BTW, Dad is mending nicely. Thanks for the flowers and cards. Oh! And thanks so much for the plane tickets for my boys. You guys are the best! I'll repay you somehow, I don't know how. I'll think of something.

The next few months will be busy. I have to sell the house and pack up. Should anyone be visiting the Greater St. Louis area in the next few months, I could use some extra hands. Hey, if we get anything close to market value on home-sweet-home, maybe I can pay you back with the proceeds. In the meantime: Garage sale, anyone? J/K – no *really*.

Marcus is looking forward to moving to Florida. It's going to be a fresh start for all of us. I'm so glad we have a plan.

Finally.

Love you guys, Laurel

***

To: shootingskye, laurelextonsbunch, missymom, jannasbananas, celiasunshine, AsheMacD
From: ally1234
Subject: Oh, no, here we go again...

Girls, I don't know how to say this without saying this... (scroll down)

...

...

...

...

...

...

...

...

...

We're pregnant again!

Can you believe it? I'm delirious, I'm scared, I'm old (OMG! AM I OLD!?), I'm in shock. Greg is crazy happy. Vanessa is still dancing. Where's my video camera? I have to go. This is a moment I have to catch on tape.

I'll email once I've come down off my cloud.

Ally – Mom-to-Be, Again

***

To: celiasunshine, missymom, laurelextonsbunch, shootingskye, ally1234, AsheMacD
From: Jannasbananas
Subject: A Twist of Fate and Gender

I met Ashe!

Oh snap, he's on my 'to' list. Sorry, Ashe. (I'm sure you won't mind me talking about you. Hey... it's my job, remember?)

For those who are lost in their own little worlds or who have had their heads somewhere the sun don't shine (don't blame me, I'm talking like him because he was here all night), I will describe him.

He is handsome, tall (six foot something), with dreamy blue eyes. He claims to have all of his thick, sandy brown hair. It's so thick and wonderful, I thought it was a rug. ☺ (J/K Ashe, sheesh, have a sense of humor.) By far, his best feature is his voice. Think George Clooney with a bit of a Southern drawl. It's not only the accent. His voice is deep and sensual. OMG, he could melt steel with a voice like that. Ask Ally. Or charm the pants off a person (Oops! Sorry for the slip. Not sharing intimacies at this point.).

Ashe is a wonderful human being and will now be... *drum roll, please* Da da da DA da! A *published* author. Once it's released, let's all buy his book, *Love and Laughter in Bonnie Doone,* and support our Virtual… Dad.

If any of you are mad at him because he neglected to mention he's a man, put your anger away. It was MY fault for assuming he was a woman. He went along because he didn't know how to break the truth to me.

As for Ashe, he'll always be my friend. Anything else? Well, *Skye*, let's say anything and everything is possible. Whatever I do, I'm taking it one step at a time. No more head over heels stuff for me, no sir-ee-bob. (Another Ashe-ism.)

BTW, if I forgot to mention it: VMs rock!

Janna

P.S. Attached is a photo Mandy took of me and Ashe. Hubba hubba.

***

To: jannasbananas, ally1234, missymom, shootingskye, celiasunshine, laurelextonsbunch

From: AsheMacD

Subject: Virtual Moms

It's been only one short month since I was introduced to six of the most special women anyone could find. Your courage, your beauty, your common sense, and your intelligence are what kept me coming back for more. We might have met online, yet I feel like I know all of you intimately. Janna, along with the rest of the VMs, have had a huge hand in helping me mourn Mac. (Of course, I wouldn't recommend my particular approach for anyone else – another case of 'Don't try this at home.')

I must offer my sincerest apologies for being less than honest with you all. I don't know where my life is going. I sure hope you'll all be around for my journey. In fact, I'm looking forward to meeting all of you in person. With a book tour coming up, that shouldn't be so hard to do. Maybe the Virtual Dad will be the first to meet all of the Virtual Moms in Real Life. Wouldn't that be a hoot?

Thank you for including me in your group and for overlooking my obvious flaws.

Thank you for being my friends.

Virtually Yours,

Ashe MacDaniel

P.S. Tyler says "Hi!" Jim Bob, too!

THE END

ACKNOWLEDGMENTS

Writing a novel is not for the faint of heart. Why? It's not easy. That being said, it's necessary for me to thank those who have helped me on this particular journey.

A huge thank you to NaNoWriMo (National Novel Writing Month) for giving me and other writer wannabes a place to roost and commiserate. The bones of this story was written during November 2009, 1,500 words and a chapter a day.

To all the 'real' writers I've met along the way, thank you for your nags and wags, your cattle prods, your Mapquest directions to the writing reference section of the local bookstore, and all of your many Internet links. Lydia, Sandy, Dr. B., Patti, John, and all the others (you know who you are – you're too many to list here) that have touched me, flogged me, and cheered me on.

A special thanks to John J. Owens, author extraordinaire, who served as official Southern advisor.

To all my BETA readers, a huge thank you. Writers can learn so much from readers.

To my editor for life, Ralph Scott, thank you for your fabulous guidance and your ideas for the direction of this book. Way to go!

Finally, to my husband, Brad, who allowed me to sneak away from the day job long enough to write and edit (and edit and edit and edit) *Virtually Yours*. Thank you. I love you and will remain forever virtually yours.

www.ingramcontent.com/pod-product-compliance
Lightning Source LLC
Chambersburg PA
CBHW070654180626
46817CB00006B/2371